A Far Magic Shore

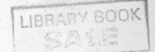

A Far Magic Shore

BOOK ONE
of
THE FALL OF THE DISENCHANTED

Keith Timson

Futura

**For Julia,
one of the Enchanted**

An Orbit Book

Copyright © 1988 by Keith Timson

First published in Great Britain in 1989 by
Futura Publications, a Division of
Macdonald & Co (Publishers) Ltd
London & Sydney

All characters are fictitious and any resemblance to real persons, living
or dead, is purely coincidental.

All rights reserved

ISBN 0 7088 4206 2

Printed in Great Britain by
The Guernsey Press Co. Ltd, Guernsey, Channel Islands.

Futura Publications
A Division of
Macdonald & Co (Publishers) Ltd
66-73 Shoe Lane
London EC4P 4AB

A member of Maxwell Pergamon Publishing Corporation plc

PART ONE
Sanctuary

Prologue

There was a time when Sanctuary was free, when the only armies which invaded its high-cliffed shores were the eternal legions of rolling, thunderous waves charging relentlessly to their destinies upon rocks and sand. There was a time when the island was a haven, safe for all. There was a time when Sanctuary was.

The Banished One had returned. His journey had not been an easy one, for a voyage across the Great Main was always perilous, yet, as soon as he had set sail from the Land of the Disenchanted in the stolen fishing boat, he was filled with a raging optimism.

While his boat had been tossed by the heaving waves of the Main, pitching and twisting in the howling winds, not once had he feared death. Never in his heart had he believed that it was Talango who ruled the seas any more than the High Lord truly ruled his Domain. No, all this was the Whim of The Wizard. Everything was His creation, His will, and only those who believed this deserved to survive. He, the Banished One, the Betrayer of the Word, had learned to acknowledge this. Such was his mission: he had to survive if the world he both knew and loved was to be saved from extinction.

The Grand Wizard saw fit to guide the Banished One's boat not only to the shores of Sanctuary but to the safety of Kingtown Harbour. To his relief none of the inhabitants recognised him, and his tale was believed when he said that he was a fisher whose vessel had drifted away from the natural protection of the bay at Marol.

Once inside the high marblon walls he thanked the Sanctuarites for their good-natured generosity, then he entered the Citadel itself where, like any other islander, he had the right to demand an audience with the King. As always, the high, pinnacled towers of the Citadel cast the bailey into deep shadow. A hundred braziers – he had once counted them – blazed incessantly. Silver armour turned to gold in the flickering light while knights stood resting upon their swords, as if posing for an artist. He wondered how any of them would fare in battle compared to the sham fighting of the tournaments. One of them asked him his business and was told a story of Gathrol the fisher, shipwrecked, come to beg money from the King. His tale was accepted without question, and the knight, his heavy armour clanking loudly, conducted him through the two open iron doors which led into the Main Hall.

It was all just as before. Daggers of light streamed in from the tiny windows set high in the ceiling, blending eerily with the orange-red light of the fire that blazed in the massive hearth dominating the far wall. As if they had never moved while he had been away, three large ranger hounds luxuriated in the warmth of the flames, leaving the other occupants of the Main Hall to shiver in its cold, damp atmosphere. To his left was a high-backed chair mounted upon a plinth. In that chair sat King Septor. His voice echoing metallically, the knight announced the arrival of Gathrol, a fisher from Marol.

8

'Come closer, Gathrol, and tell me of your woes,' the King said hoarsely.

Head lowered, the Banished One trod slowly towards his King. Despite the chilling dampness of the audience chamber he was sweating profusely. At last, nerving himself, he looked up and saw the face of a man old, sad and broken before his time. The King returned his gaze and in a startled voice uttered:

'Ruthor! Can it really be you?'

'Yes father.' His words fell like tears. 'It is I, your son.'

Chapter One

Princess Rosamile burst into the Royal Bedchamber, her
hair flying. 'Is it true that Ruthor has returned?' she cried,
taking her father by the arms and almost shaking him in
her excitement.

'It's true enough.' King Septor's voice was grim. Her
mother continued to stare down at the floor, her hands
tightly laced.

'Where is he?' Rosamile demanded.

'Downstairs.'

'Then what are we all doing up here in the Royal
Chamber?' I must go at once to greet my long lost brother!'

Queen Katrila stood up, her eyes fixed on her daughter.
'Surely you can't have forgotten why he was banished?'

'Of course not,' the Princess snapped, growing more
impatient with her parents. 'But I forgave him a long time
ago.'

'Oh you forgave him, did you?' There was both anger and sarcasm in Septor's voice. 'I suppose that makes everything all right. Never mind the Way of The Wizard.'

'You mean the Way of The Wizard according to that old crone, Orina.' Rosamile volleyed the words at her father, knowing she was probably arguing for her brother's life.

'Orina is not to blame and well you know it.' The king glared at his daughter. 'It is written that death can be the only penalty for one who abuses His Magic powers. Ruthor had those powers in abundance and, as you know only too well, he abused them.'

'But Ruthor was no Wizard!' Rosamile was now pleading. 'He was only a boy who played a nasty trick on his younger sister. Because it was he who would inherit the kingdom, I was often envious but I never wished him dead.'

'And I have, I suppose? It was I who had him banished instead of being killed.' The King shook his head in despair. 'You might think you have grown up, Rosamile, but in so many ways you're still a child.'

'I am not a child!' she raged at her father. 'And if you kill him then you had better kill me too.'

'Act your age, girl,' Katrila said sharply. 'One day you too will have to make decisions that have come from your head and not your heart.'

'It's just . . . It's just . . . Oh, I couldn't bear to see him die!' Rosamile was now fighting back her tears.

'I know.' A tear rolled down Katrila's own cheek. 'But the truth is that neither we nor Orina are in a position to judge Ruthor. All any of us can do is beg The Grand Wizard to influence the Royal Witch in his favour.

Together, the three of them linked hands, closing their eyes, and, like anyone else not blessed with Magic powers, struggled as best they could to be at one with The Grand Wizard.

Rosamile tried harder than she had ever tried before to commune with her Creator. As always it was hopeless. Or was that a faint, wind-borne voice assuring her that all would be well, that she would be Queen one day and that a forgiven Ruthor would always be at her side helping her to rule Sanctuary? Was she merely imagining words she wanted to hear? She could not be sure but at least it gave her hope.

Clinging to this hope, she hurriedly led her parents down into the Main Hall. The man who was waiting there was thin and ragged. It could not be Ruthor, could it? Her elder brother had been so fine looking. Now the tragedy of his life had reduced him to jutting bones and wind-bleached skin. The sight rendered her speechless and it was Orina, standing nearby, who spoke first.

'I read your thoughts, while you ponder upon the Royal Court's reaction to your return,' the Witch said to Ruthor, her eyes burning into him. 'But mark well, you who sought the ways of Magic and then abused them, time is our judge and judges are by their very nature resolute. Nothing can be changed, be it the past or your future, Banished One.'

'Enough!' His father could still bellow louder than anyone else when the need arose. 'No more of your malicious prattle. Ten long years have I endured torment, wondering whether my son be alive or dead. Have I not paid dearly for his folly as well?'

'The misuse of Magic powers is no mere folly –' The hideous sores upon the Witche's face had turned to a livid red – 'No one can deny that. Was it not you, King Septor, who banished him?'

'And is it not I who welcomes him back?' the King bellowed again, glaring back at her. 'Can you not deny the future for just a few blessed days?'

Defeated by his retort, the Witch cast down her glowing eyes before kneeling on the ground. Withered hands appeared from within her shimmering black cloak as she raised them up in supplication to The Grand Wizard.

'Oh Master of All, forgive us our weakness in savouring the return of one who was loved by everyone present. Yours must always be the way but tolerate our lack of resolution in doing Your bidding, this we beg You!'

The fire died in her eyes. Now staring at Septor was a sad, old woman – an old woman deformed by her powers and pained by the role that was demanded of her. In her own distant way she had loved him as much as his own family. He could tell that it was hurting her to realise that she alone was denied the one power bestowed upon others: the power to forgive.

Ruthor had been trembling from the moment he entered the hall. He ached to embrace his sister, but he could not for now the trembling was replaced by sharp, vicious spasms as every bone in his body began to clatter as if they were sticks. Terror ruled his senses as a sword thrust of pain hurled him to the floor where he writhed and squirmed, his eyes burning, his nostrils assailed by unbearably fetid odours, his stomach corkscrewing agonisingly. Throughout his entire body, searing every part of his flesh, was an invisible fire. This was the true meaning of the Whim, to know torture which would never cease. 'All is Yours!' his mind screamed before the fire scorched up into his brain. 'Let me die . . . Let me die . . .'

Watching, Rosamile knew exactly what he was suffering and she began to shudder uncontrollably, as if his pain were hers. Fists clenched, she clamped her mouth shut to hold back her screams, but she could not. This was her brother, her own dearest brother, and she had always loved him.

Then he was still. For a time he remained prostrate upon the chequered floor, the coolness of the soft stone bringing relief to his body which still felt as if it were burning. Thankfully he gasped in the cool clean air of life as his arms and legs slowly stopped their twitching. As the last pangs of agony ebbed away he heard the jagged voice of the Witch, rising above the screams of his sister as she pleaded for the torment to be ended.

'This was what you did to your sister. Never forget, errant Prince, why you were banished from this kingdom. Nor that the ways of the Disenchanted are very different from our own.'

'No, no, please forgive him, I beg of you!' Rosamile said. 'I forgave him long ago, and it is my right alone, for it was I whom he wounded! Orina, please listen to me!'

Orina did not seem to hear the Princess. For her, there

could never be any compromise: Ruthor had abused the power she had taught him, used it to torment his own sister. There was no honourable escape from that shameful revelation, however much Rosamile pleased.

'Now greet the rest of your kin,' she said in a softer voice, 'for it is only I who am cursed never to forgive you.'

His mother came to him first, while Rosamile stepped back, rubbing the shameful tears from her face. Katrila's warm brown eyes danced in the firelight as she rested her head upon her son's shoulders and wept with joy. In silence he held her small body against his own and listened to her whisper his name over and over again. Next, her composure recovered, Rosamile approached, her blue eyes wide with love – and doubt.

'All these years I thought that you would never forgive me, dear sister. If you only knew how I have longed to renew our bondship, if only for a short while.'

Now her eyes were a warm, radiant blue, and all doubt vanished as her exquisite face burst into a smile.

'Oh, you fool, Ruthor, I forgave you many, many years ago. Welcome home, Brother,' she cried loudly before stepping close to feel his arms about her. 'Welcome home!'

'A brace of women, what more could any man ask for?' the King chuckled. 'Now when they've done with their weeping we'll prepare ourselves for a banquet like no other. And that includes you, Orina. You can perform a little conjury for us.'

The Witch's sore red eyes twinkled. 'For a banquet like no other, you shall see Magic like no other.'

So Prince Ruthor was to be forgiven after all. Rosamile could not stop grinning. Her father, Orina, both of them seemed to have relented. And why not? Had she not been the one who was wronged? Never had a moment been more ripe for celebration.

Such an occasion was enough to shake the Royal Household out of its usual bovine ways. The vast kitchen became a frenzied clamour of cooks chopping vegetables, boiling blue eagle eggs by the score, baking in mead and raisin sauce enough apples to fill an orchard, peeling off the hard skins of gigantic Colidors. Servants were also busily employed in untapping barrels of well-matured Redthorn ale or filling jugs from vats containing the choicest of wines: Black Nightberry from the North, the sweet-tasting Goring Lady, or the King's favourite, Double Strength White Pear.

Those working in the Main Hall were equally busy. One of the servants even took courage in both hands by daring to chase the ranger hounds away from the fire. Standing, these beasts were almost as tall as a human, and only upon the rarest of occasions was anyone willing to risk life and limb by disturbing them. The hearth had languished in filth for long enough. Forever tolerant of their dilatory ways the King had never demanded pristine cleanliness, but tonight, all would sparkle – all would shine. Wood was varnished until arms ached, candlesticks were polished until they shone like spears, and even the remotest cranny was successfully cleared of ancient grime and spiders' webs.

Four householders were sent upon errands into the Royal City to seek out jesters, tumblers and minstrels to perform at the banquet, and soon the word spread that Ruthor had returned. There would be dancing and singing in the streets. The King had welcomed back his son. It was time for them all to celebrate.

In the Royal Chamber on a padded bench, Katrila and Rosamile sat on either side of the Prince while Septor slumped in another of his high-backed thrones opposite them. Surrounding them were tapestries depicting the beauty that was Sanctuary: the rolling hills and protected valleys where fruit and flowers abounded, the tall cliffs lashed by the ever-violent seas of the Main and the sheltered gardens near the Royal City where all could wander, feeling close to the Nature Spirits. The tireless needlework had been a labour of love; a dedication to the family who ruled them so wisely and to the very island itself.

'Now tell us why you returned, Ruthor,' the Princess

16

begged, her face alight.

The King frowned so that deep furrows formed upon his forehead. His crown had been removed to reveal a large bald patch in the centre of his curly grey hair.

'I see before me a son who was once both proud and handsome. Now, like me, he's old before his time. Was it not so many years with the Disenchanted that drove you to return?'

'And face such risks – certain death? Innocents that you all are, I had a better reason. Could I be expected to die in an alien land, knowing that this haven from all evil is in danger of being destroyed?'

His words stunned them all to silence. It was a long time before Septor could demand confirmation.

'You mean,' Rosamile gasped, 'they're planning another invasion?'

'Yes.'

'You're sure?'

'Yes.'

There was a brooding silence, but Rosamile soon broke it.

'Ruthor, you must tell us everything immediately!'

'No, bide your time,' the King said heavily. 'Be swift, and what choice do I have?'

Rosamile frowned. What did her father mean? In her urgency, she brushed his words aside. 'Tell us, Ruthor, tell us!'

'Rosamile's right. I must hurry with my tale. As for choice? I learned at Talango's court that destiny can never be cheated.'

'You were at the Supreme Fortress?' the king roared.

'I was, Father, though the lands of the Disenchanted are almost as much a mystery to me as they are to you. But let me begin with my early days of banishment.'

'Start with how you survived a voyage across the Great Main,' his mother said, clasping his hand in her own. I felt that you had been condemned to death when they cast you off in that tiny boat. I knew then that I'd be haunted forever by the image of your drowning. Praise to The

Wizard that at last I've been saved from that nightmare.'

'As have I!' cried Rosamile, leaning forward to hear her brother's tale. It was a thrilling feeling to know that everything would be all right again, and she was relishing every second.

'Except to say I survived it, there's little to tell,' he continued. 'Banished from my homeland I had no wish to live. I huddled in that boat just waiting for a wave to overturn it or a tentagoth to drag me down, or a spear fish to thrust into the woodwork. Did it matter which of these was my fate? But it was not to be. After days of wretched suffering on wild seas my boat was sucked into a channel which, in turn, sped me into a huge grotto. I assumed I was dead; thirst and hunger had made me delirious. I was convinced that despite my blasphemy, I was in The Wizard's Magic Wizardom. Then I heard the sound of paddles stirring the waters. Emissaries coming to greet me perhaps? What foolishness! How dare I imagine that one so unworthy as myself should be so exalted?'

'If forgiveness exalts your soul, Ruthor, then let The Wizard hear of my love for you.' The Princess was pressing her hands together in the form of a prayer.

His eyes shone fondly upon her. 'Rosamile, let it be enough that despite those depraved efforts of mine, you've matured into a Princess worthy of her title.'

'I interrupted,' she smiled, a smile which radiated her beauty. 'Tell me more of the Magic grotto.

'Alas no Magic, although it was pure Magic from above that guided my boat. No, enchantment was behind me. 'The Kelvi were of the Disenchanted.'

'Never heard of them,' Septor grunted.

'Father, we Sanctuarites know so little of our adversaries – though in this case these people were no enemies. They took me to some caves and restored me to health with a diet of fish, seaweed, brine cake and a peculiar drink which, although foul tasting, has restorative powers far greater than any Magic potion.'

'Blasphemy!' Angrily, the King banged his staff down upon the soft stone floor, while Rosamile said impatiently that he was to let Ruthor speak.

'To disclaim all that lies upon Disenchanted soil is foolish,' Ruthor answered calmly. 'An enemy unworthy of respect can be no proper enemy.'

The King seemed impressed by his answer. 'Continue, Ruthor, I shan't interrupt again.'

The Prince allowed himself a wry smile before continuing.

'They were kindness itself but thanking them proved difficult for they spoke in a strange language. I'd always imagined that everyone, even on the mainland, were of the one tongue but it took a long time to learn that *slerweg* meant water, *foddle* was food and *labrof* meant plenty. It's believed by the Sangorans that all men spoke this way and had a similar appearance. From this race developed the races which populate our world today.'

'More blasphemy!' This time King Septor waved his staff at Ruthor. 'You dare speak of such beliefs. The Grand Wizard created all in His image, even the Disenchanted.'

'Father!' Rosamile snapped as if she were addressing a naughty child. 'You promised to listen, now listen.'

As if he were a small boy just chastised, the King sank into his throne and bade the Prince continue.

'Maybe so,' the Prince said. The Disenchanted refute everything they can't see or feel, save the existence of the Black Unicorn. That is all we Sanctuarites have in common with them. That creature has become the embodiment of the High Lord Talango. Now it is both his other name and his symbol.'

'That I did know,' his father said petulantly, 'but perhaps you should avoid their vile beliefs lest I lose control of my temper again.'

'I tired of the Kelvi's company,' the Prince continued, 'even though they showed me hospitality worthy of the noblest islander. Because these people are regarded as imbeciles, they are allowed to continue their lives unhindered by Talango. There is great wisdom in being regarded as harmless fools in such a predatory domain. The reason for leaving was, I suspect, the Grand Wizard urging me on to fulfil the mission he had planned for me but, of course, I didn't realise that at the time.

'Alone, I wandered in the wilderness finding myself in a place of rocks and sand where little grew, few birds flew, nor did insects pester at my feet. Life had gone from this place, it was as barren and forsaken as myself. With no company but my thoughts and the renewed threat of starvation, I began to hate my family for what they had done to me.'

His mother flinched at this last remark, but he took her hand.

'Remember, I'd been banished to this bleakest of lands for what? One solitary abuse of newly learned Magic; the one and only time when my inner thoughts had manifested into a curse upon my sister. It's impossible for you who have never left Sanctuary to realise the severity of the punishment.'

'It was the Witch who insisted that you be banished,' Rosamile interjected. 'She remained adamant that it was The Grand Wizard's words which came to her. Even I begged for your forgiveness, Ruthor. Yes, I the one you tormented. How could you hate us like that?'

'Because it was what our Creator wanted him to feel,' Septor groaned impatiently. 'Can none of you see?'

'At the time I wouldn't have agreed with you, Father, only now can I see it was all The Wizard's doing. Most of us serve Him in more obvious ways but I was chosen to tread a very different path. I longed for a chance to avenge myself against you and that chance was soon to come.

'I came to a town. Talonless and cursed by hunger, I lurched up to its gates. My treatment by those Sangorans – who look no different from ourselves – was very different from that of the Kelvi. They were soon beating me and forcing me to eat the offal of a slaughtered animal after I'd told them that I never ate the flesh of land creatures. However, when I explained that nobody living on Sanctuary ate meat it ensured I suffered no more beatings. For such a spy, as they regarded me, was best

20

delivered to the Supreme Fortress fit and strong, so that he would not die upon his torturers before all information had been extracted.

'Then I discovered that I was in Etania, the place where all Sangorans originated. However, I know nothing more about it for they took me to the Supreme Fortress in a windowless metal wagon. It was like being in a black pit which rattled and jolted without end.'

Again he squeezed his mother's hand for her eyes were full of pain.

'When the wagon finally came to rest I was taken through a gigantic iron door, far larger in size than the one in our own Citadel which is nothing more than a peasant's hut compared to the Supreme Fortress. Then I was led in chains through countless corridors before arriving at the massive stone head of the Black Unicorn. The stone used for this was as black as marblon, but lacked its shiny finish. However I dally upon something unimportant. More to the point was that beyond the open mouth which served as an entrance was the High Lord Talango. Before entering, I was blindfolded so that I could not see his face. In fact I've never seen him, for all who are in his presence must lower their gaze and never raise it upon pain of death. Those privileged to have an audience with him must enter, and remain, on their hands and knees. In his Exalted Presence they are regarded as nothing more than mere cattle.'

'He must think he's The Grand Wizard Himself,' Septor scowled but, ignoring him, Ruthor continued his story.

'I decided that instead of suffering torture I would tell Lord Talango everything I knew. This I did before swearing an undying allegiance. To my relief, he accepted and it was my Sangoran captors who were to spend the last moments of their lives screaming in agony at the hands of the torturers; such was their punishment for treating me so badly.

'Freed from my chains I was allowed to wander throughout the whole of the Supreme Fortress, but no further. That mighty edifice was to be both my prison and my home. I learned to know and even love it, just as I had loved the Royal City. It was, after all, the most fascinating of places where strange plants abounded, often nurtured by even stranger people. After many years I still had not tired of this tapestry. I was given a chamber for my personal use, its walls covered in tiny stones which shone like jewels.'

'How can I think of my son as a willing convert?' the King said with a shake of his head before Rosamile bade Ruthor continue.

'To my shame, I became his adviser upon the planned invasion, although at this point it was nothing more than a mere notion; a dream to amuse him. Only much later did he decide to turn his dreams into a reality.'

'What can such a powerful ruler want with our tiny island?' Rosamile's expression was grim. All feminine grace had suddenly deserted her; it was as if she were already preparing herself for war.

'For a start there's marblon to consider. It might be the hardest stone in the world to quarry but for building a fortress or citadel, nothing will ever compare. There are still a few who rebel against his rule, and softer, less slippery stones have been known to crumble, besides being easy to scale. Also, think upon our woods and forests. Small they may be but timber is scarce in many regions, so, despite the problem of shipping those logs, their export would still be justified. But uppermost is the challenge it provides for an omnipotence who has, save for a few remote places, conquered all of the mainland. You see, he wishes for one last great achievement before forsaking his mortal body.'

'You speak of him as if he is more than just another human being; it's almost as if you believe in his omnipotence yourself.' The King fingered his grey beard. It still seemed troublesome for him to try and comprehend anything beyond Sanctuary.

'I speak of how I saw him for the last ten years. After all, he did provide what I most desired.'

'You had all that you could ever want here, Ruthor,' his

mother said, obviously stricken by this remark. For a moment he was silent, unable to construct the right words, but he had vowed to tell the truth, no matter how painful it was to their ears.

'No, I did not have all I wanted here. The only time I possessed real power was just before being banished. My opinions counted for nothing in this court. Only in the Supreme Fortress were they sought constantly.'

'Your opinions about the wholesale slaughter of your family and all our Islanders, you mean?' his mother said bitterly.

'Mother!' Rosamile cried, glaring at the Queen. 'That's not fair!'

'It was a good many years before I came to my senses and guilt came to me upon a sudden wind. It was then that my health began to decline. However, I was wise enough to keep my anguish to myself. But how could I escape? In truth I was still a prisoner, never being allowed to go beyond the walls of the Fortress. I finally managed it by hiding myself in one of the many fishers' carts which delivered their catch to the High Lord's household. The stench was unbearable as I crawled beneath sodden sacks and was taken to what I prayed would be a port. Once again I travelled through Etania without seeing anything, but unwittingly, the fishers did take me to a port although I shall never know its name.'

'If only I could have been with you.' Rosamile touched her brother's arm.

'It would not have been half so bad had you been there.' He smiled at her before going on, his voice sounding almost mesmerised. 'Under cover of darkness I managed to leave the cart, steal some food, and set sail in an unattended fishing boat. Putting my trust in The Grand Wizard I remained convinced that as I was upon the most sacred of missions, I would be blessed with survival.'

'And so it was that you, who had found favour with this tyrant, finally realised the error of your ways,' the King said, hope in his voice.

'I was also spurred by the fact that at this very moment

23

the tyrant's mighty wheeled ships are being assembled. The fleet will be upon the Main before the season is out.'

'Before Leavefall!' Septor bellowed in horror.

'So soon!' Rosamile gasped.

'Yes, before Leavefall. He's aware that not every one of these ships will survive the crossing both here and back again, but he is willing to accept losses of up to half of his force. Nor has he shunned the risks himself. He will be at the head of his army. As I've told you, though his life is run, his soul is restless and still seeks adventure.'

'Just what are these wheeled ships?' Rosamile asked.

'They're large, sturdily built vessels with removable masts and sails, which have wheels concealed in their hulls. When they reach these shores those wheels can be lowered so that they can be dragged overland to the Royal City. The boats will then be up-ended to form mighty siege towers. From these towers will leap his Flying Avengers – soldiers with wings strapped upon their backs, enabling them to float down into the City and slaughter all those defending the ramparts. Then when the City is theirs they'll lower their ships down again before dragging them through the Main Gate. Yet even if they fail in the last task, all they have to do is remain in the City and lay siege to the Citadel. They'll be well supplied and capable of living off the land which surrounds us. For those in here it will be a slow, lingering death.'

'It will never succeed!' Rosamile said, defiantly tossing back her mane of blonde hair.

'If only one half of the wheeled ships survive the first crossing, then you'll be facing an army twice the size of the last one which attacked Sanctuary.'

'You speak as if we've lost this battle before it has begun.' Rosamile's eyes were now an ice-cold blue. It was the way they looked when she was at her most indomitable.

'There's always hope. After all, Queen Landora succeeded against them in the Great Attack, but this army of giants and dwarves and all the other strange inhabitants of his Domain is indeed a mighty one. It is better to be warned.'

'Queen Landora made a channel up from the sea and

then flooded the area near the City Gate. Then, when the invaders were assembled outside, the doors were opened outwards and all of Karango's soldiers drowned,' Rosamile put in, thinking it apt to remind everyone present that they had already defeated a Sangoran army.

'No trick can be played twice. The Magicians will not be able to torment Talango's warriors, for they have all been trained to withstand such mental attacks. What was done to me downstairs would not have worked upon any of them. The Witch knew I was still a believer. That's why I was affected. Not so the Disenchanted.'

'But what else can we do but fight?' his father urged. 'Only with your advice, Ruthor, can we hope to succeed.'

'Yes, brother, we need your advice. Is that not why you came back?'

'No, my task is done. I know nothing more of the invasion than what I've told you. My mission is over. It must be the task of another to thwart this army.' Turning to his sister he said, 'Rosamile, have you not always excelled in the skills of combat, far better than most men?'

Silently, she questioned him with her sharp blue eyes.

'Ruthor is right, you can't really deny it, dear, can you?' her mother said.

'I suppose not.' She gave a shrug. 'But tournaments and mock sword play are a different matter from this. A Princess may play games but I —'

'Well this is no game for any of us.' Septor's knuckles were white from clenching his staff. 'So think upon our future, dear ones, as you've never thought before. However, despite this news, tonight . . .'

'Tonight we shall enjoy a banquet like no other,' Rosamile cried as she clasped both of Ruthor's hands. 'For at last, my favourite brother has returned.'

'I am your only brother,' he grinned.

'Had there been ten more then you would still have been my favourite,' she told him before laughing with the gusto of a man.

Although her words were laced with a slight bitterness it provided an excuse for all four of them to relieve the tension caused by his news. As one they revelled in mirth while vowing for just one precious evening that both past and future would be forgotten as soon as the wine started to flow.

Many citizens had been invited to join them after the Royal knights and those members of the household who were not serving had taken their seats. Four long tables filled the main Hall: one for the knights, one for the householders, the third for those who had drawn the right numbers in the City lottery and the fourth table for the Royal Family, who were accompanied by those Witches and Wizards who lived near enough to attend. In the centre, a space had been cleared for the performers.

But first of all, thirsts had to be slaked and whether it be upon wines of Nightberry, Goring Lady, Double Strength White Pear or Redthorn ale, jugs were soon emptied and needed to be replenished before the food arrived.

Knives and daggers were soon digging into spicy vegetables encased in a rich pastry which crumbled deliciously in the mouth, or the prized blue eagle eggs, only so many of which were allowed to be taken from a clutch. On being bitten, they turned into a warm cream in the mouth. Others enjoyed Colidor apples which were so big they needed two hands to hold them and when eaten made a crunch loud enough to be heard above the sound of gay laughter and chattering voices. Even ordinary apples were an attraction; glazed in their golden-brown mead and raisin sauce and then dipped in a bowl of cream laced with Nightberry wine, they became the sweetest of delights.

Sweet also were the ballads from Wulf of the Valleys who, to the accompaniment of his own harp, lyricised about the singing winds and the eternal loves of the beautiful fairy Medila, who was said to haunt the magic wood of Cophaven. A tear coursed down the cheek of Prince Ruthor as he listened. Was he crying through joy or sadness? None could tell and none would ask, not even his sister, whose eyes rarely left him that evening.

Then it was time for excitement as tumblers bounded in and started to leap over tables, launching themselves from one another while everyone ducked, convinced that at least one of them would crash down upon the merrymakers. To everyone's relief, the skills of these men and women had not waned. Less hectic, yet just as enjoyable, were the performances of the jesters and jugglers. The occasion seemed to bring out the very best in all of them for it was not every day that a Prince returned.

Only one variety of act had been absent so far – Conjury. Always at celebrations a respected Magician would forsake the solemnity of his Magic calling and perform a few tricks for the amusement of all. Now the Royal Witch kept her promise to the King and amazed the audience as it had never been amazed before. Snow-white doves fluttered from out of her garments, before a serpent of fire appeared from the floor and began weaving and diving about her. Then, as if of its own volition, the Sacred Orb, which was placed above the hearth, floating towards her. For a moment she allowed the black marblon sphere to hang suspended above her head before it circumvented the tables, raising all eyes. Truly, upon this most blessed of nights, Magic was in the air.

'Remember,' she told them in a loud, declamatory voice, 'above all else is The Grand Wizard. Let those who believe be regarded as His Children. Blessed are the Enchanted – strong shall they stand. For they and they alone, know that it is His Will which must be done and His alone, no matter the pain it causes them.'

The Hall was cast into silence; a moment to contemplate upon her words before the revelries continued. Then it was time for more wine and more songs, except that this time they were sung by all those present.

At this juncture, after delivering a knowing glance to the King, the Royal Witch left the table carrying a plateful of leftovers from the feast. Noting her gesture, Septor lingered with his family just a little longer.

When all were into the second chorus of 'Merry as You Go', the Monarch himself slipped away to join Orina.

27

Slowly, and swaying slightly from the effects of imbibing too much Double Strength White Pear wine, he made his way up the steps until he came to her chamber.

He had not visited her for a long time. It was easy to forget how strange and mystical her small domain was. Tame bats hung sleeping from the oddest of places: edges of tables and chairs, beams across the ceiling and anything else which could be grabbed by their tiny clawed feet. A weird, acrid-smelling incense burned his eyes as he tried to focus them on Orina and the scruffy boy who was gorging upon the food she had brought. Surrounded by her leather-bound books and jars of potions, she was brooding over a small cauldron of bubbling essence.

'Welcome, my King,' she said without looking up from the cauldron. 'How rare for us to be honoured by a visit from you.'

'Who's your little friend?' Septor asked, still finding it difficult to focus his eyes.

'An urchin I found sleeping in a chicken barn, hence his name, Barney Fowl. It was out of charity that I took him into my care but it's just as well I did. At the moment his ways are too coarse, even for your rowdy court, but one day you will be appointing this little brat as the Royal Wizard.'

'I'm not that drunk y'know.' The King said.

Looking up she gave a knowing glance before saying: 'No matter how drunk you are, my said King, our Creator has spoken to me. It is time for you to do what must be done.'

One of the bats fluttered from the chair as Septor tried to clutch the bars for support. His fingers felt hot and hugely swollen. All control had left them.

'Now? Surely we can be granted just a little more time?'

'Am I not a vessel for His word? Some will say, as before, that it was I who wanted it so but nothing could be further from the truth. Were I ever to have thoughts so wicked that they manifested into a terrible deed, then I too could expect the same judgement.'

'But he was just a boy, no more than a foolish boy,' the

28

King protested. 'Has he not suffered enough: thin, sunken-faced and haggard as he is now?'

'Have you never realised the terrible price which is paid by all those with the Magic Gift?' The strange purple light emitted by the brew in the cauldron made her look even more hideous than usual: her distorted face and bulbous warts cruelly emphasised. 'Once I was beautiful. There was even a time when, in your heart, you desired me more than your own wife, remember?'

It was true. Her beauty had once captivated him with that strange, ethereal quality which none but those with the Gift seemed to possess. Many men had longed to embrace the beautiful Witch, but none more, he suspected, than himself. Despite her ensuing ugliness there was still a warmth of feeling towards her that went deeper than mere respect. Then his bloated stomach turned as he thought of the price he had to pay.

'Orina, can there be no mistake?'

'None,' she said, shaking her head. 'By now he must have told you all he knows about the invasion?'

'You know of that?'

'Voices upon dark, secret winds told me of his thoughts. I even know that this will be a war beyond the powers of Magic. Bide well upon your son's words and remember that if The Wizard's Will is done, then you will be blessed with victory.'

Septor gazed down at Barney Fowl who was listening to everything that was being said, apple juice dribbling down his chin. Was Magic to claim this grubby innocent too? Blasphemously he found himself wishing that he was of the Disenchanted. How could he deify a Wizard who demanded so much? A warning chill was coursing through his veins. The soporific glow of the wine had been vanquished by realisation. He was sober; as sober as the chilling sea rain.

'Go now to Prince Ruthor. He has left the banquet.'

'Where is he?'

'You, his father, must know where he stands. Ruthor awaits you. There shall be no hate in his heart this time.'

Reluctantly, his feet leaden, Septor climbed the twisting staircase of the Fifth Tower. Bitter tears filled his eyes. He hated his role as King more than ever before. Spiralling round and round on the narrow stairs he remembered the halcyon days when the walls had echoed to the sounds of laughter. So many times had he chased his little son and Rosamile up and down those flights as if nothing in the world mattered more than hearing their mischievous laughter.

When finally he reached the ramparts, Ruthor was standing against the parapet, gazing out to sea. It was a vision which would haunt the King forever. Always, because of the view, Ruthor had chosen to stand upon this, his favourite tower. With a sad slowness, he went over to the Prince's side and gazed up at The Wizard's nightly creation.

'The Disenchanted don't believe that all those spangles are lights,' Ruthor said without averting his gaze. 'They think they're other worlds. It's strange, but somehow I've always liked the idea.'

I do this for you, sweet Sanctuary, Septor vowed in silent dedication. *I do this for you.*

'Did the banquet please you, my son?' he asked, choking upon his tears.

'It sang of your love for me.'

'I never realised it would have to be so soon.'

'My destiny is fulfilled. It's good to be here where my spirit belongs. How often I used to watch the seas from this tower, wondering what lay beyond. Well, unlike other Sanctuarites, I know now and I tire of knowing and seeing so much. Give me sleep, dear father. Give me sleep.'

Trembling, Septor curved his arm round the Prince's waist while with his free hand, he drove the blade of the dagger through his son's doublet directly into his heart. Ruthor made no sound as the blood oozed from his chest. Gently, the King lowered the lifeless body to the floor before kneeling beside it, his hands clasped.

'Forgive me!' he cried against the eternal howl of the winds. 'Forgive me!'

Chapter Two

Rigid with grief and bitterness, Princess Rosamile urged her exhausted steed along the Path of Enchantment. She wanted to be anywhere but on the Island. Instead of feeling protected by the Great Main she now felt trapped by its raging seas. At this moment she hated everyone on Sanctuary and none more than her own parents.

She passed quarriers who were driving carts that buckled and creaked from the weight of the marblon stones piled atop them. There was also a shepherd who to her annoyance blocked her path with his sheep. Close behind were six knights returning to the Citadel. All of these people paid homage to her. All were ignored.

Next appeared a large group of Wizards and Witches. As soon as they saw the Princess they raised their arms high towards the sky and began to praise her and the Royal Family to which she belonged.

31

Enraged, Rosamile dug her heels into the horse's flanks and rode it straight towards the wailing Magicians. She revelled in the look of panic on their faces as they scattered before her.

'Murderers!' she screamed over her shoulder as the horse carried her away from them.

The Arildan steed did not continue its gallop for long. Slowing to a canter, then a trot it finally came to a halt, standing with its head down, breath shuddering through its nostrils. Furious, Rosamile dismounted and walked away, leaving the poor beast to recover unaided.

'Oh Ruthor, why did I let them kill you?' she cried into the empty air.

There was no answer but the baying of the sea winds. How could there be an answer? Did not all the hills, fields, and trees surrounding her belong to The Grand Wizard? Overcome by her hatred of Him she threw herself to the ground and wept.

King Septor had not stirred from his bed since the death of his son. Pages would scurry nervously into his chamber with what the cooks regarded as their most tempting offerings, only to have, upon almost every occasion, the food hurled back at them to the accompaniment of his curses.

It was not long before the odour within his chamber had become almost unbearably pungent, for the King had insisted upon bathing in nothing but his own misery. As the days passed he began to care less and less for his health, spurning anything to drink save jug after jug of Double Strength White Pear wine, preferring to feed upon the bile of his own guilt. All contact with his wife and daughter was forsaken and only servants willing to endure his cruel barrage of insults and risk having food thrown at them, were allowed to carry keys to the new locks he had ordered to be fitted.

Outside his closed door, Queen Katrila had pleaded in vain for him to emerge, explaining that she had both understood and forgiven him for the death of Prince

Ruthor. In her opinion no one was to blame, not even the Royal Witch, for love was in all their hearts, from the shepherds in the hills to the quarriers who chipped away day after day at the marblon stone, to the Royal knights who were desperately awaiting the re-emergence of their leader. Then, hands clenched, and continuing to address the locked door, she would tell him of how every night, when The Grand Wizard raised the Silver Orb high into the dark sky, she would rise from her bed to pray that her beloved husband would return to her side.

The first time she uttered these heartbroken pleas at his door, she was echoing tortured thoughts which could be contained no longer; the second time being simply a reiteration of what had been said before and the third an impassioned prayer. The fourth, however, was a set announcement such as the ones made by the Town Marshals who, unheeded by the majority of citizens, would mindlessly repeat at the end of each day the Laws of Good Dwelling. Although her words had become as innocuous as the cries of these Marshals, she still persisted upon a fifth attempt, a sixth, seventh and an eighth, until her obsession demanded that she spend much of each day outside her husband's chamber repeating the same words over and over again.

Finally, although mindful that she was their Queen, the senior knights had no option but to drag their heart-broken mistress away from the door and take her back to her own private throne room. It was to be there that Katrila spent all of her waking moments in silence – a mute figure sitting with perfect stature upon her throne, mentally composing her silent laments.

At the beginning, the Royal Witch had remained in her chamber cloaked by the mysticism of her calling, and some had even dared to wonder whether she had not cast a spell upon their King. Others, however, were wise enough to discount such an absurd assumption. No, for their part they had assumed that, like the Royal Family, she had imposed complete isolation upon herself while she grieved for her Prince, who had not been entirely condemned by herself, but by the Way of The Wizard. For most, it was not in their nature to hate her for what she had commanded for it was no secret that to be so at one with The Grand Wizard was a terrible burden. In truth, all of these assumptions were wrong, for when she too had felt the blade plunge into Ruthor, remorse had flayed her senses.

To her urchin apprentice, Barney Fowl, she had suddenly become a fearful monster. The old woman had screamed out her wretchedness against the four walls of their chamber, serpents of fire lashing the air before the room had become engulfed in a vortex, causing jugs of potions to smash upon the floor, herbs swirling around as if the chamber had suddenly become a wood during a windy, Leavefall day.

Yet most terrifying of all to the child, who had scurried beneath the table like a frightened cat, was the transformation of the woman whose face, although deformed, had always possessed an aura of tranquility and widsom. Suddenly she had become the kind of wicked old hag only to be found in the worst nightmare. He saw her jaws, already twisted by the force within her, as those of a hideous beast, while her forehead elongated itself as if she were turning into something as fearful as the Black Unicorn. Yet worst of all were her eyes. No longer deep and mystical, they had become filled by a wicked fire – a surging madness which drove the storm within herself towards infinity. Trapped in the chamber, Barney Fowl could do nothing but cringe in terror and pray to the Wizard that soon she would cease her self-inflicted torment before they were both destroyed. Then suddenly – as suddenly as the rage had started – it ceased.

There was now a stillness in the air, perhaps exaggerated by the turmoil which had preceded it. Orina, his surrogate mother (for the identity of his real one would forever remain a mystery to him) and mentor had returned. He gazed up at her, still trembling with fright, until his fears were assuaged by the calm serenity now emanating from deep within her bright, feline eyes.

'Were you afriad, little one?' she asked, smiling.

'Course I was,' he scowled. 'Never seen you like that before, 'ave I?'

'Nor seen fire lashing through the air or felt a whirlwind swirl like that around a chamber, while everying is flying about you or smashing to the ground?'

Barney shook his tousled head before answering.

'No, and I 'ave never seen you change into something so 'orrible. It wasn't you anymore. You was someone out of . . .'

'Your worst nightmare, perhaps? Is that it, little one? Now let me guess how I appeared to you – a cross between a mountain beast and the Black Unicorn perhaps?'

'Know everything, you do,' he admitted grudgingly.

'Not everything, Barney,' she teased, 'but one day you might know it all.'

'Me?'

'Yes, my uncouth, ill-spoken little scamp. One day you might know of things beyond your wildest imaginings and for that I pity you.'

'I never want to turn into something as 'orrible as you became just now. Rather stay as I am!'

She knelt down before him, bony talon-like fingers clasping his shoulders while she gazed into his eyes. As always, when he looked into those emerald pools he saw things almost beyond his comprehension. He saw Time. Not the time marked by the changing of the Orbs from one day to the next but Time itself. The force of creation flowing inexorably onwards – a river upon which his own fragile destiny was being swept along. There were other destinies upon that river, yet his and his alone was . . .

'So, you read into my eyes, do you?' she said softly. 'Do you really think that everyone can do that? Of course they can't. Already you have a gift beyond that of a normal Wizard.'

'Me, a Wizard!' The urchin was stunned at the thought.

'You weren't listening, were you? Did you not hear me say a gift beyond that of any other Wizard? I spoke of this to King Septor, yet obviously you chose to ignore my remarks.'

'I thought you was just fooling.' He gave a shrug in order

35

to hide the bevy of ambivalent emotions seething within him.

'Fooling!' she said sharply, her expression now severe. 'I never fool about Magic. Now tell me, why did I allow such dark forces to assail me?'

'Because . . . because . . .' Barney fought hard to concentrate his mind upon the question until like the sudden bursting of the dawn, the answer came to him. 'Because you wanted to get all that grieving over and done with all at once?'

'There, you see.' She dropped her hands from his shoulders before clasping his hands together so that he could feel the warmth of her Magic flow into him. 'How many people do you think would have the wisdom to understand that?'

'But the Royals, they'll be doing their grieving for a long time to come,' declared Barney, now eager to impress.

'Given the choice the Royals would gladly grieve forever. But it is not our place to judge the Unblessed by the standards of Magicians, even Kings and Queens. We can but wait until remorse has been purged from them by much slower means.'

During their wait for the King's recovery, the Royal Witch ensured that neither she nor Barney Fowl were idle. Her apprentice was sent upon countless errands, not only to the kitchen for food, but to the clay workers for replacement jugs for her potions, and to the fields beyond the Citadel to gather fresh herbs.

Wizards and Witches from various regions of the Island now resumed their visits and were usually seen to leave her chamber bearing jugs containing a suitable remedy for the patient in question. What was not seen was the invaluable advice they had been given regarding the exact spell with which to cure the malaise. Not once during this period did Orina spurn the duties required of her high position. It was only the plight of the Royal Family which she blatantly ignored.

Orina had just finished stirring a potion which required attention far beyond most others. It was so easy to forget that too much of the thick, glutinous honey, which came from the giant mountain bees, would congeal the liquid into a stagnant substance too solid to be of use to the shepherds who depended upon its use to enable them to be at one with their flocks, no matter what the conditions and even when they were sleeping. Nor were any of them ever to realise the risks of preparing this mystic beverage. Just a little too much sea salt fused, perhaps, with an over-generous amount of glanfer herbs and an air bubble could form, so great as to suddenly explode the scalding contents of the cauldron over both herself and her apprentice. Upon the completion of this hazardous task it was therefore the usual practice for both of them to celebrate its completion by imbibing a cup of refreshing Hillcorn juice. However, on this particular occasion she took just one sip before declaring to Barny:

'It is done!'

'We've made some good stuff 'ere for the shepherds, 'aven't we?' he agreed proudly, for this time he had made more than just a small contribution to its preparation.

'Not that, Barney,' she said impatiently. 'I mean the King's grieving. His time for wallowing in self-pity is finished. Has The Grand Wizard never spoken to you in such a way?' Her green eyes twinkled in the half-light. 'One day He shall, and when He does, a flash of golden light will streak across your mind – a spasm of fire will singe beneath your very flesh. This time He has told me that Septor must rise again to be the King he was ordained to be and that soon his Kingship shall be tested to the full. We can do very little but pray that the Royal Family will be strong enough to lead us to victory against the forces of the Disenchanted.'

'I thought you'd be the one to do that.' Pensively, Barney was poking a grubby finger into the potion. 'You've got the gift to do anything.'

'I've many gifts.' Her hand lashed out at the offending finger, smacking it away from the cauldron. 'But I cannot lead the Sanctuarites into battle. Can I, a deformed old woman, persuade and inspire them to lay down their lives

37

in the cause of winning a terrible and bloody battle? Of course I can't! And as for military tactics, well, I thank The Wizard I'm not encumbered with skills which are more suited to the Disenchanted.'

'You'll still help with some Magic though, won't you?'

She smiled mischievously. 'This time it will take more than the simple Magic used in the Great Attack to thwart them. So closed have their minds become that I fear they will be immune to any dark spirits we can summon.'

'I don't believe that.' Barney gave a knowing look. 'You've still got a few tricks up your sleeve.'

'Tricks!' she scolded mildly. 'All this time have you been under my counsel and you still haven't learned not to refer to manifestations of Magic as tricks! Wizards and witches don't like it, Barney. Even those sleight-of-hand conjurations which some do to impress those in their care are spoken of with great reverence. All Magic flows from the power of The Grand Wizard and never forget it. But as you say, I shall still play my part in sending those miserable wretches back from whence they came. So enough of all this talking, I must go to my King and impress him with one of your so-called tricks!'

King Septor lay beneath the coarse blankets of his bed, his naked body festering in dirt and sores. It was a cruel, umbrageous world he now inhabited. His breathing had become loud and stertorous, combating the brooding silence of his thoughts. For every waking moment – although, due to his sparse eating habits, much of his time was spent in troubled sleep – he re-lived over and over again that terrible sensation of feeling the blade of his own knife plunge into his son's breast. Like a predatory dark spirit the memory lingered until it had become an all-embracing companion, acting as both tormentor and panacea. He had confiscated the shining new keys of his servants, instructing the last one to push her key beneath the door after locking it from the outside. Now he was completely alone – alone to die. He wanted only to join Ruthor and beg for his forgiveness.

Yes, Ruthor would forgive him. Had not the heir to his throne spoken of his love both for him and for their blessed Kingdom of Sanctuary? Why, they could rule the land together, spirits gliding down from the Magic Wizardom to ride upon the Singing Winds – shapeless forms sweeping through huddled villages and filling the hearts of all who dwelled in them with joy. Or, perhaps, drifting down into the busy streets to be at one with the citizens. Then again, might they not be able to create in their spirit form, one huge canopy of love shielding all from the barren cold of Leavefall and the unyielding harvests? He gazed up at a ceiling laced with the pewter traceries of spider's webs. Septor would concentrate upon those webs until his mortal life passed away, all the time thinking of Ruthor, his beloved, forgiving Ruthor. Yes, Ruthor would forgive him and he could not wait to join him.

He had almost lapsed into sleep when the door to his chamber exploded in a maelstrom of fire. Startled, the King sat bolt upright before cowering back beneath his blankets. Flaming serpents licked angrily towards him before retreating to form a blazing firmament. Standing in its centre and staring down at him contemptuously was the Royal Witch, Orina.

'Why?' Although his anger was strong his voice was weakened by starvation. 'Why have you –'

'Burned down your door?' she shouted while the fire surrounding her began to dim. 'Because, my good King, you had locked yourself in.'

'You have no right to –' Once again his rage was muted by the weakness of his voice.

'I have every right, as have the rest of your subjects, to demand that instead of wallowing in this cesspit of self-pity, you rise to the task of preparing yourself for the coming of the Second Great Attack!'

Her words stunned him into silence. Like a chastened boy he sat against the bolster of his bed, his head bowed in shame. Patiently she waited for him to speak.

'I have done a terrible wrong,' he finally admitted.

39

'What vanity it is to mourn over such a grave past when the future bodes such grave peril.'

'The winds spoke to me of an invasion before Leavefall.' Orina's eyes flashed.

'Ruthor spoke of this also.'

'Well, had you not been languishing here in your chamber then you would have known that Leafbirth is almost done and the trees are now laden with leaves stronger than ever before. It is indeed a good omen that so few of them have fluttered into the winds. The Nature Spirits have heeded The Wizard's Warning. They can do no more. It is up to you now.'

'And what of the Royal Witch and her attendant flock?' Strength was slowly returning to his voice. Perhaps, while they had been talking she had cast a spell upon it? 'Surely a few Dark Spirits can be raised for the occasion?'

'You above all should know that such Magic can only be granted when people are prepared to make an effort themselves. I know the Disenchanted are immune to much of our Magic but I'm sure that if Sanctuary does prepare herself then many of The Wizards's great forces will flow through His mediums.'

'My people will be ready, just like last time!' Septor vowed.

'Those are the words I longed to hear.' She brushed away wisps of smoke, the last traces of both the fire and the heavy wooden door which had been engulfed by it. 'Together we shall drive the High Lord's army back into the Great Main.'

Septor shuddered. There was nothing very warlike about the people of Sanctuary: there never had been. How could he suddenly be expected to mould them into an army of fierce warriors before Leavefall? His Kingdom was doomed. Only the tempests of the Main could save them. However, he had forgotten that there were many times when Orina could read his mind, just as if she were reading words upon a scroll.

'It would be foolish to rely upon the Great Main to do your work for you,' she now said. 'No doubt a few ships will

40

flounder but Talango will have taken this into account. I expect your son confirmed that this time the vessels will be much sturdier than before?'

'He did.'

Septor's voice was now as strong as it had ever been. His assumption had been right. Orina had been weaving a spell even as she spoke to him.

'What else did he say?' The Royal Witch asked as an icy chill blasted in through the open doorway, billowing out her black robes.

'He said . . .' Septor clutched the soiled sheets to himself as the wind swirled about him . . . 'that this time they'll be using ships with wheels so that when they land, the vessels can be dragged ashore right up to the walls of the City. Then the hulls will be up-ended to form tall siege machines from which flying soldiers can leap down onto our defenders.'

'Cunning!' Orina arched one brow, her feline green eyes twinkling. 'Truly those who forsake Magic can create the wildest inventions.'

'Wild?' Septor growled. 'Ruthor did not think of such inventions as wild. It is only fools who think of their enemies as fools.'

The draught now seemed to be even colder as Orina, angered by his insult, stared at him with deadly menace. Yet Septor knew that a King could not show fear of anyone, not even a Witch. He returned her stare, determined that she should face up to the fact that there were other clever and powerful people in the world besides Magicians. They continued with their staring match – Septor's eyes the dark, ancient hue of fallen leaves, a symbol of rustic eternity, contrasting with Orina's glowing green ones, symbols of warm, verdant days when Magic breathed gently through the air. It was not long before their hardened expressions softened and they burst into laughter.

'At last! We have our King back,' she announced, her eyes now dancing with joy and reminding him instantly of the beautiful girl she had once been: the girl he had almost fallen in love with.

'Yes, my Queen of Enchantment, you have your King back,' he told her. 'Now fetch me my servants so that I might enjoy some food and perhaps wash it down with one of your famous potions. Then tell my family that my door is open to them.' Pointedly he directed his gaze to the smouldering doorway. 'For, thanks to you, my door will be open for a long time.'

'Good exercise for your carpenters,' she retorted. 'It'll help them to become fit enough for soldiery.'

'Everyone in the Island is going to be fit enough for soldiery, Orina. Everyone!'

'Then there is hope for us all.' The Royal Witch smiled before turning her back upon him and walking out through the doorway, her black robes fibrillating as another questing gust of wind whistled into the chamber.

At first Rosamile assumed that it was the pangs of hunger that had woken her. Then she heard the sound of small twigs cracking. Blearily, she raised her head yet saw nothing but the trees of the woodland. It was probably her imagination. Curling up, she decided to return to sleep, to try once more to dream of a world where there was no grief, no heartache. Afterwards she would make some kind of effort to find something to eat but for the moment . . .

'Wake up! Wake up!'

Startled, Rosamile opened her eyes to find that she was being shaken by her mother.

'At last I've found you!' The Queen's face was white, her hair wild.

Rosamile wrenched herself free and leapt to her feet. Angrily she glared at her mother. 'Leave me alone, you murderess!'

Katrila stared back. How often this rebellious child had disturbed her with her fiery tantrums. All the same, she would face her now. 'Leave you alone to dwell in the woods until it is time for you to go to the nearest village and demand that you be fed? That way you can keep on ignoring the suffering that goes on about you, can't you?'

'What else can I do?' Rosamile demanded bitterly. 'How can I ever forgive you or Father for what you did?'

'Like you, I never expected Ruthor to die.' The Queen's voice shook. 'It was as much a shock to me when it happened as it was to you.'

'Oh so that makes all the difference, does it?' Rosamile flipped back the mane of blonde hair that was now tangled and greasy. 'If that's all you've come to say then never has time been more wasted.'

Katrila again stared hard into her daughter's eyes. 'Had you been in your rightful place in the Royal Citadel instead of wandering aimlessly about the Island, you would have seen a father who was so stricken with grief that until the last few days he had not moved from his bed. Like yourself, no doubt, he was hoping that The Grand Wizard would take his life.' The Queen shuddered before continuing. 'As for me? While my husband spurned me, I took to the silent singing of the same laments over and over. In short I had gone quite mad. It took the magic of Orina to cure us both.'

'So now you've both recovered?' Rosamile said coldly.

'With no help from you, Rosamile,' the Queen retorted with equal coldness. 'Where was our daughter when we needed her most?'

'Your daughter was grieving for Ruthor!' the Princess retorted.

We should have been grieving together!' The Queen put a hand to her forehead as she fought to keep her balance. Habit made the Princess rush to her aid and help her exhausted mother to rest against a nearby tree.

'Surely, instead of wallowing in self-pity your time would have been better spent preparing for the invasion?' Rosamile said.

Katrila laughed bitterly. 'Only you, Rosamile, would have the arrogance to criticise others for doing exactly the same as yourself. You could have been preparing us all for the invasion had you stayed. Even though you are young, the people would have listened. They respect their Princess.'

Rosamile gazed up at the Golden Orb glowing between

the trees. She could feel its penetrating light deep in her bones.

'Yes, I do have a destiny to fulfil and you were right to come here and beg for my return. None of us can afford to dwell on the past when our future is such a perilous one.'

She squared her shoulders as if she were bearing the weight of armour.

'That sounds more like my daughter,' the Queen said wryly. 'You always did have a high opinion of yourself. Now is the time to show just how worthy of that opinion you can be.'

Rosamile looked at the woman who, like herself, had paid a terrible price for Ruthor's death. Only one person seemed to have been unaffected. 'And how is the Royal Witch?' she asked.

'There's no need to ask like that,' the Queen replied. 'Wizards and Witches pay the highest price of all, as well you know. The Grand Wizard will soon be wanting her life. It has always been the way that, as well as the judged, the judge must also perish.'

'The Way of The Wizard,' Rosamile spat. 'How we are all cursed by it.'

'So that's what you've been doing then?' Katrila shook her head. 'Why should you want to rebel? You are part of us, part of this very Island. Forget your blasphemies and return with me, and no more shall be said.'

There could be no argument against such wisdom. Rosamile could not deny that there was a powerful bond between herself, her parents, and the Sanctuarites. At this time of crisis they needed someone with a flair for military matters.

She took her trembling mother in her arms and held her close. 'It's time we went home, Mother,' she said softly. 'It's time we went home.'

Upon her return to the Royal Citadel, Princess Rosamile greeted her father warmly and swore that they would never be parted again. To celebrate the re-uniting of the

Royal Family they dined together and King Septor drank a toast to the daughter who would help him gain victory over the invaders.

Victory? It soon became apparent to her that no one, including the King, had any real idea as to how they were going to defeat an army of highly trained soldiers who would be arriving in ships that could be converted into massive siege towers.

As soon as they had finished eating she went to the scroll chamber. She planned not only to study the accounts of previous invasion attempts, but to remain there, in the scroll chamber, until inspiration released her.

Of all the subjects written there, none were dealt with more copiously than the tale of the High Lord Karango's abortive invasion of the Island. No fewer than twenty scholars had produced their interpretations of the event and Rosamile had read them all. Yet in truth, compared to the works of Algris of Kingtown who, although born much later than such contemporaries as the verbose Chadstar of Goring, the reputedly inaccurate Wizard Gorg, or the indulgently lyrical poetess, Dedrilla, all lacked his welcome terseness backed by a commendable authenticity. She could think of no better way to marshal her thoughts than by studying, once again, this testament to the valour of Queen Landora and her subjects.

Diligent research had revealed that Karango, in the tradition of the Disenchanted, had defeated and killed his three brothers in mortal combat, and thus had inherited the Autocracy from his Father, the High Lord Pagado. To the relief of all those who served and benefited from the Grand Autocracy, Karango proved himself a leader who was both capable and ruthless in the suppression of those who dared to challenge his rule.

Yet there was one vital difference between himself and the deceased Pagado. Instead of simply being content with three quarters of the known world, Karango was obsessed by gaining the final quarter as well. Algris of Kingtown had gleaned from the recorded interrogations of Sangoran prisoners that it was not unknown for him to burst into uncontrollable rages whenever the Island of Sanctuary was mentioned. Any reminder of the defiant nation that, protected by the savage seas of the Great Main and unscalable marblon walls, had always been regarded as impossible to conquer was inflammatory to Karango. Such was his obsession that he took the unprecedented step of publicly reviling all previous High Lords for never having attempted to bring the Sanctuarites to their knees. Karango was to be the Great Champion who was to invade the Island with a staggering display of military strength.

Even those who meekly abased themselves before their ambitious master had warned him of the hazards soon to be faced by himself and his army. Fearlessly, Karango had dismissed all warnings, declaring it to be his destiny to vanquish an enemy who blasphemously still believed in and practised Magic.

So while the subjects of Queen Landora were working hard in the golden, Orb-filled days of Leaftime, a vast navy of thirty ships heavily laden with soldiers, horses and siege equipment had set sail upon the hostile waters of the Great Main. It was The Way of The Wizard to bring upon this fleet a tempest like no other. Mountainous waves which all sailors upon the Main were forced to brave suddenly increased to three times their height. Dangerously overloaded ships were tossed mercilessly by the seething waters, causing ten of them to sink.

It was then the turn of the sea monsters to take a further toll. An exceptionally large tentagoth had risen up, wrapping its tentacles around another ship, dragging its victims down to its undersea lair. Then, when the black marblon cliffs were in sight, a giant spear fish skewered yet another ship, creating a hole so big that it went down to the bottom instantly.

At that point Scholar Algris took an almost unbiased approach to his subject by actually praising the High Lord and his forces for, despite everything, almost managing to stay on course. Not unsympathetically, he described how soldiers who were frightened, exhausted, and suffering

46

from a variety of debilitating ailments, were now expected to find a way of actually getting on to the Island, after drifting too far to the north. Rising formidably from the seas were tall, black, insurmountable cliffs. It was to be a whole day before they discovered a fissure leading up from the beach and onto the cliff tops.

No doubt they had all been looking forward to a well-earned rest once they had filed up the fissure and on to Sanctuary itself. It was not to be. Forewarned by captured spies, Queen Landora had arranged the cruellest of receptions. It was said that the screams of the invaders could be heard fifty tree lengths away and that the stench of burning flesh, carried upon the sea winds, could be smelt even further as vat after vat of boiling oil was emptied upon a panic-stricken rabble. There was little sign then of the highly disciplined army which had left the land.

The torment of the Sangorans continued until eventually they managed to drive back their attackers and reach the top. Reluctantly, Karango had granted his exhausted men a full day's rest before their long march to the Royal City. This decision was described by Algris as folly for it was not only the well-organised peasant militia who were to ensure that few of the invaders would get any sleep.

While sentries fell prey to the skilful arrow shooters, those allowed to sleep were tormented by nightmares created by the Magicians who, by invoking the Dark Spirits, had ensured that the army which embarked upon its march the following day was in a worse state than before. Encouraged by their success they summoned even darker spirits and on the weakest of the invaders were able to inflict a madness which was to have a devastating effect upon their ranks. A solider would suddenly discover huge, festering warts sprouting from his skin and then he would be overcome by a frenzied desire to kill as many of his comrades as possible, his comrades having no alternative but to put him to death for their own safety.

The practice of Magic had of course been banned by the Grand Autocracy and it was therefore with keen

47

embarrassment that Karango was forced to plead for anyone with knowledge of these arts to come forward and cast a spell that would act as an antidote. Like all other scholars Algris was vague as to how someone of the necessary skills had been able to claim their reward by expelling these curses. However, it was an undeniable fact that Magic had indeed played a vital part in the defeat of the Disenchanted.

Although brave skirmishers – principally from the towns of Kingstown and Goring – had successfully harassed the enemy it was reasonable to assume that the army which assembled before the walls of the City was still optimistic. Victory, they assumed, would soon be theirs. Despite everything, the inferno timber, obtained from the combustible forests of Nordag had been successfully protected by a constant soaking in water and once allowed to dry could be ignited and catapulted over the walls, thus ensuring that all those Sanctuarites who, foolishly, had taken shelter within the City would be burned alive.

Blazing volleys had filled the sky before raining down upon the defenders; the cruel Karango relishing the prospect of hearing their screams as they became engulfed in an all-consuming inferno. But instead of screams, great clouds of steam gushed up from behind the parapets. Somehow, they had managed to flood the whole City. Then the two main doors opened outwards and a powerful torrent was released. Directly in its path, men and animals drowned in the ensuing deluge. Amongst the victims was Lord Karango himself. Algris wondered how differently the survivors would have been treated had it been the Sanctuarites who had lost the battle, and not themselves, for Queen Landora commanded that the few Disenchanted who had escaped death might either be allowed to settle on the Island and provide information about the Autocracy they served, or return to their homelands.

Ten of them chose to remain and, living as outcasts, did oblige by telling the scholars everything they knew about the Domain, while the rest returned in shame; those who survived the voyage being able to tell of the fate which had befallen their comrades. Following this disaster came a period when many others of the Disenchanted braved the waters of the Main in order to seek a life upon the Island. Although, like the invaders, they were treated as outcasts, scholars had benefited from their accounts of the world that they had left behind them.

Through these accounts Algris then learned of how the Heir Lord, Cicero of Wergan, managed to kill each of his brothers in ritual combat, thereby deciding who was the strongest and worthiest to rule as the new High Lord.

Although successful in single combat, he had soon proved to be a weak ruler over nations that, after the ill-fated attack, had begun to challenge the Autocracy's authority. One by one the fiefdoms had fallen to insurrection until Etania itself was forced into slavery by the rising Mystics who, although at one with Magical Ways, had defiled the image of The Grand Wizard by demanding repeated blood sacrifices to sate their lust for power over their people. This power was short lived for under the leadership of the present High Lord, Talango, the Sangorans had rebelled and regained their former domination of the Mainland.

Without pause, Rosamile had read the entire account from beginning to end. As always, she found it immensely inspiring. If an invasion could be repelled once, then why not again? Except that all the lessons of the past would now have been learned by this new army. This time, Ruthor had told her, the Disenchanted would be totally immune to any mental assaults by the Magicians. Nor would they be able to flood the Royal City again. As before, it would require the building of an enormous channel from the sea. The invaders would seek for evidence of the same ruse being repeated, and act accordingly. No, all the mistakes of the past would have been noted. This time the Sanctuarites would face a far more wily enemy. How would they succeed? Now that she had recovered she could see more clearly, and the truth was that a nation of basically peace-loving people could be no match for an army which had no doubt been trained for years to accomplish these tasks. The Island was doomed. In her heart she knew it to be so. What chance did they truly have?

Rosamile slumped onto the desk. It all seemed so hopeless. How could a young girl like herself ever hope to solve the most insurmountable problem the Island had ever faced?

Yet who else had ever given any real thought to the art of warfare? Whenever she had fought a knight in mock combat not only had the fleetness of her feet been an ally, but also the quickness of her mind. Now that mind would have to be used for other purposes – to think of some way of counteracting the cunning inventions of the enemy. She knew of no other than herself who had such an ability. She had vowed to stay in the chamber until she found the answer. Perhaps it would take days, even weeks. No matter, she would stay until her work was done.

It was not until the third night of her self-enforced incarceration that Princess Rosamile charged into the Royal Bedchamber and woke her parents by declaring exultantly,

'At last I have a plan!'

Chapter Three

Leaftime was upon the Island, every vale and hedgerow blossoming with the joy of The Grand Wizard's creation. Although the Singing Winds of the Great Main tore in from the shores, the young leaves held fast upon their branches and, unlike the previous year, hardly any fell at all. Naturally, there were some who, in their darker and more brooding moments, saw it as ironic that Sanctuary should be at her most beautiful upon the eve of an invasion. Even so, such thoughts (deemed more worthy of the Disenchanted) were rarely voiced publicly. No, it was the opinion of those who lived through these fleeting days that in the future they would be venerated by generations to come as the victors of an epic ordeal. Songs would be composed and poems written about the Second Great Attack until, no doubt, many would tire of hearing them. Soon, the Militia would be calling them to arms and the captains – the only ones who had constantly practised the skills of warfare – would be haranguing them until they could cut and slash with their weapons to the same deadly effect. It was a time of fear and uncertainty but it was also a time of elation. The people rightly considered themselves as the most important to have lived since the First Great Attack.

Amongst those waiting to be called to arms were the quarriers of Deepcroft. For the moment, their days were spent toiling upon the hardest rock of all, marblon. Kraag and Cena had just finished seven days' solid labour and were now looking forward to a well-earned rest in the company of their son, Athrum.

'So what are we going to do with ourselves, little man?' Affectionately the broad-shouldered quarrier tousled Athrum's hair while his wife stirred patiently at the vegetable broth she was preparing for them.

'Let's go up on the hills!'

'The hills?' Kraag chuckled. 'It's always the hills with you.'

'I reckon he's going to be a shepherd when he grows up,' Cena said. 'He might be strong enough when he gets older but even so, he'll have no mind for quarrying.'

'Is that so?' Kraag pretended to sound angry. 'My son a shepherd? Never!'

Athrum looked guilty. 'I like the hills best of all,' he confessed. 'It's my favourite place.'

'Well, my one and only son, if you want to be a shepherd then a shepherd you shall be. Right, Cena?'

'Can't change folks from what they are,' his wife agreed. 'My mother always said that, and she was right.'

'And my mother always told me that a change is as good as a rest,' Kraag responded. 'So tomorrow we'll be doing something else besides wandering over hills. I reckon a nice day by the stream will do us all a lot of good.'

'But –'

'No buts, young Athrum,' Kraag's expression became grave. 'Because of this invasion we've all got to make the

52

most of our times together. Understand?'

Athrum nodded before flinging his arms around Kraag's thick neck. During these past weeks he had sensed the developing of his own maturity. Not long ago he would not have truly understood what his father was saying but he did now. Only too well.

Flowing down the Hill of the Fine Lady was a stream that vanished into a copse where the trees now glistened with fresh rustling leaves on colidor, prime oak, and, draping over the water's edge, the haunting, sad willows which, be it Leaftime or Leavefall, always possessed a mournful quality. This is why they had become a natural symbol for the passing of those who had gone before to the Magic Wizardom. It was a place much loved by the inhabitants of Deepcroft who on such days as this would laze, talk, laugh, or simply watch the silver waters of the stream swirl over a fascinating world of bright green weeds and pebbles of all shapes and sizes. Besides Kraag, Cena and their son, eight quarriers were enjoying such delights when the messenger disturbed them.

His name was Vargol and by trade he was a farmer, toiling upon the land at the foot of Dark Gown. He had thought it suitable to deliver his message in his armour, a crude and shapeless breastplate fashioned from heavy lacklustre metal, and a battered helmet perched uncomfortably upon his exceptionally large head, stiff, sprouting hairs jutting out at forehead and ears. Darag, a hearty and generally impolite companion wasted no time in pointing to this metal pimple and bursting into raucous laughter. He was not joined by the others. Even the three children were pondering upon the message which Vargol was about to impart. They included the usually boisterous Athrum.

'You'll soon be laughing on the other side of your face, Darag,' the farmer was quick to riposte.

'Tell us the worst, Vargol.' Athrum's father stood up respectfully and braced himself for the King's decree.

'It might be worse than all you quarriers think,' Vargol

53

said, directly addressing his words to Kraag. 'Like the rest of us you're all bound for the City, too. The King reckons that just like the last one, Talango will be wanting to take the capital before trying to invade the rest of the Island.'

'We were expecting it to be so,' Cena said, having raised herself to stand beside her husband. 'When it comes to wielding axes we quarriers take a lot of beating.'

'That's good to hear.' Vargol stroked the luxuriant grey beard which spread over the whole of his breastplate. 'Because some folks seem to think that only its citizens will be called to defend the capital, but that's not so. This time they reckons the Disenchanted will land in the south, and make straight for the City, so there'll be no need for skirmishers.'

'Well as long as we can take our families with us then happily, if it be the Will of The Wizard, we shall fight for our King.' The speaker was Sedral, a man who had sired no less than eight children in his time.

'That might well be the Will of The Wizad but it's not the will of the King.' Awkwardly, Vargol fingered the matted strands of his beard before continuing. 'He says that young 'uns, old folks, or anyone else not fit to fight, should stay put.'

'Unprotected!' Cena took Athrum's hand in her own. 'I'm not going to leave my son behind. What if everyone's wrong and the Disenchanted do land here, just as they did before?'

'They say there isn't room for everyone in the City.' Vargol was still fingering his beard. 'Besides, you quarriers have got a special job to do though nobody seems to know what it is. Anyway, you're to take your quarrying tools with you.'

'But we can't leave our families behind!' Sedral protested, his face flushed.

'Look it's not me who's giving these orders, you know.' Vargol's voice was half impatient and half filled with heartfelt sympathy. 'Maybe the King thinks that those who don't have to do the fighting are best off out of it. Besides, I've got a family too, and that includes a wife who's too lame to fight. I shan't be looking forward to saying my goodbyes tomorrow any more than you will.'

Some noticed a small tear drip down onto Vargol's beard and knew that very soon, tears would be swelling in their own eyes.

'It's tomorrow, then?' Chaag and his wife, Krona, asked in unison.

Vargol nodded while snuffling into his beard.

'Then best we make the rest of this day one never to be forgotten,' said Rifla, a cheerful widow who had always enjoyed the reputation of casting out any sorrow before the burden became too heavy. 'I'll go down to the quarry and get the others, then I'll run down to Deepcroft and bring over everyone who's there. I'll make use of Old Slow Trot and that cart of yours if that's all right with you, Kraag?'

Nodding, Kraag told her to bring the flagon of Redthorn ale from his hut. Following the example of his generous gesture, others now insisted upon providing donations in the way of food and drink. There would still be plenty of time before The Grand Wizard lowered the Golden Orb beneath the horizon, and even then the night was warm enough for them to eat, drink, and to do their very best to be merry before the dawn of an ominous future arrived.

The party was begun by a rousing singsong of favourites extolling the virtues, together with a few vices, of their beloved Island. A traditional starter was their jolly anthem, 'Merry As You Go', which told of the 'merry folk' of the Island who never failed to be jolly. This was followed by 'The Leaves of My Heart', a romantic ballad echoing not only thoughts of love but also the change of the seasons and of how, as those seasons changed, so did the course of love. Then it was time for the myths. 'The Goats of Cophaven' was always a popular fantasy, telling of how some Islanders, ignoring the teaching of the Magicians, strode boldly into the Magic Wood of Cophaven only to find that when they emerged, they had all turned into creatures that were half human and half goat.

It was a foolish little song, for every Islander held too much respect for this sacred place even to have dreamed of entering it. An even more ominous myth was 'The Black Unicorn', a song telling of the legendary beast which was said to roam the cliff tops known as the Forbidden, impaling any trespasser with the sharp black horn protruding from its scaly head. It was common knowledge that although he had dispelled all Magic from his Domain, the High Lord Talango used such a beast as his emblem, yet few knew the reason why. Nevertheless, sung in a certain way this refrain could be both frightening and dramatic. Curiously, it was a perennial favourite of the children – as were the songs about the white unicorns that were said to dwell in Cophaven.

When their singing was done, it was time to quench their thirsts: Redthorn ale for the adults, herb or wild fruit juices for the children. It now seemed that the Orb shone as never before as it twinkled brightly in The Grand Wizard's unseen hand. It was to become a day of bright songs and laughter, clouded only by a gentle haziness induced by the ale. It was only when the last drop of that ale had been drunk and the Orb became ocherous as it was lowered down towards its nightly home, that sadness drifted into their hearts like a sudden shadow.

Those who had been called to arms now clutched desperately at their children and old folk while singing the haunting lament, 'The Tide Takes My Body, The Hills Have My Heart'. Rarely had it been sung with such poignancy just as never before had the whispering trees and trickling water played host to such tragedy. By the morning the visitors would be gone from this place – some for ever. Out of respect, many bright young leaves fluttered down from their branches to die upon the soil of the Island. It was a gesture largely unnoticed by the copse's weeping guests but one which, nevertheless, had to be made.

Sombrely, and in reverent silence, they wandered back to Deepcroft, there to try and sleep as best they could before loading up their carts ready for the journey to the

Royal City. They began this task at the break of dawn, taking any food or drink left over from the party, and, as requested, the tools of their trade together with the heavy axes that were soon to be used for hacking at the flesh and bones of the Disenchanted instead of timber. Unfortunately the work was completed all too soon and it was time to make their farewells.

Athrum had been granted some sleep during the previous night. There was a short time when, contentedly, he had dozed upon his mother's knee, his soft blond hair splaying out over her thigh, his cherubic face illuminated by silver Orb light as both parents gazed down upon their happy, innocent son. As soon as he awoke, that look of tender peace was gone, fear and apprehension now in those wide blue eyes. Already the Disenchanted had succeeded in catapulting one young boy into the brutality of a new life.

'Why do you have to go?' he asked, gazing up at them with trembling mouth.

It seemed impossible to explain to a small boy why they should leave him here to the mercy of his enemy. How could they, the very people who had cared for and nurtured him, justify this act of misplaced patriotism?

'*Why?*' Athrum demanded again, tears flowing down his cheeks.

Again his parents were silent until Kraag knelt down before his son and clasped his tiny shoulders.

'Listen here, little man,' he said slowly. 'Yes, that's right, little man – because that's what you are now. Not a boy, but a little man. The last thing in the world we want to do is to go away and it's the last thing in the world you want us to do as well, right?'

Athrum nodded, making a brave attempt to smile.

'Well, we will be back soon,' Kraag told him. 'And there's plenty of people here to look after you. You've always liked Granny Wena, haven't you? You'll be safe here with her.'

Cena's heart was now pounding loudly in her breast. Her hands were slimy with sweat, her throat parched with sorrow. It was wrong what they were about to do. She would refuse to go. Yes, she would refuse to go!

'Don't lie to the boy,' she cried to her husband.

Kraag wheeled round, glaring at her angrily.

'Watch your tongue!' he said sharply before anger flashed from him as quickly as it had come. Realising how much she grieved, he hugged her and whispered into her ear: 'I know how you feel. But tell me, precious, just what sort of a chance would Athrum have if we didn't fight, eh? Besides, Talango's never going to land near Deepcroft again. This time they've got better ships and sailors. They're bound to make straight for the south. I reckon this village will be the safest place on the whole Island, you mark my words.'

Cena tried to feel ashamed of her outburst. Kraag was right – the King was right – Vargol was right – all of them were right! But was it right for her to walk away from her own flesh and blood, from the child she had taught to walk, speak, laugh at his own frustrations just as loudly as he laughed at his successes? Together, they had breathed the airs of this world. Athrum was her only son; he belonged by her side, nowhere else.

It took the combined strength of Kraag, his friend Darag and his sister, Retha, to pry the wailing Cena away from her little boy and heave her up onto the cart while Athrum pathetically tried to cling both to the legs of his mother and father. Theirs was one of the most heart-rending farewells but many tears were shed as the carts, laden with wretched quarriers, finally trundled away from Deepcroft.

Using the Path of Enchantment and taking little rest, the journey would take them a good day and a half to reach the City. During this time they intended to sing their songs, laugh at oft-repeated jokes and do the best they could to take each other's minds off their unseen future. Yet it was in silence that they began their travels, their dark moods reflected by the towering blackness of Eagle Mountain before they reached the equally sombre Hills of Dark Gown which, until now, had never succeeded in depressing travellers to such an extent by the casting of its long shadows. This brooding silence remained with them as they passed the Caves of Forgotten Spirits, before trundling on towards the mystical woods of Cophaven.

Then at last, their spirits were lifted. Shielded from sea winds by the high cliff tops of the Forbidden, Cophaven was, as always, uncannily still. They stopped on the high road of the opposite hill. There could have been no more inspiring sight than the colourful display of deep turquoise and emerald merging into a bright background of apple-green together with leaves which were almost silver, sparkling brightly in the Orb light. They climbed down from their carts and stood upon the Hill of Good Measure, gazing reverently down at Cophaven and to the cliff tops of the Forbidden that lay beyond.

'No,' Kraag suddenly announced, loud enough for all to hear, 'this is a place which will never belong to the Disenchanted!'

Sedral reminded them jestingly that should invaders enter these woods, then the chances were that they would all turn into half-goats. It was a feeble joke but it did help him to forget for just one precious moment that, back at Deepcroft, he had left behind not only a dying wife but eight small children. Pilna, a girl barely out of her teens but having already developed the thickset physique of a quarrier, rendered an impression of a Disenchanted who had suddenly turned into such a creature, making squealing, bleating sounds, and running on all fours. They knew very little about their enemy, or what the half-goats looked like, but they managed gales of laughter and felt some of their depression leave them.

They journeyed on now in slightly higher spirits. Even those in the third cart, amongst them the often taciturn Grubel, began to sing as they hastened to Kingtown, pausing for the briefest of rest periods before driving their weary horses onward. Upon their arrival they found the town virtually deserted of all the able-bodied. Only the slippery marblon walls surrounding them would offer any kind of protection should the enemy decide to attack. The quarriers paused only long enough to purchase food and drink before completing the rest of their journey.

In contrast to Kingtown, the area surrounding the Royal City seethed with people. On the field which formed the approach to the Main Gate, men and women were swinging axes against specially erected wooden poles, testing both their strength and their accuracy, while others hurled spears into straw bales. There were heavily armoured knights lumbering at one another in mock sword fights, weapons clanging. It was a strange, almost unnerving sight to see so many people gathering like this in one area, trampling down the grass until the ground was a quagmire of mud. Yet it was reassuring to see that the Sanctuarites were determined to prepare themselves as best they could for the coming battle.

Before the Main Gate was a small tent made from a cloth which they guessed might well have been the colour of gold before it had faded. The opening had been pulled back to reveal, sitting inside, their King. They clambered down from the carts and bowed before him respectfully.

'Greetings, good quarriers,' Septor said heartily, 'for with burly shoulders such as yours, quarriers you must surely be. Am I not right?'

'Quarriers no more I fear, Sire,' Kraag replied. 'Till all of this is done think of us as men and women of the axe, ready and willing to show you that Deepcroft shall be a name never to be forgotten!'

'Ah, but you know nothing of the secret plan.' Septor raised his bushy eyebrows.

'We were told that you had something special in mind for us, Sire,' Robag, the eldest of their band told him, 'but none of us is afraid of death. We're ready to play whatever part you want us to.'

'I wonder,' he said, looking at them with eyes glazed by warm affection, 'if any sovereign has ever had such loyal subjects? Each and every one of you seems to think of your own lives as nothing more than leaves to be blown away by the Singing Winds. What courage! Well, my loyal ones, I have good news for you and, perhaps in another respect, some bad also. The good news is that I shall not be expecting you to take any more risks than the others. However, I must urge you to make the most of this Orb light, before living the lives of moles, burrowing deep into the ground. It is not axes you will be wielding but the tools of your trade. You must work fast at your task, which I daresay will be both tiresome and dull. However they do say that those other quarriers down there make fine company.'

'Then tell us where we might leave our horses and carts, Sire, and we shall begin our work straight away,' Darag boldly declared, much to the silent annoyance of those who would have preferred to take a short rest before starting.

'Your horses can serve as carriers for men and materials. As for your carts . . .' The King paused awkwardly for a moment. 'They will have to be broken up and then used as bracing for the walls, just in case the Disenchanted do decide to try and batter them down. A strong shoulder of wood and earth will be needed to absorb the blows. Solid marblon might take some breaking as well you quarriers know, but Challid, who professes to know about these matters, assures me that we can't afford to ignore the possibility. So how can I argue?' He gave an exaggerated shrug. 'There's nothing to stop you from challenging him when he shows you the tunnel.'

'There'll be plenty of time to make some new carts after the battle's been won,' answered Darag, who had now appointed himself as their spokesman.

'Then let The Wizard's Blessing be upon you all,' the King responded.

Challid was waiting for them by the Western Wall. In comparison to them he was thin and absurdly small but nevertheless he seemed amiable enough, and he promised to do his best to get them some small compensation for their carts once victory was achieved. Cheered by these assurances they lowered themselves by means of a rope ladder down into the dark tunnel. Sparsely lit by weakly flaring torches, it resounded with the sound of picks scraping against stone.

Having conducted the last intake of quarriers to the tunnel entrance, Challid returned to the Royal Citadel to find Princess Rosamile. She was with the Sangoran, Zagro, a direct descendent of those of his kind who had remained on the Island after the First Great Attack. The outcast was now enjoying a new-found status as advisor to the beleagured defenders. Having learned that they were upon the fourth turret, Challid climbed breathlessly to the top of the battlements. The Princess was standing against them, her lithe body silhouetted against a bold blue sky, while her hair flowed in the Singing Winds. She was, without doubt, the most beautiful young woman he had ever seen. His regained breath was almost taken away again when she turned round to reveal a face of utter perfection in the whiteness of its soft, unblemished skin and the exquisiteness of its oval bone structure. Most stunning of all were her eyes: bluer and deeper than the sky itself yet as bright as the most golden days in Leaftime. Her radiance shone like a beacon to his heartfelt desire.

'How goes it, Challid?' She smiled, a smile which he fantasised was for him and him alone. 'Is the work in good progress?'

'More carts are being broken to reinforce the walls, Highness, and everything else seems to be going as planned. I've come to tell you that the quarriers of Deepcroft are now amongst us.'

'Good.' She gave another smile that would haunt his thoughts for the rest of the day. 'Tomorrow I shall visit the tunnels, and our Sangoran friend can come too.'

Suddenly she was no longer a girl with the wisdom of a woman, she was a child again, beautiful and desirable beyond measure, but a child all the same. True enough, Zagro and his kind had lived upon this Island for many decades but they had never been allowed to integrate and until now had never been granted the opportunity to stand at a Princess's side. It occured to Challid that this alien, with his unnaturally silken hair, might well suddenly

62

decide to brave the perils of the Great Main and warn his fellow countrymen, especially now that he knew of their secret plan.

'I know what you're thinking, Challid,' the Sangoran said wryly. 'Can't say I blame you really. I'd be thinking exactly the same in your position.'

'Yes, I can see you don't approve, Challid. Am I correct?' Rosamile asked.

'Your Highness, it is not for me to say that Zagro might have divided loyalties, although it would only be natural for him to do so.'

She leaned against the battlements and gestured for the Sangoran to speak his mind.

'I daresay you suspect that having discovered the secret of the plan I might scurry out of this City, steal a boat and sail out across the Great Main? Of course, assuming that I survive the passage, I might then find that the fleet had sailed from its port before I got there.'

Challid was unconvinced. It was equally possible that Talango's fleet might first hear all that Zagro could tell them. He made no attempt to conceal his scepticism.

'Please, I beg of you,' there was something in Zagro's almost almond-shaped eyes which demanded trust. 'I swear to you that I have no alliegance to Talango. Outcasts we might be but your people have treated us with a certain respect if not affection. What respect can anyone expect in the Great Domain? Dearly I love this Island and what it stand for, as much as you. Perhaps, being an outsider, I love it even more, if that's possible? Although I could never fully accept your Enchantment there is nowhere in this world which I hold in deeper admiration.'

Challid was moved by the Sangoran's words. 'I'm sorry to have mistrusted you, I'm sure that your knowledge of enemy tactics will prove invaluable.'

'From distrust to misplaced flattery in one great leap?' Zagro lifted an eyebrow and smiled. 'I can but tell you what stories have been passed down from the generations of Outcasts. It's believed that Karango did not take full

63

advantage of the many races under his rule, preferring to use only Sangorans in his army. Yet according to what we have been taught, Talango, if he so wishes, can bring with him the deadliest of enemies. Take the Moberane, for instance: giants who are twice as tall and twice as wide as any Sanctuarites. If he's trained them well then we really will have a fight on our hands. Then he might also use the service of the Clavitars from Sudelia – a race that has taken the example set by the lizards that live in their land and have developed tongues which can lash out and pick off a flying insect or, worse still, rip away the flesh from a man's face.'

In silence, Zagro waited for Challid's reaction to his words.

'Globins?' the Princess put in. 'Some of the scribes wrote of Goblins.'

'Indeed,' Zagro said, 'nasty, half-sized little people, too big to stamp on yet often too small and fleet of foot to kill with a sword or axe. They may have been called to arms. Of course, unlike ourselves, they might not be at all willing to fight but it would be foolish to make this assumption. No doubt the promise of loot will be enough to lure most of them to their deaths.'

'What do you think would happen if Talango were to be killed?' Challid asked.

'I doubt if his death would make any difference.' Zagro paused to stroke a beard which grew to a natural point without the use of any brush or comb. 'His four sons will remain on the Mainland and whichever of them gains the High Lord's title would execute as many of the defeated as was practicable. I reckon the forces of the Domain are mightier than ever before and they would have no difficulty in hunting down those who tried to escape from their master's harsh justice. They won't have any choice but to fight to the death.'

'But fear of retribution can be no substitute for the will of our people,' the Princess announced regally.

'My father always taught me that,' Zagro said. 'He regarded the spirit of the Sanctuarites as indomitable.

After all, deep in their hearts the Disenchanted must truly know that there is a better life than one under such a tyrannical rule.'

'Your people have been on this Island for long enough. Please, Zagro, bathe, in our Magic. If you did but know it, your sincere ways are at one with our own.'

Zagro fell to his knees. In the same manner as her mother, Rosamile gracefully extended her arm so that he could kiss the Royal Seal upon her finger. Challid knew this to be time for him also to swear fealty. He felt the delicate touch of her fingers on his own palm as he kissed the seal, fighting to suppress an emotion which far exceeded a natural love of his Princess.

'Arise, both of you,' she commanded, 'and gaze down from this turret upon all that we defend.'

There was no need to say anymore, the vista before them said it all. Directly below they saw Sanctuarites carrying more earth for shouldering, then their gaze travelled to the walls where the actual task of reinforcement seemed almost complete. Beyond that was the field where, their armour glinting in the Orb light, the knights were training. It had been the Princess herself who had insisted upon such intensive sessions both for the knights and the Militia and it was also her idea that the King, often accompanied by his Queen, should take station outside the gate and mingle as much as possible amongst his subjects, offering words of encouragement and good cheer to all those who had so willingly forsaken their homes and families to fight for the cause. It was a glorious day with no dark clouds invading the tranquil blue sky, and with the Orb lovingly pouring golden warmth upon them all. It was a day when the winds sang of hope.

Barefoot, yet ignoring the pain from the callouses and blisters upon their feet, pilgrim Magicians from the Island were walking to the sacred wood of Cophaven. Many found it tiresome that Orina had insisted upon the words of the Magic Scroll being strictly adhered to. To emphasise their humility, she instructed that no footwear of any kind should be worn. It was equally tiresome for the young apprentices who were forced to slow their pace so that they would not outstrip their elderly masters and mistresses. Yet, instinctively, the youngsters realised they were being taught the art of patience; something that all aspiring Magicians were required to learn.

On the ordained day, known as the Blessing of the Season, held on two occasions yearly – when the first leaves appeared upon branches and then when the leaves began to fall – all were assembled before the vast wood. Cophaven was now a spectacular diffusion of bright, verdant leaves mingling with the glinting golden hues of those beginning to fade. First there was the chanting of litanies when all apprentices were expected to give responses that were word perfect. Then the Serpent of Destiny was formed.

Much to Wizard Althigor's chagrin, for he had always regarded himself as holding a position second only to the Royal Witch, Orina insisted that her own apprentice, Barney Fowl, would be directly behind her in the human chain. Althigor was not alone in his resentment, for while all Wizards, Witches and even their apprentices had managed to ensure that the ceremonial symbols of their office, the tall pointed hats and long flowing robes, remained as clean as possible, the urchin had already daubed his newly acquired garments in so much mud and slime that they looked as filthy as the clothes he wore beneath them. It was regarded as an insult by all present and an even greater insult that such an obnoxious child should be so exalted in the eyes of their leader. Even so, none dared to voice their opinions to Orina, although it was generally accepted that she was perceptive enough to realise exactly what they were thinking.

In accordance with what was written in the Scrolls, the long Serpent was formed upon the western side of Cophaven. Orina then began to lead them around the perimeter, towards the foot of the Forbidden. Now different incantations were being sung in an order which had been followed since the very inception of the Blessing of the Season ceremony at Leavefall.

> *The trees are life*
> *The birds our brethren*
> *Suffer the fall of leaves*
> *The trees are life*
> *The birds our brethren*
> *Suffer . . . .*

It was ensured that each word, each syllable, lingered upon the air, carried upon soft, amiable breezes into the Magic Wood. Slowly and rhythmically, the hundred-and-five-fold train of worshippers began to circulate, gazing deeply into the arboreal haven which had remained inviolate since the birth of their race.

The Orb had now dimmed to a tender glow as it was lowered down by His great hand against a background of bronze-striated clouds rippling across a golden sky. They reached the slopes which led up the cliff tops of the Forbidden, their blistered feet now sinking down into boggy marshland as the subject of their incantations became the Forbidden cliffs themselves.

It was the fifth in line, Pricina, the elder Witch of Colwan, who first saw a flash of white amongst the densely packed trees. She remained silent. Neither did Milgar of Kingtown or his apprentice, Tilna, say anything when they too noticed something moving in the wood. It was not until the Royal Witch saw it that the Serpent was drawn to a halt. Most of the Magicians were too far back in the chain to know the reason for their being stopped but those nearer the front waited with baited breath to discover just why this unprecedented decision had been made.

Eerily, soundlessly, the White Unicorn emerged. Although shaken by what they saw, all had the presence of mind to fall to their knees in the soggy morass. They watched in amazement as the pony-sized white beast cantered out upon cloven hooves that were as golden as the long horn projecting from its forehead. It veered to the left before trotting along a chosen path around the perimeter until all had seen it. Then it disappeared into the woods again.

'So there really are unicorns in there!' Barney Fowl exclaimed.

'Yes, there are,' Orina answered loudly enough for a good many of them to hear, 'and anyone who has ever doubted their existence should never have taken their Magic Vows. Those with the True Gift would have heard the Magic creature telling us that the secret of its existence must remain. It is the wish of the Unicorn that no one be told of this, and we must regard it as a sign from The Grand Wizard that we who do His direct bidding must have faith in our own Magic.'

Their cloaks were now as muddy as those of Barney Fowl yet it did not matter, for upon this day they had witnessed something never seen by any of the generations before them and, perhaps, never to be seen by any generation to come. Implanted in all their mortal memories, for as long as they lived, would be the sight of the Unicorn trotting past them with elfin daintiness upon its cloven hooves, haughtily jabbing its knurled horn towards the sky as it tossed its soft white mane and swished its tail with joyful exuberance while its sapphire blue eyes met theirs with a deep understanding. Its beauty had surpassed even its own myth. It left them speechless.

Soon Sanctuarites would be fighting to preserve all that they held dear. Yet the Magicians would be fighting to preserve something else – they would be fighting for the preservation of that fabulous creature. For now, above all else in their hearts, was the pledge to ensure that no harm should ever come to the Unicorn of Cophaven.

Chapter Four

It was at Dore Point in the north west where the mighty fleet was first sighted. An old shepherd was gazing absently out to sea from the cliff tops when he saw a dark speck amongst the rolling grey waves. Then he saw another and another. It could only be the invading fleet. Doing his utmost to ignore the restraints imposed by age and leaving his sheep to roam wherever they pleased, he struggled down to his village as fast as he could. The moment that he had imparted the news, a Militiawoman mounted her fast Arildan steed and rode at full gallop to the next village. While another rider was taking the message to the next place along the Path of Enchantment, she eased her pace. The relay system had been instigated by Princess Rosamile to ensure that within the day the defenders were ready for the Second Great Attack.

As predicted, the long ships of Talango's fleet landed at

Blue Bay, a place near enough for all five towers of the Royal Citadel to be seen. A minimum force of skirmishers were waiting for them and it was they who were first to witness the awesome spectacle of the mighty fleet appearing over the horizon. Trembling with anticipation as they counted seven ships pitching and rolling their way towards them, they wondered how many of the others had been engulfed by giant waves. A rumour had spread amongst their ranks that should there be less than ten, then there was a chance of victory. Seven seemed a good number. At that point they had not lost heart.

It was only when the ships drew nearer to the shore that fear almost overwhelmed the watchers. They really were huge – massive superstructures each one big enough to house its own army. When the prow of the first ship to arrive towered up towards the sky, they cast horrified looks at one another. Even higher now, as if the top was almost touching the clouds, was a mast supporting a vast canvas of sail emblazoned with the huge forbidding emblem of the Black Unicorn. Tiny silhouettes could just be seen on the decks. It would be impossible to beach these gigantic vessels upon the shore and it was obvious that those they could see were all engaged in the task of weighing anchor. Above the whining sound of the chilling winds, they heard giant winches being operated, followed by the whirring of ropes as two great anchors splashed heavily into the sea.

A second ship was now at the side of the first and once more they saw tiny figures busy themselves beneath the high sails before it, too, was secured to the sea bottom.

Nervously, arrowshooters fingered bowstrings and axemen and women gripped the handles of their weapons whilst those in the Spear Militia clutched tensely at their spears, their knuckles white. The invasion was here and it was a terrifying vista of wooden giants yawing in the heavy tide.

'So how's they going to get themselves on land?' an arrowshooter asked his wife as they watched from behind a pile of marblon rocks.

'Search me,' she answered, her eyes transfixed upon the

scene, 'but they'll have a way and there won't be much we can do to stop them.'

Her words were soon proved right. They did have a way. Even at such a distance, above the sound of the winds, they could hear again the noise of cogs grinding against each other before two square, box-like devices emerged from open flaps on either side of the prows. Projecting towards the sea, they rapidly became immersed in the waves. Then, appearing upon rumbling castors, they came out from the waters again and onto the black pebbles of the beach. It soon became apparent that the ends of these strange objects were sealed, thus making them watertight. In effect, they were tunnels leading from the ship to the shore.

Although it could mean certain death, twenty-two Sanctuarites waited at the entrances to those boxes and, as the seals were forced outwards, the first blood of the battle was spilt.

It was evident that these tunnel boxes could only be operated initially with a small number of occupants, and the unfortunate Sangorans chosen for the task of opening the seals were soon slaughtered. They were unarmed, and the Sanctuarites thrust their spears into stomachs which folded inwards on impact as their dying victims retched blood, or struck axeblades heavily into unprotected necks. For those born of a gentle land it was cruel and heartless work, but they performed their tasks without mercy, knowing that very soon it could be their own turn to die.

Amidst the corpses of the slain, they waited at the entrances, comforting themselves with the prospect of living forever in the Magic Wizardom. Soon they heard the sound of running feet echoing towards them. The Disenchanted spilled out of the exits. Wearing spiked armour, the Sangoran soldiers resembled oversized hedge-hogs. Upon their heads were tall, gleaming, scythe-shaped helmets with face plates in the design of ferocious beasts. The deliverers of their deaths could not have been more formidable.

Yet the Sanctuarites stood their ground, swinging their

axes and jabbing out with their spears. A sword arm spun through the air as an axewoman fell upon her enemy, accounting for the life of another. Despite his spiked armour, she had gashed open the stomach of a third solider before the point of a Sangoran blade was rammed into her mouth, killing her instantly. It was not long before they had all fallen either to the sword or, in some cases, been impaled by the elongated spikes that their enemy wore upon their elbows, knees and boots and in the centres of their stomachs.

Instead of fleeing to safety, the arrowshooters, inspired by this sacrifice, stood their ground and volleyed their arrows into the armoured mass as more and more of the enemy emerged from the tunnels. Not all these arrows found a proper target. Skilfully, the Sangorans parried many of them with their petal-shaped shields or took advantage of the spiked protection of their armour. Then, in retaliation, these enraged soldiers charged at them, firing from the centre of their shields small, deadly bolts. These bolts accounted for many of the ill-protected arrowshooters, before the rest were put to the sword.

It had been a useless, perhaps pointless, gesture. For those who had been watching from a safe distance it had become all too apparent that any skirmishing by them would have little effect. Yet skirmishers they were, and however Talango's men intended to haul in their mighty ships they had all vowed that the attempted invasion would be performed under constant harassment. When least expected, arrowshooters would pick off random victims while Arildan-mounted riders would suddenly charge out and hack down many of the enemy before retreating with the same speed.

Soliders of all shapes and sizes were now marching out from the boxes. In addition to the countless Sangorans were swarms of little men only half the size of normal humans, yet sturdily built and bearing, like many others, well-fashioned pieces of wood. Larger pieces were dragged out by giants bent double as they emerged from the tunnels but twice the height of any other man when they stood up. Every one of these pieces was to be fitted into place so as to form some kind of device. Whatever this device was, the skirmishers intended to hinder its construction as best they could.

It soon became clear that the Disenchanted were assembling, piece by piece, large, heavy wheels directly opposite the tunnels. The sound of hammering was echoing against the cliff walls. These giant wheels were obviously winches which would be used to drag the ships up onto the shore. If they could be stopped, then the invasion need never take place. Arrowshooters concentrated upon the tighly armoured giants as arrow after arrow thumped into arms, legs, and occasionally an exposed neck or face. Often it took as many as six arrows to lodge into these ogres before they fell from their labours. It was futile work for the arrowshooters, many of whom strayed too near to the enemy and fell prey to Sangoran shield bolts.

After a hasty discussion, it was decided to allow the Disenchanted to assemble their great wheels and even wind their ropes around them. Waiting for the right moment were the forty riders armed with axes, spears and glavors – heavy, two-handed weapons resembling a cross between a sword and an axe. For those who could handle them, they were the most destructive killing tool of all. None would survive when the time came, but if they executed their move quickly enough, then they would certainly have played a major part in defending the Island.

Unhindered, the enemy was allowed to assemble its winches while the Sanctuarites watched and almost marvelled at such organised efficiency as the wheels were built upon wooden supports. Then ropes were passed around the wheels before the opposite ends were carried by scurrying dwarves back into the ships. As expected, it was not long before the giants took their positions at the long-handled cranks and, with synchronised movements, turned the wheels. From the ships came the sound of the anchors being raised.

Tensely, the riders waited for a signal from their three captains. One of them, a woman whose silver hair flowed out from her helmet, nodded to a red-bearded companion who rode a bluish, dappled Arildan. He nodded back before turning to the burly man on his right who raised his glavor high into the air before bringing it down in a sweeping movement.

The charge was on. Hooves clattered for footing upon slippery black pebbles, yet the practised skills of both riders and horses ensured that little momentum was lost as they galloped from behind the boulders. The cords on the winches were now as tight as bow strings. Those armed with glavors would aim straight for those ropes; the rest would do their best to protect their comrades while they severed them.

Unprepared for the attack, the Sangorans involved in the beaching of the first ship scattered before the charge. Virtually unimpeded, the glavor-wielders reined their horses to a halt before dismounting. Then, with quick, impatient movements, they sawed away at the ropes with the jagged edges of their weapons, working frantically until they were severed. One huge ship slewed to its right and crashed loudly against the nearby jagged rocks. With luck the hull would have been punctured. Quickly, the glavor-wielders remounted and charged towards those winching in the second ship. This group was better prepared and the Sanctuarites were now forced to fight heavily towards ropes which had been deliberately slackened off in order to make their task that much harder. In this action all were to die, even though the arrowshooters had joined their cause and were doing their best to kill as many of the winch-defenders as possible. Men and women, dying from deep wounds, dragged their bloodied bodies towards ropes which, due to the unavoidable rolling of the ships, had tightened again. Although at this point most of the riders and their horses had been slaughtered, somehow the thick cord was severed and another ship was cast back out into the Main. A panicking skeleton crew released the capstans but before the anchors could lodge, a series of giant waves broke against the ship's side, forcing the vessel to wallow out into the deep again. Although the fate of the other ship was avoided it would take the enemy much time and effort to winch this one back in again. The sacrifice of the valiant forty had not been in vain.

Enraged by the loss of so many riders and horses, the lightly armoured arrowshooters forsook their true purpose as random skirmishers and volleyed their arrows into the Disenchanted. No longer committed to the hauling in of ships, the first two invasion parties were now able to give these attackers their full attention. Filled with vengeance for their own dead, they charged at the men and women whom they totally outnumbered. Most of the arrowshooters were killed either by the swords or shield bolts of the Sangorans while others were broken upon the knees of giants after being hoisted up from the ground as if they were nothing more than small children. The least fortunate were to suffer the worst death of all. The little men would delight in thrusting their short knives up into the genitals of a victim before leaving the unfortunate man or woman to writhe in agony in a pool of their own blood.

For the five observers it was a harrowing sight. Instinct told them to return to the City, yet it was their duty to remain and watch the beaching of the ships, for their King may wish to know how it had all been achieved. As the vessels were hauled in, prow first, so the boxes retracted until they were back inside the hulls again. Sails were lowered before each ship was dragged and the keels were virtually out of the water. Then, with amazing skill and strength, the dwarves swung themselves up on ropes and, using both arms and legs, worked their way toward the prows until they were back on the decks again. The purpose of their return to the ships soon became apparent – more hands were needed to operate more mechanisms. To the now familiar sound of grinding cogs, the ships began to rise up out of the sea. Had the Disenchanted embraced Magic again – a Magic which somehow could lift ships out of the water? Yet it was not Magic which caused this but something even more fantastic. Emerging from each keel were eight wheels. The ships rose higher and higher until three-quarters of the mighty wheels became visible. Then the winching was resumed and this time they heard the sound of the heavy wheels grinding down rocks and pebbles as the ships were rolled onto the shore. To the right of the observers was open ground. No wonder the invaders had chosen here instead of a sandy place where ships could be more easily beached. There was little doubt that these incredible craft, which could be converted into siege towers, would soon be at the walls of the City. Hastily, the five rode back to tell of the selfless sacrifice of their fellow Sanctuarites and to warn their King of what was now inevitable.

'If only we'd realised how they were going to land those ships and how vulnerable those ropes were!' Angrily, King Septor shook his fist up at the grey clouded sky before returning his gaze to his companions.

'Think again, Father,' Rosamile said levelly. 'Had a larger army assembled upon the shores then the Sangorans would surely have dealt with it before attempting any other manoeuvre. You've just heard how well organised they are. It would probably have meant the end of us there and then.'

'I just pray to The Wizard that you're right,' the King told his daughter, 'and that this plan of yours works. We'll stand little chance if it doesn't.'

'Do you think I don't know that?' she snapped. 'So let's not waste any more time and get ready for them.'

Not only did Rosamile immediately regret this retort to her father, but she also realised the foolishness of her statement. Of course they were ready; they had all been ready since Talango's fleet was sighted. As she stood upon the battlements surrounding the Main Gate, the Princess turned first to her left where she saw a triple layer of Sanctuarites huddled against the cold winds. Some of the more polished helmets caught the dull Orb-light which filtered through the clouds and flashed like beacons. To her right was an identical scene. All were silent and resolute, their eyes fixed upon the horizon. Below the walls and directly behind them, occupying the outer streets of the City, were the rest of the defenders. She and her people were prepared for everything. There was nothing else to be done but wait.

In the distance they heard the sound of rolling thunder before six tall masts appeared on the horizon. Those with good eyesight could just see a thick black shadow spreading over the land. The shadow grew until they realised it was an entire army dragging the ships towards the City. Then the vessels themselves appeared: huge, gargantuan battleships. Just as the skirmishers on the beach had done, so those on the walls shuddered inwardly at the sight of craft of such a daunting size.

'What sort of people could build such monsters?' Queen Katrila said, turning to Zagro.

'It is believed, Your Highness, that the Goblins could be the ones clever enough to design them, while the Elves would have been involved in the more intricate work. Probably all manner of races would have been employed in their general construction.'

'Elves?' the King said sharply. 'You've never mentioned Elves before. Must we face them as well as all this other riffraff?'

'I doubt if they'll be here, Sire,' Zagro answered mildly. 'They might have a good reputation as slaves but they are useless as fighters. I would say that it will be an army mainly of Sangorans, Moberane giants, Goblins, and perhaps a few hundred Clavitars if they can endure our cold climate. Most of the other races who are servile to the High Lord's rule will remain, in order to maintain order in the Domain.'

'The old fool should have sent them all,' Septor declared with false gusto, 'then we could have a really decent fight on our hands. Now, where's Orina? Surely she should be up here watching all this?'

'I expect she's down there with the rest of the Magicians.' The Princess pointed to a circle formed by a number of cloaked figures wearing tall pointed hats. Distinguished by a crimson hat, and standing in the centre of them, was the Royal Witch.

'She must have some kind of Magic up her sleeve, even if it only means the bringing of good luck.' There was desperation in the Queen's voice.

'According to Ruthor, they're all so Disenchanted now that Magic can't influence their minds,' Septor said sombrely. 'Don't you agree, Zagro?'

Zagro brushed some of the windblown dark hair from his forehead before answering.

'I'm afraid I do, Sire, for even we Outcasts find it hard to be at one with the Magic of the Island. To our enemies, cold cynicism is a way of life. Since the rise of Talango I believe them to be completely immune. Most in his army will have been trained to shut their minds to such influences.'

As they spoke, the tiny figures on the horizon had become full-size soldiers. It was just possible to make out the petal-shaped shields and pointed helmets of the Sangorans. Easier still to spot were the Moberane giants who loomed over them, while, at their feet, Goblins swarmed. Those with really keen eyesight could see that further behind the six ships was the effigy of the Black Unicorn, also running on wheels. Inside that metal horse would be the High Lord himself, of that they had no doubt.

'If they're going to upend those ships then the sterns should be facing us,' a knight growled through his helmet.

'And what are they going to do about those masts? I reckons they've got other ideas than using those boats as siege towers,' an axeman said to a companion.

'Such as?' a spearwoman asked mockingly.

'Well . . .' the axeman lifted up his helmet and scratched his wrinkled brow . . . 'maybe . . .'

'Maybe, they're going to turn the things around,' the spearwoman jested half-heartedly as they watched the six ships being drawn to a halt.

To her surprise she was proved right. Yet another demonstration of ingenuity was given as the wheels began to turn inwards. By shifting all their efforts to the right hand side of the ships, the enemy could now begin to turn them around. Wheelwrights were momentarily able to forestall their growing fears by marvelling at the skills of a people who could create such adaptable devices. By being able to turn the wheels, they had actually steered their vessels to the City.

As soon as the ships had been turned, the ropes fastened to the sides were taken up again. Now stern first, they were being dragged to the walls surrounding the Main Gate. The invasion was truly upon them, changing a familiar and much loved vista into a frightening world of gigantic ships and hordes of murderous Disenchanted. Now all could see the spike-armoured Sangorans and, in contrast, the more scantily clad giants who wore little armour to impede them in their contribution towards the larger part of the pulling power. The Goblins could also be seen – vile little demons babbling and scurrying about. In lesser numbers were even stranger men who had dark faces and elongated jaws. They wore gold-plated armour in the design of a woman's gown.

There was also much activity on board for it was obvious that the ships were to be raised up until the decks rested against the walls. But how was it to be done? The ships continued to grow in size as the rumbling of the wheels drowned out all other sounds. Soon, they were almost beneath the watching Sanctuaries. In a way the worst part was over now. The waiting was done; the fighting would soon begin.

The invaders were now in range and the arrowshooters could begin their work. Volleys of arrows were rained down upon the assembling army but despite well-practised accuracy, the defenders could do little to reduce the enemy's number.

The bare masts now rose high above them while the square-ended sterns were all but half a tree length's distance from the walls. It was time for the oil. The hot pitchers were lifted up. Unfortunately those below had been prepared for this and most of the oil splattered down harmlessly upon the ground. It was only the cumbersome giants who, too slow to take avoiding action, fell victim. As the boiling liquid seared through their flesh they emitted terrible baying sounds more like those of animals than of human beings. It was not long before many Sanctuarites were gagging upon the pungent stench of burnt flesh as it wafted up towards them.

Those who had nurtured the hope that the ships might be inflammable had, with an extra effort, cast some of the oil onto the woodwork. Where the pitchers had managed to reach the ship, arrowshooters directed flaming arrows onto the soaked timbers. The wood must have been of a rare kind for it hardly burned at all and the feeble flames were easily extinguished.

The defenders had become too engrossed in their efforts to notice that the masts were becoming shorter and that the decks were slowly rising up to them. For many the realisation did not come until they saw that where there had once been tall poles, there was now a darkening grey sky. Why were the masts being lowered and what was happening to the sections which were rapidly disappearing beneath the decks? These masts served another purpose – they were also stanchions, lifting up the ships, deck first, to the walls. Now that the baying of the dying giants was over, they could hear the sound of cogs grinding against each other. Sanctuarites had used cogs for milling but never had they conceived such usage as this!

Soon the ships were gone, transformed into awesome siege towers, rearing up towards them. The prows now became formidable arched heads, blocking out the sky. The defenders prayed harder than ever before for The Wizard's Strength. The battlements juddered as the towers came to rest against the walls. For one hopeful moment it seemed as if the third tower was going to topple as it slithered precariously against the hard, slippery surface, but its heavy weight ensured that it rocked itself into position. The six towers were now in place – massive and immovable. Heavily armoured knights, most of them wielding glavors, assembled before what should have been a drawbridge, leading straight from the towers and onto the battlements where the attackers would charge out.

The Princess cursed their stupidity. Had they not seen that the only exits from these towers were the hatches in the arched heads? In their moment of foolish panic they had forgotten her warning of 'flying warriors'. She gave a command to be passed along to every defender that they should steady their glavors, pointing them up into the air in order to impale the invaders, just as the spearmen and women intended to do.

Throughout this time the Royal Family had remained upon the walls of the City. It was now time for them to hasten back to the Citadel.

'I'm staying here,' Rosamile shouted above the din as she saw down below that the Disenchanted were assembling into long queues behind each tower. 'It's safe enough. Once more weight is added to those towers then –'

'It should have happened by now,' Septor shouted back while grabbing her arm, 'and if it doesn't work, then you'll be the first to die if you stay here.'

'Then so be it. You'll just have to appoint another heir to your throne. I'd rather die in battle than wait to be captured. Besides, Challid here is confident that just a little more weight should do the trick. Aren't you, Challid?'

Challid nodded in agreement, yet the King was far from convinced. Fear was a bedfellow of impatience. He wanted it to happen now and he wanted his only daughter back in the comparative safety of the Citadel.

'Rosamile, I . . .'

'No!' The Princess stamped a heavy boot down, causing her armour to rattle. 'If I can't show confidence in this plan of mine then who can?'

'But what if it doesn't work, then what shall we do?' the Queen pleaded.

'We shall all die, Mother, be it here or in the Citadel. If they succeed at the walls they'll lay siege to our home while feeding off the whole of the Island. All of you will be slowly starved to death.'

Septor listened, realising now that his own beautiful daughter was the bravest of them all. Despite the restrictions of their armour he held her close to him, her golden hair flowing into his face. It was perhaps a time for dying, a time for The Wizard to take them all up into His Wizardom. Yet without doubt it was also a time for bravery and as he watched Rosamile embrace her mother he knew that with such a Princess, Sanctuary could not be served by anyone more courageous.

It was the moment for Orina and her chosen Magicians to take their places upon the ramparts. The Dark Spirits were with them now. Orina had delved her mind deep down into the black cesspit where the manifestations of every wicked thought, no matter how perfunctory, dwelled in loathsome eternity. Lining themselves along the walls, the Magicians linked hands so that the evil summoned by the Royal Witch could flow through them. Soon, on their tongues, was the taste of a bile too repellent to be of the mortal world. Seconds later, it flooded through their veins, drenching every part of them in its horror.

Orina's eyes turned black while her face became a maze of dark veins. Soon the others were the same, including her boy apprentice, Barney Fowl. Like the rest he glared down at the Disenchanted with a malevolence which was not his own. The power born of a million forgotten hatreds rippled through the bodies of those at his side before exploding into his own body. It blinded him instantly, engulfing him in a darkness that was deeper than the night – a bottomless void that was alive with the unthinkable. Then it was gone. He was blinded by the light of life itself and back in his own world again, watching for the result of the Summoning.

Alas, very few of the enemy were affected. However, he did see one giant clasp his head before starting to attack his comrades in a wild frenzy. Before he could do any real damage, he was killed, as were the other two Sangorans and the one Goblin who had also succumbed. Yet, besides a few isolated cases, the Disenchanted remained unaffected and, laughing, waved at them. This army was immune to their Magic and now the Magicians were being cruelly mocked. A fresh hatred burned within Barney but this time it was not due to the Summoning of the Dark Spirits.

Orina had not expected total success but failure such as this was degrading. In desperation, she summoned the birds of prey. Following the Royal Witch's example, the others stretched up their arms to the sky and began their incantations, willing their brethren of the air to swoop down from the leaden skies. To their dismay, nothing happened. Even the birds had forsaken them in their time of need.

Then they saw a solitary blue eagle emerge from the clouds, drifting on the Singing Winds. It soon became obvious that, through her mind, Orina was conversing with the creature, yet none could tell what she said, save for Barney Fowl. All they knew was that suddenly, the air was filled with predatory birds: blue eagles, falcons and Main gulls.

The majority of them dived to their deaths for, with disciplined precision, the Sangorans formed circles and lifted up their petal-shaped shields to the sky so that most of the birds were impaled by the tiny bolts fired from the centres of those shields. Several Goblins fell prey to the beaks and talons until one of the giants rushed to a victim's aid and tore off the wings of the attacking birds. It was also apparent that the dark-faced men with elongated jaws had a unique way of dealing with the birds. They lashed out with their tongues, ripping away the heads, stomachs or wings of the poor creatures. Too many of their number were now lying dead on the ground in heaps of bloodied feathers. Before their species could be forced into extinction, the rest flew home. Despondently, the Magicians watched the last blue eagle fly off towards the horizon, knowing that their leader would be mentally thanking it and all the other survivors for their brave attack and sympathising with them over the loss of so many of their kind.

Once more the Disenchanted made defiant gestures of

mockery as the Sangoran warriors became busily engaged in attaching floppy, sack-like objects to each others' backs. Once secured, these sacks would float upwards, almost lifting their bearers off the ground.

'Bladders,' Challid announced. 'Animal bladders cut in a certain way so that when the Sangorans jump out of the towers, the air lifts them up, thus breaking their fall.'

'I don't care how it's done,' Rosamile said impatiently, 'all I want to know is when can we expect the plan to take effect?'

'There can't be enough weight for it to work yet,' he said, visibly shaken by her rebuke.

'That may be, but it must happen soon, Challid, or we're doomed. You know that the Citadel could all too easily be laid to siege.'

'They might not even have to lay siege to the Citadel, Your Highness,' Zagro put in. 'Supposing they have a way of dismantling those masts then, once they've opened the Main Gate, the towers could be converted back to ships, dragged on their wheels all the way to the Citadel and then re-erected as towers again.'

'You're forgetting about the moat,' Challid said. 'Not only would they have to fill it in but also ensure that it was strong enought to take the weight.'

'Silence!' commanded the Princess. 'All that matters is what happens at these City walls, nothing else. While you two have been arguing, men have already started to enter the towers and are climbing up to us. Look!'

She gazed up at the six prows and studied the double doors which would soon be springing open, enabling the Sangorans to fly out like birds. Then realisation came to her. The Disenchanted had no intention of doing any fighting on the battlements at all. The flying warriors would all be landing inside the City itself. As for the plan? It had failed; they had simply underestimated the loading needed for it to work. She had no choice but to assume it to be so. In rapid succession she did two things. Firstly she told the knight she knew as Peringor to take all those who were on the battlements down below, with the exception of

84

the arrowshooters who were to pick off the Sangorans as they descended. Then she commanded Zagro to hasten to the Citadel and tell her father that, in her opinion, all those defending it should forsake their posts and help to fend off the invaders here, beneath the City walls. Her father would rage and curse at poor Zagro, but she knew that eventually he would concede to her wishes. What alternative was there?

As they hurried down from the battlements, spearmen and women were reminded again of the importance of steadying their spears upright in order to impale the Sangorans. Axe carriers were also reminded that the foe would be at their most vulnerable upon the impact of their landing while they had yet to regain their breath. It was planned that those who escaped from either of these two fates would have heavily armoured knights to deal with.

Rosamile also realised that it had been a waste of time reinforcing the walls, for no battering rams were in evidence and some of the flying warriors might even be able to use the piles of broken wood and mud to break their fall. Yet they were now powerless to do anything about it.

In her mind Rosamile could see the first wave of attackers scaling ladders. Were they so eager because of promises of an easy victory, perhaps? Or were they, like herself, shaking beneath their armour, knowing that very soon all the horrors of war would have to be faced? There was nothing else she could do now but join the others below the battlements.

The doors of the third tower from the left were the first to open. Sangorans swarmed out, bladders rapping loudly on the air as they opened, allowing the soldiers to drift down. The arrowshooters started their work, arrows hissing towards their targets while below them, spearfighters looked up to see the metallic faces of fearful beasts descending upon them. Some succeeded in skewering the warriors on the points of their spears whilst others managed to rip open armour so that, as their wounded victims landed, they could be axed to death. The Sanctuarites took a heavy toll upon this airborne force but the toll of their own number was even heavier.

Now launching themselves from all six towers, the Sangorans appeared in their element. The small bolts fired from the centre of their shields proved more than useful in killing or wounding the defenders as they drifted down. They were now also proving adept at avoiding the spearheads before crashing down heavily upon the Sanctuarites, gouging or stabbing them with the elongated spikes upon their elbows, stomachs, knees and feet, or crushing them beneath their spiked armour. Many even managed to avoid the volley of arrows fired from the battlements by steering themselves in midair towards the piles of wood and mud banked up against the City walls, thus enabling them to slide down into the mêlée below.

More and more of the Disenchanted fell from the skies while the arrowshooters' task became increasingly difficult. Now many of their arrows were striking harmlessly against the white, mushroom-shaped bladders which had been released by those who had landed and which were now drifting upwards again. With constant reinforcements of not only Sangorans, but also Moberane giants, Goblins and the deadly-tongued Clavitars, they could not see themselves holding out for much longer.

Orina had commanded that most of the other Magicians flee to safety before the battle commenced, retaining only those whom she considered capable of enduring what was to be her final act. Barney Fowl had been amongst those whom she had dismissed but he had defied her orders, wanting to be nowhere else but by her side. Above the din she had shouted and raged at him before realising it was hopeless to persuade him to leave. Something told him that she did not want to quarrel any more. There were times when it was important not to. With their lives under this constant threat, this was such an occasion. Yet her thoughts also told him more that he didn't want to face.

On the narrow confines of the battlements six of the Magicians formed a circle round the Royal Witch. Barney tried to become part of that circle but was pushed away. He tried again, but still he was shunned. He gave a pleading glance to Orina. She broke from her trance and stared back at him, her green eyes shining with love. Then they reflected a deep sadness and he knew that she was saying goodbye to him forever.

He opened his mouth to protest but she was gone, locked in that place between their own world and the Wizardom, where the forces could flow through her. The circle of Magicians began to turn faster, then faster still. Suddenly a Witch, a Sangoran shield bolt protruding from her head, fell away. Barney tried to replace the dead woman, but the gap was quickly closed up and the circle started to spin again, as fast as before, becoming a human vortex, hurtling round at an impossible speed. In that moment the horrified urchin knew exactly what was to follow.

The intense heat could be felt even before the fireball was created. Barney was gagging and retching upon the stench of human flesh before the first flames spiralled out to him. Arrowshooters nearby backed away from the blazing sphere as it began to rise upwards towards the top of one of the siege towers.

Unable to stop themselves, many of the Disenchanted fell out of the doorway and onto the rising fireball, there to perish instantly. Others did manage to take avoiding tactics but the intense heat of the flames melted the bladders on their backs and they plunged to their deaths.

Then it was the turn of those within the tower to die. The sickly stench of burning flesh intensified as the flaming sphere rolled into the tower. Flames licked out of the doorway while black smoke drifted across the sky. The screams of those inside could just be heard before the whole construction became an incandescent pillar of fire.

Sparks showered down upon the arrowshooters, one of whom was dragging a stupefied Barney as they fled to safety. The child was now crying out the Royal Witch's name. It was pitiful both to hear and see this pathetic little urchin mourn for the only person who had ever cared for him. However, to waste time in comforting the boy would have meant that all those brave Magicians had died in vain. Momentarily, the Sanctuarites had been given the advantage. Encouraged, they loosed arrows upon those soliders descending from the remaining towers. It was no time to pity the boy. It was no time to pity anyone.

Challid and the quarriers were running to the East Wall on pounding feet, Cena and Kraag amongst them. All the efforts of the invaders seemed to be concentrated upon the walls of the Main Gate. Challid could only pray to The Grand Wizard that all the surrounding areas were unoccupied, for a small force comprising only himself and thirty or so volunteers could be no match for an army. As they ran, the sound of their thudding boots echoed against the narrow walls of the streets while their eyes scanned from side to side, searching for any sign of the enemy. Fortunately, they reached the wall unhindered.

Like all the other smaller gates, the East Gate was heavily reinforced. Realising this, Challid had instructed every quarrier to obtain a bladder, either from the corpse of a dead Sangoran or by catching one that had been released before it started to float back up into the air. Clutching at these strange devices, together with their own axes, they hurriedly clambered up the steps and onto the battlements.

Now was the time for doubt. The thick-muscled quarriers had hoped to obtain the larger bladders used by the giants, but time was too precious to waste in searching for them. All they were able to do was snatch the first one they could find, and, when the time came, take hold of the strings and jump. Cena and Kraag looked at one another lovingly. These might be their last moments together.

Having wished the others success in their task and thanking them for the sacrifice they were about to make, Challid jumped. Gracefully, the Battle Adviser floated down to the ground unharmed. Although he was considerably lighter than most of the quarriers this was encouraging, especially as one of them had pointed out that a Sangoran warrior, fully armoured, would weigh almost the same as themselves. Quickly, they followed Challid's example and experienced the strange sensation of floating down like fallen leaves. It did not take long before they were all outside the East Walls.

Nearby would be the concealed entrance to the tunnel which they had dug to run around the perimeters of the City. Unfortunately, it was situated in such a place that it could easily be seen by those of the Disenchanted who were queuing up to enter the towers. The defenders' first task was to chop up the bladders into manageable pieces before burying them in the ground, for to allow them to float back up into the sky would have revealed their presence.

Having done this, they ran over towards the entrance of the tunnel, throwing themselves to the ground as soon as they were in sight of the invading army. The importance of what they were about to do became even more apparent now. Thousands were still waiting to join in the battle. Unless they succeeded, victory would be assured for the High Lord.

It was almost as if they belonged to that army, for so near were they that they could actually hear Sangoran officers barking out orders to their subordinates. They could also see and hear the Goblins babbling incessantly, presumably to counter their fears, while the giants stood in silence, their massive heads hung low. Then there were the dark-skinned ones, who, turning their weird faces up to the sky, were either practising or easing their tension by lashing out with their tongues. All, in their own individual ways, were too preoccupied with thoughts of the coming battle to take any notice of Challid, who was rolling himself over to the entrance.

Five other quarriers rolled over to join him. Now would follow the riskiest part of all. The hole leading down to the tunnel had been blocked by heavy wooden boards and then covered over with soil. All of this had to be removed, in total silence.

Although they were able to scrabble away the soil with their bare hands the boards themselves had to be lifted out. This could only be done if they got up onto their knees to gain greater purchase. With baited breath the others watched while the task was performed, all of them praying to The Wizard that their companions would not be noticed. As soon as the boards were lifted up, Challid disappeared down the hole. The others followed before, one by one, the remaining quarriers rolled over to the entrance and clambered down the rope ladder into the black confines of the tunnel.

This time, there was no means of illumination. Engulfing them was a thick darkness. Gasping upon what little air there was, they could not see anyone at all, no matter how close they were to them. Those who secretly harboured doubts of The Wizard's Teachings shuddered at the prospect that this soundless darkness might be all there would be after death, while Kraag took Cena's hand in his and grasped it tightly.

Yet without faltering, they followed one another, knowing that Challid would be counting the stanchions until he was satisfied that they were directly beneath the siege towers. As they neared their destination they could even hear the creaking of these pillars as they heaved under the massive weight of the towers above. Perhaps it would not have taken much longer before they gave way, but by then it might have been too late. No, their sacrifice would not be in vain. It was the only way.

Blindly, Kraag and Cena located with fumbling hands the two poles which they were about to sever. Then it was time to say goodbye.

'Poor little Athrum,' Cena wept in the darkness, her tears wetting her husband's cheek. 'What will become of him after we're gone?'

'Granny Wena will look after him,' Kraag whispered in her ear. 'He'll grow up into a fine young man, proud that he was born of parents who saved Sanctuary from being invaded.'

'I love you,' Cena said, holding him as tightly as she could and never wanting to let go.

'And I you,' Kraag answered, choking upon his own tears. 'Now let's be done with this so the both of us can meet again in The Wizardom.'

Along the tunnel, axe heads were being driven against the supports. Kraag was one of the first to hear the sound of wood splintering apart before the whole weight of the roof and what was above fell down upon him.

*

90

The second tower from the right swayed and rocked, prematurely casting out those about to leap down, before the ground beneath it caved in. As it toppled, those inside were compressed against each other, the spikes of Sangoran soldiers being driven into the bodies of those beneath them while others became fatally mangled by the cogs of the machinery. Panic-stricken, many struggled to free themselves before the tower rolled backwards, killing not only most of those within but crushing those queuing up to enter as well. The tower to its immediate right fell in exactly the same way, but faster. Hundreds more, both inside and out, met their deaths for few had any chance of escaping. Two of the other towers fell against each other while the remaining one slithered against the shining marblon walls before it too fell to its destruction. Survivors outside the towers tried to flee to safety but, as Challid had predicted, the collapse of the tunnels had caused a landslide and many more perished as they were crushed by the tumbling bodies of their own comrades.

Almost too late, Rosamile saw the massive spiked mace descending upon her. Hurling herself to her left, her foot slipped on something. The full weight of the weapon's impact jarred the ground as it missed her. Looking up, she saw, partially unprotected by his breastplate, the navel of a Moberane giant, and instantly she thrust her sword upwards. The mace fell from his grasp as she twisted the blade into him with both hands and wrenched it out again. The huge, lifeless corpse flopped down onto the disembowelled intestines she had slipped on. Seconds later, she found herself surrounded by Clavitars.

   She hacked open the exposed face of one of them before the tongue of another lashed out at her head, now unprotected after the loss of her helmet. It was about to rip away the flesh of her face when a glavor appeared from nowhere and smote the long tongue in half. She wasted no time in thanking the knight who had saved her, but drove home her own blade straight into her attacker's throat before hacking off the sword arm of another.

Then it happened. There was a thunderous crash as the tower fell. The Sangoran she was fighting turned to see what was happening. Rosamile ensured that it was the last thing he ever saw by ramming the point of her sword into his eye. Instantly, she regretted this method of killing him for the blade became lodged in the dead man's cranium. Before she could extricate it, two Goblins were upon her.

Lying on the ground was a Sangoran helmet. While battering her assailants with her shield, she picked it up with her free hand. There was a small grab handle inside, thus enabling her to grip it and use the sharp curved blade at the top as a sword. The first Goblin tried to run but she was soon upon him, slitting open his tiny back as he fled from her. His companion pleaded for his miserable life before she beheaded him in one perfectly timed movement. Discarding the helmet, she picked up the miniature head and then dodged her way through the mêlée until she was clear of the battle. Her fighting was done.

Triumphantly she ran towards the Citadel, her golden hair soaked with the blood dripping from the Goblin's head as she waved it jubilantly above her own. Perhaps it was wrong to feel this way. Should she not have been grieving for Challid whom, she knew, had always been secretly in love with her? Or maybe poor Orina who had destroyed a tower by turning herself and her brave companions into a fireball? Then of course, there were the quarriers who had chopped down those poles, knowing what fate would befall them as soon as their task was done. So many had died this day; and more would die before the Disenchanted were vanquished. But the grieving for them all would have to wait. The drawbridge had been lowered. Standing upon it were her mother and father. Ignoring the pangs of her exhausted body, she ran joyously to celebrate with them. They had won – they had won!

PART TWO

The Four Sons of Talango

Chapter Five

All those who had survived the battle fled back to the beach where the one ship which had not been dragged ashore was anchored. It was the High Lord Talango's own personal vessel so those in the lower ranks knew that very few of them would be allowed to board. As it turned out, only twenty were hastily chosen as crew members; the rest were left to the mercy of the Sanctuarites.

Both the ship and the High Lord managed to survive a crossing that could not have been more savage. By the time the vessel had reached Etania only one of its three sails remained, while Talango's once indefatigable spirit had succumbed to the shame of his defeat. As quickly as they could, his serviles conveyed him to the Supreme Fortress where, as all now knew, his life would shortly be coming to an end.

*

Talango sat miserably upon his high throne, longing to return to the bed he had been forced to vacate. Nothing but sleep could bring any comfort to the bitter pain of defeat. With new eyes he surveyed his chamber. The wall draped with gold-edged ebony curtains now reminded him of the high marblon walls of the city he had failed to occupy. The beams of light streaming in from the crescent moon windows ironically cast him back to the bright optimism he had first felt as the siege towers had been raised against those walls. The flickering braziers, just above floor level in order that serviles could tend to them without standing in his presence, reminded him of the sudden shock when one of the towers had suddenly burst into flames. Could the fireball which destroyed it have been created by Magic? If anyone knew the truth he doubted if they would dare to tell him, any more than he would have dared to ask.

Would any of them realise that just as they were all slaves to his rule, so he too had always been a slave of their expectations? His gaze drifted to the unicorn-shaped fireplace, and he pondered yet again upon his own fragile mortality. The High Lord Talango was dying.

There had been a time in his life when he had foolishly believed himself to be immortal. It had seemed impossible that one so strong and dominant in every aspect should age and die. Insects, he had reasoned, died because they were, in general, small and insignificant, so, as the seasons changed, it was time for them to be replaced. Animals, he felt, died because if they had not been eaten by mankind at the appropriate time then their flesh would decay and they would weaken. As for man himself? Fear was his destroyer. It was this to which those who served him eventually succumbed, their insides rotting away until the bones began to contort and the flesh to wrinkle. Eventually, their fears defeated them completely; their minds finally embracing the Nothing. In those halcyon days when all the world was his, he had shown no sympathy – even to the most useful of serviles – as he swaggered about the Supreme Domain assured that he, Talango, would live forever.

Then like a slithering, insidious snake, something had

begun to course through his veins. His skin had started to wrinkle, wisping hair had drifted down upon his shoulders like falling leaves. He could feel his bones contracting, drawing his body inwards and hunching him down towards a black empty void from which there could be no escape.

From his high throne he gazed down upon the backs of those who enjoyed the privilege of serving him in his chamber. The mere utterance of one word and obediently all these Chosen Serviles would shuffle upon hands and knees to await his command. How pathetic they were! He could only assume that for many of them the Nothing could even provide some kind of release. Perhaps they were unafraid of it? For the first time in his life he envied them.

With the advent of old age, he had become obsessed with the thought of conquering the island of Sanctuary. He knew of Kalango's abortive attempt and how, indirectly, his defeat had brought about the fall of the Grand Autocracy, but the man had been a fool. Only a fool would have attempted such an invasion with ships that were unseaworthy and an army that was so ill-prepared.

When he realised that, even for him, the Nothing was inevitable, he had chosen to face it in battle rather than remain in the Supreme Fortress and rot away in his chamber. The Nothing could be kept at bay by military conquest, and Talango's invasion would succeed – or so he had thought.

It had been one of his sons, Giraldo, who had discovered what he thought to be the unique talents of the Goblin, Nym. This discovery had pre-empted his decision to invade; it had seemed logical that the dwarf's talent for creating ingenious devices should be put to good use. To this effect the diminutive servile, whom he found particularly loathsome, presented him with a plan for ships which could not only run on wheels once they were beached, but could then be raised up to form siege towers. Dazzled by such a concept, he had ordered the construction of thirteen, a figure chosen as a deliberate defiance against the teachings of the Mystics who had always preached that this particular number was unfortunate. Even if in this instance, obviously through sheer coincidence, they were to be proved right.

Six of these ships had sunk in a storm during which, unseen by serviles, Talango had cowered in terror within the twisting confines of his cabin. What excuse could there have been for such behaviour? After all, he had surely known the risks involved, even being prepared to forfeit his own life if necessary. Yet he had quickly recovered and was soon to take a more positive attitude. The worst was over and he had survived. Victory would soon be his, of that he had no doubt.

So the temporary disablement of the seventh ship when they had landed had merely been dismissed as a minor setback; six towers, placed against the city walls, would still be sufficient. It was only when the towers fell that his spirits had sagged down into a mire from which they would never rise again. Only one man was truly to blame for this – that was if he could even be called a man.

Despite the blazing fires and the thickness of his foul-smelling robes, which even the constantly burning aromatic spices could not expunge, he felt cold. Even so, he did not seem to have the energy left to shiver. The Nothing would soon be upon him. There were matters to be attended to. He would hurry.

'Serviles!' he commanded.

Despite the weakness of his voice all scurried to him. For one moment a memory returned of how, when they were younger, he had taught his four sons how to playfully whip serviles whom they considered to be moving too slowly. That, too, was a long time ago. Now all games, including the game of life itself, were coming to an end.

'Tell the Bringer of Pain to deliver to me that accursed Goblin,' he croaked, a spasm of pain attacking him.

The Bringer of Pain was, of course, wearing the obligatory black attire expected of his profession and, also in keeping with his comparatively high status, he sported a moustache with elongated, thickly waxed tips. Yet, as always, the most striking feature of those of his calling were the two sockets where once there had been eyes. Voluntarily, all Bringers of Pain would have both eyes burnt out by hot irons so that they could not only stand before their High Master without gazing upon his face but also, or so it was believed, apply torments with even more sensitivity. There had been times when Talango had watched one of them at work, marvelling at the intricate patience which could prolong his victims' agonies until their pain-filled eyes were pleading for the Nothing.

Beside him, the miserable little wretch Nym huddled in chains. The Goblin was to suffer even worse and longer torments than any Talango had ever witnessed, or the Bringer of Pain himself would be tortured.

'And how is your charge?' Talango enquired of his most feared sevile.

'High Master, I have kept him in good health so that he might endure his sufferings for as long as possible,' the torturer replied.

'Get to your feet, Nym,' Talango ordered with a voice which could no longer boom out across the chamber, but nonetheless made the Goblin shake with dread. 'Let me gaze upon the face of a servile who dared to trick his master!'

The Bringer of Pain jerked at the chain attached to the iron collar around his prisoner's puny neck with such a force that instantly the dwarf was yanked onto his feet.

It had been a long time since Talango could remember actually seeing the face of a Goblin. He had almost forgotten just how ugly and obscene they were compared to Sangorans, or even Elves for that matter. In this instance Nym's eyes which, like all of his race, were unnaturally red, had become crimson with terror. His broad nose, with hairs bushing out from its nostrils, twitched nervously while his thick-lipped mouth gaped open, revealing rows of yellowing, pointed teeth.

'Tell me, Nym, what do you see?' Talango asked.

The Goblin tried to stutter a reply but could not manage even a croak.

'Then I shall tell you,' Talango wheezed. 'You see before you a High Lord who is broken with grief over a shattered dream. It all began when one of his sons brought before him a Goblin who was said to be the key to that dream. Brazen in his own cleverness, this undersized parody glorified himself, strutting around my fortress, thinking himself a full-sized man; wearing clothes which were garishly bright and jewellery more suited to a High Lord's station! Yet this despicable little worm bloomed on the folly of his inventions – ships which could be turned into towers that fall down! Thanks to him my dream will remain unfulfilled.'

'Mercy, mercy,' Nym squeaked as he fell to his knees before the Bringer of Pain jerked him to his feet again.

'Mercy?' For one moment the tenor of Talango's voice was that of a much younger man. 'What mercy have you shown to me by bringing me such a bitter defeat? Now that I have seen how ugly you really are you may go to the Chamber of Exalted Suffering and ponder upon the disgrace you have brought to this Domain before your torments begin.'

Even before Talango had finished speaking the Goblin writhed and squirmed in his chains, begging pathetically for a swift death. Using the symbol of his office, a wooden staff fashioned in the shape of a twisting serpent, the Bringer of Pain cracked it against the whining wretch's head before Talango ordered his High Guard to assist the torturer in dragging him out. Then he called for the Heir Lord, Giraldo, the son who had so unwisely recommended Nym's services.

Upon entering, Giraldo angrily kicked aside one of the Chosen Serviles before glaring up at his father.

'I suppose you're going to blame me for Nym's handiwork?' he growled, folding his broad arms and stretching apart his muscular legs in a stance of pure defiance.

'Who else should I blame?' Talango said bitterly. 'Was it not you who enthused so eagerly about his ideas? Did it never occur to you that if the Sanctuarites were to build tunnels beneath those towers then they'd collapse?'

'No, Father, it did not, any more than it occurred to anyone else. I dare say it was Ruthor's advice that inspired our enemies to think of it.' There was sheer malevolence in his son's dark eyes.

Ruthor! Talango had almost forgotten about the exiled Sanctuarite from whom he had gleaned so much about the Island before the prince had treacherously fled the Fortress. His soldiers had searched everywhere in the land but had failed to find the traitor. It had been assumed he was dead, for even though there was a report of a fishing boat being stolen how could anyone have survived a lone voyage across the Main? No, this was simply a cunning ploy by his son to turn the blame away from himself.

'How can I be sure, Giraldo, that you did not send spies over there to warn them, or that you yourself weren't in league with them?' he retaliated.

'Nonsense!' as was his habit when emphasising something, Giraldo pummelled a huge fist into the air.

'Why is it nonsense? What could have been a more perfect ploy to get rid of me?'

'I think this audience should be conducted in private,' the Heir Lord suggested before kicking at another servile with the toe of his highly polished boot.

'Would that include the High Guard, perhaps? One word from me and you would be dead. I need that kind of protection when you are in my presence, you see.'

'Now why should I bother to kill a dying old man?' his son sneered. 'Your days are nearly over, everyone agrees on that if nothing else. Then it will be time for the Supreme Contest. Even you have to agree there can be only one winner.'

The High Lord was now too weak and cold to argue, realising that to harangue Giraldo would only incur more taunts. Anyway, the last word could still be his.

'I'm not dead yet and your contest is yet to be fought,' he reminded him. 'As it was you who first brought Nym to my chamber then it shall be you who will supervise his end. Remember that arrangement of pipes that he tried to impress me with? The ones that enable me to be heard in every part of the palace?'

'I do.' Giraldo stroked his black beard. Like his moustache it had been trimmed to squareness at the edges.

'Good, then you can organise its extension down to the Chamber of Exalted Suffering.'

'It shall be done. I too will be interested to hear what kind of sqeals the little vermin makes.'

'Then see to it with all haste so that I can be soothed by his wailing while I'm in my bed. A possible remedy, would you not say?'

Giraldo gave a shrug of his burly shoulders, promised to attend to it and took his leave.

It was now time to deal with the Supreme Combat Lord, Begridido. Having just returned one prisoner, the Bringer of Pain was now expected to collect from the Chambers of Penance yet another. However, this time the torturer's task would be much simpler for although twice the size of Nym, Begridido would carry himself with dignity and composure to the very end. While he waited, Talango mused sadly on the trusted Lord who had failed him on only one fatal occasion.

To their surprise no doubt, all serviles, guards and even the Bringer of Pain himself, were dismissed when Begridido was brought before him. Save for a bolt-launcher, which had been detached from a shield and was now loaded and resting on his knees, the High Lord was completely alone with the deposed Supreme Combat Lord.

'Begridido,' he commanded quietly after regaining his breath from another chilling spasm, 'get up off your hands and knees and onto your feet.'

The heavy chains clanked loudly as the prisoner did as he was bidden, careful to keep his face turned away from his High Master's.

'To think that just over a hundred years ago, you, who have always been at my side, once gazed upon my face,' Talango reminded him.

'I have cherished that honour all my life,' Begridido answered. 'Yet I cherished even more the moment when you were rightly acknowledged as our High Lord. Although I could never be allowed to see it, I knew that glory shone upon your face like no other; a just reward for defeating the strangest of enemies.'

'There are still stranger enemies lurking in the far corners of the Domain. If only I had concentrated upon those instead of being beguiled into trying to invade Sanctuary.'

'The Island would have been yours, High Master, had it not been for my folly.'

'Incredible!' Talango said hoarsely. 'You who have succeeded where all others have failed, you who have denied yourself nearly all the rewards worthy of your high station so that selflessly you could serve me even better than I demanded; yes you who have done all of these things now blame yourself?'

'High Master,' Begridido almost collapsed to his knees again, 'how can so unworthy a servile deserve such praise?'

' "How can so unworthy a servile deserve such praise?" ' Talango mimicked. 'Oh my dear Begridido, who else deserves it? Is it not ironic that I, the omnipotent ruler of his Domain, must have you brought before me in chains, you, the one man who above all else has helped to keep me in this position?'

'I could expect no more, High Master. Who else could be blamed for such a loss?'

'Well, to start with there's that vile little Goblin. It's a pity you won't be able to hear his screams when his tortures begin.'

'It is indeed,' Begridido agreed, and Talango imagined his lips curling up into a wry smile. 'I too would have gained much pleasure from listening to his squeals.'

'Both of us would have enjoyed it, my . . .' He then used a word he had never used before, 'friend.'

Silence pervaded the chamber, save for the crackling of the fires. Talango had felt foolish uttering that word and now regretted it. How could a man who demanded such servility refer to anyone as a friend? It was absurd. He,

103

High Lord Talango, had always been destined to spend the whole of his life alone. Nobody could ever be his friend, not even his four sons. Yet he could sense that Begridido was deeply moved by what he had said. In that silence he could feel it, as if the man really was a friend.

'In the very beginning, High Master,' Begridido said slowly and hesitantly, 'I almost thought of you as a brother. It was only when your Domain grew and you were rightly recognised as the Black Unicorn, solitary and powerful beyond measure, that I, like so many others, was honoured to become your servile.'

'Then tell me, my friend and servile, did you in all honesty accept the legend of the Black Unicorn?'

'I . . . ' Predictably, Begridido found it hard to express his true thoughts upon such a sensitive issue.

'The truth now,' Talango insisted, ignoring yet another chilling spasm within his body.

'I . . . I confess that I have always thought it a brilliant ploy of yours to gain the support of those who still believed in the foolish teachings of the Mystics. By identifying yourself with one of their mythical beasts you became acceptable to them. It would have been unwise in the early stages to refute all their beliefs. Only now, and rightly so, is it a blasphemy to believe in any such thing. Yet as an emblem I can think of nothing more inspiring.'

'And that, no doubt, is what most of the population believes. Well, what if I were to tell you that every word of the legend is true?'

The Supreme Combat Lord was stunned into silence.

'Yes, everything,' Talango continued. 'How can I ever forget being a child tied to a sapling and knowing that within the next few moments a blade would cut into my little stomach so that my innards could be drawn out of my still-living body and then tied around that very tree? Until that day I had never seen the beast of legend. Then, as if from nowhere, it charged out at the priest who was about to perform the sacrifice, impaling him on its black horn. Nor have I seen it since. But I tell you this: as I too approach the Nothing, I have finally realised the true significance of the Black Unicorn.'

'And what is that, High Master?' Talango could tell from his tone of voice that Begridido had been amazed by this information.

'The Black Unicorn is a catalyst of change,' he told him. 'Think of our world as a living entity. When it sees danger caused by those who walk upon its soil it will demand change. It is then that the dark creature appears.'

'So that's why it has not been seen again? It knows that the Domain can never fall.'

'Who can say?' Talango gave a shrug. 'But do you really think that any of my four sons will be strong enough to rule in my place?'

'Giraldo is bound to win the contest.'

'Agreed, but you're forgetting that the Mystics came to power because, after Kalango's death, the High Lord who replaced him was incapable of ruling the Grand Autocracy.'

'The Domain is far stronger than the Autocracy ever was. Giraldo has strength enough.'

'Giraldo might be strongly build and he even has a good brain. However, was not Ferigo physically superior to most men as well as having a reasonable amount of intelligence? Yet under his rule, the Mystics rose to overthrow him. No, I sense an imminent change and whoever faces it must be strong, as strong as myself, perhaps stronger. Somewhere in Giraldo is a lack of foresight and in some respects I wish it could be one of the others to take my place. Take Vestudio for instance: no doubt you have seen someone who is fat and hopelessly indulgent, but I have sensed an exceptional ability at organisation. With Sigaraldo, I see beyond his deformed, crow-like appearance and find a ruthless patience which would be a priceless asset in the seeking out of rebels. Even fey Karabano has a better understanding of the finer tactics of battle than the impulsive Giraldo. Can you not agree?'

'Perhaps I can, High Master, but at the Supreme Contest nothing would deter me from betting heavily upon Giraldo being the winner.'

'And you would be wise, my friend whose judgement I have cherished above all others. Soon, whether I wish it or no, I will be joining you in the Nothing and then – like yourself – I shall want to leave this world knowing that one way or another it will still be ruled by a High Lord worthy of his title. Rest assured that upon my deathbed my last thoughts will be of this problem, for that is something which can never be blamed upon the worthiest of Supreme Combat Lords. You may also rest assured that it is the Domain itself which demands retribution, not I. Now let me look upon the face I have not seen for a hundred years.

Begridido turned slowly until the two men were looking at one another. Talango now realised that the rule of master and servile had been the basis of a long and sustained illusion. His friend, like himself, had grown old. Yet deliberately, perhaps, he had allowed these obligatory circumstances to help him forget this fact.

Warily, Talango allowed his eyes to roam over his friend's robes of office, once so fine but now dirty and stained, then up to the gold-plated helmet which no longer shone brightly but was dull and battered. Finally he looked into the face of a stranger. Gone now was the freckle-faced boy with eyes which always burned with such zeal. Instead, there was an old man with a moustache which, despite careful waxing, drooped limply down as, with faded eyes, he stared back at his High Master. Like his own, Begridido's body was rotting away; there was nothing else to be said. In silence they stared at one another before the High Lord nodded and the servile turned his face away from him for the last time.

Weak and with shaking hands he raised the shield bolt-launcher and aimed it at his friend's heart. Thankfully, it was a clean and instant kill. Chains clattered loudly as Begridido fell to the floor, a bolt protruding from his back. Then, heavy with sadness, Talango tugged at the cord beside his throne. Serviles and guards scurried back into the chamber to remove the body. Then he retired to his bed, knowing full well that he would never rise from it again.

*

As he had predicted, his condition rapidly deteriorated, yet the delay in his final passing allowed enough time for him to enjoy the benefits of having the Goblin's auditory system linked to the Chamber of Exalted Suffering. He thanked Giraldo for providing such a satisfying entertainment and was pleased that there was a way of muting the device so that upon occasions he could ponder upon the last remaining problems in his life without the disturbance of Nym's screams. He also commanded that he was not to be disturbed by anyone, save bringers of food which he rarely touched, for he intended to die in peace. The only other persons allowed to attend him during this final period were two Serviles of the Word who were instructed to record vital alterations to the Grand Rules of the Domain. Then, once this last task had been completed, the High Lord Talango, Ruler of the Supreme Domain, passed away during one cold Leavefall night into the place which all mortals dreaded – the Nothing.

Willingly or otherwise, the entire Domain went into mourning as soon as the news of his death reached them. All were told how his revered body had been placed in a massive effigy of the Black Unicorn which had then, with great effort, been dragged up to the very peak of the Exalted Mountain, the place where it was said the mythical beast had dwelled before saving their High Master from being killed by a Mystic. It was then set alight, the flame of the pyre burning up into the night sky to illuminate the surrounding countryside.

Below, all those who had held exalted ranks abased themselves in misery at the place where once a small boy had been saved from sacrifice. Then it was time for men of the High Guard, as a final gesture, to lay down their arms at the foot of the mountain before the procession of the Lords reverently began to walk around it. They were led by Talango's four sons, the Heir Lords, who, so that none could see their faces, were all masked. Then came the four Custodian Lords of Etania, Sudelia, Nordag, and Wergan, and behind them followed the newly appointed Supreme

Combat Lord, together with the fifty Combat Lords who could be spared from their posts.

Many feared that when the Supreme Contest was fought beneath the Exalted Mountain one of the three weaker Heir Lords might win instead of Giraldo, but it was virtually inconceivable that anyone other than the ruthless Giraldo should succeed. However, there were some who did express secret doubts to their most trusted confidants that he might not have the ability to rule the Domain with the same authority as his father.

Eventually, the fire died down to become smoking embers. For a while there was total darkness, reminding all of the Nothing to which Talango had now passed. Then the moon emerged from behind the clouds and stars shone brightly. It had become a cold, clear night, thus heralding the birth of a new dawn when the Supreme Contest would be held and Giraldo, having slaughtered his weaker brothers, would take his place upon the High Lord's throne.

Chapter Six

There was nothing wrong with the armour that Karabano, the Heir Lord of Wergan, was wearing. Nevertheless, it was ill-fitting. There were some people who adapted easily to armour and there were those who were simply not made to be encased in metal plating. It was Karabano who was ill-fitted for this armour just as, in many ways, he had been ill-fitted to the life he was about to lose.

Awaiting the dawn of the day which would see his execution, Karabano shivered against the cold chill of the night. The closed visor acted like a door, shutting out the world he was soon to leave. Alone, he savoured for the last time the simple acts of breathing, of seeing a bright moon illuminate a landscape of sweet-scented plants and of hearing the voices of those who would live beyond that dawn. It hardly · seemed possible that all this would suddenly be replaced by the Nothing – a black emptiness where everything was rendered meaningless. Death was such an unkind trick.

At least for him immortality would be partially achieved for it was doubtful if any future scholar would ever be as prolific in such a short space of time. Already his works were regarded as the definitive histories of the High Dynasty, the Grand Autocracy, and the Supreme Domain. Due to his cogent and readable interpretations, many more would become acquainted with the dithering yet curiously effective Gopoto, and the bellicose Veldigio who loved fighting above all else. Then there was Talastio, the first ever to totally conquer Sudelia, and, of course, Kalango who had launched the first invasion upon Sanctuary. If only there was a place beyond death where he could meet them all, an imaginary world where the poets and playwrights also dwelt and all the artists he had admired so much. Instead of the Nothing he envisaged a vibrant tapestry unfolding before him. If only such could be true. If only . . .

'Master.' Encroaching upon his thoughts came a familiar voice. Karabano wanted no intrusion. He was about to push the servile away when he spoke again. 'Master, I beg audience with you.'

'What is it, Bezulo?' the doomed Heir Lord enquired of the servile who had been his main assistant during his researches. 'Can't you tell that I want to be alone?'

'Yes, Master. I have only dared to crave your attention to tell you how much pleasure I gained from being in your service. Should the outcome of the contest prove –'

'Don't be a fool,' Karabano snapped. 'You know what the outcome will be as well as I.'

'When the time comes I shall avert my gaze,' Bezulo told him. 'Then after, when I'm about my business in the Spiral Towers of Learning and of Knowledge, I shall feel your presence urging me in my quest to find the truth, no matter how vexing my task.'

'Of that I approve.' Karabano gave a half smile which none could see. 'Giraldo has no skill at learning and dismisses the acquisition of knowledge as if it were unimportant. Yet wisdom can be a great asset in ruling the Domain. I have learned of the many mistakes made by others; will he ever be able to claim the same?'

'Master, if only . . . '

'If only nothing,' Karabano retorted, gritting his teeth. 'I have applied myself to mock combat. I could almost feel your regrets when my father berated me for my miserable attempts to compete with Giraldo. At first I thought your reaction to be mere disappointment that you had no chance of becoming a favoured servile to a future High Lord. It was a long time before I could accept that you were actually grieving over the prospect of my death.'

'May your death be swift and painless, Master.' A tear trembled on Bezulo's cheek.

Through the slit in his visor, Karabano gazed down upon Bezulo's back and saw that his orange cloak had been brightened by the first rays of daylight. It would not be long before the Supreme Contest would begin.

Sigaraldo, the Heir Lord of Nordag, had a plan. He had always excelled at making plans, but so far they had all failed or, to be more precise, the Elves whose skills with poisons were reputed to be unsurpassed had failed. True enough, the poisons created had all proved to be spectactularly fatal. One Servile of Lesser Worth who had been force fed with the most toxic potion had died almost the moment it was forced into his mouth. Yet the smell of the mixture had been too pungent and proved impossible to disguise. Sigaraldo had made several subtle attempts to poison Giraldo but for one reason or another, all had been foiled.

At the first ray of daylight he had begun to sweat profusely, and even the most generous gulps of water could not moisten his parched mouth. It would soon be time; the waiting would be over. He had but one chance to survive. Beside him was a little casket with a lid which could easily be flipped off by the blade of his sword before he dipped it into the poison.

All he then had to do was to inflict the smallest of cuts

upon Giraldo and the only Heir Lord he feared would die instantly. Should his first duel involve either Karabano, or the fat and clumsy Vestudio, then he would not risk revealing his ploy. Even with a wizened body which had always been prone to illness he was still confident he could beat either of those two. No, the poison was reserved for Giraldo.

All the same, he had many doubts: doubts which would not be banished until he was standing over Giraldo's corpse. At a very early age he had learned that his Etanian brother could defeat him in any sword fight, although he realised that his physically superior opponent did have a weakness. Giraldo's confidence was abundant – too abundant; one day he would over-reach himself. So far, his superior sword-fighting skills and sheer brute strength had enabled him to parry any counter moves with ease. But if Sigaraldo should encourage his arrogant brother to think that he was bound to win, that he could not fail, then his guard would drop, thus allowing for the penetration of the poisoned blade . . .

So there was hope. He decided to increase that hope by summoning the five Chosen Serviles waiting nearby. Through his visor he watched them scurry on all fours towards him, yet there was a hesitancy in their movements. Somehow they seemed to know.

He studied each of their orange-cloaked backs. Two of them were mere boys, only recently appointed from the ranks of the Ordained. It was not difficult to tell that they were all afraid. One of them would have every reason to be. He chose.

'Onto your feet, servile,' he commanded of the well-built one he had jabbed with his foot. 'Get up!' he insisted before kicking out at the servile for a second time.

A lifetime of servitude could not be ignored; duty prevailed. In the next instant the man leapt to his feet.

'Now turn and face me. What do you fear? As I am visored you cannot see my face.'

Shaking, the man turned and faced him. Whether this particular servile was the strongest was debatable, yet did that matter for his plan?

'I think you have been around long enough,' Sigaraldo told his victim, who was now looking down in terror at the sword blade pointing at his chest.

He fed upon the servile's fears as he studied the wide staring eyes and noted with relish how the wet lips quivered. Yet to one so deformed as himself, delivering a singular killing thrust had always presented a problem. Now, difficult though it was, he must do it.

Ramming the blade into the servile's belly caused him to reel and almost lose balance. For a moment it had actually seemed as if he had killed him outright. Yet it was not to be. As he yanked out the blade, he discovered that the servile was still breathing. However, in one respect it did not matter. None of his opponents, including Giraldo, would realise this. Still alive, his victim collapsed into a heap on the ground where he made loud gargling sounds as blood seeped out of his wound and his mouth. Momentarily, he considered killing the other four just to see if he could improve on his initial attempt. But then in his mind, he could hear Giraldo's mockery.

'What's this, brother Crow? Are you going to kill all your serviles just to show us how afraid you are?'

This taunt would then be followed by the cruellest of laughs, its imagined sound twisting him upon a spike made of his own bitter hatred for his brother. Upon reflection it had been foolish to attack the servile. Now all he could do was hope that the wretch would soon be done with his gargling and pass quickly into the Nothing. The Nothing! It was all too terrible to contemplate. Once again he checked that the little casket was concealed from view. Cunning and guile had always been his most valuable assets. He had need of them as others had need of meat and drink. Somehow he would kill them all, including Giraldo. Somehow.

Vestudio, the Heir Lord of Sudelia, was feeling nauseous. Perhaps when the time came he would be forced to vomit

113

inside his armour? On learning that his father was dying he had known that his own death would soon follow so he had chosen to gorge on huge amounts of food, cramming toasted red lizards, dragon fillets and honeyed jellies into his slack mouth. Such was the practice he had gained over the years that he was able to eat and drink until his belly visibly swelled. Through an alcoholic haze was the most comfortable way to see life. Only his ability to enjoy the voluptuaries had waned. Those paraded before him had either been too plain to be of interest or if they were acceptable, had not performed to his expectations.

It was said that when a man knew he was about to approach the Nothing, then all his senses were heightened. Strangely, part of him had almost relished that prospect. However, the statement had soon proved to be woefully untrue. The overriding fear of death had in fact dulled his senses. Pleasure no longer provided the escape it once had.

Yet the shadow of death had never been far from his side. Since early childhood he had known that his gross and indolent body would always hamper his efforts to defeat the wily Sigaraldo, let alone Giraldo. There had been a brief period when he really had made an effort to lose weight while gaining both in strength and fitness. It had all been to no avail. When he fought Giraldo again in a mock sword fight, he had merely forced his Etanian brother to make a slightly greater effort to defeat him.

From that day onwards, Vestudio had indulged himself in every imaginable delight, his only respite from these indulgences being the occasional study of the past. Not that this had taken any effort for he had only to listen to his similarly doomed brother, Karabano, who always welcomed any opportunity to relate his latest findings. Another diversion had been to test his skills in board games against the cunning Sigaraldo, who would rage and sulk if prevented from winning. Even his eventual executioner, Giraldo, occasionally provided good company. When tired of bullying his own serviles, he would enter Vestudio's chamber and bully some of his.

When the encumbrance of his great weight had not seemed too burdensome, he had even undertaken some travelling. Despite protests from his father, Vestudio had ventured into the place from where his mother came, Sudelia, there to endure the oppressive heat of its climate. In contrast, he then explored the frozen lands of Nordag before moving on to the eerie, forested regions of Wergan. Exploration of the Domain had proved to be a fascinating experience, full of surprises both pleasurable and frightening. For most, the various gardens within the Supreme Fortress depicting the diverse forms of life within the Domain had proved an adequate adventure. Sigaraldo had never bothered to travel, while Karabano always preferred to explore long-forgotten scrolls rather than come into contact with the real world. In short, Vestudio's had been a full life where little had been achieved yet much had been enjoyed.

Now it was over. Through the slits in his visor he looked out across the arena and over to the two mountains beyond. There were too many clouds to see the sun. This would make it impossible for the four Supreme Custodian Lords, so charged with the task, to declare when it had risen above the twin peaks. It would seem that yet another of the now deceased Nym's inventions would have to be used to calculate the exact moment when the contest should begin.

Perhaps upon the first delving into the Bowl of Stones it would be decreed that he fight Karabano? What an entertainment that would provide for the serviles who, for the first time in their lives, would be allowed to raise their heads in their Masters' presence so that they might watch the duels! What sport they would both provide, he thought bitterly – an overweight sluggard battling it out with an effete weakling. Yet at least it would encourage him to fight to his full abilities. Better to die at the hands of Giraldo than be disgraced by a death inflicted by someone so inept at fighting as Karabano.

He clasped the pommel of his sword as if it were life itself. Sweet memories had fled. His thoughts were now dominated by the dread of how it would feel when a sword blade sliced into his neck before separating his head from his body. Yet at least that would be a quick and merciful death. Could it be guaranteed that Giraldo would be so merciful? Before the need to vomit became too great, Vestudio wept alone and silently over the imminent passing of a life he had once known and relished. Then he had no alternative but to open up his visor and empty out the contents of his stomach. For one precious moment he found relief. Then thoughts of the Nothing returned and once more he became obsessed by the cold vacuum that was sucking him nearer all the time.

Giraldo, the Heir Lord of Etania was confidently seated upon a stool, his armoured legs wide apart. Through his visor he had watched the pathetic Vestudio vomit. The ability to gorge without any ill effects had been one of the few traits he had admired in his brother. Now the approach of death had robbed the imbecile of the one good quality that he had possessed. Had it been he who had wished to vomit then he would have ensured that the contents of his stomach spilled out over the back of a servile. That at least would have displayed a sense of humour. Yet despite everything he had always been fond of that useless lump of blubbering flesh. For old times' sake he would make Vestudio's death a quick one.

Not so Karabano. No doubt that pole-shaped weed would be expecting a swift despatch. Clearly, he showed no intention of fighting for his life. When the time came he would be presented with an unpleasant shock. In Giraldo's view, there was something altogether too smug and clever about scholars. There had been times when his father had sought advice upon matters by using his brother's knowledge of history. Yet what had been gained from these studies? In this world, the Heir Lord surmised, there were doers and there were thinkers. Thinkers did not deserve a quick death. After all, he thought wryly, it would only be fair to give them time to think while they were dying.

Yet Karabano's death would not be the slowest of all.

116

That privilege was reserved for Sigaraldo, the brother to whom he always referred as the Crow. Truly, this deformed aberration was just like the bird he had named him after, with his rounded back, his long beaky nose, and a voice which sounded just like the cawing of his namesake. Such was his loathing that Giraldo had even indulged in savouring the moment when he would have him, the Crow, at his mercy. Yet before any fights between himself and his cunning brother could begin, he would demand that the blade be tested upon a servile, thus proving if it was poisoned. Did the Crow really think that he, Giraldo, would be foolish enough not to suspect him of such trickery?

Although slightly pacified by reflecting upon how the title of High Lord Giraldo would suit him, his patience was now at snapping point. Just what was delaying those imbeciles? Surely the sun would have risen high enough above the peaks by now? Very soon the whole Domain would be his. It could not be soon enough.

Before them was a square, box-shaped object which, vainly, Nym had called a Nymoter. By the means of a measuring plate and the operation of a complex of wheels and pulleys they could actually calculate where the sun would be at any given moment. The four Supreme Custodian Lords nodded to each other. Although the sun was behind clouds they knew it was time.

They ran as fast as they could to the outer perimeter of the arena. Upon reaching the prescribed distance of their journey they continued on all fours. It was Jepero, the Supreme Custodian Lord of Nordag, who enjoyed the honour of reaching the centre of the arena first, and uttering the historic words:

'The sun has risen!'

Immediately a Servile of the Word scurried out to join him and unfurled the Grand Scroll. It was then Jepero's honour to remind all present of the origins of the custom of four brothers duelling with one another to decide who would be the next High Lord.

It had begun in the early days, long before the Supreme Domain and the Grand Autocracy, when the ruling power was known as the High Dynasty. The High Lord Dorito had sired twin sons who were born within moments of one another, and both had seemed equally capable of taking their father's place after his death. So it was decided that a duel would be held and the winner would then become the new High Lord. Wisely, the victor, Egatto, who had been despised and treated with contempt by his parents, had then killed his mother, the far too influential mistress of Dorito.

As she lay dying, his mother had cursed him.

'I will live again in your son and when the time is right, I will kill you!' she had hissed.

How could he forget such a threat? No woman would ever win his affections; no son would ever enjoy his love. How could he love a boy who would raise his arm against his own father? He would simply pleasure himself on any woman of his choosing, and when sons were born, they would be slaughtered immediately.

As he grew older and realised that his lands would be open to any ruthless conqueror, he had softened. He would allow four sons – one born in each of the regions – to live, but they must be boys of particular appeal. Upon his death, these four brothers would then decide by mortal combat who was to succeed him. And so it was and had been ever since.

This reading was followed by a brief chant from all serviles present:

> 'Death is the Divider.
> The strong shall live.
> The weak shall fall.
> Death is the Divider!'

It was then time to bring forth the bowl containing twelve equal-sized tablets. Blindfolded, the newly appointed Supreme Combat Lord would then take one out before passing it to Jepero, who would declare whether it was blank or inscribed with a name. The process would be repeated until two names were to hand and the first duel could take place. The winner would then be expected to turn his back while the second contest was fought, thus denying himself the advantage of studying any newly acquired technique his next opponent might employ. After a brief rest period, when wounds could be attended to, the deciding contest would begin. However, before the Bowl of Stones was used, it was the duty of the Supreme Combat Lord to read out any final decrees made by the previous High Lord. To the further annoyance of the impatient Giraldo, this was to be such an occasion.

Yet could he not wait for just a few moments before becoming the greatest High Lord of all time? The entire Domain would then be under his control; even those annoying little havens where rebels could still be found. During the past years Talango had grown old and foolish. Now was the time to replace him by someone who was both stronger and bolder – himself.

Neither did Karabano have any interest in hearing his father's words, knowing that they could only concern the victor. All he wanted to do was run from this place of pain, but that was impossible; fate had decreed otherwise. Despite his terror, he still had an imagination which could transport him to the freedom of the mountains. During his life he had hardly ever strayed from the confines of the Fortress. There were so many things he should have done instead of spending every waking moment at his work. It was all too late now. Only the regrets remained.

Sigaraldo was less confident than before. Constantly plaguing him was the uneasy question as to whether Giraldo did in fact suspect his ploy of using a poisoned blade when the time came. If only his hated brother were not visored, then, perhaps, even at this distance, he might be able to judge from his expression whether he suspected anything. Trembling with fear, he felt no wish to hear the old fool's last words. All he wanted to do was get it over with. For better or for worse.

Having defecated inside his armour, Vestudio had

been forced to raise his visor even higher in a vain attempt to expel the terrible stench. Yes, let Talango's words be read out again and again. Let it be the longest scroll ever written, and let the reader bide his time. What could be waiting for him at the end of the reading but death?

The newly appointed Supreme Combat Lord shifted his knees until his position was more comfortable. Arching his back he raised himself up slightly, and although still maintaining the required crouching position, he was now able to read out the scroll so that all could hear Talango's decree.

' "It is tradition that only while two Heir Lords are actually engaged in combat, may underlings gaze upon their masters," ' he began. ' "I hereby decree that this day shall be an exception. As this scroll is being read out, all may raise their gaze and look upon the visored faces of my four sons.

' "My reason for allowing this change in the rules is because no combat will be taking place. Lying upon my deathbed has given me time to ponder upon the state of the Supreme Domain as it is today. Thankfully, it has expanded further than the early Dynasties. It is also resting upon far stronger foundations than the Grand Autocracy which, due to misrule, allowed a brief rise of the Mystics. Yet it is the fate of the Autocracy which has forced me to come to my decision." '

The old fool is going to make me High Lord without having to fight for it, Giraldo cursed to himself. Does he want me to spare the other three, perhaps? What right did some old nonentity drifting in the Nothing have to tell him what to do?

Having paused for breath the Supreme Combat Lord continued:

' "It is assumed by all, no doubt, that the Heir Lord Giraldo would be an easy victor in the deciding contest. I shall not dispute it. Yet I would dispute whether one man can now subjugate not only his own fieldom of Etania, but also three other lands as well. My four Supreme Custodian Lords have served me well by maintaining control over such vast areas without the constant presence of a High Lord. In the future this may prove to be an impossible task. I have the utmost faith in the Heir Lord Giraldo's ability to rule his native land, but to impose all four regions upon him would be too great a task. To this effect I bequeath to the remaining three Heir Lords the lands from which their mothers came. Sigaraldo shall become High Lord of Nordag, Vestudio, the High Lord of Sudelia and Kara – " '

Before the rest could be read out an enraged Giraldo got to his feet and hacked open the back of the nearest servile.

'Enough!' he bellowed while waving his blood-stained sword in the air.

Despite Talango's decree, all serviles lowered their gaze in horror. Under such circumstances it was the safest thing to do. The only exceptions were the duty-bound but confused High Guard.

In his wisdom, Talango had realised how impetuous Giraldo could be. All present were now being given a convincing demonstration as the Heir Lord furiously kicked away the scrolls from the Supreme Combat Lord's grasp before throwing down his sword, foolishly disarming himself. Those members of the High Guard whose eyes were not fixed upon this display of petulant rage had noticed that Sigaraldo had dipped the blade of his sword into something buried in the ground before advancing upon his brother.

'Perhaps the contest should take place, Giraldo?' he cried triumphantly. 'So much better to face an enemy who has no sword while being armed with one whose blade has been dipped in poison, don't you think? Just one little scratch upon the skin and . . . '

'And the High Guard would launch their bolts! Is that not so, Rortino?' Giraldo rasped at the Supreme Combat Lord.

'It is, High Master,' Rortino replied, already addressing the new High Lord of Etania by his correct title. 'As a servile it is my duty to protect my ruler.'

'Well, all four rule the Domain. Therefore, all four must be protected from one another,' Sigaraldo emitted a long caw, tapping his beak-like nose.

'That is so,' agreed the Supreme Combat Lord who, to Giraldo's annoyance, had not reverted to the full crouching position of total obeisance. 'What would any of we serviles gain if the Domain were to fall? By his decision our High Master Talango has shown that he cares for the welfare of *all* his serviles.'

'Talango never cared for any of his serviles,' Giraldo scoffed. 'You were put upon this earth for one purpose and one purpose only: to serve your ruler! Now, Rortino, fetch me my sword so that I can despatch these three imbeciles or your body shall provide work for the Bringer of Pain before this day is out!'

'Then I shall assign some of the High Guard for my own protection,' Sigaraldo put in, his beady brown eyes darting nervously from side to side. 'Remember, it is the right of all four of us to seek protection. Is that not so, Rortino?'

'Consider it done, High Master,' the Supreme Combat Lord answered. 'Each Lord will be protected from the others.'

'You . . . !' Giraldo kicked out at Rortino. Skilfully, the Supreme Combat Lord managed to avoid the spike at the end of the Heir Lord's toe being jabbed into his face by diving aside at exactly the right moment.

'Must you continue to act so foolishly, Giraldo?'

The words had been spoken by the unarmed Karabano who, his visor now lifted up, was staring straight at his irate brother. To Giraldo's exasperation neither fear nor anxiety were showing in the weakling's face.

'Stay out of this!' he roared.

'Might I suggest that we all throw away our weapons and adjourn?' Karabano said, ignoring the threat. 'Then our situation can be discussed. Clearly, we are no longer in a position to fight one another.'

'And aren't you thankful?' Giraldo sneered.

'Karabano talks sense.' Vestudio had joined them. In a trembling hand he was still carrying his sword. 'We cannot

122

fight each other now.

'Cowards all of you!' Giraldo growled, punching an armoured fist into the air.

'Brothers!' Deliberately, Karabano continued to ignore Giraldo. 'Why not join me at my corner so all this can be discussed away from the hearing of serviles?'

Both Vestudio and Sigaraldo dropped their swords to the ground before going with the new High Lord of Wergan to his corner, where they were joined by Giraldo. Bolt-launchers at the ready, the High Guard followed. Giraldo, face scarlet with fury, rounded upon them.

'Remember,' he snarled over their cowered heads, 'the rules of the Domain still apply! To see one of our faces for just one moment will mean certain death for the offender.'

'You may rest assured, serviles,' Karabano told them all with a new-found air of authority, 'that the words of the High Lord Talango shall be honoured. Now, stay your distance so that we might discuss how best his great words can be put to good effect.'

His bidding done, Karabano took a seat, thus forcing the others to remain standing. As a sign of trust he removed his helmet, and Vestudio and Sigaraldo did likewise.

'The way I see it,' Karabano began, 'is that we must always show agreement before our serviles. If we fail to rule with the same authority as our father then in time the Domain will, as he feared, suffer the same fate as the Grand Autocracy. From the very beginning the success of our society has depended upon the omnipotence of its ruler. It must remain so, or there is no future for any of us.'

'Exactly,' Giraldo said, his dark eyes glaring down angrily at Karabano. 'It has always been under one ruler, not divided up as the property of four High Lords.'

'Well, it is now,' Sigaraldo said, tapping his nose again. 'And there is nothing that you can do about it. Karabano speaks reason. Doesn't he, Vestudio?'

'Yes, yes,' the High Lord of Sudelia blubbered nervously, all too aware of the humiliating stench seeping out from his armour. 'I agree.'

'Good,' Karabano said smugly, first turning to Sigaraldo, then Vestudio, but avoiding Giraldo's malevolent gaze. 'I shall make a suggestion now.'

'And what is that?' Giraldo sneered, his fingers clenching and unclenching.

'Let us all now retrieve our swords and summon each of the four Supreme Custodian Lords to abase themselves at our feet. Then . . . '

'Of course!' Sigaraldo gave a conspiratorial caw.

'Exactly,' Karabano confirmed before turning to Vestudio.

'I agree too,' the High Lord of Sudelia put in, wrinkling his bulbous nose.

'And what about you, Giraldo?' Karabano asked, looking his brother straight in his brooding, hate-filled eyes. 'Remember, all of Etania belongs to you and that includes the Supreme Fortress. Yours is by far the largest and most prestigious of the four fiefdoms. I suppose that does make you slightly more important than the rest of us.'

'True enough,' Giraldo preened.

'Then let us not forget our father's words when he reminded us of how the four Supreme Custodian Lords served us so well. Was he not suggesting that we show how capable we all are of standing on our own feet?'

All of them nodded in agreement. Now helmeted and visored again, they strode out to the centre of the arena and retrieved their swords. Then, standing side by side, they ordered all serviles to raise their gaze.

'Supreme Custodian Lord of Etania, Costito!' Giraldo bellowed. 'Come and abase yourself at my feet.'

'Nebidio of Wergan,' Karabano called out for all serviles to hear. 'You may do likewise.'

Vestudio and Sigaraldo then summoned the Supreme Custodian Lords of their new Domains. When all four Lords had abased themselves at their feet, Giraldo wasted no time in raising up the point of his sword. Immediately the others followed his example. With practised ease, Giraldo despatched the Lord at his feet. Sigaraldo, who was using the poisoned blade, also used little effort; as soon as an incision was made, the poison took immediate effect. Simply by leaning his heavy weight down upon the pommel, Vestudio was able to exert enough pressure to drive his blade down into the Sudelian Lord's back, out through his chest and into the ground. Only Karabano, much to Giraldo's contempt, had to feebly hack and stab at his victim several times before eventually managing to kill him.

Yet for the benefit of all serviles, the point had been made. Like their father, they too now possessed total power of life and death. As he had stated, the four Supreme Custodian Lords had served the Domain well but their purpose was over: deep down all of them would have resented having to surrender the comparative independence that they have previously enjoyed. To ensure that all understood, the brothers declared in unison:

'We the four High Lords are now as one. All shall serve us in gratitude, fear, and subjugation!'

The bolt-launchers of the High Guard were no longer aimed at them. Their role was now the same as it had been during Talango's rule, that of protectors of their High Masters. A new era had begun. Now four High Lords would rule, not one.

Chapter Seven

Nym had been working all through the night. As had always been his way, he neither stopped for food nor rest. Even now, all he needed to see him through the rest of the day was a little fresh air. The creature they were experimenting on was still bellowing out its agony when he left it to the charge of the Elves who were assisting him. Blood was pouring from its wounds and there was always the risk that it might bleed to death. As in all matters of vivisection, there came a point when all that could be done was to hope.

Outside, the bright sun was rising above the surrounding plains, the misty haze clinging to the ground heralding the entrance of another warm day. For a moment he thought back to the place where he had been a child. At this time of year, it would be blossoming with trees and flowers. Why had they not built the Supreme Fortress there instead of in this wasteland, he wondered? At least then, when he allowed himself respite from the stench of blood and animal fear, there would be something to view from what had recently become his home – the Spiral Tower of Beasts.

Yet he was able to cheer himself by reflecting upon his skills and those of the Elves under his command. They had all improved enormously. Fewer and fewer of their subjects were dying from their operations. In the beginning thousands of different species of beast had been inadvertently sacrificed and the temptation to become disheartened was strong. Giraldo had grown impatient. Yet again, the Bringer of Pain had beckoned Nym, even though his High Master had been delighted with the creation of the Stormrider ship. He hated to remember how terrified he had been, begging on his knees, having to remind the High Lord of his other talents. Desperately, he had spoken of the Nymoter which enabled anyone to calculate the exact position of the sun even on a cloudy day. Then he had reminded him of the sunwheel, a device which enabled solar heat to be used more effectively. Fortunately he had succeeded in convincing Giraldo how invaluable he was and had been granted just a little more time to experiment. Now, to his relief, success was in his grasp.

His thoughts were suddenly interrupted by the sight of something shining in the distance. Emerging through the dawn haze was an army. They had arrived prematurely. There was no time to lose. He must change from his bloodstained clothes and put on his finest garb.

He hurried down the spiral staircase of the tower, past where the limbs were being removed from others, to where his most successful transplants were caged. There, he ordered one Elf to bring him a hip bath of scented water and ordered another to lay out his magenta tunic with its pronounced lacework together with the matching silk hosiery; his velvet cloak of the deepest purple, and the casket containing his most spectacular jewellery so that he might choose something suitable for the occasion. Then, upon his arrival at the cages, he selected from his unique menagerie the three creations which he would present to Giraldo's brothers.

From a tower which was no longer referred to as the Tower of the Black Unicorn but as Giraldo's Tower, the High Lord of Etania watched the spectacular approach of his three brothers. It appeared that they had journeyed through his fiefdom together. No doubt fear and mistrust of him had caused them to travel in unison. He was flattered that even after five years they should still fear him so much.

It also pleased him to note that their entourages, like his own, were more colourfully attired than in his father's day when Talango had set a gloomy precedent for the wearing of blacks and greys. Thankfully, the only prominent black now on display was the black and yellow flag of Sudelia beneath which crouched serviles who bore bright jade shields which were almost as luminous as the fins of a tentagoth and glittered in the bright sunlight. In shining contrast were their gold and silver cloaks and the opalescent clothes that were draped over both oxen and horses. Perhaps it was to be expected that the indulgent Vestudio would create the brightest spectacle? However, it had to be admitted that neither Karabano nor Sigaraldo lagged far behind in putting on a good show.

Within the Nordagian camp everything was stripes. Not only had the Black Unicorn emblem been replaced by one of red and green stripes but everything else was now striped as well, including the armoured wagon in which Sigaraldo travelled. Giraldo wondered whether the furs his brother would be forced to wear in winter were also striped? In a way, this trip would serve as a welcome relief from the frozen winds of his own fiefdom.

No treat for Karabano though. Wergan's climate was similar to that of Etania. Yet to give his hated brother credit he had ensured that although he, no doubt, was attired in his usual drab grey robes, his entourage appeared spectacular in their orange and white liveries.

128

It was written in Talango's final decree that all four Lords should meet at the Supreme Fortress every five years. To ensure that no foul play took place, each Lord was to donate a number of his most useful serviles to another to be kept as hostages. Reluctantly, Giraldo had done this. For the moment he intended to play everything straight but one day he would become High Lord over all, just as his father had been. However, for the moment his forces were not strong enough. First he must make the one conquest which had eluded them all, and for this he needed his brothers' help and, with a little persuasion, he intended to get it. Giraldo would wait for them sitting upon his throne, where he knew that he looked his most handsome and impressive.

Perversely, he chose black. Yet although reminiscent of his father's garb, this puff-sleeved doublet was ostentatiously dappled with bright orange circles. Complimenting the matching black hose were his favourite knee length boots which, although made of leather, were painted to appear as if they were pure silver. As a token to these silver-sheened boots, and dangling from his square-brimmed hat, were tassels actually made from the prized metal. The square tips of his moustache and beard had been dyed orange to match exactly the circles on his doublet. He stood before the tall, polished metal mirror which Nym had made for his personal use, and admired his handsome countenance. Vainly, he reflected that should any voluptuary ever be allowed to gaze upon her High Masters then undoubtedly she would find him the most attractive of the four. Before seating himself on his throne, he picked up an ivory bolt-launcher encrusted with jewels and ready for use. Then he bade his High Guard – who, in deference to Talango's decree, were unarmed – to open the doors of his chamber before taking their leave.

The three brothers entered. Each of them, in accordance with their father's instructions, carried a bolt-launcher fully loaded and ready for use.

As Giraldo had expected, Karabano was dressed in miserable grey robes and seemed the same mournful individual whose slaughter he had been denied five years ago. Vestudio wore an almost blinding lurid green which, despite careful design, still failed to hide the fact that he had grown even fatter. Nor could Sigaraldo, garbed in a striking red and white striped outfit, hide the fact that he still resembled a crow, and always would.

'I daresay the bolts in that launcher of yours are all poisoned,' Giraldo observed caustically, nodding at his Nordagian brother. 'However, as I trust you have no intention of using your weapon here, I welcome you and my other two brothers. I also trust that all goes well with you all?'

Sigaraldo could not keep the suspicion from his eyes as he said, in his unforgettable cawing voice. 'My fiefdom does well enough, dear brother, and given time I shall have an army strong enough to launch an invasion.'

'It is reassuring to find you as predictable as ever.' Giraldo gave an enigmatic smile before turning to the fat oaf at Sigaraldo's side. 'And how about you, Vestudio? Aren't you planning to invade me, too?'

'Don't tell me your spies haven't been keeping you informed!' Vestudio wrinkled his bulbous nose. 'I'll lend you some of mine if you like.'

Giraldo gave a hearty laugh. There had been times – rare it was true – during the past five years when he had missed his brother's wry humour. However, he never had, nor ever would, miss the doleful company of Karabano.

'Before you ask me,' the High Lord of Wargen said in that superior and effete tone which had such power to irritate Giraldo, 'I have no intention of launching an attack upon Etania. Even if I were to succeed in conquering your land, I would still have my other two brothers to contend with. The truth is, and well you know it, that each one of us is too committed to ruling our own fiefdoms. As much as we all might harbour ambitions to become as omnipotent as our father, the sheer impracticality of such a task is too overwhelming. We all have our problems and that, according to my spies, includes you, Giraldo.'

'What a speech!' Giraldo crooked an orange-tinted

eyebrow. 'I'm pleased to find that your spies – like my own – are well informed. However, they also tell me that while you immerse yourself in your scrolls your fiefdom is falling apart.'

'As ever, you both lie and exaggerate,' Karabano said disdainfully. 'I'll admit there are one or two problems. Keeping control of such an area, much of which is dense forest, is not easy but it has always been so. The Fiefdom of Etania has also been plagued by uprisings. All the same, neither fiefdom is in danger of falling at the moment.'

'The trouble is,' Vestudio put in, 'Talango meant so much to the serviles. That symbol of his, the Black Unicorn, seemed to have a kind of mystical influence over them. Would you not say?'

'Mysticism does not, and cannot, exist. We were right to discard it!' Sigaraldo said. 'No doubt your spies have told you that we did suffer a brief uprising in Nordag? Well, after it had been quelled I taxed those living in the offending area into starvation. There's been no trouble since.'

'Yes, but what use are dead serviles?' Giraldo turned to Karabano. 'Would the historians not agree with me?'

'They would,' the High Lord of Wergan replied, visibly surprised at his brother's astuteness. 'Such tactics, if carried to the extreme, could even cause the collapse of a fiefdom. The art of subjugation consists of invoking a certain willingness in serviles to *be* subjugated.'

'Spoken like a true thinker.' Giraldo punched a huge fist into the air. 'I myself am beginning to find that rewards can be much more effective at times. Whenever Talango made a fresh conquest, he always ensured that those who had played a major part in the victory were well rewarded.'

'My, my, just where did you find this new brain of yours, brother?' Vestudio taunted. 'Can it really be possible that you worked all that out for yourself?'

'Coming from such a wastrel that is the limpest of jibes,' Giraldo scoffed. 'Yet I trust that my other two brothers have enough wit to think upon what I say.' He looked at them meaningfully.

'And just what are you saying?' Sigaraldo demanded. 'I was far from willing to attend this meeting. In truth I care not for what was written in Talango's decree.'

'I doubt if any of you came willingly.' Giraldo eased himself back into the seat of his throne. 'Yet are we not blood brothers and just a little curious to see one another?'

'I came merely because it has been written that we meet every five years,' Karabano said. 'No other reason.'

Giraldo stroked his beard which had not only been tinted orange for the occasion, but had also been waxed to perfection. 'Of course, I had almost forgotten your obsession with the past and its protocols.'

'Just to escape from that dreadful heat in Sudelia was enough to lure me.' Careless of his own protection, Vestudio gestured with his bolt-launcher. 'Oh yes, also a change of diet and, who knows? A chance to –'

'Don't worry, you great ugly lump of pig fat.' Giraldo grinned at him. 'Not only shall I give you a feast never to be forgotten but afterwards, should any of you be in the mood to pleasure yourself upon voluptuaries, then I have twelve of the finest for you to choose from. Needless to say, if any become pregnant then I shall see to it that their children are duly spiked.'

'*Such* generosity,' Sigaraldo said sarcastically. 'To think, just five years ago you wanted to kill us all. How can I be sure that the food offered will not be tainted, or even that the women you make available have not been impregnated with poison?'

'Oh, come now, you of all people are bound to have brought along your tasters. As for impregnating the women with poison? Well, that's a chance you'll have to take but do you really think I'm that clever?'

'Well, you do seem to be thinking a bit more these days,' Vestudio smiled, but it was more a threatening rictus than a pleasant upturning of the mouth, and the bolt-launcher gripped tightly in his fleshy hands was now aimed straight at Giraldo's heart. 'You were a big enough threat to me when all you had was brawn,' Vestudio went on. 'The world forbid that you've now got brains now as well!'

132

'Haven't you been listening, Vestudio? A stalemate exists between us. I'll admit that thoughts of invasion have crossed my mind occasionally. But even I realise that I must bide my time before even contemplating the invasion of another fiefdom. Talango, the crafty old fox, realised that a forced unity would exist for a decade, even longer perhaps.'

'Nothing to conquer? No battles to fight save the crushing of a few half-hearted rebellions? I'm quite sure that, despite this newfound patience of yours, you're bound to get bored sometimes.' Karabano was interrogating him with the same air of self-importance that he had shown five years ago in the arena. 'I concede that it would make more sense for you to wait until your forces are strong enough to take on all three of our fiefdoms, but fighting is in your blood. Can even this improved patience of yours endure such a strain?'

'Yes, time is no friend of yours, brother,' Sigaraldo agreed. 'After all, had we not delivered such valuable hostages to one another then we should all be dead now, I don't doubt.'

'That's where you're wrong,' Giraldo sneered, 'because those delivered to you were not hostages. They were gifts.'

'Gifts!' Vestudio laughed.

'Then they cannot be as valuable as you claimed,' Sigaraldo cawed angrily, prodding his bolt-launcher at Giraldo's chest. 'We've been cheated!'

Giraldo allowed his ivory bolt-launcher to drop upon his knees and extended his hand in an expansive gesture of trust before declaring, 'Sigaraldo, how can you say that when you have in your charge the man who helped to save your miserable life in the arena?'

'Hmm, I assume you mean Rortino, the Supreme Combat Lord at the time? Well, I did recognise his voice when he crawled before me, but I assumed that he was no longer of any importance to you.'

'What an insult! If I choose to get rid of people then I let the Bringer of Pain deal with them. There's nothing wrong with Rortino, provided his insolence is kept in check.'

'Then why this grand gesture, brother?' Vestudio

frowned. 'You never do anything without good reason.'

'Because I will be requiring a generous contribution to the invasion of Sanctuary.'

'Sanctuary?' Karabano shook his skeletal head in amazement. 'Have you not learned your lesson from our father's folly? When you attack Sanctuary it is not only the inhabitants whom you fight but the very Island itself.'

'To be exact –' Giraldo now learned forward on his throne, adopting the pose of one who was confiding in friends – 'our true enemies are the Great Main and those damned unscalable walls. Yet I'll show you a ship which is completely unsinkable and a foolproof way of scaling those walls. This time success will be inevitable!'

'Sounds like the same old story to me,' Vestudio said. 'Don't you agree Karabano?'

'That I do.' His brother nodded. 'Besides, what could any of us gain from such a venture?'

'Its conquest would be to the benefit of us all,' Giraldo told him.

'How come?'

'Because, my indulgent Vestudio, it would show the serviles of Sudelia that their master is not merely a fat and lazy slug, but a ruler who has helped to achieve something which eluded even the mighty Black Unicorn himself.'

'Yet you yourself admitted that any weakness shown by us would be to your advantage,' Karabano said. 'After all, is it not your intention to invade at least one of our fiefdoms in the near future?'

'Who knows?' Giraldo shrugged. 'But at this moment Sanctuary beckons. Just think how my name will appear on one of your precious scrolls, Karabano – especially if I do win all your fiefdoms as well. Then no longer would it be known as the Supreme Domain but as the Magnificent Domain.'

'As I see it, your intention is to gain not only marblon but a few extra serviles as well, together with supplies of timber and grain. Then, reinforced, you'll invade our lands. Do you expect us to tolerate that?' Karabano asked.

'Well said,' Sigaraldo exclaimed. 'I for one want no part of it.'

'Me neither,' Vestudio agreed.

'That's just what I expected you all to say, yet I notice that, despite his words, Karabano has not declined. Is he secretly hoping for my downfall, I wonder?'

'Perhaps we would all like to see your downfall,' the High Lord of Wergan said. 'However, I await your inevitable threats before I make my decision. Although you're showing a little more self-restraint than before, Giraldo, I sense that a willingness to reason with us can only last for so long.' He cast a knowing look at the others before continuing. 'You obviously plan to use our serviles in your army, thus ensuring that you're not only commanding the most suitable soldiers for the task, but that you will not be leaving your own fiefdom undermanned. Yet I conclude that even should we refuse, no matter what the outcome, you will then attempt an invasion of at least one of our fiefdoms.'

'Could any one of us ever achieve the omnipotence of our father?' Sigaraldo asked as he gazed up at a ceiling which was no longer painted black but decorated in garishly bright crimson shapes. 'I very much doubt it. I think we should be realistic about this.'

'Perhaps in our hearts we all know that,' Vestudio said. 'He was, after all, his own legend.'

In silence, Giraldo glared at the three of them. Karabano had been perfectly right in his assessment of the situation. Really, it could only be expected from such an introspective brother. The truth was that he would never be safe while his brothers lived. One day – and soon – he would crush them and having done so he would become more powerful than any High Lord before him. Yet for the time being the quiet force of persuasion would be his ally. He pulled the cord at the side of his throne and immediately the chamber was filled with serviles scurrying towards him on all fours. He commanded them to fetch not only the three living gifts, but their creator as well.

The central area of the chamber was soon cleared. Into

that space crawled a purple-cloaked goblin.

'Allow me to re-acquaint you with Nym,' Giraldo gestured towards the strange little figure.

'But surely . . . ?'

'Was he not tortured to death five years ago?'

The brothers looked at one another in surpise.

'A Goblin was tortured to death, that I'll grant you. Yet, in truth, one Goblin's squeals sound very much like another. It seemed such a waste to dispose of this one's talents so I substituted another in his place and Talango never knew the difference. However, Nym knows well enough what would happen to him should this invasion fail. Don't you, my clever little servile?'

'Yes, High Master,' Nym squeaked obsequiously.

'Good, now show our esteemed guests the three presents you have for them.'

Nym left but soon returned. Following behind him were three of the strangest and most mystifying creatures ever seen. The brothers did find some semblance to a dog in these aberrations: heads, necks, and ears were all very canine, but there the similarity ended. Instead of being supported by legs these pathetic mongrels had long tentacles which flapped down loudly upon the stone paving as they painfully tried to drag themselves along the floor. Even though the brothers were immune to the slaughter and torturing of serviles, they found themselves regarding these animals with an unusual degree of pity.

In awe they watched their unwanted gifts sloping at their feet, the sucker pads on their tentacles making loud and squelching sounds. And looking up at them were eyes which registered a pain-filled bewilderment at their hideous predicament. For a moment the three brothers studied the aberrations in silent sympathy, these frightened and bewildered dogs which had now been changed into such tragic deformities. Yet, like Giraldo's patience, such compassionate feelings were soon exhausted and it was not long before they were relishing the assumed suffering of the creatures.

'I think I'll take mine cooked,' Vestudio guffawed.

'Ugh!' Sigaraldo contorted his face into something even uglier than usual. 'I'll not go near it, let alone eat the thing!'

'I hope they can't breed.' Karabano retreated hastily as a green-scaled tentacle slithered towards him.

'So far none have done so,' Giraldo told him. 'But as you can see, in Nym's hands, the art of grafting has reached perfection.'

'What good news!' Vestudio guffawed again. 'Where would any of us be without our tentacled dogs? How about tentacled giant oxen? Now that really would be something!'

'Yes, why not?' Sigaraldo said mockingly. 'What better way can there be to plough a field or drag a wagon than by using oxen with tentacles instead of legs?'

'This will soon be achieved,' Giraldo snapped, visibly angered by their derision. 'Surely Karabano has delved into his ancient scrolls and thought of a likely reason for these experiments?'

'Since when has history ever included dogs and oxen with tentacles?' the High Lord of Wergan said sarcastically before leaping aside to avoid yet another tentacle which was slithering towards him.

'Sucker pads!' Giraldo shouted, pointing both a finger and his bolt-launcher down at the dogs.

'And what is that supposed to mean? All we know is that your clever little Goblin here has been able to make a few obscene playthings.'

'The herd of giant oxen I intend to use when the time has come will be no playthings! Has it not occurred to you that sucker pads will enable them to carry themselves up and over marblon walls?'

'Why don't you graft a tentagoth's brain into a giant oxen, then it might be able to do your fighting for you as well,' Sigaraldo cawed.

'Nym is working on that, too,' Giraldo said, eyes narrowed.

At this remark the three brothers burst out into fits of derisive laughter.

'*Silence!*' Giraldo bellowed. 'Silence, I say, or I'll . . .'

'Ah,' Sigaraldo cried trumphantly, his beady eyes

darting. 'I see the Giraldo of old has returned. Yet surely you forget that if you want our help, you will have to treat us with a little more respect.'

Checking his temper, Giraldo forced an amiable smile. 'Look everyone, I haven't gone into this casually, you know. These dogs are merely for your amusement or, in Vestudio's case, consumption. Yet you will soon learn that they can climb up on walls and even ceilings. Or cast them into water, and you'll find that they can swim better than any dog.'

'Then I suppose I ought to be grateful.' Vestudio's attention was riveted on one particular hound. Pathetically it was trying to bark even though no sound came from its mouth.

'You can also show gratitude over the feast that awaits you. Eat well, dear brothers, for tomorrow I'm taking you on a most unusual fishing trip.'

'Me on a boat? Going fishing?' Sigaraldo protested. 'Why should I risk being drowned?'

'Because in a Stormrider ship there is no risk of drowning,' Giraldo replied coolly. 'And it will provide you all with something that's been missing from your lives – sheer excitment!'

There had been many times during their father's rule when the family had feasted together. Such occasions were always special. Giraldo had ensured that not only was the memory of those occasions invoked, but even surpassed. Such was the exuberance of his hospitality that the tasters belonging to the three brothers ended the evening with bellies that were almost as full as their masters'. The choice of meats seemed unending. Not only were there oxen glazed in Etanian peach sauce, but also lamb in an imaginative variety of cuts and served upon burning strips of aromatic honey-tree bark so positioned that the flavour of the wood simmered into the meat. Then there were red lizards skilfully stuffed with herbs and placed upon a gigantic platter to surround the most spectacular of the offerings: a delicious baby dragon.

There were also fish swimming about in huge, water-filled tubs, waiting to be killed and roasted. It was amusing to watch small tentagoths contorting their tentacles in fascinating patterns as they were dropped into boiling water, where they turned from green to a succulent pink. Then a spear fish was brought before them, of a size which until now had been regarded as too large to be caught. Giraldo wasted no time in boasting that this monster had been caught in the deep waters of the Great Main by the crew of the new Stormrider ship.

Vestudio in particular showed a voracious thirst for the unique herbal flavoured Etanian wine that was served from huge jugs which were constantly being replenished. Yet despite this excessive consumption, the Sudelian High Lord was fully able to appreciate the parade of voluptuaries which followed the meal.

From behind a speedily erected wooden wall with concealed viewing slits, the naked girls were studied. Vestudio, the connoisseur of females, was impressed to see a well-balanced selection. In contrast to girls with fair skins and corn-gold hair were those with a light tan and tantalisingly thick black manes. The group could then be divided between those with generously endowed bosoms and hips and the thinner, more delicately boned specimens, each one possessing her own particular charm. It was indeed a tempting selection. Once more the three were invited to pleasure themselves upon any of their choosing, with the repeated promise that should any children be borne by these women then they would be impaled upon spikes at birth.

As Giraldo had predicted, the ascetic Karabano showed little interest in the women, while Sigaraldo complained of indigestion before muttering something about having been poisoned. Despite assurances not only from himself but also from his other two brothers that all the tasters were still alive, the High Lord of Nordag retired to the chamber provided for him, his hand clutched to his gurgling belly.

Only Vestudio indulged. Always a lover of contrasts he had chosen one woman with rounded curves and fair hair and one slimmer brunette with dark eyes which were flashing with an exquisite fear. He studied them for a long time before eventually ordering them to be conducted to Giraldo's Chamber of Pleasure – a place of total darkness where a High Lord could indulge himself upon a woman without the fear of her seeing either his face or his naked body. To his satisfaction he found that the plump girl performed well enough. However, the brunette seemed to have little talent to provide any real kind of ecstacy. Had she been one of his own voluptuaries then she would have been handed over to his Bringer of Pain. Yet as he was a guest he generously conceded that he might have been a little too indulgent with the wine. Besides, despite his love of sailing on rivers and lagoons, he was feeling too apprehensive about the forthcoming voyage to enjoy anyone to the full.

Giraldo, now dressed in a doublet and matching hose of spruce green, was no longer carrying a bolt-launcher. This was a grand gesture upon his part to display his complete trust in his three brothers who, as expected, were still carrying theirs. Despite Vestudio's sleepy protests and Sigaraldo's complaints that he had spent the entire night vomiting, the party set out at dawn for the port of Karang.

They rode in an armoured wagon which had been made for the exclusive use of the High Lord Giraldo. All save Karabano, who had spent virtually all of his time within the walls of the Supreme Fortress, had travelled this road before. Once more they saw the honey-trees which now, in Leaftime, looked their finest, as gross bees buzzed heavily around them. There were also the splendid hills of Rojang to admire and, nestling in the valley below, a walled town of white spires called Drong; a place where many serviles did their trading. Many of those same serviles were also to be seen fishing upon a vast nearby lake for anything that swam, such were their desperate attempts to delay the inevitable starvation of many of their kind.

At last they reached the port of Karang. In addition to the natural shelf of rocks which helped to keep the violent seas at bay there were massive walls which needed constant reinforcement. Yet it was not only the walls of the harbour that needed reinforcing but also the walls surrounding the actual city itself. Through one of the concealed viewing slits in the wagon, Sigaraldo noticed that a small part of the eastern wall had crumbled away. Attacks by rebels of some kind? It could be the only answer. So Giraldo really was having difficulty in keeping his fiefdom in order. No wonder he needed an outside supply of soldiers for this ridiculous venture of his.

Yet other than that, Karang seemed to have changed little since Sigaraldo last saw it. As the wagon trundled through the main gate he looked up at the rooftops of the dwellings and at the fly-covered bodies of errant serviles who had been executed by the resident Custodian Lord. Then he saw that, built in the dock area for some reason, was a massive wooden fortress. Surely his brother did not have rebels attacking the city from the sea as well?

'Whatever is that edifice I can see by the docks?' Vestudio asked as he too noticed it. 'I hope for your sake it's not made of honey-tree wood. Too much sunshine will soon dry the timbers and it will crumble away to nothing.'

'The answer to the first part of your question,' Giraldo began, 'is that the wood has been specially treated and the second point is that the outer timbers could never become that dry anyway because they are exposed to a constant soaking. What you see before you is a Stormrider ship.'

Nobody replied. Save for the sound of wheels grinding over the stone-paved road, there was complete silence. Surely Giraldo was lying? A vessel as big as that could not possibly float! Besides, it looked nothing like a ship, nothing at all.

'No doubt you think I'm jesting.' Giraldo fondled the now green-tinted edges of his moustache and beard. 'Well, I can't say I blame you. In your position I'd probably be thinking the same. However, I daresay you will believe me when we set sail. By the way, I've brought along some masks for us to wear as I've relaxed the rules concerning the crew. I thought you might find it interesting to wander around the vessel and see for yourselves how everything is operated.'

'You have relaxed the rules?' Karabano protested. 'But it is written in the scrolls that only during a Supreme Contest may any servile raise his gaze!'

'Yes, yes, Karabano, and have I not bullied them more than any other? But when needs must it pays to be realistic about such matters. Remember, I am supplying both ships and their crews so I want you to see how well it all works.'

'I am yet to be persuaded upon that score,' Sigaraldo said.

'Me as well,' Vestudio added with a self-satisfied chuckle. 'I may well be prone to a little over-indulgence at times but that doesn't mean that my brain is so addled by wine that I'm going to donate part of my army to you.'

'I'm not asking for an army,' Giraldo insisted. 'All I need is a thousand hand-picked men from each of you. Now what is that from a force of ten thousand or so?'

'More than enough,' Karabano wagged a thin, stick-like finger at him. 'Yet I wonder if an army of only three thousand will suffice? According to those who survived the last attempt, the Sanctuarites are determined fighters. Not only do their men fight, but their women too. There are also knights, as they call them, who wear heavier, more protective armour than any of our own soliders, and who are more than capable of wielding gigantic two-handed weapons with deadly effect. And they have arrowshooters who can –'

'Enough!' Giraldo snapped. 'I know full well what we face, yet you forget that on the last two occasions almost half the invading forces were lost at sea. This time there shall be no such losses at all. That I can guarantee.'

'Ridiculous!' Sigaraldo thrust his face forward, jabbing out at his brother with his beak-like nose in the true manner of a crow. 'Of course you'll suffer losses. At least one ship is bound to be sunk. Hopefully, it'll be the one you sail on!'

'Well, if such a prospect persuades you to contribute to my army then I'll not discourage you. However, I'm sure that a brief little trip in the Stormrider will convince you otherwise. So, dear brothers, why not prepare yourselves for the experience of a lifetime?'

Even as they were about to enter Nym's gigantic creation, it seemed impossible to them that it actually was a ship and not a building. True enough, the long ships used for Talango's attempted invasion had seemed incredibly large when they had first seen them, yet they were merely small models compared to this. At close quarters it looked even less like a ship than before. The whole structure of the vessel was fully enclosed.

Inside, it was like being in a vast underground city lit by countless braziers. In the centre was a wooden version of the spiral staircases in the Supreme Fortress. Presumably it twisted its way right up to the top deck or, in the case of this vessel, the roof. The old, long ships had only had three lower decks, yet as they stood at the bottom of the Stormrider it was impossible to see just how many decks tiered above them. Giraldo suggested they climb the staircase which, with its padded rails, did seem impossible to fall from even in the roughest of storms. He also told them to keep wearing the masks he had provided, reminding them, once again, of how the crew had been instructed to continue with their work unhindered by having to go down on their hands and knees. However, he assured them that should any servile be seen gazing at them unduly then they would be thrown into the sea without delay. So that the brothers' sensibilities upon this matter were not too outraged, both Nym and the Sea Lord in attendance were to remain at all times in the position of full obeisance.

First of all they were shown what Nym described as 'the tiller mechanisms'. Unlike the usual crude lever arms associated with boats, this weird conglomeration of cogged wheels and pulleys was claimed by its designer to hold a required course no matter how fierce the waters they were sailing upon.

'Let's hope it stays on course during this trip,' Sigaraldo wheezed as the dampness of the atmosphere caused him to cough violently.

'Of course it will,' Giraldo said. 'I assume that none of you wish for a demonstration of how the whole vessel can be overturned, only to right itself again without shipping water?'

'Impossible!' Sigaraldo spluttered beneath his mask, which Giraldo had ordered to be made in the image of a crow.

'There is a way of deliberately capsizing her,' Giraldo said. 'I shall ensure that for your benefit it is done.'

'You shall do no such thing!' Sigaraldo shouted angrily. 'Now let's get on with this conducted tour. I daresay you'll want to do some more boasting. Besides, I fail to see the advantage. Judging by this atmosphere, most of your army will soon die of suffocation if not by drowning!'

'Comfort was never promised. Was it Nym?'

'No, High Master,' Nym said, addressing their feet, 'yet there are enough small ventilation holes to ensure that all can breathe throughout the voyage.'

'Nor must any of you ever forget that the voyage to Sanctuary is really not very long, merely a few days in fact. So it will be worth suffering a little discomfort to invade a place which has fascinated every red-blooded Sangoran since time began.'

No one replied. The others had obviously been convinced. As for himself, Sigaraldo was already longing to be back on land again. To him it seemed as if he were inside some gigantic womb from which there was no escape. The air was pervaded with the stink of sweat and damp timber and menacingly lit by the specially shielded braziers, their erratic flickering causing it all to become an alternating abyss of darkness and light.

Noisily – for everything echoed like the inside of a bell in this giant ship – they explored the ten decks. Most of them were empty yet each one was in size almost comparable to a floor in the Supreme Fortress. There was no denying that just a few of these ships could transport a whole army. They were also shown crews winching up what must have been the largest anchors ever made. Although none of them would ever have considered praising Nym's incredible achievements, all were astounded. It was a long time before Karabano could think of a possible criticism.

'Surely ships such as this cannot be beached?' he began, 'so how do you intend to transfer your men and their equipment onto the Island?'

'Good question.' Giraldo turned to his brother, his dark eyes seemingly nothing more than two black holes in the gloom. 'But I shall allow Nym to answer.'

'By tentaoxen, High Master,' Nym said from beneath them. 'As you will discover, the pets in your care are far more skilful at swimming than ordinary dogs. Oxen with tentacles will enjoy the same advantage. It will not be hard to train them to swim but a few tree lengths while carrying wooden fortlets, each containing twenty of your best men. Not only will their occupants be protected from the waves by these constructions, but also from the defenders as their mounts carry them up over the walls and into the city. The rest of the army will be ferried to the shore by transporter boats: scaled down versions of the vessels you are about to sail in. By the time these additional soldiers reach the city, the tentaoxen will be ready to carry them over the wall as well.'

'Incredible!' Vestudio sneered. 'Surely it's only foolish Sanctuarites who believe in all that Magic nonsense?'

'Bide your tongue when addressing me in front of serviles!' Giraldo snapped. 'I shall not be called a fool, especially by one so blind as you! Inventions have nothing to do with magic, they are reality. Can none of you remember those days before our Goblin here invented his Nymoter, thus enabling us all to calculate time accurately? And what about that bolt-launcher still aimed at my heart? It'll never replace the bow and arrow – that's what many said.'

'Bolt-launchers are one thing,' Vestudio protested, 'but this is taking things too far.'

'With application anything is possible. I deal in realities, not flights of fancy. Now, best we set sail for the Great Main.'

The brothers were silent. With one command from Giraldo the crew set to work. The sound of grinding cogs as the anchors were being raised was deafening. Yet the well-drilled precision with which the crew performed their duties could only be admired. Often when a boat's anchors were freed, the vessel lurched violently. Yet such was the size of the Stormrider ship that when the chains became locked on the spools there seemed no real sensation of floating.

Even when they gently drifted out from Karang and caught a high wind that swept them into the surging cauldron of the Main, the ship hardly seemed to pitch and roll at all. Sigaraldo was forced to admit that compared to any other sailing he had endured, this was less violent and might even be described as comfortable had it not been experienced in semi-darkness and while breathing in a foul, rancid atmosphere. Yet, as in all voyages, the further they went out the rougher it would become. It soon became apparent that Giraldo was quite prepared to take them right out to where the worst storms would rage. Nym had invented the long ships, hadn't he? Weren't they supposed to be unsinkable? So why should he trust in the stability of this vessel either? His brother could have a thousand men without further argument; let them suffocate upon this floating nightmare, not he!

'Very well, Giraldo, I've seen enough. I'm convinced,' Sigaraldo lied. 'A thousand men from my fiefdom are yours. I've no real wish to spend any more time in this abominable thing.'

'Nor I,' Vestudio put in.

'Still the same old cowards, I see,' Giraldo scoffed. 'Only Karabano and myself seem to have any sense of adventure. That is if you can call sailing in an unsinkable ship an adventure.'

'Courage has nothing to do with it,' Karabano said. 'I see life as a historian, but in this case, I have the chance to see history being made at first hand. I may be one of the first to witness the beginning of a new era when men will actually go out fishing for giant tentagoths instead of trying to avoid them.'

'A man after my own heart!' Giraldo looked pleased. He was beginning to gain a little respect for his ascetic brother. 'I'm sure you'll be impressed. So while we sail out to their lairs I'll let Nym explain some more about the design of this unique vessel.'

Still on his hands and knees, the Goblin boasted, with an annoying lack of respect for their high positions, of how the 'wet boat' principle had suddenly come to him. Why build a ship, he reasoned with himself, to stand as high out of the water as possible, thus not only exposing it to the elements, but also to the risk of capsizing? His amphibious long ships had gone a little way to combating this problem by being of a lengthy and low design. Yet it was no good making such a vessel if it was not watertight. Nym had decided to re-think every single law of ship-building that there was and question them all. He soon came to the conclusion that most of them were wrong. High, square sails might well catch the wind more easily, but who wanted to catch winds in a storm? No, the Stormrider would have but one large mast and carry a sail of triangular shape with a few much smaller ones to help keep it on course. The hull itself would be of the strongest timber, thicker than those on the long ships, and virtually enclosed. His design would also be what he called the 'Half and Half' principle. This in effect meant that the measurements had been so calculated that the weight of the ship was balanced out into two equal halves. Should it capsize, then the weight of the keel would force it to right itself again. To achieve this he had spent countless long and tiring days embroiled in a multitude of calculations and making test after test with model vessels until he was satisfied. Now, whether fully laden or empty, in the unlikely event of the ship being overturned, it would automatically revert to its original position. Yet all this, he claimed, was purely academic, as it would never capsize. A ship of the 'wet type', so called because so much of the hull was beneath water that the decks were constantly awash, would always remain upright even in the severest of storms; of this he was sure.

Karabano asked how the sails could be lowered and raised if the decks were always awash and was shown yet another conglomeration of winches and cogs which enabled the crew to adjust the sails without venturing from below decks. In short, the Stormrider was a floating miracle. Eventually they were all convinced.

Access to the lookout post was also internal. Inside the partially hollow iron mast was a small upright ladder. Only Goblins were small enough to squeeze themselves up the vertical tunnel until they could reach the crow's-nest at the highest point on the ship. When they were far out to sea, the order to 'stay in wind' was given. The boom of the main sail was winched out to the left as far as it would go while the additional sails were angled in the opposite direction. Nym explained that the tiller mechanism would be locked over to the left, thus turning the massive rudder over to the right so that it could be used as a brake.

The ship lurched violently in the heavy seas of what was now the severest of storms. It was time for the appointed Goblins to go about their unenviable task and climb aloft.

Clutching for dear life upon the rail of the lookout posts, they stood high above their ship as it rode against the gargantuan rolling mountains of water that completely buried the hull. These howling winds were no ordinary winds. Storm winds possessed a strength which terrified. What kind of force was it that could tear through the most protective of clothing, instantly reducing its wearer to a frozen stalagmite? Should any grip be slackened only slightly from that vital rail then the winds would whip their victim right out of the turret and hurl him down to his death in the swirling cauldron below.

How could they be expected to see anything at all amidst such a wild scene of dark, rain-lashed skies and angry waves hammering below them? Yet despite all this one of them did manage to catch a glimpse of the tell-tale, luminous green dorsal fin of a great tentagoth. Taking the risk, a Goblin let go of the rail but before the winds could catch him, he had grabbed the rope by the entrance and had begun to tug at it as hard as he could.

Down below, bells clarioned out their discovery. The order of 'Pumps!' rang along the decks. In this dark and twisting world, crew members stumbled and lurched their way past the watching brothers. Nym, who was now having difficulty in remaining on all fours as the ship swayed and lurched from side to side, tried to explain what was about to happen. The tentagoth would be lured by what it would assume to be its natural prey, for trailing behind them was the carcass of an enormous spear fish caught on a previous trip. However, the insides of the fish had been completely gutted and replaced by air. It was their plan, by means of pumps, to draw out that air and thus create a vacuum as soon as the sea beast's tentacles embraced its victim. Instead of the tentagoth being able to use its pads to suck out the living essence of the spear fish it would find itself being drawn inwards and would be unable to release itself. While in this state it could then be netted. To watch this event they were conducted to the observation portholes at the stern.

They had all seen the small tentagoths that were kept in a pool at the Supreme Fortress, but these creatures seemed completely harmless by comparison with what was now attacking the giant spear fish. From out of the foaming waves rose a massive, green-scaled tentacle, as thick as the largest tree trunk, whiplashing up into the sky and then slapping down onto its victim's silvery back before the whole fish became encased in tentacles.

'*Now!*' Giraldo barked.

There was a hissing sound as crew members strained against the pump levers. From a thick metal tube linking the ship with the mouth of the spear fish, the air was quickly drawn out.

'Instead of doing the sucking the tentagoth is being sucked itself,' Nym said, and burst into fits of laughter. He continued to laugh until Giraldo booted him in the backside and ordered him to explain what was about to happen next. 'While it is in this vulnerable state,' he went on, 'the net can be released. Once the creature is enveloped then the net will be tightened so that our catch remains wrapped around the spear fish and is rendered helpless.'

'Ingenious,' Sigaraldo said while his stomach churned yet again. 'Now, can we get it over with and get back on dry land again?'

'Such impatience!' Giraldo mocked. 'However, you may

rest assured that once the netting has been completed then we'll not tarry. We'll be wanting to have the tentagoth safely confined in our purpose-built lagoon as soon as possible.'

'How do you intend to feed it?' Karabano asked.

'With as many spear fish as we can,' Giraldo told him, 'and of course, with any errant serviles that come to hand. At the moment my Bringer of Pain is almost redundant. Yet what else can I do? Until it's time to graft their tentacles onto giant oxen they need constant feeding.'

The nets were cast. By a clever arrangement of pulleys and winches a vast, weighted carpet of rope was ejected from the stern. For one bizarre moment it hung in the winds, a weird, rippling landscape, before collapsing with perfect accuracy over the tentagoth. Instantly, the monster's luminous green fin retracted inside its body as the order to tighten the net and release pump pressure was given. Below them came the sound of more winching and as a massive wave rolled past they momentarily saw that the creature had now been drawn into the shape of a huge, green ball.

The homeward journey proved as stormy as the outward one and it became necessary to close most of the portholes. To reduce the risk of fire, many of the braziers had also been extinguished so that much of the ship was in virtual darkness. For Sigaraldo in particular, it proved to be an even worse nightmare than the outward voyage. No one was more relieved than he when the sighting of the mainland was announced.

What intense relief when the portholes were opened and welcome light flooded back into the ship. Immediately, Sigaraldo rushed over to one of them and inhaled long, thankful gulps of fresh air. He could now see that the Stormrider ship was approaching a newly made harbour. Remaining at the porthole he witnessed the ship's entry into a wide canal before they were sailing across another vast expanse of water. This could only be the lagoon to which Giraldo had referred. Once more he was forced to endure the infernal sound of cogs being turned as the monster was released from the nets.

Besides Giraldo, his other two brothers had now joined him, neither of them carrying a loaded bolt-launcher, but the High Lord of Nordag maintained a grip upon his own weapon. He no more trusted his brothers than he did the sea, but this did not prevent him from enjoying the demonstration Giraldo had arranged. A large raft, overflowing with tethered serviles, drifted towards them. Amidst calm waters and set against a peaceful pastoral background, they could hear their wailing. Suddenly the whole scene exploded into a flurry of foam and greedy tentacles. In the next moment both the raft and its occupants were gone.

'Now I can see why you want those donations of a thousand men,' Vestudio chuckled. 'At this rate, save for yourself and your precious Nym, there won't be anybody else left in your fiefdom.'

'Oh, this was just a little treat,' Giraldo said. 'As I explained, most of their diet consists of spear fish.'

'When will you want these men?' Karabano turned away from the porthole to stare directly at his Etanian brother.

'Then you will let me have them?' Beneath his mask, Giraldo was grinning triumphantly.

'What choice do any of us have?' Karabano sounded resigned. 'It's in your blood to go to war. Better for everyone that you channel all your efforts into an unconquerable island than to try and destroy both us and the Supreme Domain.'

'Well said!' In celebration Giraldo punched a fist into the air. 'Here's praise for the wisdom of historians.'

'I too shall agree,' Sigaraldo announced reluctantly, as did his brother, Vestudio, by emitting a begruding grunt. 'However, I'll want something in return. No doubt after your victory you'll be shipping marblon back to Etania. Well, there's no reason why you can't ship some of it to Nordag as well.'

'That's as good as done,' Giraldo said. 'All three of you will be given enough marblon to build all the unscaleable castles you'll ever need!'

'I fear it to be more likely, despite my brother's generous promises, that every piece of marblon taken from Sanctuary will be used for the sole purpose of building castles in Etania,' Karabano said. 'Then, when he is ready to launch an invasion upon one of our fiefdoms, his victim will find himself up against unscaleable walls when he tries to retaliate. Perhaps I'd prefer it if you donated some of these so-called tentaoxen you plan to create.'

Giraldo threw back his head and roared with laughter. Karabano really was impossible to fool. Chuckling, he replied, 'Never fear, my historian brother, some day all this will fill a fine scroll. And now I must consult with my crew before we dock.' Bowing, he strode off.

'It will indeed,' Vestudio agreed before joining in with the laughter. 'What say we get off this infernal boat and return to the Supreme Fortress? Then we can enjoy another feast and drink a toast to the failure of Giraldo's venture.'

'Quite so,' Sigaraldo gave a conspiratorial caw. 'Indeed we must do all we can to encourage our brother either to get himself killed or at least to lose control of the fiefdom he already has. Who will inherit Etania, I wonder? Myself? Vestudio, perhaps? Who knows? Even Karabano might.'

'Don't be fools,' Karabano interrupted disdainfully. 'If Giraldo fails, so will the Supreme Domain. I can see nothing but brother fighting brother. Then while they busy themselves upon their greedy tasks, a festering evil will become whole again. From the icy caves of man's innermost fears, from the hot and muddy Sudelian swamps where underlings breed their desires to rise up from their hated lives of subjugation, and from the deep rivers where flows the very blood of rebellion, the Mystics would rise again.'

'How poetic!' Sigaraldo said sarcastically while flapping his arms as if they really were the wings of a crow. 'But like most poetry I find it nothing but pretty words without substance. As far as I'm concerned, Giraldo shall have his thousand men, so that he might get himself defeated by this mad venture and in time not only shall I have Etania, but also the Supreme Domain.'

'Over my dead body!' Vestudio folded his arms in a defiant stance.

'Then so be it,' Sigaraldo said with relish.

At their feet Nym had listened to every word of the brothers' conversation. What fools these three were to think that the invasion was doomed to failure. Yet it did not matter. His own High Master had succeeded in dragging out of them the promise of one thousand well-trained soldiers from each of their fiefdoms. Now all they had to do was build some more Stormrider ships and begin the creation of the tentaoxen. Then would come the day when he would be recognised by all as the one (second only to the High Lord Giraldo) who was responsible for this, the grandest of all victories, and the Island which had remained unconquerable would be theirs. Let these simpletons enjoy their freedom for just a little longer, he grinned to himself. Their days were numbered.

PART THREE
The Black Unicorn

Chapter Eight

Although Leaftime was virtually upon them, high on the hills there was still a biting chill in the Singing Winds. Yet like any other shepherd, Athrum had learned to endure it and that included the icy storms when, for day after day, both he and his flock were forced to seek whatever shelter they could. It was a hard life, of that there could be no doubt, yet he would not exchange it for any other, not even for the life his parents had endured: that of toiling against marblon, the hardest rock of all. Neither did he crave for the excitement of being a fisher, daily running the risk of drowning. No, his was a pastoral leaning although farming had not been to his taste when he had been forced to survive it for three arduous years after his grandmother had died.

For as long as he could remember, the brooding, silent hills had beckoned. He had always sensed that one day he would adopt the lonely and ascetic life of a shepherd. As a child he had known both love and companionship and days which had glowed with the Magic of life. But the courageous sacrifice made by the quarriers, Kraag and Cena, during the Second Great Attack had left their bereaved son with what many saw as a self-imposed burden – the burden of isolation.

It was not that he disliked the company of others, it was just that, from that day onwards, some inner voice strengthened his desire to spend much of his time without human contact. It was said that shepherds often lost their minds and it was not uncommon to find one who was totally incapable of speaking to anyone but his sheep. However, for this handsome, blond-haired youth, a solitary life simply seemed the most natural.

Today was an unusual day. Today he would actually mingle with the people of Sanctuary. It was once more a time for his friends to be shorn of their Leavefall coats. As he had been trained to do, he called out to them all with his mind, their reply of obedience echoing through his thoughts. It was still hard to accept that these animals were in a sense insensate. Perhaps that was why he had become a shepherd? Did he not envy the simplicity of their ways? Theirs was a world of grazing upon grass and gorse, of drinking from streams, and mindless sleep. Although he could touch and control them all with the tendrils of his thoughts, he never understood them. Yet was there really anything to understand? Were their heads not only empty chambers in which anything but the most basic of concepts aimlessly blew around like winds in a valley?

When he had first been shown how, by solid practice, he too could acquire the magical gift possessed by all shepherds, he had relished the prospect of actually being able to explore the innermost thoughts of these woolly beasts. How disappointed he had been to discover that sheep did not really have any innermost thoughts. There was, however, a deep satisfaction in being accepted by a flock as both its leader and its mentor. It was he and he alone whom they trusted to keep them together and to save them from the consequences of their own ignorant follies. Who else was there to prevent them from climbing upon slopes which were too dangerous? He was also expected to tend, as best he could, any injuries they sustained, often performing miracles with a skill he liked to think bore comparison with that of a Magician.

Despite their enjoyment of the solitary life, even shepherds needed a little respite from life on the hills. Tantalisingly, Kingtown spread out before him. On such a day as this, when most of the Golden Orb was shrouded by veil-thick cloud, the black marblon walls of the town served to emphasise the sobriety of the scene. With a hint of sadness he remembered the words of his quarrier father: 'If you keep yourself happy, my lad, then every day will be a bright one.'

Athrum had cherished those words just as he had cherished, and always would do, the memory of his parents. True to Kraag's words, he had tried to ensure that every day had been a bright day. Today would be a particularly bright one. The wool from his flock would fetch a good price and he would have money to spend.

'Besides the lambs, I've counted twenty-three going into that pen,' the man with only half a face declared.

'Twenty-three it is, at ten talons a head,' Athrum said, brushing back the strands of thick blond hair from his face.

'Ten talons! Do you really think I'm going to get two hundred talons worth of wool from that mangy lot?' the man croaked from out of the side of what remained of his mouth.

'I daresay you'll make four hundred talons from the deal, leaving you with two hundred talons clear profit!' Athrum riposted. 'Do you take me for a fool?'

With the one eye he had left to him, the man with half a face scrutinised the lad before pronouncing slowly and deliberately, 'I see before me no fool. At least, even if I do see one, then there will come a time when he'll be wiser than most.'

'What do you mean?' Athrum asked, slightly troubled by such a strange statement.

'I wish I knew'. The man gave a casual shrug, yet even the mutilated side of his face showed a pensive expression. 'I honestly wish I knew what made me say that. However, talking of other matters, I daresay you're loath to admit that one of your sheep is dying. Best to put the poor thing out of its misery. Wizard Rograth can put it to sleep without any pain. The meat can help feed some of the cats around here.'

Athrum winced. Like all good shepherds he cared deeply about each and every one of his flock. Yet it had to be admitted that there was little kindness in watching a ewe that was now far too old and lame to keep up with the others. Up on the hills its death would be both lonely and painful. In the hands of a Magician it would be painless and peaceful. He strode into the pen and summoned the ewe to him with his mind. It stared up at him with tired, sad eyes. Somehow, he knew that it would actually welcome death. Heavily, it laid its head upon his knee while the young shepherd pressed his face against its muzzle and bade it farewell, wishing it an eternity of contented grazing in the Magic Wizardom.

'Death is never pleasant, is it?' the man with half a face comforted as a tear fell from Athrum's eye.

'I daresay some Redthorn ale might bring a bit of comfort.' Athrum forced a smile. 'So I'd be obliged if you could pay me my money now.'

'My pleasure.' The man gave a nod. 'And I'll do more than that. It's high time my partner did some work for a change. He can do all the shearing while I take the rest of the day off to buy a new customer a drink.'

'Do all your customers get such good treatment? The last time I took my sheep to Marol all I got were sour looks when I demanded a proper price for my wool.'

'What else can you expect from a place like Marol?' The shearer waved a hand that was missing a little finger. 'Mind you, they're no better in the Royal City for that matter – miserable toads the lot of them. I tell you, Belrag of Kingtown is the only shearer worth dealing with. And who should know better than Belrag himself?' he added with a chuckle, slapping his chest.

'Who indeed?' Athrum laughed, placing one of his broad hands upon his new acquaintance's shoulder. 'So best we celebrate at an inn of your choosing.'

His cloth pouch now bulging with talons, Athrum offered to pay for the two mugs of Redthorn ale which had been brought to them by an innkeeper who was quick to remind them that her particular brew was both the strongest and best to be found in the whole of Kingtown. However, Belrag insisted upon paying.

'I suppose you must be wondering what made me so beautiful,' the shearer said without either bitterness or rancour. 'Well, I had the misfortune to come up against a Clavitar during the second Great Attack. I got him straight in the neck but that was only after he'd ripped half my face away with his accursed tongue.'

'I lost both my parents in that battle,' Athrum told him. 'They were quarriers. It was their job to hack away the supports in the tunnel beneath the Disenchanted's siege machines. They knew that as soon as the poles were chopped in half, the whole lot would come down on top of them.' His throat tightened as it always did when he spoke of Kraag and Cena.

'And so you became an orphan.' Belgrag was sympathetic.

Athrum took a long, steadying gulp of the potent brew before replying. 'My childhood ended that day. It broke my heart, though I was proud of the way they died.'

'You've every right to be proud,' Belgrag agreed. 'More than anyone, those quarriers saved us from being invaded.'

'I reckon they might even be proud of me when we're all together again in the Magic Wizardom. My mother always said I'd end up being a shepherd, said it was the right kind of life for someone as dreamy as me.'

'Well none of us knows what The Grand Wizard has in store for us. Enjoy each day for what it is, that's always been my motto.'

'Mine too,' Athrum replied, his mind now enveloped in a blissful alcoholic haze. 'Although if I keep drinking this stuff then I'll not be enjoying tomorrow very much. I can't take it like you townfolks.'

'Tell you what –' Belrag's distorted face broke into a smile – 'instead of getting aled, why don't we go to the tournament that's on today? I bet you've never seen the Nameless Knight in action, have you?

Athrum shook his head. In truth, he had no wish to see him in action anyway. As a child he had once been taken to watch a tournament and after three or four contests had soon become bored. Yet he knew, despite his large build, that an afternoon spent supping this powerful brew would prove his undoing. A tournament, watched in the company of Belrag, would be a pleasant enough way to spend the rest of the day. He would go and perhaps this time would find it just a little more exciting than before. First he would get in another round. One way or another he was determined to enjoy himself.

One thing which had impressed him during his childhood visit to the tournament was the size of it all. Now, seen through the eyes of an adult, everything seemed much smaller, and appeared to him to be of even less consequence than before. Belrag might even have sensed this reaction for he went to great pains to explain that after the Second Great Attack many people had forsaken this particular form of entertainment because it reminded them too much of their recent ordeal.

So, in order to boost flagging attendances and so raise funds for their upkeep, the Royal Order of Knights had invented a touch of mystery and excitement in the form of the Nameless Knight. It seemed that the idea had not been a total success for, according to Belrag, the crowds were still smaller than those that had preceded the Attack. Yet it could not be denied that the spectators present were all ardent enthusiasts, most of them, according to their chants, supporting the Nameless Knight. None seemed keener for the proceedings to begin than Athrum's companion, who, when asked of the true identity of the legendary knight, was unable to tell him.

Overhearing their conversation, a man from behind, who had also gained ugly scars during the Attack, interrupted and told them both that in his opinion the Nameless Knight was actually several different knights. He laid claim to this statement by boasting that he had actually seen the scroll that was soon to be read out by the Town Crier. They were told to listen carefully for the announcement of each contestant and to note the absence of Sir Redgarth, a large and jovial warrior who always acquitted himself well. It was the man's theory that, instead of wearing his own armour, on this particular occasion the big knight would be encased in the Nameless Knight's black breastplate and helmet made from steel fused with marblon. It was also his theory that on previous occasions the role of the Nameless Knight had been performed by such sturdy fighters as Sir Lathum, Sir Peregod, Sir Jactor, and Lady Calmile.

To Athrum, the explanation sounded reasonable enough. However, he suspected that Belrag was unwilling to have his illusions shattered in such a manner, preferring to believe that the occupant of the black armour would remain forever mystically anonymous. Even so, when the lists were read out, the scarred man's theory did have some validity, for noticeable by its absence was the name of Sir Redgarth.

The trumpets sounded and the first joust of the day began. On the third run Sir Dogarad was unhorsed. It was either due to his skill in falling, or the skill of his armourer who had made such a strong and protective suit, that he was able to heave himself up onto his feet and continue the contest by using the wooden glavor attached to the saddle of his steed. Even despite such determination, he was eventually forced to yield to his opponent Sir Bogadin.

Throughout successive bouts Sir Bogadin remained the champion while Athrum became increasingly bored by it all. It was with relief that he welcomed the heralding of the final and most popular contestant. The crowd cheered as the Nameless Knight rode out before them upon a long-haired, black Havelot steed. Despite the scarred man's theory, there seemed to the shepherd a fearful anonymity about the nameless one. Unlike the others, it was difficult to imagine that there was anyone inside that menacing black armour. It was as if it contained some faceless spectre. To Athrum he seemed a bringer of retribution, terrible beyond all imaginings. Shuddering, the shepherd allowed his gaze to roam over the jet black visage of this most formidable of adversaries. The surface of the helmet glistened like marblon cliffs freshly washed by the sea; never could any metal have been burnished to such a sheen.

It was not only the helmet which seemed to have been created by the unparalleled skills of master craftsmen. The rest of the armour bore the same immaculate sheen. How shoddy and roughly fashioned Sir Bogadin's armour now seemed compared to the suit which, incredibly, seemed to have no joints and to have been moulded as one. The wearer of this dark creation must surely regard himself or herself as a walking fortress.

It was then announced that the final contest of the day, would be fought, this statement being read out in ringingly grim tones, as if it was a real fight to the death.

Upon the first joust both knights broke lances while still managing to remain in their saddles. Exactly the same happened upon the second and third attempts. It was not until the sixth clash that Sir Bogadin, for the first time that afternoon, was unseated. Heavily, he crashed to the ground, while the menacing silhouette of the Nameless Knight watched pitilessly.

It would now become nothing more than a heartless ritual. The crowd cheered when the Nameless Knight dismounted. A black glavor was drawn from his Havelot's saddle. Sir Bogadin also drew a glavor from the scabbard attached to the saddle of his own horse and, although still reeling from the effects of the fall, prepared to do battle.

Now that the heavy, two-handed weapons were being wielded against each other it became apparent that the burden of the armour made the movements of the Nameless Knight even more ponderous than those of Sir

Bogadin. Yet this extra weight proved to be of no disadvantage compared to the extra protection the armour provided. The black warrior was making little effort to repel Sir Bogadin's blows. The tactic was obvious. Very soon the victim, who had already fought four contests in order to win the privilege of facing this dark adversary, would find that all his energies were spent. It would then be time for his execution.

At the appropriate moment, the Nameless Knight swung his glavor in a deadly arc and, in one powerful movement, toppled his opponent. Such was the impact that Sir Bogadin's helmet became unhinged and rolled away along the ground, leaving his head exposed. Above him the black glavor was raised. In the next moment it would be swept down and the vanquished's exposed head would be split in two.

Athrum could watch no more. Closing his eyes, he felt the bile rise into his throat. In the next moment he was vomiting between his knees, while, somewhere, a voice was complaining about such disgusting drunken habits. To his dismay, he now found that he lacked any kind of control over himself; his senses had become invaded by the nausea of death. It was as if by merely observing this terrible scene he had actually killed Sir Bogadin himself. As he gasped for air, he felt a hand gently touch his shoulder.

'Couple of jugs of Redthorn too much for you, my lad?' Belrag's voice seemed to come from another world.

'No stomach for it, eh?' a strange voice chided. 'I say, what would you be like if it was for real?'

In that other distant world Athrum could hear laughter. Why were they laughing? A man had been slain, hadn't he? Dreading what he would see, he opened his eyes. Reality sprang upon him. Standing at the side of the Nameless Knight was Sir Bogadin, now miraculously recovered. It had been a sham contest, just like the others. But why had he, a simple shepherd, suddenly identified himself with this formidable slayer of men? It must be, as Belrag suggested, that his stomach just wasn't accustomed to dealing with Redthorn ale. He vowed never to drink the brew again.

Whatever the reason, much to his relief, his recovery proved a swift one. By the time he and his half-faced companion had left the tournament, Athrum was fully recovered. Belrag wasted no time in pointing out that a now empty stomach should be filled as quickly as possible. To this effect, the shepherd was invited to supper.

'It's a fish night,' Belrag enthused, 'not one to be missed by someone like yourself. That is, unless you treat yourself to a crafy bit of meat occasionally?'

'Never!' Athrum said, shocked. 'I follow all of The Grand Wizard's rules. I know it to be a blasphemy to eat anything that has walked across this sacred land. Even the thought of eating meat has been banished from my thoughts.'

'No wonder you have no need of a woman at your side when virtue's your bedfellow!' Belrag put an arm around him in a manner so paternal that it reminded him heart-wrenchingly of his father. 'But fish come from the sea and it's our poor friends the fishers who have paid the price for us. I was taught that hunting can only be deemed right if there is a danger of the hunters being hunted themselves. None can deny that the Great Main and its monsters don't do their fair share of the hunting, can they? Did you know that no less than twenty of those foolhardy folk were lost at sea during Leavefall?' He gave Athrum a paternal shake of the shoulders, just as his father would have done. 'I too never touch the flesh of any animal, though I know of some who have indulged. As for you, well, killing of any kind is just not in your nature, is it?'

'It's kind of you to offer to share such a precious treat, but as you say, I find it impossible to eat anything that's been slaughtered, be it on land or water.'

As they made their way back to the pens, the townfolk of Kingtown were preparing for the evening. From behind the clouds The Grand Wizard was lowering His Golden Orb. Opposite, above pearly puffed clouds now bordered by a mountain range of white cumulus, could be seen a sliver of the Silver Orb. It was to be a night when only a section of it would be visible, the rest being grasped in His great hand. Now was a time for merchants to make that all-important last sale, for shoppers to grab that final and most valuable bargain, and for wanderers to cease their pursuit of idle amusement. The day was done; it was a time for all to return to wherever they belonged. Athrum had no dwelling and never would have. His bed was a sward of dew-blessed grass, his roof the twinkling jewels cast from The Wizard's free hand against a clear night sky, his only companions the faithful flock which yielded so obediently to his leadership.

'I can tell you want to be back on the hills,' Belrag shouted above the din of a trader and three women haggling energetically over the price of some Colidor apples. 'Well, I daresay your sheep have now been shorn of their Leavefall coats.' He glanced at the fruit stall before saying, 'Here, let me buy you some Colidors for your supper, it's the least I can do. But I'll do no haggling for them. My wife reckons no apple is worth more than a couple of talons. You watch, I'll show you how to get them for a fair price without all that screeching of abuse.'

Belrag kept to his word and paid but a few talons for six of the giant apples. His secret was that the stall-holder was his brother. Keeping one as a present for his wife, he donated the other five to Athrum, who piled them into the sack he always carried upon his back. Then they returned to the pens. Well before he reached them, his flock welcomed their leader as their minds became linked in that symbiosis upon which both they and himself depended. Having given sincere thanks to Belrag and promising to visit him soon, Athrum collected his sheep and drove them, by using his thoughts, through the narrow streets of Kingtown while a wind corkscrewed between the walls, beckoning both himself and his flock back to the hills.

Yet for all their strengths the winds were already feeling warmer. Leaftime was imminent; the leaves were already starting to thicken upon the branches. Very soon would come the time when The Grand Wizard would no longer cast the Island in shrouds of dark cloud and the rain of His

Tears. Then all, from the smallest insect to the largest of Havelot steeds, would benefit from the warm glow of His Golden Orb. There was only one place to be during such a season and that was as far away from any town or village as possible. Quickly, Athrum found a sheltered spot and, with his flock surrounding him, he drifted off into a contented sleep. With nothing but thoughts of the coming balmy days to encroach upon his mental cocoon, he was able to ensure that not one of his sheep would stray during the night.

After breakfasting upon one of the Colidor apples, he decided to herd his flock towards the west, in the direction of the Sacred Wood of Cophaven; there was always good pasturing around Kedydale and Yorn Valley. As he had predicted, it was a much warmer day than the previous one. How could anyone wish for more than to spend such carefree times amongst fields of grasses rustling dreamily in the wind? Both he and his friends made their way towards Yorn, between whose hills was hidden a rushing stream. Athrum liked to secretly pretend that it belonged to him and nobody else. He looked forward to washing himself in the coolness of the crystalline waters.

His sheep were in a hurry; it was often the way after they had been shorn. Athrum transmitted a reminder to them all: Life is for the savouring, not merely the living. Dutifully, they accepted his assertion although he doubted whether any of them really were wise enough to appreciate the true philosophy of this favourite saying of the Sanctuarites. Not for the first time he wished that these simple creatures could display just a little more intelligence, there really were times when he needed human company. Why had he left Kingtown in such haste? Belrag had proved an amiable and kindly acquaintance and perhaps he should not wait so long before seeking civilisation again? A shepherd had once warned him that even the most solitary of persons needed the occasional company of beings who had just a little bit more brain than sheep.

So while their master pondered over 'the shepherd's dilemma', as it had once been referred to, the flock flowed freely over the open hill. It was not only this matter which occupied Athrum's thoughts. Running strong-boned fingers through his thick, curly hair, he reflected on his over-reaction to the performance of the Nameless Knight. Somehow there seemed to be a connection between the image of the knight and the terrible memories of his parents' death. Yet how could death have an image? It had all been brought about by nothing more than downing a drink which was too potent, coupled with allowing his imagination to run away with him. The whole business had been a foolish relapse and something that he vowed would never happen again. His own thoughts were supposed to control these sheep. How could he expect to remain in charge if he allowed his so-called superior brain to get out of control? As the day drew to an end he resolved that in future he would exert more discipline over his reactions.

That night he slept at the edge of a copse and, having regained confidence in his abilities, wove control of the flock amidst the tapestry of his dreams. On the following day he insisted that they all keep within much tighter boundaries than before. As a reward for his improved performance, he treated himself to a thorough wash in the clear, glacial waters of his secret spring in Yorn Valley. It was his intention that they linger in the valley for many days. Usually it was what his flock desired, but not this time. For some curious reason they wanted to move on. He had once been advised that should they ever be subject to such an overwhelming instinct to roam, then it was best that the shepherd give them their head until they calmed down; all that should be done was to make sure the flock stayed together.

Reluctantly, Athrum followed them as they went on towards Kedydale. Such was their haste at times that ewes almost left their lambs behind to fall prey to any blue eagle or mountain beast in the area. How long would this ridiculous urge of theirs last? The shepherd was beginning to lose his patience and was exhausted when they finally reached Kedydale. To his anger, the flock showed no desire to graze but simply carried on. Thankfully, the coast was not too far away and then their wanderings would be halted whether they liked it or not. His limbs were aching, while the sack strapped to his back seemed to become heavier and heavier.

It was not until they were in sight of the cliffs of the Forbidden that, to his horror, he realised that the whole flock was heading straight for Cophaven. Now he really would have to stop them. Were they to wander into this, the most sacred of places, then no longer could he regard himself as a shepherd, for it was firmly believed that any animal that strayed into the mystical wood was liable to vanish forever. 'Never plead, always demand,' he had been told. Athrum followed that advice, determined that their empty, stupid heads would be bombarded by his rage until they came to their senses and turned back.

14   His anger was swept towards them on the winds. They paid no heed as they raced over the Path of Enchantment. Stop! his mind shrieked. *Stop!* Ignoring him, the entire flock charged towards Cophaven. Not only was he now begging with his mind but with his voice also. He had lost complete control. His shepherding days were over. Soon, many of the sheep were vanishing into the wood.

Yet there was still a chance of saving some if he moved fast enough.

In a desperate frenzy, he chased after those heading for the trees. His mind a vortex of fear and frustration, he forced his exhausted body onwards in the hope of catching the ram that was bounding along before him. Desperately, he dived towards it. The creature fought itself free and continued running. Athrum could do nothing but try again.

He was almost in the woods now. He had already made three attempts to wrap his arms around its neck and all had failed. He was determined that his next attempt would succeed. He fell upon the ram again and clung tenaciously to its neck.

Suddenly he was no longer being dragged through grass. A dazing collision with a tree trunk separated him from the ram. Reeling, he got to his feet. He had become so obsessed with retrieving his flock that he had committed the ultimate blasphemy. Inadvertently, he had trespassed into the sacred and forbidden wood of Cophaven.

Chapter Nine

The ram was gone. He was alone, enveloped in an eerie, silent world. Shaking both from his own fear and his collision with the tree, he looked about him. If he got out quick enough then perhaps there might just be a chance that he would not change into a goat-man, the supposed fate of any trespasser. After all, he had not actually gone right inside. His days of being a shepherd were done, but not a normal life, not if he hurried.

Tearing at his face was a vicious lacework of twigs, twisting and curling from out of twisted branches. An anger both at his own stupidity and at the twigs caused him to tear at them in a frenzy, as he fought to return himself to the world he knew.

It proved impossible. Not only had he to contend with the hardened twigs but also the gorse bushes which he was sure had not been there before. Their prickles were as sharp and obtrusive as spikes.

Athrum tried once again to force his way out but once more the branches and prickles prevented him. Was it the Will of The Wizard that he should remain here for ever, for what greater punishment could there be than to spend the rest of his life rotting away in a wood? Yet even on that count, was he not being too optimistic? True enough, as a shepherd, Athrum had learned to eat virtually anything, but would a place which so magically produced twigs and gorse bushes from nowhere allow him to feast upon any of its fruits? Perhaps starvation was to be his punishment . . . Could it be that many had strayed into Cophaven in the past and it was these lost souls that had become the trees? The thought made him shudder uncontrollably.

There was no actual path. However it did seem possible to go deeper into this umbrageous kingdom of tall, mute sentinels. As he could not escape, he clenched his fists and struggled to assemble his courage in readiness to discover just what had lured his flock into the bosom of the wood.

Externally, Cophaven had never impressed him as being particularly large. Yet now as he wandered through it, both frightened and dejected, it seemed to carry on forever. It was a world within a world. He was pondering over how this world had succeeded in luring his flock so eagerly into it, when something large and bright fibrillated past him. As it half-buzzed, half-fluttered, into a tree he realised that it was larger than any insect he had ever seen. Without doubt, Magic was all around him.

Looking up he saw the Golden Orb shining down between the peaks of the trees. Despite his fears, the wood no longer seemed quite so forbidding and gloomy. It was now filled with an all-pervading golden glow that gilded both the trees and the ground into which they were rooted. The unnerving thought came to Athrum that upon entering the wood he had left life behind, that this actually was Death. Never in The Wizard's Teachings had there been mention of any form of retribution in the Magic Wizardom. Yet even so, in his case, punishment might well be due. All he could hope for was that he would not be denied the sight of his parents in the world to come.

Another bright creature fluttered past – a gigantic butterfly perhaps? He doubted it, the thing had too bulbous a body and besides, its wings were not only too large but seemed transparent. In outer world terms, it was too early for moths to be seen, so what was it? He had always held the illusion that the Magic Wizardom, unlike Sanctuary during Leaftime, would not be infested by annoying insects. To his chagrin it now seemed that here they not only arrived earlier but were of a dismaying size.

The wood still seemed endless. His spirits sinking, he wondered whether Cophaven was not a wood at all but simply an entrance to the Magic Wizardom. It suddenly became apparent to him just what his punishment would entail. For his folly, The Grand Wizard would demand that Athrum spend his time, perhaps all eternity, languishing in here.

He would never see his parents again. If only he had followed their example and become a quarrier! It was a cruel irony that he had been beguiled into becoming a shepherd. It had been cruel to allow him to hold the dangerous belief that he actually did possess the shepherd's gift of controlling his sheep before demonstrating his shortcomings in the most disastrous of ways. Athrum cursed his Creator. Blasphemously, he demanded an answer as to why he had been treated so harshly, his words raging into the mysterious battlements of trees, and then, stricken with remorse, he cried, 'Please forgive me! Please spare me!'

Begging forgiveness, he clasped his hands together in prayer as he sank to his knees. Then he wept as strenuously as he had done on the day when his parents had left Deepcroft to fight the Disenchanted and, later, when he had been told of their deaths. Surely it could not be true that he would never see them again?

His weeping continued until he was disturbed by the cracking of twigs. Something was moving between the trees. Raising his head, he searched with eyes that were screened by a misty haze. At first he saw nothing. Then he glimpsed part of a white animal foraging just ahead of him before it vanished into a large thicket. So his sheep were still in the wood!

It surprised him that they too had not been admitted into the Wizardom. Surely such empty-headed creatures could not have been judged so harshly? It needed brains to commit any real blasphemy against The Grand Wizard's Teachings, didn't it? Once more hope returned to him. Could there not be a good chance of gathering up the whole flock? Of course, that was it! He had been a shepherd, hadn't he? Would it not be fitting for a shepherd to enter the Magic Wizardom with his flock running before him?

He would round them up. By now it was more than likely that they had all flocked together again, as was their custom when grazing in a strange territory, and there could be no stranger territory than this. With just a little application on his part he might yet enter the Wizardom.

Despite being eerie and mysterious, Cophaven still had some resemblance to the world he and his flock had vacated. He saw birds, all of them familiar – rooks, thrushes, sparrows, and plenty more. It was all as a wood should be except for those enormous flying insects which, to his relief, had not been seen again. What he did eventually see was the smooth, shorn rump of one of his sheep. He called out to it both with his voice and his mind before scrambling through the dark brown bracken in pursuit, ducking between branches and snapping away many more clutching, thorny twigs. There were times when it vanished but instinct and determination encouraged him to keep up the chase. He did not lose any real contact with it until reaching the stream.

No Wizard had ever mentioned that a stream coursed through this Magic Wood. Yet here it was, and even more bright and sparkling than the one in Yorn Valley. Athrum would have admired it longer had he still not been searching for his sheep. He hoped that he would find them nearby, lapping at the water thirstily. Then to his intense relief one of them slowly emerged from the trees. He had been right. They were all there.

Athrum now realised what he had been following. Perhaps he had been fooled by the familiar sound of its cloven hooves, yet as it lowered its slender neck to drink of the waters, he could see that this was no ram or ewe. It was a unicorn. With bated breath, he marvelled at its gleaming white skin which glowed brightly in the Orb-light. Flowing from its neck was a mane unlike any other horse's, layers of fine, soft, silk threads streaming down from its head. Its eyes were a remarkable sapphire blue and they glinted like rare jewels. Most impressive of all, however, was the knurled, golden horn protruding from its head. He could do nothing but admire it in awe and delight. Athrum remained transfixed until he realised that it was beckoning him, turning its head like a gesturing arm. It seemed that the unicorn had assumed the role of shepherd and he that of a sheep.

Like an obedient member of his flock he did its bidding and started to wade against the flow of the waters as they lapped around his thighs. Ahead of him the unicorn tripped daintily over the pebbles of the stream with an air of playful exuberance, now and again tossing up its golden horned head haughtily and swishing its silken tail. Their journey continued until they reached a curve in the stream beyond which Athrum could not see. The young shepherd trembled in anticipation. For some reason he had the feeling that beyond that curve there would be more than just woodland.

She was undoubtedly the most beautiful woman he had ever seen. This vision of beauty was sitting upon a throne-like rock set in the centre of the stream. Paralysed by such a sight, he marvelled at the bright, rich, sunbronzed hue of her curly red hair, adorned by tiny flowers of delicate blue and rosy pink, bright lemon yellow and snowdrop white. These flowers were all that she wore, for she was completely naked. Her skin was not unlike that of the unicorn – blanched to a milk-white smoothness. Even though he had never seen a naked woman before, he doubted whether any other could have been created to such perfection. Still knee-deep in the swirling waters, he was unable to find his voice. All he could do was stand there, mesmerised by this vision from a dream.

He was finally shaken from his trance when a stone loosened by the current hit him on the ankle, causing him to stumble backwards and struggle for his balance. Yet almost immediately, he became transfixed again by the aquamarine eyes that twinkled and danced with life. Suddenly their hue changed to a deep and mystical indigo, reflecting an introspective shade of her aura which was just as captivating. When their colour returned to aquamarine she smiled, the most enchanting of smiles, her lips curling tantalisingly.

'So it would appear that I have a surprise visitor,' she said, her voice soft and mellow. It had a timeless quality, or was it that time as he knew it did not exist for her?

Athrum was still unable to say anything when she smiled another smile, this one warmer than a crackling fire on a snowy day. He now realised that all his past values of beauty had vanished. Before, the only real beauty he had seen was in the hills. In those days nothing moved him as much as the sight of a rippling sward of new-born grass, with the hollow sound of the winds echoing through the valley. Or the sudden banishment of night as the Golden Orb was lifted up into a dawn sky. All these sights and sounds had made him happy to be alive. Now they were but barren delights, paling before this vision of sheer wonder.

'It seems that I must come to you,' she said to him very softly, yet her voice carried to him like echoes on a clear Leaftime day. 'I think that in the past you've had little to do with women, just as I've had little to do with men. We must learn together.'

With a sensual ease she stepped down from the rock. Her curling hair was no longer draped over her bosm but by her movements had become parted to reveal even more of her nakedness. Athrum doubted whether other women's breasts could be so ripe and full. Just like the first apples, he longed to touch and caress them, to revel in the sweet roundness of their shape.

It was not only her breasts which stirred him. Every part of her seemed to have been created in a perfect harmony. Her arms were neither too thick nor too thin and, like her shapely legs, seemed to be imbued with a feminine but virile strength. Beneath an exquisitely tapering waist and between silken white thighs he saw to his embarrassment the soft red hairs of her womanhood. He blushed like a young girl as he watched her dip her tiny feet into the stream before she waded towards him.

Still motionless, he could do nothing but gaze into her aquamarine eyes and catch his breath as she stretched out her hands. Cool, slender fingers brushed against his palms and in the next moment he was holding them in his own. Only once before had he held a girl's hands. Those hands now seemed chubby and awkward compared to ones that were as delicate and light as gossamer.

'I am Medila,' she announced, scrutinising him closely as if she wished to absorb and memorise every part of him.

'I'm . . . I'm . . . ' hopelessly Athrum fought to remember his name.

'Do not worry, my nameless stranger,' she smiled. 'As the days pass all that's gone before will recede into nothingness.

'I want to stay here forever!' he blurted out, unable to stop himself.

'Only the trees can stay here forever.' Her eyes had now changed to their deeper, more reflective indigo. 'I do not even know how I got here. Was I born of an egg like the birds? Did I just drift into this place carried upon the winds from the sea? I really have no idea, any more than do the unicorn or the faeries here.'

Athrum was reeling over the revelation that in this wood were actual faeries, people who, despite the teachings of Magicians, he had never believed could exist, when a giant moth buzzed between them. Then he saw that this was no moth but a tiny naked figure supported by gold-tipped, translucent wings.

'That was Lightnip and . . . ' Another babylike figure

buzzed between them . . . 'that little lady was Brightle. Silly names I know, but what else can you call people who can appear and disappear whenever they fancy?' Medilia's eyes were aquamarine again, dancing, sparkling.

'Faeries!' A unicorn and a beautiful Faery Queen to rule over them all!' Athrum gasped. 'I always showed proper respect towards Cophaven, just like any other, but I never realised that all this went on inside.' He felt a strange, tingling excitement deep in his stomach.

'All this doesn't go on during Leavefall,' she answered, her eyes reverting to their sad and troubled indigo again, 'but let's not concern ourselves with all that. Leaftime has many days and best we make the most of them all. Now, come and sit on the bank with me.'

Athrum obeyed, leaving a discreet gap between himself and her naked body. Opposite, he now saw two of his sheep drinking at the water's edge.

She looked at him and gave a knowing grin before saying, 'Just like you, they are free to go as they please and go they probably will, once Gallant realises they're here.'

'So I am not dead and this is not an entrance to the Magic Wizardom?' he said. 'But who is Gallant?'

'Now I could hardly give all the faeries names and then ignore the unicorn, could I?'

'No, of course not.' Her nearness was having a powerful effect on him. He could barely take his eyes from her white, silken beauty and yet he knew that he must not stare so rudely. How relaxed she seemed, despite her lack of clothes. He wished that he could say the same for himself.

'I call him Gallant because although he's the most lovable and harmless unicorn you'll ever find, he likes to imagine that sometimes he's as aggressive as his fearsome relation, the Black Unicorn.'

On cue, Gallant reappeared. Haughtily, he tossed up his head and stamped his cloven hooves. His blue eyes were ablaze with mock fury but, instead of lowering his horn as he charged at the sheep, he swept it around in the air. Even such a mild display was enough to frighten them off, and they galloped into the trees. He then trotted back and forth, snorting over his victory and giving Athrum the chance to release his uneasiness by laughing at the unicorn's antics.

'See how the wood has already changed you,' she told him. 'You've just watched two of the animals in your care being chased away. Have you stopped caring for them?'

'I suppose I have.' He gave a shrug. 'Many of those sheep originally belonged to another flock. I've no doubt that some other shepherd will soon find them wandering about. When they ran into this wood our relationship ended.'

'Such is Destiny. It was the Will of The Wizard that you came.'

'It was?' Athrum almost gasped at her words. 'But what can He want of me?'

'What does He want of any of us?' As she spoke she took his hand once again. 'All I know is that in the outside world you would have missed out on many of life's riches, yet before you leave this place forever, for just a brief and precious spell you will be blessed with everything you've ever desired.'

'I never want to leave!'

'How soon you forget that at first you never wanted to come here.' She looked up at him. 'I wonder if you really do know what you want out of life, my handsome stranger?'

Once more he tried to remember his name, but again he found it impossible to do so; his recollection of everything that had gone before was fast receding.

Medila gently squeezed his hand before saying, 'You must accept whatever Destiny lies before you.'

'You've no idea what it might be, then?'

She shook her head, causing a few of the tiny flowers to fall from her hair onto his hand. Her eyes were indigo again, and there was both a sadness and a wisdom in them. Then she said, slowly and deliberately, 'I fear our time together will be all too short but very precious.'

Somehow, Athrum knew she was right. As magical as all this was, there was something ephemeral about it. The

179

seasons of the year never lasted. Time and life were always changing. He had misinterpreted that timeless quality she possessed. Time was her master as much as it was his.

Such thoughts were instantly expelled when she spread herself beside him. Desire for her swept through him. Although it was out of wedlock, an instinct of wanting stabbed through his loins. With a dry throat and shaking body, he watched her breasts rise and fall above a stomach that he longed to palm with his hands before stroking those alluringly taut thighs. No longer chilled by the waters of the stream, he felt the sap rise within himself.

'Don't you envy those faeries and the unicorn? Simple creatures who care nothing of what will become of them?' she said softly. 'Well, we must care for nothing but each other now.'

'Is this all a dream?' he whispered.

'No.' She pouted her lips slightly. 'It is not a dream. But I fear you might race ahead with your emotions, Stranger. What good is ardour if not just a little chilled? I know nothing of love but some forgotten memory tells me that it's best if we first bathe ourselves in the stream. Then like the faeries and the unicorn, we shall be cleansed of any thoughts but those of our own happiness.'

Self-consciously, Athrum unlaced the cords of the thick tunic he wore and after pulling it over his head, cast it down upon the backpack he had used as a headrest. Then he took off his boots before, with a blush, the virgin youth removed his hose. Despite strong mental efforts he was forced to reveal an erect manhood which, to his relief, was unseen by Medila who had tactfully turned her back on him.

Yet although saved from this embarrassment he found himself subjected to another. Suddenly arriving upon the scene to gawp at the spectacle were the two faeries. Lightnip had an unruly mop of golden hair, while his diminutive female partner, Brightle, was a perfectly scaled down version of a baby girl. Both of them were soon joined by others. They hovered just above him in a wide arc, gazing down at his protuberance and, in unison, making

180

loud o-o-ing sounds.

Cursing their mockery, he wasted no time in plunging feet first into the stream, creating as large a splash as he could. As he had suspected, the faeries did not like being sprayed with water and fled back into the trees. Never before had he welcomed the coldness of a stream with such relish. As he ducked his head beneath the swirling surface he knew that his ardour was bound to be cooled by such a change in temperature.

But then another body brushed against his own. Medila rose up before him and wrapped her arms around his waist. As his mouth fell upon hers, he drank of a wine that swept him into a frenzy of wanting. It was an ecstasy more pure, more divine, than anything he had ever expected from his first kiss. With one palm against her wet, silken-sheened hair, he kissed her wildly, pressing his lips tirelessly against her sweet tasting ones.

'I had intended that we stay in the stream for a while but . . .'

'I know,' he said tenderly, 'I know.'

Then in one strong movement he scooped one hand under her thighs and one round her waist and lifted her back to the bank where he gently placed her down, treating her as the most precious object he had ever held. Then he knelt beside her. Not embarrassed now or ashamed by his feelings, he was proudly aware of his swelling desire as she arched her body up towards him.

Her eyes were no longer those of a mystical faery queen, they belonged to a young girl as innocent as himself. He knew that she wanted him to break that innocence – to break his own, too. Around them was a magical stillness; nothing stirred. Without knowing why, he became afraid.

Then he was being pulled down towards her. His lips brushed against her cheek before his mouth was upon hers and he closed his eyes, shutting off the world outside. These first kisses were nothing like what he had expected. He had always imagined they would be soft and slippery, but there was a hardness to the sensation which made him want to drive his mouth against hers until both of them were forced to gasp for breath.

Then he was kissing her eyes, her nose, her cheeks in rapturous adoration. No longer did they seem two separate people; slowly, hesitantly, they were becoming one.

Her body was now curving up against his rigid manhood, tormenting him with an exquisite desire. Tiny fingers, still chilled by the waters, were actually guiding him deep inside her as she opened her legs. It was a sensation that was even more incredible than kissing – paralysing him with both fear and passion. The fear went as Medila began to move her thighs in a slow rhythm.

That rhythm pulsated through his body as if it were the driving force of life itself. He found himself becoming part of it as he pushed against the barrier that was still separating them.

'I love you,' he gasped. 'I love you!'

Medila was now crying in pain. He was hurting her but he could tell from the way she was holding him that she wanted him to continue. It was only the torrent of his own passion that had to be stopped. Unless he fought to hold it back it would flood out from him. He didn't want that, not yet.

There was an urgency in their movements as Medila cried louder and louder. He was now pushing with all his strength. Suddenly, she was bursting open like a flower and he was even deeper inside. Something moist and sweet was now flowing from her and the torrents could be held back no longer. Love gushed from him like a wild flowing stream until, finally, it ebbed, leaving him wrapped in a haven of warm and tranquil peace.

In blissful silence they lay huddled in each other's arms. Medila was now sleeping, her long hair draped over his chest as he looked up and contemplated the trees above, the familiar sky of deep, everlasting blue. Would that all this could go on forever! Without warning, his life had changed completely – the Nameless Knight incident, the unexpected behaviour of his sheep, his entry into Cophaven, his encounter with the unicorn, and finally, Medila.

So much had happened in so short a time.

At a moment like this he should have been happier than at any other time in his life. He recalled that in the world outside it was normal for those who had just made First Love after wedlock to be revelling in the prospect of spending the rest of their lives together. Yet for all he knew, Medila might suddenly vanish even now as she rested upon his chest. Today he had learned that, come what may, nothing was forever. Yet he vowed to himself that no matter what was to follow, the memory of this and what ever further days he would be granted with Medila, would stay with him for the rest of his life.

Chapter Ten

It took time, but the Stranger to the wood did eventually manage to familiarise himself with each and every name Medila had bestowed upon the faeries. Beside Lightnip and Brightle, who were by far the tamest of these errant little people, there was Teardrop, so called because unlike the others, he never sought shelter when the Wizard's Tears fell, and Night Flower, so called because she preferred night to daytime. Then there was Tipple who favoured tip-toeing along the ground rather than flying, and Bluebell, who always managed to find a flower of that name large enough to fit over her head.

Although by now the Stranger could not remember whom he had been, he suspected that he had always found the constant buzzing of insects during Leaftime particularly tiresome, although these annoying bugs paled by comparison to the faeries who loved to hover around him and babble incessantly. Fortunately, their small voices were barely audible but they burst out into fits of giggling so often that he suspected their conversation could well be about himself.

It did not matter. If Medila was capable of tolerating them then so was he. The wood was without doubt the most beautiful place he had ever seen, yet curiously, its mysteriousness had paled a little. Nothing about it now seemed quite so unnatural as at first. Once again he was capable of seeing it as part of the Great Island. Yet the knowing of who he was, and what he had actually been doing on the Island before he came here, was now beyond his reach. To Medila and her ever-attendant faeries he was simply known as 'The Stranger'. It seemed an acceptable enough name for someone who, deep in his heart, suspected that he may well be cursed with the role of outsider forever.

'What are you thinking about, Stranger?' Medila asked him one warm and blissful day as they strolled amidst the trees.

'Now what was I thinking about?' He took her hand in his own. 'If only I knew! It didn't concern me what happened before I came here, that's for sure.'

'I did not think it would.' While Medila spoke, some high branches parted so that they could pass more easily. 'So it must have been something about us.'

'I suppose I was thinking about building us a home.'

'What's a home?'

'Something where we can take shelter during Leavefall.'

She stopped in her tracks. Her eyes were now a deep indigo, and he knew he had troubled her. Without delay, he took her in his arms and drew her naked body to his own, but for once that did not banish her dismay.

'Stranger, there is no point in that,' she said impatiently. 'When Leaftime is done, so are we.'

He stared at her, not comprehending, while the woodland sounds around them faded and grew still.

'Please . . . ' Tears were now coursing down her cheeks . . . 'Don't waste the rest of your life hoping for my return. All

185

of us here are fated to pass you by. Next year all will be gone and the wood will be empty save for the animal visitors.'

'But even if you have to go during Leavefall you can still come back next year, can't you?' He could feel his face reddening and there was a choking feeling in his chest.

'Oh, what a fool you are!' she bunched her little fist and struck it against his throat. 'Only when we are invoked by a special calling can we appear. It is possible we might never take form again.'

Although it was difficult for him to accept the full import of her words, her meaning was all too apparent. When the first leaf fluttered down to the ground he would know that it was ended.

'I can't accept that!' he cried. 'You're so alive. I can touch your soft skin, can't I? I can feel your sweet breath against my cheek, can't I?' He was almost shouting now. 'You're not something out of a dream, you're real flesh, real, warm flesh!' He gripped her by the arms, almost shaking her.

'Yet I'm afraid that's exactly what I am, a dream,' she said sadly. 'The pure in heart have created me. I can sense upon the winds that far from here there are those who have turned their backs upon the Magic of their dreams. Perhaps if they were to return to all they have forsaken then I might become real, who knows?'

Choking upon his tears, the Stranger could say nothing for long moments. Then finally, his voice raw, he croaked, 'I love you, I love you, Medila!'

'And I you,' she wept, 'as much as I dare. I, the faeries, Gallant, we are all passing clouds. To those who grow fond of us we can only be thought of as dreams, unless the whole world is changed.'

'Then I shall change it!' the Stranger vowed. 'Before I am finished everyone will believe in Magic whether they like it or not!'

'Now you are sounding as silly and petulant as my faeries,' she rebuked. 'It is impossible to change everything. Nobody can do that.'

'I suppose not.' He gave a defeated shrug. 'When you're gone I'll have nothing, nothing at all! And what purpose has all this served? None at all!'

'There must have been a good reason why you were led here. Make no mistake about that. You have no choice but to love me now while you can and then to cherish my memory for as long as you live. If you can do that then you will be keeping your dreams alive.'

After saying this she arched herself against him, throwing her arms round his neck. Beside them a soft bed of ferns had formed. Medila gave a knowing smile. He would make love to her, and afterwards, despite any protests, he would build a home to shelter them from the snows. Nothing could be more futile than such a gesture, yet she knew that he had to do something – to fight in some pitiful way against what would not only be the end of Medila's life, but his own as well.

To his surprise she didn't protest when, on the next day, he told her that he intended to begin his self-appointed task. It was only at this stage that the problems of actually building the home occurred to him. Would it not be sacrilege to even think of removing a single branch from one of these trees? And even if such an act were permissible then what tools did he have to do the job, save his own bare hands? Medila had obviously pondered upon this already. Sensing that his frustrations needed an outlet, she suggested that he exercise more and set him the challenge of moving the rock that was set in the middle of the stream; the one she had been sitting upon when he had first seen her. He knew it would be impossible, however. Even if he were twice the size he was, he doubted whether he would have had enough strength to shift it.

'The challenge is too hard for you, then?' she teased.

'I didn't say that,' he grinned and then was prodded in the back by the horn of the unicorn, who seemed to be urging him on too.

Eager to satisfy them both that it was actually impossible he waded out into the stream and squared one bronzed

187

shoulder against the rock. Taking a deep, determined breath, he heaved and pushed as hard as he could. Then he tried again, then a third time. Still it would not move.

'It can be shifted, my beloved,' Medila called out to him from the other side of the bank.

'And how do you think I'm going to do it?' he retorted with a grin.

'By practice and perseverance. All you have to do is keep lifting up stones, tackling heavier and heavier ones and very soon you will succeed.'

'Just like that?'

She did not answer but smiled an enigmatic smile.

'What will be my reward should I succeed?' he asked.

'Now I had not thought of that.' Her aquamarine eyes twinkled mischievously. 'But I'm sure I can think of something.'

As she had suggested, he started to lift some large stones he found nearby before tackling larger ones and then larger still. As if this were not sufficient exercise, Gallant began to take more seriously their game of parrying his golden horn against broken branches. This was in addition to the races they ran against each other along the banks of the stream. In what seemed an amazingly quick time he found himself becoming both fitter and stronger.

It was not long before he felt ready to test his now muscular, nut-brown body against the rock. Solidly, defiantly, it remained in the same position. He tried again. This time there was a slight movement. Cheered by this achievement, he gave another heave, succeeding in pushing it further. Then, with one mighty effort, he actually managed to roll it along against the flowing force of the waters.

Medila was delighted by his performance and told him immediately what his reward would be. Although he was too exhausted to claim it at once, that night she demonstrated new skills in her lovemaking.

From that day onward his strength increased. Medila seemed obsessed by his getting fit, but when he asked her the reason for this she became sadly reflective. All she

would say was that in the future he would need great strength to survive. Once more the Stranger insisted he had no wish to survive anything after she had gone; his remark upset her and she chastised him for his insensitivity. Was it not his own welfare she was caring about? He felt obliged to apologise and to continue to impress her with his prowess. Soon he was lifting even heavier rocks and constantly proving himself to be the more skilful opponent when playing the game of thrust and parry against Gallant.

'If only there were some wide open spaces where I could run more freely,' he complained to her after finding the races against Gallant along the riverbanks now rather limiting.

'Oh, but there is,' she told him.

'Where?' He asked eagerly.

'Beyond the wood and up a slope are cliffs which are never frequented by people from the outside world. Where else do you think Gallant vanishes to? There is no reason why you can't join him. Tomorrow you must stay with him all day, until he shows you the way out.'

'Why don't you join me?'

'Could you ever see me running as fast as you two?'

'Not up to it, eh?'

'Take care!' She gave him a playful slap across the arm. 'Just you remember who climbed up that tree with more speed and more grace than someone else not very far away from here.'

'But this is your home. It's trees for you, and running for me.'

'Such wisdom, my beloved Stranger. Yes, this is my home and I never want to stray from it. But you are different. Remember how you came to this place with those animals you call sheep?' Well, you must have roamed all over the hills together. Something inside you is bound to yearn for that kind of exercise again.'

The sheep! He had forgotten all about them, but now that she had said that, he knew it to be true.

Their supper that night was a feast of wild garlic and

berries, followed by Colidor apples and white pears. Without being tended, everything seemed to grow in abundance in this wood. Vaguely he recalled that outside nothing was ever so easily obtained as here. After the feast he presented her with a posy of woodland flowers.

'How delightful,' she exclaimed. 'Stranger, you think of everything.'

'What else is there to occupy my mind but you?'

'Doesn't that ever bother you?' she asked.

'I can't remember much about anything that went on before I came here.'

'And that would be the trouble should you spend an eternity with me,' she said. 'Cophaven has no past, neither does it have a future. I suspect that a permanent relationship needs such things. Only in the Magic Wizardom can there be true enchantment.'

'I wish we could go there,' he half-teased.

'Maybe, but the trouble is, neither of us is dead. Nor am I alive – not as you think of it.'

'To me you're life itself!' He took her hands in his own.

'Of course I am!' she said it totally without vanity. 'I have been born from the hearts of people who hold this land sacred. Even when I am gone my spirit will still be in the woodlands and hills of this Island.'

A tear was forming in the Stranger's eye. Knowing she would be upset by his grief, he turned away and contemplated the sight of the faeries flitting in and out of the trees, their gleaming wings flickering in the silver Orb-light. It was an eerie sight. Woods had always impressed him, especially this enchanted one. Was he, for the first time, seeing it for what it really was – a place that was both cruel and forever without an answer for him?

'Who knows?' she continued. 'In the future you might find my spirit in the people you meet. It could be that in the coming times, I shall serve as part of your strength.' She gave a forced smile. 'Now enough of all this sadness. Tomorrow you will go for a run on the cliff tops, but tonight . . . .'

*

190

Although they had made love several times, the Stranger awoke early to the warbling of birds and the irritating buzz of the faeries. Medila stayed sleeping at his side while he watched Lightnip lead a single file formation around the trunk of an oak tree. The pace then became so fast and noisy that two of the participants flew away from the rest before becoming too giddy. It amazed him that anyone could still carry on with their sleep amid such loud droning but his enchanted lover did not stir.

Gently, he lifted his arm from her shoulder. After tenderly kissing her forehead he got to his feet. Somewhere, near to this spot, would be the clothes he had discarded when they had first made love. It took a little time but eventually he did find the pile which was now reeking of woodland smells and infested by insects. He also found his boots and when one of them was upturned, a huge, fur-spined spider scurried out. He was reluctant to wear either the boots or the clothes but even on such a warm Orb-filled day as this, instinct told him that there was still the risk of catching a chill on the cliffs.

As if to confirm his decision, a wind breezed over his naked flesh. Vigorously he shook out more insects from his clothes before eventually putting them on. He would begin his search for Gallant after taking just one more glance at Medila.

'Sleep, my precious,' he whispered. 'Sleep my precious nature spirit, for nothing can be more sacred than your dreams.'

Once more, gently touching, he marvelled at the luxuriant softness of her red hair, the whiteness of her tender and innocent flesh, the warm and generous breasts which rose and fell to the rhythm of her breathing. It seemed impossible that one so beautiful, one so real, could ever vanish at the arrival of Leavefall. Again he wondered bitterly just what would be the purpose of taking her from him like that. Given time she might even have borne his child, several perhaps. Why could they not have started an enchanted family, living in a sweet harmony with the faeries, the unicorn and the wood itself? Had not all of them been created by the power of positive thought? Well,

191

it would be positive thought that would keep them in this wood! Today he would be running for her. Perhaps there was a way of fighting off the inevitable. Someone strong and fit enough might just stand a chance of altering the world. It was an absurdly optimistic way to react to the situation, yet what else was there to be done?

As expected, Gallant was not very far away. The Stranger slapped the unicorn's flanks, thus signalling that it was time for some exercise. Except that this time, he did not run but merely jogged through the woodland at an easy pace while the unicorn trotted just ahead of him. The wood was now lit by the first golden rays from the Orb. Winds whispered softly through the leaves, while birds and animals fluttered and scurried, perhaps oblivious to how magical this place was.

Then, finding himself in a part which was unfamiliar, he realised that the unicorn was now out of sight. Quickening his pace, he took up the chase. As always, gorse bushes and bracken, as well as twigs and branches, all parted as he ran, weaving his way between the trees. Was Gallant trying to lose him?

There was now an extra brightness ahead of him. At last he had come to the edge of the wood. Gallant was out there already. Although an uneasiness had come over him, he did not hesitate, dashing out from the undergrowth and into the open.

Initially, he was dazzled by being in a place without shadows. Then an overwhelming sense of freedom came over him. It was good to be running over open ground instead of having to dodge past trees and bushes and to gain an unimpeded view both of the powder blue sky and the Golden Orb spilling its warmth.

Rising gently before him was a hill. Gallant had already started to climb it. The Stranger chased over the grassland and, still running, began his own climb. The unicorn could only have become disheartened by such an effort for, upon his catching it up, the creature stopped in its tracks. Taunting his rival, he slapped it on the flanks as he carried on up towards the summit.

Gasping for breath, the Stranger stood upon the clifftops. It came to him that once before he had stood upon cliffs like these and revelled at the sight of the sea. Amidst wind-torn heather, he stood and gloried in the full force of the winds that howled in from the seething turmoil. Without doubt, the wood was a beautiful place of gentle shadows and quiet harmony yet pounding before him was the very wildness of life itself.

Now recovered from his running, the Stranger strode into the winds towards the cliff edge. He went as far as he dared before the risk of being blown over the top became too great, gazing in wonder at the powerful, heaving waves rising up against each other to form great mountains of water before being dashed against the shore. Walls of spume shot high into the air, causing thousands of sparkling droplets to fill the sky and tingle coldly against his face.

Behind him, he heard an impatient snort. So Gallant had ventured up here after all! Well, the unicorn would now have to wait before he got some attention. He had decided to watch the sea for just a little longer before running on.

The unicorn snorted again, an altogether more imperious sound, deeper and more commanding. Slowly, and dreading what he might find, he turned around. He gasped with horror. Behind him there was indeed a unicorn, but it was not Gallant. This monster was at least twice Gallant's size and covered in glistening black scales. Its eyes were not blue but red, a fierce and fiery red. Jutting from its forehead was a tall, powerful black horn which tapered up into a deadly point. Slowly, menacingly, it pawed at the ground with its cloven hooves as it prepared to charge straight for him.

Chapter Eleven

The mighty beast charged, its long black horn aiming straight for him. Mesmerised by the sight, he could almost feel the terrible sharpness spearing him as its eyes blazed with a wild, destructive fury.

At the last moment he moved to avoid the thrust of the horn, yet he still made contact with its forehead. All breath was hammered out of him as he was knocked sideways, those thundering hooves just missing his legs. For a moment it was gone, and then he heard the sound of its pounding hooves. It was charging again.

This time its snorting nose was brushing over the heather as it lowered its horn down towards him. Although still breathless, he was quick, very quick. In one lithe movement he rolled to his right and kept rolling. His timing was perfect, just as it was when he had played a similar game with Gallant. If he could continue to think of it as nothing more than a game, he might have a chance of survival.

He got to his feet for the next charge. Before the horn could impale him, he dived to the left. So did the unicorn. By some miracle they avoided one another. The next time he tried to outwit it by first feinting to his left, before leaping to his right again. The beast was almost fooled – almost. Despite its heavy, bull-like physique the monster was far from stupid. As he tried to feint again he was caught by the horn. Its deadly point ripped through his tunic and into his left shoulder, gashing it open down to the bone. As the beast charged away from him he felt his own warm blood being chilled by the cold winds.

Inevitably, the beast would win. It could not be long before the bleeding would weaken him. There could be no death more terrible than being impaled upon that horn. Yet he was determined that to the very last he would give this ugly monster a worthy fight. Twice again the unicorn attacked him. Twice again he survived, despite the throbbing pain.

He felt strong enough to face the challenge of a third charge but the unicorn waited. Now it stood eyeing him in exactly the same way that it had done when he had first seen it. The red eyes blazed maliciously. The Stranger could see himself writhing in his death throes upon that horn, his arms and legs flailing helplessly before his limp and dying body was tossed up into the air.

Both beast and prey studied one another while the winds howled a pitiless requiem. The unicorn remained still and relaxed, turning its head to one side to study him. For one moment they were as one. The hunter and the hunted were to play out their final death rite. The Stranger prepared himself, as best he could, to die.

For the last time he watched the rippling muscles of the powerful body as it charged towards him. Its cloven hooves hardly seemed to touch the ground as it gathered speed. The rhythm of its snorting grew louder until the howling sound of the winds could no longer be heard.

The Stranger braced himself. The wound was now

taking effect. As before, he would do his best to avoid the horn but the pain and exhaustion were dulling his mind. The beast was now upon him. His vision was filled with the horn, the shining black forehead, the eyes blazing with a lust for his death.

This time fear got the better of him. For one fatal moment he was frozen into immobility. The deadly spear of the horn was pointing towards his stomach. He came to his senses only just in time and threw himself sideways. He was hit by its neck. Although winded again, he still managed to grab at its thick mane. With whitening knuckles he grabbed at the coarse black strands of hair while his feet were being dragged along the ground. The pain in his wounded left arm was excruciating but he did not let go.

The beast continued to gallop at full speed while in agony the Stranger locked his grip upon its mane. In a world of blind pain he panted for breath while his feet continued to be battered along the ground. Suddenly, it drew to a halt. This was his chance. He pulled hard on the strands with his good right hand. Then he jumped as high as he could, kicking out with his leg as he went, but as it made contact with the smooth, scaly back it slithered off again.

So he kicked up again, using all his force, and launched himself high. Now he was astride the beast. Enraged, the Black Unicorn gave a loud bellow, a fearful contrast between the whinny of a horse and the roar of a mountain beast. Rejecting him, it rose onto its hind legs and angrily scythed at the air.

The Stranger clutched desperately at the coarse mane, digging his knees deep as he fought to stop himself from slipping off. Gritting his teeth he stayed on. Again and again the beast reared up, yet each time it failed to throw him off. Eventually, the unicorn appeared to relax and the terrible scything stopped.

Save for the howling of the winds there was silence. The Stranger could do nothing but wait for the next move. He could almost feel the beast's loathing for him flooding through its dark veins. Any moment that hatred would explode again. The wound in his shoulder was now pouring blood. His head was spinning.

Suddenly, the unicorn bolted forward, its rider being thrown up against its neck as it began to kick out with its hind legs. Every bone in his body was jarred as it bucked and kicked in a wild frenzy. Unceasingly, he was tossed in all directions as the beast tried to free itself from the burden on its back. Yet despite having now soaked its black flanks in blood, the Stranger refused to be unseated. The beast bellowed once more before it bolted forward again.

At full speed the unicorn galloped along the cliff tops before starting yet another session of bucking and rearing. Still, the rider somehow remained upon its back. Now it began to charge round in smaller and smaller circles. Neither did this tactic succeed. Mindlessly, the Stranger had become part of the beast. Despite all the agony, all the throbbing pain and the loss of blood, he continued to be its master.

Then, without any kind of warning, the beast charged towards the slope he had climbed. As they plummeted down, the Stranger was thrown backwards, his legs kicking forward around its neck. It was virtually impossible to hold on for much longer after that but he hurled himself forward, almost pitching himself over the beast's head and onto its horn.

It was now harder than ever to stay astride as dislodged stones battered at his face and the pain in his shoulder turned to a burning fire. He was hurled forward, winded by the constant battering of his chest against the bull-like neck, slithering about on scales that were glistening with sweat and blood. His vision was now beginning to blur.

It stayed a blur when they reached level ground where the unicorn swerved and galloped around the perimeter of the wood. He was feeling dazed but despite this, he refused to let go of the tangled mane.

In this bleary stupor he saw the world to which he had once belonged. They were now upon some kind of pathway. He thought he could remember something about that path, something from the past, yet he couldn't think what it was. The constant soporific rhythm of the beast's hoofbeats were all he could hear now. His strength was leaving him. Would he bleed to death? Fall? Or finally be impaled by that horn? It didn't matter. Nothing mattered to him now but sleep. Yes, that was all he wanted to do, go to sleep.

King Septor sat upon his second throne and troubled over his daughter's words. In his heart he knew them to be true. Now in her mid-twenties she was more beautiful than ever, and even more wilful. She could also be crushingly right about many matters, as in this case. Even so, he intended to argue, to fight her if he could.

'Listen, Rosamile!' He banged his staff upon the stone floor so that the noise echoed against every wall of the Royal Chamber. 'In Sanctuary, firstly there is the power of the Magicians, secondly there is the power of the Magicians and thirdly there is the power of the Magicians . . . !'

'All right, Father.' Angrily, the Princess flicked back the long strands of her blonde hair. 'You've made your point but now I'll make mine.'

'I thought that was what you'd been trying to do all this time,' Septor groaned.

'But that doesn't mean you've been listening, does it?' She crooked an eyebrow and stared at him quizzically. 'Why can't you admit that Barney Fowl's nothing more than an ignorant little imbecile?'

'He's got time. Don't forget he's younger than you are,' he reminded her.

'Then why did you appoint him?' she snapped.

'Because he has the Gift. Orina told me that his powers will be far greater than any other Magician in our history.'

'Hah!' With exaggerated drama Rosamile stamped her booted foot upon the floor, creating a sound that in loudness almost competed with the banging of the King's staff. 'Then are you claiming, dear Father, that virtually everyone in the whole land has the Gift? Surely you realise that at the time she spoke Orina was not in full command of herself? She probably knew that she was about to sacrifice her own life.'

Anger swelled inside the King. No one had the right to make such a claim about the martyred Witch, not even his daughter.

'Bide your tongue,' he growled at her. 'I can only be pushed so far, as well you should know.'

Visibly she smarted from his rebuke, yet he knew that harsh words would never be enough to deter Rosamile. There was a long pause before she replied.

'I'm sorry, Father, I didn't mean it to sound as harsh as that. I was only making the point that, sometimes, people lose sight of things when they know they're about to die. I, like most others, will always remember Orina as the bravest and most courageous person I've ever known. That's why it's so wrong that Barney Fowl should have taken her place.'

'She was in full command of her senses when she told me he had the Gift. She was convinced he was Gifted above all others.'

'*Gifted*!' Now that she had apologised Rosamile obviously regarded it as her continued right to berate her father. 'There is as much Magic flowing through his veins as my own, probably less. Have you ever seen him perform anything Magical whether it be mere conjuration or any other kind of miracle? He can't even make potions!' Her blue eyes flashed. 'Do you know that during Orina's time all shepherds were supplied with a potion which aided them in controlling their flocks by the mind?' She glared at him with her piercing blue eyes. 'Well, no more. Thanks to his laziness whole flocks have gone astray, something which never happened in the old days. There's even been a case where not only did a flock run amok, but the shepherd who was supposed to be in charge of it just vanished into thin air.'

'So this shepherd was probably attacked by a mountain beast, or maybe he fell down a crevice.' Septor gave a shrug. 'There are all sorts of things that could have happened. It's absurd to blame something like that on the Royal Wizard.'

She glared at him mockingly. 'Why not? Everybody else does, just as they're blaming him for last year's poor harvest. Not only that, but according to the reports, this year more people have been dying than ever before. It was never right to make a child like that a Royal Wizard and even after all these years he's not improved.'

'Death is something we all have to face,' Septor said bitterly. 'I refuse to blame the fact of life – or death – on the Royal Wizad, or any other wizard for that matter.'

'Father, Magic is life. Isn't that what we've always been taught? Don't you realise that if this situation continues for much longer, we could even have civil war in our land?'

'Now you really are being ridiculous, child.' It was the King's turn to mock. 'The only way this Island will ever get involved in a war is with the Disenchanted. And after what we did the last time, I don't think we'll ever be troubled by them again.'

Rosamile said nothing but stared at her father coldly. Equally cold was her tone of voice when she asked, 'Did you know that Althigor is trying to usurp Barney Fowl?'

'Never!' Septor's voice boomed out. Many of his subjects backed away when he gave full vent to his anger and on occasions that even included Queen Katrila. Yet, no matter how much he raged, Rosamile always stood her ground. In a more level tone he asked, 'And who would ever be so bold as to go against the wishes of their King?'

'I don't know.' She continued to stare at him in defiance. 'I don't know how far he and his supporters would be prepared to take it, but to say that there's unrest amongst a lot of people would be no exaggeration.'

Pensively Septor stroked his beard with jewel-ringed fingers. It seemed impossible that Orina could have been so wrong. True enough, he had most vociferously expressed his own doubts about appointing a filthy urchin as the Royal Wizard. Yet the Witch had not been prepared to argue with him. Adamantly, she had assured him that it was not her own wish that Barney Fowl replace her but that of The Grand Wizard. According to her, it was Destiny that he should succeed her and that to ignore this prophecy would have caused disaster. Despite a garrulous display of reluctance, Septor had finally conceded. Yet from the very first day that this uncouth child had inherited her role, he had regretted it.

'Well?' Rosamile insisted. 'What are you going to do about it? Remember your own wise words – "All troubles cease at the Royal Chamber because that's where they have to be solved".'

Septor almost grinned at her last remark. It was, after all, fair comment. He had used this favourite adage of his many times. It was an excellent way of cornering him and well he knew it.

'Mark these words well, young lady.' he finally said. 'When the time comes for you to sit upon this throne then I daresay you won't be seeing all matters in the nice clear black and white you seem to do at the moment.'

She sighed and then said, 'The truth is, Father, that it is you who sit upon the throne, not I. I've nothing personal against Barney Fowl. In his own way I find him quite –'

'Quite unpleasant and disgusting?' he suggested. 'I know my own daughter well enough to know that she has never suffered fools gladly and never will. And there lies her weakness, for upon this Island dwell many fools. As a future ruler you must find it in your heart to love them all.'

For a moment, she actually seemed to pay heed to these last words before rallying with the riposte. 'It wasn't fools who beat the Disenchanted during the last attack and it won't be fools who beat them again!'

'As I've told you before,' Septor said, now tiring of her belligerence, 'we'll be left alone by them from now on.'

'Be that as it may, this Island must still be run efficiently. Surely Althigor was always more suited to the post of Royal Wizard?'

'I've always disliked Althigor as much as you've disliked Barney Fowl.'

'Can a King afford to have any preferences?'

She had won. Common sense had won. Perhaps deep down inside he had even wanted this confrontation. There was nothing like a self-assured daughter who knew that she was right to help him make a decision. She had not got her way yet, but she was certainly getting there. 'Rulers can never have preferences.' Of course, those, too, were his own words, weren't they? He started to laugh while she stood bemused by his reaction.

'I've taught you too well,' he roared, 'far too well!'

Then they laughed together, putting animosity temporarily aside. Later, the King decided to join his Queen. Although it was still evening both he and Katrila would be in their bed well before the coming of nightfall. Rosamile might imagine that she was the only woman with any real influence at his court but she was mistaken. First Katrila would be entitled to her say and then, finally, he would make up his own mind, preferences or not.

As they lay in their bed, bathed in the warm orange glow from the Orb as it was being lowered down towards the horizon, he told Katrila what Rosamile had said to him, knowing full well that she had already spoken to her mother upon the subject. He waited for her reply but the Queen remained silent.

'Look,' he said impatiently, 'I know you don't like Barney Fowl any more than anyone else seems to, but can I really deprive him of a position that was ordained by Orina?'

Katrila placed a slender hand upon his coarse-haired chest and looked at him with the turquoise eyes that were not only unique in their colouring but unique in their understanding and wisdom. She began to speak in the soft and gentle tones that still beguiled him, even after all their years together.

'It was never easy for me to respect the views of Orina, and you know why.'

Septor's patience was now being tested to the limit. He pushed her hand away.

'We've been into this before,' he said. 'I swear to you that I never – '

'Of course you didn't.' Katrila turned her back to him as she spoke. 'What temptation could someone so deformed and shrivelled before her time present? I know you've never been unfaithful to me. Yet long ago there was a time when Orina was the most beautiful girl imaginable. And during those days though while in body you were at my side, your heart was yearning for her. Deny it if you dare.'

'Look, I was not the only one to be captivated by her!' he protested.

'Exactly,' she said sharply. 'And all that time I remained the faithful and dutiful Queen while you longed to be with her. It's a terrible thing to admit, but I almost rejoiced when her Magic took its toll and she became ugly. Perhaps I feel uneasy about Barney Fowl because he too is so repulsive. It's almost as if she had spawned him.'

Septor's anger went as quickly as it had come. He had, after all, sought his wife's advice and now he would listen to her.

'So you would prefer to see Althigor in his position?' he asked.

'He's a good Magician – one worthy of the title of Royal Wizard. He spoke to me upon the subject recently while you were watching a tournament. I was most impressed by him.'

'He doesn't seem to lack cunning, does he?' Septor noted. 'Well, I suppose you and Rosamile are right. I guess we can't keep going on without a proper Wizard, can we?'

'The trouble with you, Good King Septor, is that beneath that bark of yours there is no bite at all.' Katrila's voice was honey now as she snuggled up to her husband.

'True enough,' he chuckled, but he was half listening to the sound of the Singing Winds howling outside. Suddenly they seemed very loud. 'I won't deny it. I'm not looking forward to telling the lad that he's being replaced. It'll hurt him. He might even take to wandering and sleeping rough again.'

'There are plenty who do that, you know. They're just as happy as we are.'

'Impossible!' He put an arm around her shoulder and

squeezed her tightly against him. 'I never loved Orina, you know. Not really, not in the same way I love you. You're the one who has always made me happy, nobody else.'

'I believe you,' she whispered softly.

For a little while they lay side by side in silence. It was well before the arrival of the night when they drifted off to sleep, still locked in one another's arms.

Meanwhile, Barney Fowl, now mockingly referred to by many as the 'Wizard Without', sauntered sadly upon the battlements of the fourth tower of the Royal Citadel. Miserably, he reflected upon his ineptitude. Orina, the one person he had ever looked up to and trusted, had assured him many times that he possessed a Gift greater than any other Magician but it had proved to be the cruellest of lies. Ever since she had died he had been unable to perform even the simplest of conjurations. He was no Wizard, nor ever had been. When Orina had died, so had her Magic.

The sleepy city was preparing itself for the night. People were on their way home. Their day was over while his own – for sleep had become virtually impossible for him during the night – was about to begin. Probably he would stay up here on the battlements and brood, for brooding had become a self-imposed occupation now. He seemed incapable of thinking anything but bitter thoughts about a lonely past without anyone to care for him, and a future which now seemed equally bleak. Yet if he were to escape from this place then at least he could revert to the person he had once been and continue to live the life he had been doing before Orina interfered. A life of sleeping in barns and open fields – could there really be any other way for him now?

Tomorrow, he would go and see the King and tell him that he no longer wished to be the Royal Wizard. No doubt his statement would come as a relief to them all. Nobody, save Princess Rosamile, had ever publicly intimated any dissatisfaction with his inability to prepare even the simplest of potions, yet how much longer could he endure their secret ridicule? What made them so superior, anyway? Just what was so special about washing your body and clothes all the time? High on the Singing Winds the stench of the city was carried to him. How could people object to the odours of their own bodies yet tolerate the stench of excrement and rotting vegetables? He remembered how Orina had once warned him that people were often hard to understand. How right she had been! Yes, tomorrow he would go and see the King and have done with it all.

Mentally preparing himself for his return to the world beyond the Royal City, he looked far out to the darkening countryside. Many folk were actually afraid of being out there when night came. Not he: why be afraid of a place which was not populated by stupid humans but by the living things he really did understand – animals? Soon bats and night birds would be winging through a darkened sky and the creatures of the night would emerge from their lairs. He could even sense that, far away, a mountain beast was stirring from its daytime slumbers to do a little nocturnal hunting. Contrary to what so many fools believed, even these fearsome predators were not that dangerous. If a person took a bold enough stance against them, then they would simply run away.

Suddenly he could sense not so far away the presence of a very different animal. This beast was not afraid of anything or anyone. Mingling with the grime in his nostrils was the scent of something that did not belong to the everyday world. For some reason it was coming to the city, slowly and deliberately. What could such a beast be?

Quickly he descended the spiral staircase and ran out into the bailey of the Citadel. Two fully armoured knights turned and watched him as he hurried out over the drawbridge and into the main street. There were still plenty of people lurking about but they all seemed unaware of what was about to arrive.

Gasping for breath, he reached the Main Gate. Somehow, he still managed to scramble up the stairs to the battlements. Even before he spoke to her he was aware that the woman guard standing immediately before him had seen something.

'What is it?' he asked.

'Tell me,' the woman begged him in a shaking voice. 'Am I really seeing what I'm seeing?'

Barney looked out and found his breath being taken away from him again. Walking towards them upon cloven hooves was a monstrous black horse with a spear-like horn protruding from its forehead. It seemed to be carrying something on its back and even at such a distance he could see its fiery red eyes. There was no doubt in his mind that this beast was indeed the fabled Black Unicorn.

'So what should I do?' the woman asked. 'Please, Royal Wizard, just what am I to do?'

There seemed a genuine respect for him. Perhaps she found it reassuring to seek the advice of someone in high authority at such a time, even a failed Wizard? He wondered if she was going to be so reassured by his answer.

'We open up the gates and let it in,' he told her.

Chapter Twelve

The two massive wooden doors of the Main Gate were dragged open by twelve city guards. Trembling, Barney Fowl stood and watched the approach of the Black Unicorn.

It did not falter. With the same slow deliberation he had watched from above, the unicorn advanced. There could have been no greater contrast between the dainty and fragile beauty of the White Unicorn he had seen emerge from Cophaven, and this fearsome beast. Yet for some reason he was unafraid. Perhaps it was because he knew that, like the other unicorn, it had been born directly from the earth and was therefore a creation in the very purest of senses.

Not all Sanctuarites had acknowledged its existence in their hearts. True enough, most of them had listened to the songs and poems about this fabled monster. Some had even wondered just why the ruler of the Disenchanted, the High Lord Talango, had identified himself with the creature. Yet, he asked himself, how many of them believed in their very souls that it truly existed? He might be known as the 'Wizard Without' but he did have an instinct which ran deep in his bones. Perhaps Orina was right after all – perhaps he really was blessed with The Wizard's Magic?

Behind him the city was coming to life again as panic-stricken guards bawled out. They were right to be afraid. Sanctuarites everywhere had now been rudely awakened to the heralding of a new beginning, for that was what the appearance of the beast really meant. Perhaps only he, this outcast who was so derided by others, willingly embraced this new dawn.

As slowly and deliberately as the Black Unicorn was approaching, Barney ventured towards it. The beast stopped in its tracks. He was tempted to do the same but resisted. Instead, his body trembling, he kept on walking while the red eyes glared at him malevolently. Then it lowered its horn and threateningly aimed it straight at his heart.

But fear had never been Barney's master. Although afraid, he continued to advance towards the Black Unicorn. It was now pawing at the ground with its cloven hooves and snorting menacingly. The Royal Wizard was determined not to show any fear, even though his breathing was now laboured and he could hear the sound of his own pounding heartbeat.

Barney could not stop himself from wincing when the point of that horn was jabbed against his chest, yet he was determined to stay as calm as possible. He moved over to the right. The unicorn's horn remained pointing straight ahead while a cruel red eye watched. Bracing himself, he stared back. He saw that within that deep red pool burned not only the fires of death, but of life also.

Now, almost without fear, he allowed his gaze to fall upon the shiny black scales of its head and neck. There he saw, illuminated by the Silver Orb, that its neck and flank were soaked in blood. Slumped over the nape of its neck was a dead body. Was it a man or a boy? It was hard to tell. The thick mop of youthful blond hair suggested that he had been killed in his early prime. Barney wondered how many others in the Magic Wizardom could claim to have died upon the back of the Black Unicorn.

What had been its purpose in bearing this corpse upon its back? It seemed absurd, but it was almost as if the beast had actually brought the body here. No wonder it had approached so slowly.

So what was to be done with the corpse? Did the Black Unicorn want it buried at this very spot or did the monster want to carry it into the City? Was all this a portent of some great message? How Destiny tantalised. Surely, it would not have come all this way if it had not wished to enter. This legendary creature was a great deal more than some rampant predator, lunging wildly at everything that moved. It was a living catalyst – a dark emissary of change. Yes, it was the future that Sanctuarites should be afraid of, nothing else.

Fearlessly, he turned his back on the Black Unicorn and began to walk back towards the Main Gate. The beast followed. The Royal City was deserted now. Only a few of the citizens were brave enough to watch from their windows with furtive eyes. What cowards! What a way to face a new and uncertain future! Contemptuous of them all, he continued to lead the beast onwards until they were approaching the drawbridge of the Citadel.

To their credit, the two knights standing guard stayed resolutely at their posts, raising their glavors. The Black Unicorn stopped and eyed them. One glare from its fierce red eyes was enough. The guardians dropped their mighty two-handed swords. The Wizard and unicorn clattered loudly onto the wooden bridge as both knights fled inside. There were at least twenty other knights assembled in the bailey. Barney assured them all that provided the Black Unicorn was shown respect, then no harm would come to anyone. To his surprise they heeded his words.

*

King Septor and Queen Katrila had to be told the news three times before it registered. All they could then say in unison was, 'Impossible!'

Suddenly, her face flushed, Princess Rosamile burst into their chamber; she too was shaken.

'I've j-just seen it!' she said, stammering. 'It's terrifying, even worse than all those songs and poems about it!'

'Where is it now?' Katrila clutched at her husbands' arm.

'Still in the bailey, just standing there with a dead body on its back. It seems to be waiting for something.'

'Waiting for what?' the King said impatiently.

'Waiting for us,' Katrila told him. 'We are the King and Queen of the Island, you know.'

'Then Barney Fowl had better be there, too. After all, he is our Royal Wizard.'

'Barney Fowl is already there,' Rosamile said, now having conquered her stammer. 'It was he who was foolish enough to actually lead the beast into the Citadel.'

'He did?' Septor roared. 'Whatever possessed him to do that?'

'You can ask him yourself, Father. He's standing at the Unicorn's side.'

The King and Queen flung on their robes, nervously fumbling at the laces. It was now outside, yet the silhouette of the Black Unicorn with its tall, pointed horn jutting out from its forehead could not be mistaken. Holding one another's shaking hands they went closer.

It was more terrible than their worse imaginings. The reactions of Rosamile and the servant could not have prepared them for the sight of its awesome strength, the menace of its scales glinting in the Orb-light, the cruel and deadly point of its horn. Worst of all was the blazing fervour of its blood-red eyes as it glared at them. Standing calmly at its side, a hand resting upon its neck, was Barney Fowl.

'Why did it come here?' Septor asked him nervously.

'Don't know, Sire,' Barney sniffed loudly. 'Must 'ave something to do with this dead body though.'

Katrila tried as best she could to ignore the scrutiny of

those fiery red eyes while she looked at the corpse upon its back. In the Orb-light she could just tell that the darker shadings on the beast's neck were caused by caked blood. She guessed that the poor dead rider had barely reached manhood.

'Who was he, Barney?' she asked.

'Don't know that either, Your 'Ighness.' The Royal Wizard gave a shrug.

'Then best you get him down from there so he can be buried,' Rosamile ordered. 'That is, if you're brave enough.'

'I'm brave enough.' Barney's spotty face was grim. 'But I could do with a bit of 'elp if Your 'Ighness ain't too scared.'

'I'm certainly not scared,' the Princess lied. 'And how dare you speak to me like that? This beast hasn't skewered you, but it doesn't stop you from being a failed Wizard.'

'It was still me who was bold enough to go near it in the first place though,' Barney reminded her.

'Well, I can be just as bold,' Rosamile said, forcing herself to go nearer. 'Now, are you going to give me a hand with this body or not?'

Before she got any further, the Black Unicorn turned its head towards her and glared. She froze in her tracks.

'Nothing to be afraid of, Your 'Ighness. Would've killed us all by now if 'e wanted to.'

Her mouth dry, her knees trembling, Rosamile advanced again. Those red eyes seemed to be boring into her very soul. It took all the courage she could summon not to back away. It took even more courage to help Barney in pulling the body down, before they gently placed it on the ground. Relieved, she stood back quickly.

Barney stayed near the body while the Black Unicorn stared at him implacably. It seemed to trust him. Princess Rosamile was incapable of giving him credit for anything, yet the Royal Family would now be seeing him as a mediator. Although ignorant of its wishes, he realised that he had better say something.

'We'll bury him right 'ere,' he announced.

'Are you sure?' Rosamile asked.

'Yes,' Barney said uncertainly.

'Then best it be done,' Septor grunted before commanding the two knights brave enough to be at their side to tell the others to start digging a hole.

The two knights began by chastising their companions for the cowardly way they had all kept their distance. Silently, Septor approved of this and vowed that at a more suitable time he, too, would chastise them. However, to the knights' credit, it did not take long before a hole was made.

Now came the time which Barney had been dreading. Orina had always done her best to try and make him speak properly, hoping that in time he would be as capable of addressing a group of people as well as any other Wizard. Foolishly, he had ignored her efforts and not for the first time was beginning to regret it.

'Your Royal 'Ighnesses, men and women of Sanctuary,' he began, trying to sound as imposing as he could. 'The Grand Wizard must be proud of what we just done, 'cause we've all shown the courage to do what was right. The Black Unicorn brought our departed brethren 'ere so as we could give 'im a proper burial. Yet none of us must ever forget that it's only the body that's been discarded, 'cause anyone brave enough to ride upon the back of the Black Unicorn will be exal – ' He struggled to remember the rest of the word but failed. 'Regarded very 'ighly. In the Magic Wizardom 'is spirit will be blessed with the power to do whatever 'e wants. So let's all raise up our 'ands to the Silver Orb and give thanks both for the life 'e's led and the life 'e's living now.'

In silence, everyone followed his example and raised their hands in reverence to the greatness of their Creator. The silence was suddenly broken by a snort which resonated menacingly against the marblon walls. They took this as a sign of the beast's impatience and immediately picked up the corpse. Then they chanted the words:

'We return this body to the earth from which all life springs.'

As they were about to lower the corpse into the grave,

the Black Unicorn charged. Everyone scattered in terror except Barney Fowl. Although it bellowed at him, he stood his ground. It bellowed again, that same fearful cross between the braying of a horse and the roar of a mountain beast. Still he faced it without moving a muscle.

Red eyes glared at him. There was both confusion and anger in them. Just what else did it want him to do with the corpse but bury it? Unless . . . Had this person not ridden upon the very back of this magical beast? Perhaps, by some miracle, he was still alive. He knelt down and felt the throat of the corpse for any sign of a pulse. There was nothing.

'When the heart stops then so does the body.' It was a rule which even an ignorant orphan like himself had learned. So just what did the monster expect of him? No Magician could ever bring back the dead, especially a 'Wizard Without'. Somehow he had to try and communicate.

Deep in thought, he was totally unprepared for the second charge. This time he ran for his life. Stumbling over his own feet he made for the entrance to the keep, praying that someone would be brave enough to open the door. Thankfully, someone was. Hands dragged him safely inside and slammed the heavy door shut, seconds before the Black Unicorn rammed its horn into it with a jarring force. Then he heard it canter back. Relieved, he turned round and confronted the others.

'Like I said, if it 'ad wanted to kill me then it could 'ave done so.' His teeth chattered as he spoke.

His remark was greeted by silence. Nobody seemed very convinced.

It was suggested by King Septor that everyone should at least try and get some sleep and, dutifully, all tried. An exception was Barney Fowl who sat pondering miserably in the chamber filled with the equipment required for a calling he would never understand. True enough, there had been just one moment of glory when he had led the beast into the city but after that his usual ineptitude had

213

returned. Finally, he decided to do something that he should have done in the first place: he would relinquish his position as Royal Wizard and return to where he belonged, the countryside.

At dawn he went to the Main Hall. It was empty save for King Septor who, dressed in his nightrobes, sat musing upon his throne, his fingers knotted tightly together.

'I suppose you've still no idea just what it expects us to do with that body?' he asked as soon as the failed Royal Wizard entered.

'I wish I knew Sire. That's why I'd like an audience with you, if you're willing to listen?'

'Willing to listen?' The King looked bemused. 'A Royal Wizard should have words that are important enough to be heard at any time.'

'That's just it though, ain't it, Sire? My words ain't important like they should be.'

Septor remained silent, deep in thought, while outside the winds howled. He thought hard upon those words and what had been said by Rosamile earlier. It was the perfect opportunity to rid himself of someone who seemed incapable of performing his duties as the Royal Wizard. Yet something besides what he knew to be a too kindly nature was forcing him to think otherwise.

'Well,' he finally said, 'there's no denying that things haven't been working as well as they might for you. Yet tell me this, who else would have had the courage to go out and greet the Black Unicorn like that?'

'To a true believer it can do no more 'arm than a white one, Sire.'

'I'll try to find some comfort in that,' Septor sighed. 'But it still doesn't answer my question. Just what are we going to do with that body?'

'A proper Royal Wizard would be able to tell you.' Barney lowered his eyes in shame.

'And you're not a proper Royal Wizard, I suppose?'

'I reckons most of your subjects would agree with that, Sire.'

'I'll not deny it. I suppose there must be some good

reason to call you the "Wizard Without". Don't ask me why, but I've always seen beyond their complaints.' He trugged at his matted beard which was turning from a silvery grey to a magnificent white.

Barney, who had always liked the King best of all, now found himself warming to him even more. Although he was determined to beg for a release from his position he would certainly miss the wisdom of this, the kindest of monarchs.

'Alas, Sire,' he told him, 'I reckons that it should be Wizard Althigor in my place. No doubt about it, 'e's the man for the job – speaks proper, dresses proper, and does proper Magic.'

The King leaned forward on his throne and bade Barney to come closer. 'Between you and me,' he whispered, 'I've always found Althigor a pompous bore. At least you are never that.'

'That's very kind of you, Sire,' Barney said, flattered that the King had such an unexpectedly high opinion of him. 'But truth is, 'e would do it all much better than me.'

'Well, I don't want him,' Septor said glumly. 'Now let me tell you what I think you should do.'

'Sire?'

'Get out of the city. Wander over the Island for a bit.' Barney remembered that he had been planning to do just that. 'The riddle of that body is never going to be solved here, you know.'

'I knows that, – Sire.' Barney was frowning as he spoke. 'Just as I knows that the Black Unicorn is as real as you and me, even though it ain't never 'ad a father or mother. The Grand Wizard created us all so we could keep on breeding. He can also make people and animals out of nowhere if 'e wants. I reckons 'e does that when big changes are going to come about.'

'Quite a lecture!' Septor smiled. 'How that all reminded me of Orina. Who says you're not fit to be the Royal Wizard?' He banged his staff down loudly upon the stone floor. 'Now be off with you on your wanderings. I'll hold the appointing of Althigor off as long as I can.'

'No need for that, Sire. I suppose Magic just ain't for me.'

'That's not what Orina thought. She told me you had a Destiny like no other, and I never knew her to be wrong about anything.' The King's eyes were determined.

Barney remained unconvinced. All he could say was, 'I'll do my best to find the answer, Sire. I promise you that.'

'Then I suppose I can ask for no more.' Septor gave a shrug of his burly shoulders. 'Except to wish The Wizard's Blessing upon you.'

Barney bowed reverently and was about to take his leave when Septor called him back.

'The Black Unicorn – while you're away what are we supposed to do about it?'

Barney thought carefully before answering. 'I don't reckon it'll do any 'arm, not if folks treat it with respect. Mind you, just 'cause it's born of Magic don't mean it won't need feeding.'

'Fed with what?'

'Usual things you feed 'orses with, I suppose.' Barney tugged at a grimy ear. 'After all, when you think about it, it's just a big, nasty 'orse. Mind you, if we don't find out what to do with that body then it's going to get a lot nastier. I'll lead it to the stables before I go and someone can drag the body into the Main Hall.'

'Very reassuring, I must say. No wonder I'm so concerned about your success.' Septor grinned valiantly. 'I really do wish you a lot of luck.'

'I think I'll need it, Sire.' Barney returned the King's grin with a lopsided one of his own. 'I think I'll need it.'

Barney went to the kitchen and got himself a good supply of bread, Colidor apples and cheese. He put it all into a sack and, after saying goodbye to a small, white cat he had befriended, he risked going out into the bailey again. The Black Unicorn was still there, guarding the body. With a renewed confidence in himself, he walked fearlessly past it, even though it was watching his every move, and then stretched out his arm in the direction of the stables. The beast turned and, like an obedient dog, did Barney's bidding.

'Don't worry,' he called back to it as he stepped onto the drawbridge. 'Somehow I'll find out what we're all supposed to do with that body, then you can stop frightening people.'

Away from the Royal City the air was bright and clean. He was free at last of his marblon-walled prison. As he strode along the Path of Enchantment, the Island pulsated. Above him birds wheeled and dived against the Singing Winds and a swarm of gigantic mountain bees, which had strayed down from their high nest, buzzed past him. This caused a rabbit he had seen emerging from woodland to scurry in fear back into the trees again. Life was around him, both terrible and beautiful. He loved it all.

Although he had never been physically restrained from leaving the confines of the City, he had felt bound to stay there, apart from when his duties demanded he go out. Such an imprisonment had been in his mind, but nowhere else. Now, at last, he was free.

Still enjoying this freedom, he decided to leave the crude road which led to the north, and trod through a sea of flowing tall yellow grass until he reached the village of High Thorn.

Just why it was known as High Thorn was a mystery. He regarded thorns as nasty protruberances which always seemed to be low enough to scratch away at flesh and clothing. Nor in any way could this village be described as being set upon high ground. Still, he reflected, just what would life be without its little mysteries? This place had been his only home since the day he would always want to forget.

It had been populated mainly by chicken breeders living off the earnings from the eggs they sold and he assumed it still played that role. Certainly it had not changed, with its shambling, weather-beaten huts and the muddy path that led through its centre. People from better kept villages had often referred to High Thorn as a disgrace. Yet, as far as he was concerned, the people here had been the kindest of all. He recalled how, lost and alone after his parents and sister had been killed by falling rocks, he had wandered into a chicken barn. There he had slept in some straw until being discovered on the following morning. Many had offered to take him into their homes but the orphan preferred to remain in the barn. Gladly, he accepted his new name of Barney Fowl as his previous name of Gerdrun no longer seemed right for him. Thinking back, those times seemed such happy ones. All he had been expected to do was to keep the chickens amused, play with the other village children, and eat the food that was brought to him. If only he could have forsaken the promise to his King and returned to that simple life. How tempting it all seemed.

He did not recognise the first villager he saw, a knock-kneed youth with an exceptionally long jaw. With him was a young girl who was quite pretty in her own way but, once again, she was not someone he remembered. Of course, it was a long time ago but nevertheless, surely one of them might have borne just a faint resemblance to the children he had played with? He saw six more strangers before, at last, he did see someone whom he recognised.

Fergal was now a very old man. Barney hoped that someone was looking after him, for, in some respects, he had also been an outcast from the others – at least that was how, with a child's intuition, it had always seemed. Not that Barney had ever given much thought as to the reason why.

The Wizard stood in the old man's path, deliberately blocking his way. Although he was carrying a stick, Fergal teetered unsteadily.

'Out of my way!' he croaked, his voice sounding as hollow as wind blowing through the trunk of a fallen tree.

'It's me, Barney Fowl.'

'Barney who?' The old man squinted at him with faded eyes. 'Looks like a Wizard's hat you got there.'

Judging by their reactions, none of the others had recognised his battered hat as that of a Wizard. Fergal always did have a keen sense of observation. Obviously it was still there even if his sight was fading.

218

'That's 'cause I *am* a Wizard,' he said proudly. 'But I daresay you remember me as the little boy who used to sleep in the barn with the chickens.'

'Who'd ever want to sleep with chickens?' the old man asked impatiently. 'Who'd ever want to do that?'

'Well I did, if you remember.'

'Can't.' Fergal shook his head. 'Knew lots of people before the Disenchanted came here and killed them all off. Too many to remember – too many.'

The old man stared down at the ground while Barney thought of the villagers who had been wiped out by the Second Great Attack. Sanctuary would be safe forever but at what a price. He realised how foolish it was to expect nothing to change. He had wanted to reverse time itself. Even a failed Wizard like himself should have known that it was impossible. For old times' sake he would spend the night in the barn and breakfast on a few eggs, but that was all. He wished Fergal well and went on his way to ask the owner of the barn if he could spend the night there. She took a little persuading, for youths were obviously regarded with less sympathy than small orphans, but finally she relented. The barn was just as he had remembered it, only he had changed. Sleeping amongst chickens no longer held the same charms and he spent much of the night scratching.

He left early in the morning, planning to rejoin the Path of Enchantment, his mind no longer cluttered by longings for the past. King Septor had displayed great faith in his talents and he did not want to disappoint him. He began to think hard about the dead youth, who had been no older than himself. Where had he come from? What had he been doing when he encountered the Unicorn? And why had the beast carried the body to the City after killing him? All were questions which seemed unanswerable. Yet he was no longer the 'Wizard Without'. He was now determined, more than ever, that he would return with the answers.

Chapter Thirteen

Barney did not return to the Path of Enchantment.
Although he would be heading north he decided against
having any kind of order to his route. Nobody should
spend their life travelling on a road which ran the whole
length of the Island; he would never find the answer there.
So he strolled through the countryside, allowing his mind
to question just who and what the rider might have been.
Could he have been a fisher perhaps? A farmer, bleaching
that blond hair of his in the rays from the Golden Orb as
he toiled upon the land? As he revelled in the songs of the
winds and the birds, he dismissed these occupations.
Neither seemed suitable. Remembering the strong build,
Barney wondered whether he had been a shearer, or
possibly a quarrier. Yes, a quarrier seemed more likely.
That was the answer. He was almost sure – almost. He
thought again. The deceased might even have been a

knight who, caught wandering the cliffs without the protection of his armour, had been attacked by the Black Unicorn. It was an absurd theory. All his theories were absurd. As the Orb was being lowered, his spirits sank with it.

Even so, Barney still found it easy to identify himself with the mystery rider. For some inexplicable reason he was at one with him. Then, like the sudden swoop of a blue eagle, the revelation came. Of course he could identify with him. That lad had been just like himself – a wanderer!

From that moment onwards Barney felt as if he were roaming across the fields and valleys and hills in the company of someone else. He could sense that instead of dwelling in the Magic Wizardom, the soul of the rider was still upon the Island. Why? The riddle vexed him yet he still allowed his thoughts to ramble aimlessly through his mind, remembering Orina's words, 'Never hurry the brain for it is the very soil from which all ideas grow.'

In a mood of enforced relaxation, he spent the night beneath a wide oak tree. As soon as the Golden Orb was raised above the horizon, he continued. By the time it was being lowered again he had reached Copenhaven. He hoped in vain that he would once again see the beautiful White Unicorn emerge from the trees, before he reminded himself that this had nothing to do with the true purpose of his pilgrimage. Until that day nine years ago he had never really thought of the place as anything but a wood which people believed to be special. Now it filled him with excitement whenever he saw it. He realised that, on this day, it was not the footsteps of his fellow Magicians he was following but that of the nameless youth. Although exhausted by his wanderings, he suddenly started to run. Then he collapsed to the ground and fought to regain his lost breath. What impulse had made him suddenly want to do something so childish? It didn't make sense. It seemed like an eternity before he managed to get up onto his knees, raise his arms, and utter the three obligatory words:

'Blessed is Cophaven!'

Then, just as Orina had taught him, he closed his mind to all but that which lay within the Magic Wood. It was said that not only did the White Unicorn dwell there during Leaftime, but faeries also. He had often wondered just what faeries looked like. It didn't matter. All he needed were answers.

After meditating without any success he opened his eyes. He gazed at the trees, glorious in their colours, and wondered just how many different kinds there were. Although he was familiar with oaks, elms, and birches, it was now all too easy to sense that this was no ordinary wood. He might not have had the Gift but at least he was at one with Cophaven; he did comprehend its significance.

Just as he had done at the Blessing of the Season ceremonies, Barney started to chant. This time he actually got the words right, or at least most of them. It was a pity that Wizard Althigor was not there, for it was he, in particular, who delighted in correcting Barney whenever he erred. He continued to chant, mindlessly repeating the words over and over again, until, finally, sleep got the better of him.

He awoke to discover that the Golden Orb had been raised high above the horizon. There was also something on his hand. Drowsily, he looked down. Perched upon it was a tiny bat – a blood bat.

'Now there's a lucky thing,' he whispered softly, for it had always been regarded as exceptionally lucky to be visited by such a creature.

The little bat continued to sip tenderly at his blood while he wondered whether it lived in Cophaven or whether, like most on the Island, this one had come from the Caves of Forgotten Spirits.

'So just where 'ave you come from? he asked more to himself than the blood bat.

To his amazement it answered him. 'Eek-ga-eek-ga-eek-eek.'

It was pure animal talk and impossible for anyone to understand. As it sipped some more of his blood he tried to communicate with it by using his mind. 'Remember, we all share the same thoughts be we human, beast, or insect.

The Island is one. We are one.' Once again he recalled Orina's words.

'Eek-ga-eek-eek', the bat continued to squeak out its message.

Barney tried to think like a bat. He imagined flitting from one creature to another; taking a little blood here, a little blood there. It was no use. Despite the claims of people like Wizard Althigor who had often declared that he too could communicate with all living things, there had only ever been one person who had been truly capable of such a feat: Orina. Most shepherds were able to understand their sheep, even though he'd forgotten the formula for the potion which helped them to do this, yet sheep were simple creatures. Blood bats were much more difficult to understand.

Go! Perhaps 'ga' meant go? Yes, that was it. The little bat was telling him to go. But go where? To the bat's home? What else could it have wanted him to do? The Caves of Forgotten Spirits? That was where it had come from. Usually blood bats did their work at night before flying home when the Golden Orb was raised. This one must have stayed to give him the message.

'Off you go, then. I reckons you'll be there well before me but I'll not dally. That I promise you.'

It took another day before he reached the Caves of Forgotten Spirits. He had seen the caves only once before and Orina had described them to him as high-walled, pitch dark, and seemingly going on forever, deep into the earth. Now, all three of the entrances seemed like sinister black maws ready to suck him inside. Certainly, it had always been regarded by everyone as a place to fear; not only did bats and all kinds of insects dwell there but, worst of all, the Forgotten Spirits. It was believed that, although rare, there were a few Islanders whose behaviour had not been deemed worthy of admittance to the Magic Wizardom. Was the Black Unicorn's rider just such a person? He might soon be finding out.

For no particular reason he chose the middle entrance. The cave reeked of cold, malodorous air. It was a dark and forbidding place. Then his fears were overtaken by repulsion. At his feet a thousand legs were scurrying. Insects! There were times when he hated them. He wanted to commit the ultimate blasphemy and stamp upon them all. The only way he could think of conquering the temptation was to shout out as loud as he could.

'The Wizard made everything for a purpose!'

These words proved little comfort. With a frightening clarity, they echoed around the walls. Going deeper, he found it darker still and there was a rancid stench which made him gag and cough – each cough cruelly amplified.

Yet for all this there were few other signs of activity. The atmosphere was eerie. The prospect of being confronted by the Forgotten Spirits was too terrible to contemplate. Few Sanctuarites had ever dared to enter before, none in living memory except Orina. She had been the exception. She would stay the exception. He would get out of there.

It was not to be. He had ventured too far. There was no escape. He could sense something behind him. The realisation froze him to the spot. Tendrils of ice seemed to be gripping him when he heard the Spirit's voice.

'Help me!'

The voice could not have belonged to any human being. It was the baying of a mountain beast on a cold, wind-torn night; it was the plaintive cry of a bird trapped by the talons of a blue eagle; it was, worst of all, the wail of a grieving widow.

All Barney could do was close his eyes and pretend in vain that it wasn't happening. Once again the Spirit spoke to him.

'Help me! Help me!'

'J-Just leave me alone, will you!' Barney croaked while his body shook from head to toe.

'How can I? Only you can help me,' the voice insisted.

The physical death of someone was bad enough but to encounter their spirit form was even worse.

'What do you want?' Barney said, his voice a little firmer.

'Turn and face me.'

Barney lost control of himself and fought hard to say

224

the words, 'I – I'm not doing that.'

'You must. It'll make you less afraid.'

Barney found that hard to believe. Nevertheless, with quaking legs, he forced himself to turn around. To his surprise and relief he saw nothing but darkness. Was it all his imagination? No, that was too much to hope for.

'I'm no Magician, you know,' Barney said, addressing the dark, thick air surrounding him. 'I can't even do a single trick properly. They call me the "Wizard Without".'

'You're kindred with all that's Magic,' the voice moaned, 'if only you knew it.'

Barney shook even more. At any moment the voice might take form – hideous form. He wanted to shut his eyes again but some compulsion he didn't really understand forced him to keep them open. He now realised that the Spirit had power – an awesome power which knew and understood all that was upon Sanctuary, including himself.

'Just who are you?' he begged. 'Just what do you want of me?'

'I want your help,' the voice moaned again, this time loud enough for it to echo eerily around the walls of the cave. 'It was you who vowed to help me. It was you who searched both the Island and your heart to find the answer. You've got to help me.'

'Then you must be . . .'

At first it was nothing more than a light, a weird spectral glow. Barney cowered before it, knowing that in the next instant he would actually be seeing the Spirit. The glow became a formless shape, losing its dazzling quality before turning to a softer grey. Trembling, he watched it transform into a human figure. At first it was nothing more than the outline of a head and trunk. Then arms started to appear before the bottom half parted to form two legs. Shimmering against the ebon background, it turned into a real person. Although the image was colourless, Barney recognised at once the identity of the Spirit; the youthful face, the thick and tousled hair, the broad shoulders, the strong legs. He knew then that his quest was over.

'You m-must be the rider of the Black Unicorn?'

'Who else?' the Spirit said impatiently.

'Then you are not in the Magic Wizardom?'

'That's because I'm not completely dead. My body is drained of blood, yet I am not dead.' For one moment the ghostly shape almost became whole. Although still a pearly silver he could now clearly see the outline of the youth. There was a wry smile on his face which made the Spirit seem more human than before. 'But you must make me come alive again.'

' 'Ow can I do that? They call me the "Wizard Without" 'cause I can't do any proper Magic. They had no right to make a boy as young as me Royal Wizard. No right at all.'

'You were clever enough to find me here. So now my rebirth is in your hands,' For a moment the Spirit paused. 'I think in most cases when either the heart or the brain stops then so does life, but I've got a Destiny. I must earn my entry to the Magic Wizardom more than any other.'

'Then I don't envy you,' Barney told him, suddenly relaxed in the Spirit's company. 'I know myself what a burden Destiny can be.'

'So you should, for your Destiny's linked to mine. Surely you must have realised that?'

A cold chill ran through Barney Fowl. A sacrifice was required, his own. Somehow the blood was to be taken from his body so it could feed the veins of the dead rider. He became afraid even though he knew that the laying down of his own life would ensure he would go straight into the Magic Wizardom. With a heavy reluctance, he said.

'My blood belongs to you?'

'Yours and that of thousands more,' the Spirit replied. 'Perhaps that is why I lost it all in the first place, so I could take on a little blood from everyone on the Island.'

'How are you going to get all this blood?' Barney asked, greatly relieved that he wasn't required to die after all.

'From the blood bats, of course. If they take blood but don't drink it, they can give it all to me.'

'Then you'll live again?'

'With your help.'

'But what am I to do?'

'Be at one with them.' The voice and shape of the Spirit were beginning to fade. 'Be at one with them. You've got the Gift – '

Barney was alone again. Now there was nothing but darkness, the pungent stench of droppings, which was making his eyes water, and insects crawling over his feet. He knew that, above him, the blood bats would be sleeping. To rouse them would be easy enough, but what then? How could you order thousands of such creatures to go and take a little blood from every Islander and then deposit that blood in the corpse of a dead Sanctuarite at the Citadel? He tried to speak their language again.

'Eek-eek-ga-eek.'

It was hopeless, he sounded nothing like a bat. Then he recalled how he alone had seemed to be able to communicate with the Black Unicorn. Through that fearful beast he had felt the very Magic of The Grand Wizard. Suddenly words flowed into his brain – Magic words. It was the language of those in the Magic Wizardom.

'Cragameva, digsha, sogoreta, elka-elka-elka!' The words raged through him.

They seemed meaningless. It was the language of another world, another place. Yet he could feel those words driving through him, consuming his very being. Then he was able to speak again, using the words of his own language, knowing that now at last the bats would understand. In his mind he had become a bat. Now he knew what it was like to fly upon the night air, searching for the right host to feed a hungering body. He could almost feel his own arms and legs wither into tiny wings and clawlike feet as he whispered.

'You've got work to do, me friends.'

Suddenly the silence was broken by the exploding sound of wakening bats. A multitude of warm bodies and cold wings brushed against him as they fluttered past, making him feel that he was at the centre of a living whirlwind. The blood bats belonged to him. For one blasphemous moment he almost felt as if he were The Grand Wizard

227

himself, that all creation was under his divine rule. Cresting upon a wave of revelation he gave his commands while striding back out into the daylight. It was just as dark outside. Bats were everywhere, pouring out from all three entrances, darkening the skies.

Then they were gone, swarming over the hills, flying onwards upon their quest. Just as he had often seen Orina suffer, so he too was forced to endure the pangs of withdrawal. Without the force of the Magic which had been flowing through his veins he was no longer protected from the agonies of bones twisting unnaturally in their sockets, of eyes being pressed hard by invisible thumbs, or of fingers and toes locked in excruciating, clawlike positions. By the time his sufferings were over all the bats had gone.

Not far away was the village of Apples-by-a-Stream. There, he finally managed to exert his authority as Royal Wizard by holding up his shabby cloak directly against the Golden Orb, having scrubbed it clean of dirt so that the villagers could see the discreet gold crest of crossed briar twigs surmounted by the Royal Crown.

The villagers loaned him one of their prized Arildan steeds and told him that it would be collected the next time one of them visited the Royal City. The young mare was a good horse, fast and with plenty of stamina. It was not long before she was carrying him through the Main Gate and up towards the Citadel.

'You've missed some right goings on,' a doughy faced male servant told him as he took the reins of the exhausted horse. 'We've had thousands of bats all over the place. Never seen anything like it in my life!'

'Don't suppose you 'ave,' Barney grinned. 'But where did they all go? Did they go to the Main 'All?'

'That's right, they did.' The servant looked stunned. 'So it was you who sent them here then? Now that really is Magic! But what was the purpose of it all? If you don't mind me asking, that is.'

'Why, to bring that corpse back to life again,' Barney

laughed, before leaving the baffled servant to work it out for himself.

He found that the Main Hall was full of blood bats. Their droppings littered the floor. He hadn't bargained for that. The complexion of the corpse was no longer as white as it had been but, nevertheless, it still had the drained pallor of a dead man. Much of the blood-stained clothing had been torn away by the bats' tiny claws so that they could get to his flesh. Some of them had settled on his legs, others his chest, and others his arms. Somehow, they were all injecting him with the blood they had brought. It was truly Magical.

Barney was about to kneel down and give thanks to The Grand Wizard when King Septor burst in.

'*Barney*!' he cried as he slipped on the bat droppings and was sent sliding across the floor.

'I see my Magic is working, Sire!' Barney rushed to the King's aid.

'Is it you who's responsible for all this?' Septor said angrily. 'I know it's supposed to be lucky to play host to one of them but these wretched things have been making a nuisance of themselves throughout the whole Island! The Main Hall has become nothing but a bat cave for the past day. The whole place reeks of them!'

' 'Ave the Queen and Princess Rosamile also been visited by them?' Barney asked.

'Yes, yes, of course they have. Everyone in the whole of Sanctuary seems to have been visited. Now, let's get out of here so I can find out just what possessed you to stir up all this madness.'

A cold wind was howling through the corridor. Shivering, Barney wished he was back in the Main Hall. Yet he was relieved to find that, now they had left, the King's anger seemed to have subsided.

'So what is the purpose of it all?' he said, his manner calmer.

'Every single one of the bats 'as taken just a little blood from a Sanctuarite,' Barney explained.

'I know that!' The King's anger and impatience was returning.

229

'But they ain't been drinking it.' Barney fought the temptation to scratch away at a flea-bitten arm in the King's presence. 'No, Sire, what they been doing is saving the blood to put it into the veins of that dead rider.'

'So that's it!' King Septor looked stunned. 'I'd never have known, I mean, there were so many of those creatures in there it was impossible to tell just what they were doing.'

'Now that 'e's got blood in 'is veins, all I have to do is to start up 'is 'heart.'

'You mean bring him back to life? Impossible!'

'I've seen 'is Spirit in the Cave of Forgotten Spirits. It's waiting for me to do some Magic. But I'll be 'onest, Sire, I ain't got a clue 'ow it should be done.'

'What about the Black Unicorn? Can't it bring the lad back to life?'

'No, Sire.' Barney shook his head. 'It might 'ave been born of Magic but it can't do any. It's down to me.'

'You've been doing well enough so far, Barney. Lucky I believed in you when nobody else did.' There was now an endearing twinkle in the King's eye.

Barney asked about the Unicorn.

'Oh, it's taken itself to the stables,' the King told him. 'Funnily enough, the other horses don't seem that afraid of it, not like we humans. Fortunately, there are some people who are brave enough to take it some fodder. Still, what am I doing telling you all of this when you can go and see for yourself?'

Barney took leave of his King and went straight to the stables. The place was populated by Havelot and Arildan steeds. The stalls at the far end were empty, save for one. The horses might not be afraid of the Black Unicorn but neither they nor their handlers cared to go too near it. Confidently, the Royal Wizard strode up to the stall the beast had chosen to occupy.

Such arrogance was soon punished. Red eyes glared back at him with an awesome malevolence before it gave a loud and angry snort which startled the other horses and made them stamp their feet.

'Look, I've got all the blood bats to fill 'im up again, but 'ow am I supposed to make 'im come alive?' Barney asked, doing his best to look unafraid.

The unicorn snorted again, before jabbing its horn in his direction. Barney tried to remember the Magic words that had suddenly come to him while trying to communicate with the bats. It was no use. The Magic would not come to him. Glumly, he retreated.

Outside, the sky was grey and The Wizard's Tears had started to rain down. Barney's first instinct was to withdraw inside the Citadel. He decided against it. Instead he would climb the fourth tower and, upon its battlements, concentrate on the problem.

Beneath wild, rain-lashed skies Barney racked his brains. He considered the idea of just pumping away at the corpse's chest with his fists and hoping that the heart might begin to beat again. Ridiculous! If that were the case then everyone who died could be brought back to life. Alternatively, there were the extremes of hot and cold. He thought of lowering the body down into the deepest and coldest part of a pool and then, as soon as it had been dragged up again, subjecting it to the intense heat of a fire. Even more ridiculous! Maybe all that had to be done was to return him to the back of the Black Unicorn? No, somehow that solution sounded all too simple.

The clouds were no longer a steely grey but had become a dark and wild cauldron. Barney heard a distant rumbling. Very soon Sanctuary would be shaken by The Wizard's Rage, and on this occasion he was sure that Rage would be directed at himself. Magic might well have been bestowed upon him in the most spectacular of ways, but unless he discovered what his next move should be, The Grand Wizard's impatience at such ineptitude would surely be wreaked upon him.

With such anger came Jagged Fire. Within that fire was born the very source of all creation. In wet clothes, Barney dashed down the spiral stairs. At last he had the answer.

Kneeling over the corpse in the now bat-free Main Hall were Queen Katrila and Princess Rosamile. Both of them looked at him with contempt when he entered. Barney didn't care. He had to tell them.

231

'I know 'ow to make 'im come alive again, Your 'Ighnesses!' he blustered. 'I'm going to get somebody to 'elp me take 'im up to one of the towers.'

'You'll do no such thing!' Rosamile snapped. 'He's staying right here where the Queen and I will tend him. He looks such a mess after all those bats have been at him. Mind you, even though he's dead he doesn't smell as much as you.' Disdainfully she pointed at him. 'Now that your clothes are wet you stink even more than usual. No wonder The Wizard is so angry with people like you around.'

'But Your 'Ighnesses 'e don't smell like a real corpse 'cause 'e ain't dead,' Barney insisted, ignoring the insult.

'So that entitles you to drag his body up to one of the towers and expose him to the full force of The Grand Wizard's Rage?' Queen Katrila said angrily.

'Rage is life,' Barney argued. 'From the Jagged Fire that splits the sky comes the very force of creation!'

'What a revelation from the Wizard Without!' Rosamile scoffed. 'What do you know of such things? If you'd been a proper Royal Wizard then you wouldn't have vanished like you did, but stayed here and done something about all those bats.'

14 'It was me who summoned the bats,' Barney said through clenched teeth.

'Hah!' Rosamile turned to her mother for support. 'What utter nonsense. Those bats came here of their own accord. You're not really suggesting that it was – '

Before she could finish her sentence there was a clap of thunder which almost seemed to vibrate the solid marblon walls of the Citadel. Then came the sound of The Wizard's Tears raining down more heavily still.

'We must take him to the tower!' Barney urged. "Rage is Life."

Rosamile tossed back her golden hair. 'If we say that this body isn't going to be moved from here, then it's not going to be moved.'

'Then I fear The Wizard's Rage will be lasting a long time.'

The words were spoken by King Septor. Thrusting out his corpulent stomach he strode over to them, just in time remembering to avoid the bat droppings. 'I overheard

232

what Barney was saying and it makes sense.'

'The Wizard will not thank you for showing such disrespect,' Katrila said. 'It's sheer blasphemy to carry this body up to the top of a tower.'

'It's even more disrespectful to ignore The Grand Wizard's wishes, wouldn't you say?' He turned to Barney. 'Go and get some people to help you. As far as I can see, the sooner we get the dead rider there, the better for all of us.'

When Barney returned to the Royal Chamber both Queen Katrila and Princess Rosamile were still arguing with the King. Septor told him to ignore it all and, with the help of the two servants, to begin.

Barney decided to carry the body up to the tower where the King had been forced to slay his son. This seemed appropriate, for, from death, would now spring life. It was an awkward and tiring task to carry it all the way up a spiral stairway. If only carpenters would have the wit to devise something to ease such work, he thought as they struggled up, while the King followed behind, wheezing and puffing.

As soon as they emerged onto the battlements the full force of the tempest hit them. It was almost impossible to stand up in such a maelstrom of hammer-force winds. The wild sky erupted and Jagged Fire stabbed down onto the parapet. Momentarily Barney was blinded by the brilliant flash of silver. Then he saw that part of the marblon stonemasonry had actually been split. What a mighty power is possessed in His great hands! he reflected before preparing himself for what had to be done.

Assisted by the heavily built woman and the young male apprentice knight, Barney defied both the torrents and the winds. They managed to drag the corpse right out into the open and prop it up against the broken wall. The two helpers seemed exceedingly relieved when he told them to return to the shelter of the doorway. Then all he could do was wait.

There was another burst of thunder. Shaking with terror, Barney waited for the Jagged Fire and probably his own death. Even before it began its journey he knew that this would not be the one, so he opened his eyes and watched it lance through the sky. The body was momentarily bathed in a silver light. He felt reassured that if he was to die now then it would not be in vain. Whoever this youth was, he had a Destiny greater than his own.

'Oh Grand Wizard,' he called up to the sky, his words drowned by the screech of the winds. 'Let 'im receive the Fire of Life so 'e can fulfil 'is Destiny!'

Suddenly the winds died. The heavy downfall of Tears softened. It was time. It was as if the whole sky had been rent asunder. The floor beneath him trembled while his bones seemed to rattle against his flesh.

Then the moment came. From His great hand sped a jagged knife of fire. Even before it reached the corpse Barney could feel the blazing heat. Then he himself was that heat. As the point of the knife scorched into the corpse so he too received it. Writhing upon the floor he felt a million serpents of pain twisting through his veins. He wanted to scream but the agony constricted him. It became greater still as he felt nothing but the searing torment before, suddenly, the pain began to ebb. Once again he was aware of The Wizard's Tears raining down upon him. Once again he could feel the clammy dampness of the stone floor. Once again he could feel his mouth open as he fought for breath.

'Barney! Barney!' a familiar voice was calling through crimson mists.

He tried to respond but it was no use. His body was still burning, his senses stunned. It seemed like an eternity before he could open his eyes. Staring down at him, his beard and his long hair wet and bedraggled, was the King.

'Don't speak unless you have to,' he heard him say.

' 'As it worked?' Barney managed to gasp out.

Septor bent over the rider. 'There's a terrible burn on the lad's chest but his heart's beating,' he answered.

Barney breathed a sigh of relief. Jagged Fire had jolted the body to life again. The youth was alive. He had succeeded. The image of his King began to fade. Everything was fading. The full force of that Fire had been conducted through his own body. His own life was done. As his mind began to close, he had no regrets. His reward would be found in the Magic Wizardom where he would be re-united with Orina.

Chapter Fourteen

In the driving rain of The Wizard's Tears, the apprentice knight and the female servant picked up the still lifeless body of the rider. Nearby, Septor was desperately shaking an equally lifeless Barney Fowl. Refusing to admit that the Royal Wizard was dead, the King continued to shake and shout at the unresponding youth as if he were his own son and he loved him.

Saddened by the spectacle, the apprentice knight and the servant struggled down the spiral staircase and carried the rider's body into the Main Hall. Reverently, they placed it upon the chequered floor.

'What happened up there?' Rosamile demanded of them.

'And where's my husband?' the Queen asked.

'Barney Fowl took the rider out onto the ramparts,' the apprentice knight began, 'so that The Grand Wizard could direct Jagged Fire into his body.' He swallowed, his mind filling with the memory of what he had seen. 'All of a sudden, fire shot down out of the sky and struck the rider. It seemed as if the Royal Wizard wanted to use himself as a channel so that the fire could pass through him.' He pointed to the corpse lying motionlessly before them. 'It doesn't look like it worked, but the King is still up on top trying to bring Barney back to life. I reckon he's dead, too.'

'Poor Barney!' The Queen put her fingers to her lips. 'It sounds as if we all misjudged him. If only he'd succeeded! People would have venerated his memory instead of calling him the "Wizard Without".'

'For this sacrifice he's bound to be exalted up there in the Magic Wizardom,' Rosamile said softly, her clear blue eyes dulled by sadness. 'All I can do is hope that when my time comes I won't be punished too severely for misjudging him so.'

'It was a miracle what he did, Your Highess,' the serving woman put in, her ruddy cheeks glistening from the rain. 'I never heard of any Magician summoning Jagged Fire like that.'

'It would be even more of a miracle if we could bring this rider back to life. Then it really wouldn't have been in vain.'

'That burn on his chest looks terrible.' Katrila knelt down beside the body.

Rosamile followed her mother's example. Cautiously she touched the blackened scar with the tips of her fingers. The flesh still felt seared but she fought the temptation to draw her hand away. An impulse told her to keep touching him.

Now Rosamile felt another impulse – an impulse from deep within his chest. It was faint but it was a heartbeat. Then his mouth dropped open and although his eyes were still closed she could sense that he was taking in air. She lowered her face until her cheek was almost against his mouth. He was breathing! Putting the palm of her hand on his ribcage just below the burn, she felt his heart beating stronger still.

'He's alive!' she cried.

'So Barney did it!' Katrila gasped.

'I shall nurse him back to health myself,' Rosamile said regally.

'Then you'd better nurse Barney as well!'

Turning, the Princess saw that the King had now entered the Main Hall, and he was supporting a white-faced, limping Barney Fowl. She turned back to the apprentice knight and the serving maid.

'Why did you say he was dead?' she demanded.

'I th-thought he was,' the apprentice knight stammered.

'As well he should have been,' Septor said gruffly. 'Performing Magic like that hasn't done Barney any good.'

'So it's The Wizard's wish that both he and the rider survive.' Katrila sounded reflective as she glanced first at the body of the rider and then at Barney Fowl, whose head was dropped forward so that strands of his lank wet hair draped over his chest. 'Why not put them both in the third upper chamber, my beloved? Our servants here can get help. Go on, you two. Quickly!'

The apprentice knight and the serving maid gave courteous nods and left the Hall, soon returning with another five helpers.

The two youths were carried to the third upper chamber by the servants and placed on pallets. Queen Katrila supervised the removal of Barney's wet clothes and the drying of both the Wizard's frail body and that of the rider. They were then swathed in thick woollen covers and left to sleep in peace.

Throughout the rest of the night Princess Rosamile resisted the temptation to visit the rider. She did not find it easy. As soon as The Grand Wizard had banished the storm and raised the Golden Orb above the horizon she quickly got dressed and hurried to his chamber. She gave but a quick glance at Barney Fowl (now snoring loudly) before giving all her attention to the blond rider. The light from the rising Orb was streaming through the window, deifying him in gold. Princess Rosamile worshipped him with her eyes. Just who was he? For her, his attraction could only be a physical one and he did seem much younger than herself. Would he, for instance, be able to speak to her at great lengths about the Second Great Attack, giving constant and intelligent acknowledgement of the important part which she had played in that battle? She would find it difficult to respect anyone who was not almost her equal in mock combat. She needed one who could engage in discourse and, within reason, argue just a little upon how certain aspects of life could be improved. Rosamile loved life, the very joy of breathing and seeing. She loved its challenge and the sheer joy of not only meeting that challenge, but also of winning. Yes, perhaps that above all.

Before the rider's arrival the only suitor truly worthy of her attentions had been Sir Jactor. Now as she gazed upon a face that no longer had the pallor of death but was tanned to an alluring nut brown, Princess Rosamile realised that in some way their destinies may well be entwined. It was more than mere infatuation. She had long outgrown that stage. This youth had ridden into her life upon a fabulous mythical beast, hadn't he? Of course he was worthy of her!

'Your 'Ighness, Your 'Ighness!'

Impatient at having her thoughts interrupted, she glared at Barney Fowl who was staring up at her with bloodshot eyes. Feeling a little guilty, she forced herself to smile before going to his side.

'What is it, Barney?' Close to him, she could not help noticing the contrast between his sallow, drawn features and those of the resurrected rider.

'Is 'e alive?'

'Yes, he's alive. You've just proved yourself to be the finest Wizard on the Island. You have reason to be proud.'

'Sounds funny coming from your 'Ighness, that does,' he said wearily. 'Never thought I'd ever 'ear you say that.'

'I don't suppose you did, especially as it was I more than anyone else who wanted you removed from your office.'

'You was only doing what you thought was right, Your 'Ighness,' he croaked. 'And if you was to say it again then you'd still be right. The Magic's all but burnt out of me.'

'Then so be it.' She placed a hand upon his blistered forehead, hastily withdrawing it when he winced with pain. 'You'll always be respected for what you did, make no mistake about that. Now best you go back to sleep.'

Rosamile spent the rest of the day studying the stranger who had so unwittingly captured her heart, dismissing any Wizard or Witch who came to offer help. Sitting on a creaking wooden chair she eventually fell asleep, until her mother came and awoke her, and reminded the Princess that it was unseemly for an unwed girl to spend so long in a chamber with two men, even if one were unconscious and one still asleep.

The following day she returned to her normal routine. She kept herself fit by engaging in sword-fighting practice. This daily ritual was performed in the Main Street and always drew a small audience of citizens who had nothing better to do. One day she would find out just why they had so much time to idle, but not today. She was having enough difficulty in banishing the disturbing thoughts of the rider without bothering with anything else.

To aid concentration she would have to apply even more effort than usual in fighting off opponents. As always, she used her favoured single-handed sword as opposed to the heavier, two-handed glavors used by most knights. She also wore lighter armour, enabling her to be far fleeter of foot than most of her heavily encumbered rivals. Agility had always been her greatest weapon. All armour had its weak spots. Even if it meant dangerously committing herself, she would always aim for those parts. With the keen sense of survival imbued after the Second Great Attack, she invariably found them. The most difficult knight to defeat was the one who was also her constant companion, Sir Jactor. Her first contest was to be with him. Despite their friendship, no quarter was ever given during mock combat. Although wearing the heaviest of armour, Sir Jactor was able to swing his mighty two-handed glavor in impressive sweeping arcs. Rosamile ducked and swerved, skilfully jabbing with her light wooden sword. As always, victory would eventually be hers.

The whole of her body was jarred painfully when the heavy, wooden blade of Jactor's glavor banged down upon her back. Gasping for breath Rosamile fell to the ground. Recovering instantly, she aimed her blade at Sir Jactor's exposed armpit as he swung the glavor upwards for a second strike. Such a move had never failed her in the past. This time she was too slow.

The glavor hammered against her right shoulder, knocking her down again. In the next moment a foot was pressing down upon her breastplate, pinning her to the ground. Then she heard Sir Jactor, the man who had been courting her so ardently, claim his victory.

By the time he had removed his foot, Rosamile had regained her breath. Despite the encumbrance of her armour she leapt to her feet, enraged. Whipping off her helmet, she swung her mane of blonde hair free as she glared at the victor.

'You cheated!' she stormed at the knight who was holding up his glavor in triumph.

Sir Jactor dropped his massive wooden sword, whipped off his helmet, and stared back at the Princess with dark, questioning eyes.

'Your Highness, I insist that I did no such thing. It was a fair fight.'

'How dare you argue with me?' she cried.

His jaw jutting sulkily, he looked down.

'Look into my face when I address you!' she snapped, waiting for him to obey before continuing. 'Not only have you cheated but you have also shown a total lack of respect for the daughter of your King. Sir Jactor, you will no longer hold the privileged position of being a knight. You are dismissed from the Order.'

'But, Your Highness!' Those dark eyes were now full of self-pity. 'I beg you! Surely I don't deserve . . . .'

'Return your armour and weapons. You are no longer a knight!'

'But, your Highness, I . . . . '

'*Go!*'

Holding his head low, Sir Jactor clanked his way back over the drawbridge and into the Citadel. In silence the others watched. Could it be that knights were lacking in manners these days? Rosamile wondered. She had had enough of them all.

'Well, when you've all finished gawping there's more practising to be done,' she said, loud enough even for those still wearing their helmets to hear. 'And I don't want to learn of any more cheating going on – cheating is laziness. In a real battle it's the lazy who get killed.'

After delivering her rebuke she returned to the Citadel. Loudly, she stamped through the Main Hall, ignoring the greetings of her father who was holding an audience with four peasants. Animatedly they were describing how the Black Unicorn, bearing a rider, had galloped past them on the Path of Enchantment. She went straight to the chamber. To her relief she found that Barney Fowl was still sleeping and snoring loudly. Undisturbed, she could study the youth who fascinated her so much.

She looked down at the beautiful vision of manhood which was still obsessing her, recalling how much time she had wasted on Sir Jactor. How could she have been such a fool? There was just no comparison between that insolent oaf and the rider's perfection. She didn't merely find him handsome – her feelings were running much deeper than that and she was powerless to understand why. For the first time in her life she was truly in love. It didn't make sense.

Neither did her actions during the mock contest with Sir Jactor make any sense. She had behaved abominably. The truth was that he hadn't cheated. After all, in such combats there were very few rules, for in a real battle there were none at all. Rosamile had been the victim of nothing more than her own carelessness. If anyone was to blame beside herself it was this youth with his honey-blond hair. He had completely taken her over.

Although still unconscious, his vigour seemed to be

241

returning. There was more colour in his face. Once recovered, he was bound to fall in love with her. Yet what if he never recovered beyond this point and just slept his life away? Was this to be a trial for her – to fall in love with someone who would never even know she existed?

Before, her emotions had always been straightforward; now, they were being wrenched and twisted. It was getting harder to hold back her tears. Yet she would try. By The Wizard, she would certainly try!

She had almost succeeded when the eyes of the rider suddenly sprang open. They were like her own, a dazzling blue; shining up at her like the bright sky of a Leaftime day. No, they were even more beautiful than that. Her own blue eyes always sparkled with self-confidence while his were tantalisingly innocent. Her tears dried as she knelt down beside him.

'Do you know where you are?' she asked, her voice trembling.

The rider shook his head.

'You're in the Royal Citadel. Do you remember anything about the Black Unicorn?'

The rider stayed silent.

'Can you speak?'

The rider opened his mouth and made a gasping sound. He then closed his mouth, opened it, and tried again. The result was the same, as was the third attempt, and the fourth.

Gently, Rosamile placed her hand against his lips and said comfortingly, 'Don't try. You're the first person who's ever been brought back to life. Your voice will return in time.'

'You sure of that, Your 'Ighness?'

Once again she was angered by Barney Fowl's intrusion. Why couldn't he have stayed asleep?

'I'm not a fool, you know,' she snapped. 'I do know how the miracle worked.'

'Does Your 'Ighness know?' he croaked. 'Do you know that that Jagged Fire must 'ave stopped just before it got to 'is 'eart? Otherwise it would 'ave been burnt to a cinder.'

242

He sniffed loudly before continuing. 'Did you also know that if the brain don't get what it should in the way of blood and everything, then things go wrong? Least, that's what Orina told me.'

'Orina could have been wrong,' Rosamile retorted, secretly dreading that the Royal Witch had been right. 'Are you suggesting that he'll never be able to speak again? He can hear and he tried to speak when I asked him to.'

'He might not even be able to walk again. I don't know. I took Jagged Fire as well, and the way I feel at the moment I reckon I might never get up again myself.'

The thought of the strong, handsome youth being bedridden for the rest of his life was too terrible to contemplate. She even felt sorry for poor Barney Fowl.

'You mustn't give in,' she told him regally. 'Had any of us given in during the Second Great Attack then none of us would be here now. Bravery and determination pulled us through that time. It will do so again.' Rosamile lifted her chin as if she were delivering an oration before pointing to the rider. 'He was strong enough to ride upon the back of the Black Unicorn. He must possess great courage.'

'And what about me?' Barney said indignantly. 'Doesn't it matter if I never walk again?'

Rushing over to him, she took his hand in her own. 'Oh, Barney, despite our differences I could never wish that on you.'

'Well, maybe in a few days things'll start looking different,' he sighed. 'Maybe I was exaggerating about myself but the Unicorn's rider will need some looking after.'

'I shall attend to that,' she told him. 'Now get some more rest. You're just as important to me as the rider, you know,' she lied.

'Course I am.' He gave a knowing grin.

The following morning both were able to eat the nuts and slices of Colidor apple Rosamile commanded to be

243

brought for them, washing it all down with goblets of restorative herb essence. After their meal they both slept again.

The rest of her own day was spent pondering over what a fool she had made of herself in front of the knights. It was, perhaps, The Wizard's blessing that during eventide she encountered Sir Jactor. He was now dressed in peasant clothes and walking down the Main Street, his head still lowered. He looked very pale.

'If you're ready to apologise,' she said, blocking his path, 'then I might think about reinstating you.'

'I didn't cheat, Your Highness!' His dark eyes were hard and resolute. 'I can assure you that – '

'You fought both hard and honourably,' she forced herself to admit.

'I did,' Jactor said. 'How could I ever cheat the woman I admire more than any other?'

'So you're claiming that you beat me?' she teased.

'It was purely by chance,' he hastened to say. 'I've been beaten in mock combat countless times by you – '

'Now there's no need to flatter me,' she smiled again. 'I've already decided to make you a knight again. Jactor, I was in the wrong.'

'Thank you, Rosam – I mean, Your Highness.'

'You meant Rosamile, Jactor. That's how you've always addressed me when we were alone and that's what you may still call me. Have you forgotten how close to each other we've been this Leaftime?'

'How could I forget?' he replied passionately.

'Nor I,' she said with equal passion, taking his hand in her own. 'If it hadn't been for the arrival of the Black Unicorn then, who knows? Our relationship could have grown even stronger.'

'So it was the rider of the Black Unicorn who stole your heart from me?'

'He didn't steal it,' she said frankly. 'I gave it to him willingly. One day everyone will have to.'

'Already you've made him your King, haven't you?' Jactor's eyes gleamed with jealousy.

244

'How can I say?'

'You're in love with him, though.'

'That was impertinent!' She glared at him before her expression softened. 'I suppose I'd better not deny it. It seems to be The Wizard's wish that I belong to him.'

'I'd offer to try and ride the Black Unicorn myself if I thought it would make any difference,' Sir Jactor said wryly. 'But I suppose it wouldn't.'

'The last thing I want to do is watch you get yourself killed.'

'But it wouldn't break your heart?'

'You do mean something to me,' she said warmly. 'You always will.'

Jactor's eyes shone with his true feelings for her. 'Then all I can do is hope that while I lie dreaming of your golden hair flowing in the Singing Winds he'll be making you as happy as I had hoped to do.'

'Gallant as always, my brave and noble Jactor.' Rosamile was oblivious of the citizens passing her as they hurried towards the close of the day's business. 'For all I know, those times spent with you will turn out to have been the happiest of my life.'

Going down upon one knee, Jactor kissed her hand before looking up at her in adoration.

'Your Highness,' he said quietly, 'I've no wish to rejoin the Order. I will become a shepherd and wander the hills while dreaming of what might have been.'

'If that's what you want – ' She took both of his hands in her own – 'then I'll not stop you. But as far as I'm concerned a knight is what you were, and a knight is what you'll always be.'

'I'll leave for the hills right away.' He was now almost choking in an effort to hold back his tears. 'Tell the others that I admitted to cheating and that I'm still banished from the Order.'

'I'll do no such thing!' she exclaimed. 'You will be remembered by the Order as the noblest knight who ever lived. I'll make sure of that!'

'And you will be the noblest of Queens.' Turning hastily,

he headed towards the Main Gate.

Rosamile guessed that he would be travelling to Kingtown to visit his family. She wondered whether he would tell them why he had decided to change his life so completely. She wanted to let her tears flow but it was unseemly for a Princess to be seen crying in public. She remembered the times they had spent so happily together. The Orb was now a warm orange as The Grand Wizard lowered it towards the horizon. It was the end of the day: the end of a beautiful interlude in her life.

Barney Fowl was sitting up on his pallet when Rosamile arrived at the chamber the next morning. The rider was still sleeping.

'You're feeling better then?'

'Seems that way. But it's not me you are really concerned about, is it?'

'I've no time for your insolence!'

'Well, 'e was awake earlier on,' Barney said, ignoring her retort, 'and 'e still can't speak. Somehow I don't think 'e ever will. Wouldn't be wise to start him walking yet either.'

'Oh, so now you're telling a Princess what she should or shouldn't do!'

'Just advising, Your 'Ighness,' He grinned, and his forehead wrinkled. She noted that, like Orina, the ordeal of producing such Magical feats was already disfiguring his face.

'Well, I say he's ready and you are going to help me get him to his feet,' she said.

'Don't know if I can walk, myself.' Barney grimaced as he lowered his feet to the floor.

To her horror, Rosamile realised that he was naked. She threw the pile of now clean clothes over to him and turned her back while he struggled into them. He groaned and moaned while doing so, yet Rosamile had no sympathy for his discomfort.

At first the Wizard was barely able to stand but, with perseverence, he managed to hobble across the floor.

Rosamile went out into the corridor and commanded two passing servants to bring food. Quickly they did her bidding. Barney soon cleaned a bowl piled with dried catcher fish and then drank a whole flagon of herb essence waters. She then deemed it time to try and awaken the rider.

Rosamile had not really thought she would succeed but on the third, gentle shake of the rider's broad shoulder his eyes sprang open. She gazed into them, hoping that her admiration would be returned, but to her disappointment it was not. She was being too hasty. First she must restore him to health. He would not even touch the dried catcher fish she had reserved for him and Rosamile was forced to give it to Barney Fowl, who devoured it with greedy relish. She sent to the kitchens for a bowl filled with vegetables, and some nuts. To her relief, her patient ate well and drank a cupful of the herb essence.

'Let's get him to his feet,' she then commanded.

'Hadn't you better let me dress 'im first?' Barney asked, hiding a smirk.

'Yes, of course,' Rosamile snapped, angered that he should even suspect she would ever allow herself to see the rider naked.

Impatiently, she waited outside while Barney performed his task. The rider, dressed clumsily by Barney in doublet and breeches, looked very unsteady on his feet. Before he collapsed back onto the pallet she rushed to his aid and took hold of his left arm. It took the combined efforts of herself and Barney to keep him standing. It was a challenge, but she was more determined than ever before that the stranger would not be spending the rest of his life upon a pallet.

To this effect, she decided that he should take exercise right away. Barney Fowl said it was too soon. Ignoring his protests, she ordered that he assist her in taking the rider outside. As soon as they began to walk him along the corridor, it became apparent that Barney was not up to the task of helping her. A burly male servant was summoned to take his place while the exhausted Wizard tottered back to his pallet. The youth struggled to walk with increased determination, responding to Rosamile's obsessive concern. Whoever he was, he did seem to have the same brave spirit as herself. Yet it wasn't just self interest which seemed to be motivating him. There seemed to be some inner force urging him on. He was definitely getting stronger. It was time to stop. They had made enough progress for one day. The rider was returned to his chamber, where he ate some more vegetables and nuts and then collapsed onto his pallet to sleep soundly.

The following day she hurried to the chamber, and was surprised to find that Barney Fowl was gone but less surprised by the fact that he had left his pallet in a filthy and disgusting state. The rider was lying on his side but his eyes were half open.

'How are you?' she whispered into his ear.

There was no response so she shook him gently. He turned his head and stared up at her with those bewitching blue eyes. There was pleasure in them, even gratitude perhaps, but that was all. Then he smiled. So many people had what she called 'polite' smiles. Nothing could have been more genuine than his. She wondered how the smile would have appeared were he not bearded. However, the thought of pressing her cheek against the coarseness of those honey-blond strands made her tingle with excitement. That time would soon come. After all, who could resist a beautiful Princess who had the power to make the man she loved a King?

'Are you feeling better?'

He nodded.

'Have you eaten?'

Once again he nodded, and Rosamile helped him to his feet. To her amazement, he seemed perfectly capable of standing up without any means of support. Instead of walking up and down the corridor again, she decided to take him to where many of the knights would be engaged in mock battle.

Although his pace was slower than her own, the rider had little difficulty in following her as she led him down the stairs, out of the Citadel, and onto the Main Street where the knights were practising. Many of them stopped what they were doing and watched their approach. Rosamile reprimanded those who had done so and commanded that they should continue. Then, to prove to everyone that her defeat by Sir Jactor had been nothing more than a fluke, she engaged in a mock duel with the brutish Sir Bogadin.

While the rider sat himself against a wall, Bogadin slashed and hacked at Rosamile with a mock glavor which looked almost as lethal as a real one. However, he was soon defeated. She simply waited for the right moment and jabbed her smaller, wooden sword up into his exposed armpit. She heard a bellow of pain from within the metal confines of his helmet and knew that victory was hers. Her confidence now fully returned, she fought another two knights and, with consummate ease, defeated them both.

At this point the rider got to his feet, walked over to her, and pointed at her sword. Did he want to try his hand at mock combat? This was madness! Yesterday he had barely been able to walk and now he was eager to exert himself. Besides, he wasn't wearing any armour. She would forbid him to indulge in such folly.

Before Rosamile could stop her, a girl apprentice who was also using a small sword handed it over to the rider. He took the weapon and, before she could protest, lunged it towards her. Casually she parried it away. Undeterred, he made another attempt. Finding little challenge in this, the Princess parried his second attack with the same ease. It was obvious that the rider was still too weak to put in any real effort and even had he been fully fit, then no doubt his skills would have been vastly inferior to her own. She saw it as nothing more than a means of gentle exercise and there was no harm in that.

To her sudden surprise, the exercising became less gentle. His recovery was truly remarkable, as were the skills he was now displaying. Such was his improved swordsmanship that Rosamile found herself being tested to the full. She could only assume that before his encounter with the Black Unicorn he had been a Militiaman of exceptional ability. At length, she had no alternative but to throw down her sword and lead him to a nearby tavern before it all got out of hand.

Here they both enjoyed a hearty meal of stewed potatoes and blue seaweed. To quench their thirsts and restore some of that lost energy, Rosamile ordered two jugs of orbflower essence. Probably trying to thank her, he attempted to speak. Just as before nothing would come from his lips except agonised croaking sounds. Very few people except the Royal Family and scribes ever learned to write. There was no real way to communicate with him, but she would try – she would certainly try.

The top of the wooden table had been deeply scored by the knives of the tavern's clients. No harm in spoiling it a little more, she decided. Even the illiterate were often capable of writing their own names. She handed him her cherished dagger with the figure of a snarling mountain beast upon its pommel and told him to scratch out his name. He seemed to understand what she said but when he took the knife he merely drew one single line, before staring at her in a state of sad confusion. Rosamile had no alternative but to accept the fact that he didn't even know his own name. All she could do was send messengers out to scour the whole island for any clue as to this stranger's past, even though this method had no real guarantee of success. No, there was only one sure way of finding out. By Royal Decree every Islander would be told to come to the Royal City and see whether they could identify him. Thoughtfully, she watched him drain the remaining drops of orbflower essence before she paid the innkeeper and ushered her companion outside again.

As was expected of them, those not fully engaged in mock combat turned and bowed as soon as they approached. To her surprise, Rosamile realised that not only were they bowing to her but also to the rider. True enough, he was unique in having ridden the Black Unicorn. There was no denying that he had then been resurrected by the blood of bats and the Magic of Jagged Fire. But this

Citadel, this City, this whole land, was *her* responsibility. After the Second Great Attack it had been she, Princess Rosamile, who had been held in awe above all others. It must remain so. Despite her fascination with the stranger she would ensure that both he and the rest of them would be reminded of her position. She gestured for him to take a sword and picked up the one which she had thrown down. As soon as it was in her hand, she launched her first attack. This time she would make no concessions.

He parried her thrust with insulting ease. Angered by this, she launched another attack with as much venom as if it were a real battle. The rider parried her further attempts with the same ease. The situation was now becoming intolerable. Her opponent seemed to be regarding it as simply a game. Well, this was no game and she would now prove it to him!

She would lure him into overcommitting himself. Many knights had been so tricked; Lady Kagona never failed to fall for this particular ploy. It would now be his turn. She began by feinting with several seemingly ill-aimed blows at his head. He would soon be fooled into making a false move. A short, sharp stab into his chest and victory would be hers. She made her move. Then with stinging effect, her sword was knocked from her hand.

For a moment she was unable to do anything but massage her hand until the blood returned to it. First Sir Jactor, now defeat by someone who was not even a knight! It was degrading, but this time she would handle the situation with more composure than before.

'I think it best that we retire,' she said, painfully aware that many spectators had seen this defeat. 'We've done enough for one day.'

The rider seemed to want to continue. He made no attempt to follow her as she walked back to the Citadel.

She stopped in her tracks and shouted back at him, 'I said it is time for you to retire!'

The rider looked both hurt and confused. His expression melted her anger, but she was determined that, like everyone else on Sanctuary, he would obey her.

251

'We're done with fighting. Now follow me,' she comman-ded, while beckoning to him with her hand.

This time he obeyed, following her over the drawbridge and into the Citadel. It was then that she suddenly realised the reason for his disobedience. He had not heard one single word she had said. He might have been brought back to life but at a terrible price. Tears threatened to flow as she dwelt upon the irony of the brave and handsome youth who not only would be denied the chance of speaking his love for her, but would never again hear the joyful and enchanted sounds of the Island. Biting on her lips to control her tears, she now realised that the stranger was both deaf and dumb. He was obviously able to do a little lip reading but nothing else.

A Royal Decree was sent out to tell all Islanders to visit the Royal City within the next forty days. Very soon the first of these subjects would be arriving. Meanwhile, Rosamile continued to try and find out the truth from the stranger himself. Dutifully, the Nameless One, as she had over-heard him being referred to, tried as best he could to respond to her questions. It was hopeless. How could she possibly communicate with someone who could neither speak nor hear? Instead, she took him horseriding or they ran races against each other before resuming their sword-play. He excelled in all these pursuits – surpassing her many times. She no longer objected to this. What right had she to begrudge any small victory to one so afflicted? Besides, her love for him was growing stronger all the time.

The next morning she took him up to the top of the tower where Jagged Fire had brought him back to life. Not only Barney Fowl, but also her parents, warned her of the dangers of causing a bad reaction. They should all have known better than to challenge her judgement. Ignoring their protests, as did the Nameless One, who seemed bemused by the argument, she led him up the spiral stairs to the battlements.

252

Bracing himself against the windswept parapet, the Nameless One gazed out at the surrounding landscape. Just as Rosamile had predicted, there was absolutely no adverse reaction. Why should there have been? Whoever he was, the past seemed to mean nothing to him; not even his encounter with Jagged Fire. Perhaps she, too, would always be denied the chance to share in that past? It didn't matter. What did matter was that the one who had actually ridden the Black Unicorn should always be at her side. Later on she would take him to see the beast which was still residing in the stables. No doubt there would be more protests about causing a bad reaction. Just as before, she would ignore those protests. Perhaps he would ride it again, this time as its master?

One day she would rule this land while he ruled the Black Unicorn. Of course it would be more acceptable for her to marry a knight such as Sir Jactor, but a Princess had the right to wed the man of her choosing, didn't she? There would be arguments when the time came but their destinies had been forged by The Grand Wizard. She would be Queen and the Nameless One would be by her side.

Adoringly, she watched him study the vista of rolling hills before them. Why was he not adoring her? Undeniably she was very beautiful – all would agree the most beautiful on the Island. As far as she was concerned his recovery would not be complete until he acknowledged that fact. When he turned his head she hoped it was to look into her eyes. Instead he looked out to sea. Suddenly, his expression changed. He had seen something.

She turned to see what it was. Upon the Great Main were five brightly coloured sails dipping on the waves. Each one of those sails was large enough to propel a ship the size of a castle. All five were heading straight towards them.

'Oh Grand Wizard save us!' she cried, 'the Disenchanted have returned!'

Chapter Fifteen

Panting convulsively, King Septor almost collapsed after rushing to the top of the tower, his exhaustion being immediately replaced by shock when he saw the five monstrous ships. How could vessels so gargantuan possibly stay afloat? It must be a nightmare, a terrible nightmare. Even though he had just eaten, his stomach felt hollow. He wanted to vomit. That part of him that was King stood resolutely against the battlements, while the other part stood in utter terror. The Disenchanted would soon be attacking.

In a daze, he watched the ships coming closer, the triangular sails growing larger and larger. He did not need to be a skilled sailor to know that nothing could ever sink such monstrous ships. And just as they ruled the seas, they would soon – very soon – be ruling Sanctuary.

'I've sent messengers out to alert the whole Island,'

Rosamile told him, her voice hoarse.

'Good,' he wheezed. 'What do you think they'll do? Come straight to the City like last time or try and invade the Island first?'

'I wish I knew. All I can do is make a guess.' Rosamile had never sounded more despondent. She pondered in silence while Septor grew ever more impatient.

'*Well*?'

'It has been said that long ago, before our history was properly recorded, people from the mainland did try to lay siege to the Royal City.'

'I know that as well as you,' the King grunted. 'It was an easy victory for us.'

'It looks as if they have a big enough force to take the Royal City and the Citadel. I surmise that the battle will be won or lost here, and nowhere else.'

'Then it'll be won!' Septor roared his anger as an antidote to his fears.

Carried to them upon the Singing Winds were the sounds of panic as the news swept through the City.

'What chance do we have with such cowardly fools trying to defend us?' Rosamile stamped her foot angrily.

'I've told you before, not everyone can be as orderly as you,' Septor said sharply. 'Why don't you do something about it instead of complaining?'

The Princess glared back at her father, as always hating being reprimanded by him. Then she saw her mother emerge onto the battlements with tears in her eyes. Many women of her age would now be weeping, not for themselves, but for their sons and daughters who would be dying young. Her father was right. She should not judge others so harshly. She had a role to play and that role demanded she show no compromise.

'It would be better that I go and do my complaining to those who deserve it,' she said and grinned bravely at her father.

'That sounds like my girl.' Katrila patted her daughter's arm. 'You would have made such a fine – '

'A fine Queen?' Rosamile asked. 'Who knows? All is

not yet lost.'

Her parents nodded in agreement, feeding desperately upon her enforced optimism. Then she glanced in the direction of the silent rider. What role would he be playing in the coming battle? Whatever it was, it could not be compared to her own. Someone who was both deaf and dumb would only be able to fight, never lead. Dearly she would have loved to stay by his side, but she knew that it would be impossible. The people needed her guidance. She must go to them.

Her mane of golden hair flowing behind her, Rosamile ran to the stables. Momentarily, she noticed the Black Unicorn glaring malevolently at her. Ignoring the beast, she commanded a stable boy to saddle her own grey-dappled Arildan, Wild Fire. Then she urged her mount over the drawbridge and out into the chaos of the streets.

The panic was even worse than she had anticipated. Like terrified insects, the people were scurrying to and fro without reason or purpose. Even well-trained knights seemed to be part of this disorderly frenzy. Surely someone other than herself had some presence of mind? At this moment such a quality was beyond price. Through the cauldron of madness, Rosamile searched desperately for some kind of sanity. To her relief she did eventually find a group of knights and citizens who were trying to take control of the situation. As ruthlessly as an invader, she drove her horse towards them, careless of anyone in her way.

'All the able-bodied must assemble on the battlements!' she shouted to a broad-faced girl who appeared to be the most capable of the group.

'That's what I've been telling them all, Your Highness,' the girl called back, wiping a sweating brow with her forearm.

'Then keep telling them! Tell them that we've always won in the past. Why not again?'

'But – '

'Hah!' Rosamile tossed back her hair. 'They come to us in gigantic ships. Is that what's worrying everyone?'

256

A helmeted knight nodded.

'Well, surely nobody counted more than five?' she said. 'No matter how big those ships are, they can't carry that many soldiers, can they?'

It was a lie. Rosamile knew that each one of those enormous vessels was large enough to house an army, together with all the necessary elaborate equipment for scaling their walls. She could hardly blame those who looked unconvinced. She must try a different approach.

'Neither must we forget the Black Unicorn and all of the Magic on this Island,' she reminded them.

'Nor the Wizard Without,' a wild-bearded man said scornfully.

'That was insolent,' Rosamile glared back at him, 'and what's more, untrue. It was Barney Fowl who brought the Unicorn's rider back to life.'

Ashamed, the bearded man cast down his eyes and nodded in agreement.

'The Black Unicorn came to us for a reason. Everything is for a reason. Those are The Wizard's Teachings, had you forgotten?'

Was this really a time to talk of Magic? she wondered, as people jostled around Wild Fire's flanks. All she could do was hope that she had made her point.

'Never mind about your belongings,' she snapped at a woman, failing to notice that she was desperately trying to lead a child through the mêlée.

The woman glared up at her fiercely. 'I have a small girl here and I intend to save her from being trampled to death. Once she is in a safe place then I promise Your Highness that I will fight to save her precious life like no other.'

Rosamile smiled down at the woman. 'If you have the courage to talk to a Princess like that, what chance does the enemy have? Take your child away from here with my blessing, for she is our future.'

'May The Wizard's Blessing be with Your Highness!' The woman picked up the child, whose eyes were wide with terror.

257

To Rosamile's relief, more citizens now seemed to be heeding her words, heartened by the sight of her amongst them. A good many of them were assembling on the battlements fully armed, and ready to face the Disenchanted. The panic was giving way to a little order. The cold, terrifying reality of what was about to happen seemed to be calming them down.

Yet what did any of them know of fighting? Save for the knights, very few Sanctuarites had practised their military skills of late. Everyone, including herself, had assumed that after the resounding victory of the Second Great Attack the Disenchanted would be discouraged from ever making another attempt to destroy them. Sheer courage, the powers of Magic, and The Wizard's Blessing would be their only allies. She could only pray that it would be enough.

As she stood on the outer walls of the Royal City, Princess Rosamile was joined by her parents. King Septor was now fully clad in his silver embossed armour, while Katrila, (who had never involved herself in anything military) was dressed in a flowing pale cream gown – a serene antithesis to the bellicose atmosphere surrounding her. Beauty and Grace, was that not what they were all fighting to preserve? The Disenchanted must never be allowed to desecrate the tranquil ambience of the place they all loved so dearly.

Meanwhile, having heard of the monstrous ships, Barney Fowl, still weakened by the traumas of receiving Jagged Fire, had hobbled out into the deserted bailey of the Citadel. Like everyone else he had assumed that the Disenchanted would never be seen again, but his own folly was the least forgivable. Had he not known that the appearance of the Black Unicorn always symbolised the birth of a new dawn in their history? Perhaps in some way they had all strayed from The Wizard's Teachings and this was to be their punishment.

Nonsense! It was a test – the ultimate test of their

strength and resolution, and none would be more tested than he, who once again was the Wizard Without. To make matters worse, at this time of year many of the City Magicians were out visiting those upon the Island. Beside himself, only a few apprentices would be at hand to perform any defensive Magic. Their skills would be limited.

His spirits sank again as he remembered the oft-told tale of the unfaithful wife who, after confessing her infidelity to her husband, wandered out upon an open field during The Wizard's Rage. Silhouetted against its flashing light, she had appeared as tall as a tree. Then Jagged Fire had knifed through the air and killed her outright. From that day onwards men slept with no woman but their own wives and wives with none but their husbands. Truly there were times when the punishments of those who transgressed against The Wizard's Teachings were absolute.

In the Main Street, everyone was hurrying grim-faced to the walls. Perhaps this was the lesson they were all about to learn, that nothing was more important than life itself.

His ability to walk improving slowly, he reached the outer walls of the City, where there was an eerie silence. Only the whistle of the Singing Winds could be heard as the defenders lined the battlements, watching and waiting in fearful contemplation. Mounting the steps, he searched for a gap. A spearwoman moved aside so that he could take her place and see for himself the reason for the awesome silence.

He remembered how, during the last invasion, the tall masts of the invaders' ships had suddenly appeared over the horizon. How small they seemed compared to what he now saw.

So massive, so vast, were these triangular sails in their spectacular colourings of crimson, lurid green, and dazzling yellow, that it seemed as if they were just behind the brow of the hill. Millions must have been involved in their construction and thousand upon thousand must now be pouring out of the hulls. It seemed that this time the enemy intended to gain victory by simply outnumbering them.

'Doesn't matter 'ow many they've got,' Barney said, voicing his thoughts aloud. 'No scaling ladders are ever going to stand up straight against our marblon walls.'

'Course they ain't, roared a burly axeman standing to his right. 'They've come here just to get beaten, that's for sure!'

Nobody else joined in their derision of the enemy. Barney wished that, somehow, he could lift their spirits. Then a voice rose above the sound of the winds, the uneasy shuffling of feet and the nervous clattering of spears. It was a clear sound, as sharp and bright as the blue sky above them. Such a voice could only have belonged to Wulf of the Valleys. The song he sang was the most poignant and best loved of all, 'The Tide Takes My Body, The Hills Have My Heart'.

Another joined in, then another, and another, until the whole line was singing. As soon as the song was finished, they began it again. This time they did not sing with passionate fervour but with one great voice of brave defiance. When the song was finished for the second time, Wulf led them into choruses of all the other favourites. They kept on singing right until the moment that the vast army of the Disenchanted appeared upon the brow of the hill.

It was not an army in the strictest sense. Armies consisted of people, didn't they? Not – Just what were these terrible monsters? There was something about them that looked like tentagoths. Behind them, countless soldiers were following.

'What evil could have created such beasts?' a gruff male voice protested from the throng.

There was no answer to his question. There could be no answer. The main bodies of these creatures were like giant oxen. Yet instead of legs they had four massive tentacles. These thirty or more aberrations had been created. How?

Then the question no longer mattered. On turrets fixed to the monsters' backs, soldiers could now be seen. They began to fire long-stemmed arrows up at them. This was soon followed by the hiss of Sanctuarite arrows being loosed back in return. The battle had begun.

Rosamile noticed that as each monster advanced it was leaving a trail of circles on the ground. Just as tentagoths clamped onto their victims with the sucker pads of their tentacles, so these terrifying absurdities were using the same method to propel themselves along. They had now reached the walls. Below her a slimy green tentacle was squirming up the North Wall. It was only then that, to her horror, she realised what was happening.

'They're going to scale the walls!' she shouted.

'The Wizard save us!' a woman cried.

'The Wizard wants us to save ourselves,' Rosamile snapped, before elbowing her way along the wall until she reached a group manning a cauldron of boiling water.

Steam scalded at her face, forcing her to don her helmet. It offered little protection. The heat was still intolerable; those attending to the cauldrons were showing great fortitude. It gave her heart.

'Is everything ready?' she shouted above the hissing of the steam.

'Yes, Your Highness,' the young female captain answered, sweat pouring from her face. 'Can't wait to see them boil!'

'Not yet.' Rosamile shuddered as she looked down through the eye slit of her helmet and saw the tree-wide tentacles slithering up towards them. 'Wait until they're almost over the top before you pour.'

'That won't be easy.' The captain gasped as she, too, saw the tentacles.

'Just do as I say,' Rosamile ordered.

Rosamile then selected a young boy who seemed both fleet of foot and capable. His task was to ensure that all others manning the cauldrons would know of her command. Then all she could do was hope that this plan would prove to be more than a mere gesture.

The Disenchanted may well be aware of their intentions and no doubt many of these beasts would be regarded as expendable. Enough would still get the chance to clamber over the walls. It would then be the task of those soliders in the turrets to fight their way to the Main Gate and open it. Once this was done, wave upon wave of them would flood into the City. She decided to order a retreat to the Main Gate in the eventuality that the walls could no longer be defended.

To this effect she ordered the heaviest and least mobile knights to begin making their way down to the Main Gate. Remaining upon the walls, she gagged upon the pungent stench of the hideous creatures. It was the malodour of rotting fish but worse, much worse. She looked down and saw between the tentacles the large and bulbous face of an oxen. At least what she thought was an oxen. Some terrible pain seemed to have contorted its features. Its dilated eyes were too wide for the rest of its face – a face that was adorned by a tracery of hideous red veins. The Grand Wizard would never have created anything like these. In some way the Disenchanted had made these abominations themselves. Was there no limit to their blasphemy?

She selected a strong axeman to lift her up onto his broad shoulders. While arrows rained about her she raised her sword high enough for all those manning the cauldrons to see. Then she brought it down with such a dramatic gesture that the blade clanged loudly against the helmet of a spearwoman.

Before ordering that she be put down, the Princess watched as the heavy cauldrons were tipped, deluging their victims with boiling water. The effect upon the beast immediately below her could not have been more absolute. It gave a terrified bellow as it became engulfed in an excoriating cloud of steam. The steam cleared. For one incredible moment she saw the tentacles fan out to form the shape of some enormous and obscene flower as the beast fell away from the wall. The soliders occupying the tower on its back were crushed to death, as were many others when it smashed down onto the ground. Its tentacles writhing helplessly in the air, the wretched beast emitted a screaming sound which was almost human. Such was the effect of the boiling water that its body had been scalded to a livid red.

'Quick!' Rosamile commanded a spearwoman standing at her side. 'Go and find out how successful the others have been.'

While waiting for confirmation she could see for herself that beneath the North Wall, whether it be to her left or to her right, the ground was littered by the dead and dying monsters. Beyond, there was no sign of the invading army she had expected to see, but in the distance there was a massive conical tower. It glistened like a beacon. She suspected that it contained their commander-in-chief. This time, she vowed that he would not be allowed to escape with his life. This time, none would receive any mercy. Every single one of them would be slaughtered.

'Your Highness! Your Highness!'

The voice belonged to a small boy, his face ashen with terror.

'What is it?' She dreaded the answer.

'Those monsters are climbing up over the other walls!' he gasped.

She was speechless, silenced by the terrible import of the boy's words. It had been such a simple ploy. Even though many of the beasts had been sacrificed there were still more than enough to fulfil the invader's plan. It had been such an obvious ruse and she had fallen for it. Thanks to her the whole of Sanctuary was doomed. Foolishly, she had assumed that all the Disenchanted's efforts would be concentrated on the Main Gate. It had proved a fatal decision.

'Oh, what have I done?' She banged an armoured fist upon the parapet, but her dismay was only temporary. She made her way down to where Wild Fire stood waiting. Once astride, she raced the Arildan through the deserted streets until she came to the East Wall. Looking up, she saw a gigantic tentacle rise high above the battlements before slapping down on the inside of the wall. It was soon joined by another, then a third, and finally a fourth. She guessed that behind these monsters, rope ladders were being trailed. Very soon dozens of soldiers would be joining those manning the turrets on the monsters' backs.

Turning her horse, she urged it towards the South Wall. It was then that her stomach churned, her heart missing a beat. Two of the beasts were actually inside and charging towards her were at least thirty spike-armoured Sangorans. Wild Fire reared up as a tentacle stretched out towards its flanks. The horse managed to back away in time but a young girl fleeing across the monster's path was not so fortunate. She was caught by the pads of another tentacle and, with arms and legs kicking, was lifted high into the air. In the next moment her frail body caved in, to become nothing more than a morass of blood and bone. Rosamile could not stop herself from leaning over and vomiting onto the ground as shield bolts hissed past her. When her presence of mind returned, she tugged at the reins and in the next moment Wild Fire was speeding her back towards the Main Gate.

'To the Citadel!' she ordered. 'Everyone retreat to the Citadel!'

A wild panic ensued. Frightened and confused, Wild Fire reared up again. Rosamile was caught unawares and fell. Fortunately she landed on something soft. The axeman who had broken her fall was fighting for lost breath. Picking herself up, she ignored his plight. He would have to fend for himself. She had greater priorities.

Rosamile had become so involved in the battle that she had forgotten about the safety of her parents. Perhaps they had already had the good sense to retreat to the Citadel? It was certainly likely, but she had to be sure. She wasted no time in searching for her sword or the helmet which had detached itself during her fall.

Like her own horse, everyone was completely out of control. The Citadel could only house so many and they all knew it. Such a mob would be easy fodder for the Disenchanted. It was a case of everyone looking after themselves. Her own concern now was for her mother and

264

father, nobody else.

Rosamile searched for them as best she could amidst the fear-maddened crowd. She saw a woman, whose arm had been severed at the elbow, lose her balance and fall before being trampled to death. Tentacles were then seen flailing above the house tops. An axeman suddenly went mad and began to hack wildly at his own kind. He managed to kill at least two people, before Rosamile, having lost her sword, managed to slay him with her dagger, stabbing him beneath his left arm. There was no time for remorse. She had been forced to do it. She must now join the human tide flooding towards the Citadel.

Before she could do so she found herself confronted by a massive, bovine face. It was surrounded by two muscular tentacles swirling towards her. From the turret above its head arrows were flying towards her. She raced to the false safety of the crowd as the deadly shafts thumped into the ground. Any hope of finding her parents was gone. All she could do was to try and survive, for everyone's sake.

Glancing back, she saw to her relief that the tentacled monster had been speared while attacking those behind her. The drawbridge was now in sight. Another monster appeared. As tentacles weaved above them more people trampled over each other. In that frenzied moment she decided to run straight towards the advancing beast. Anything was better than being crushed to death. She had lost her sword; her dagger would be of little use. Lying on the ground was a spear. She dived at it and grabbed the handle. As a tentacle descended she jabbed at it with the bloodstained point. While the green arm twitched and recoiled, she rejoined the mob fleeing towards the drawbridge of the Citadel.

'It's the Princess,' someone shouted. 'Make way for her!'

They were sacrificing their own lives for her. She wanted to thank them for this act of courage but there was no time. The cry of 'Make way for the Princess!' rang in her ears. Even women carrying infants cleared a path for her as she ran towards the Citadel. A young boy threw himself into the moat so that she could take her place on the crowded drawbridge. Thankfully, he could swim.

There was the sound of clanking chains before she found herself sliding downwards. The bridge was being raised. Bodies were crushing down upon her as she became embroiled in a dark nightmare of screaming, thrashing people. All breath was being squeezed from her body. Death had found her at last.

'Your Highness? Are you alive?'

Through pain-filled mists she heard a familiar voice. Strong hands were tugging at her arms, pulling her free from the others. The mists cleared, the pain ebbed, as she found herself gazing up into the broad-nosed face of Sir Pendor.

'They let me through,' she sobbed. 'They laid down their lives for me!'

'They had to.' Sir Pendor was looking at her with frank devotion. 'While the Royal Family lives then so does Sanctuary.'

'They're alive? The King and Queen are alive?'

'We made sure of that.' There was pride in his voice. 'Whatever else we knights have failed to do, we did manage to save our sovereign Lord and Lady.'

'The Wizard be praised!' the news had caused her complete recovery and brought her to her feet.

At the outset of the battle the braziers had been allowed to expire. The shadows created by the five towers were casting the bailey into semi-darkness. Hurriedly she made her way to the Main Keep as somehow the packed crowd managed to clear a path for her. As soon as Rosamile entered the Main Hall she stopped in her tracks. Although many had taken shelter inside, a large space was left clear. Occupying that space was the Black Unicorn. Despite the monsters she had just encountered, this beast still terrified her. Doing her best to ignore the glare of its cruel, red eyes, she continued searching for any sign of her parents.

Emerging from the group huddled against the wall was her mother. They embraced.

'Oh, Rosamile, we thought you were dead, but now

you're here in my arms!' Katrila cried joyously.

The Princess burst into tears. She cried with relief, sorrow and guilt, for she had been spared the terrible death that those outside the Citadel would now be suffering. Then her father was approaching. His expression told her that he knew and understood how she felt.

'Come up to the Royal Chamber,' he said softly. 'It's time for a family gathering.'

Their subjects stood aside so that their sovereign King and his family could mount the stairs. Once inside the chamber the three of them went to the window.

Beyond the City walls could be seen a terrible slaughter. Carried by the Singing Winds was the din of clashing weapons mingled with the heart-wrenching sounds of the Island's men, women and children as they were killed. Rosamile covered her ears as the screams became louder. She could no longer look upon that bloody slaughter. Turning away, she hunched her shoulders as if taking the blows herself.

'I can see you're blaming yourself for all of this.' Septor took her in his arms.

'What else can I do? It never occurred to me they would attack the City from all sides. Yet it should have done – it should have done!'

'And what if you had realised?' Septor was now holding her as tightly as their armour would allow. 'Do you honestly think you could have done anything about it?' There was a deep sadness in his voice. 'It was sheer arrogance to believe they'd never return.'

'None of us thought it possible.' Katrila was now standing near the door as far away from the window as possible. 'We're all to blame and now we're all paying the price.'

Rosamile no longer held onto her father. With an effort, she managed to take control of her senses. Although tears were still in her eyes she managed to stand proudly and lift up her chin; a habit she had when declaring her views.

'The Grand Wizard must save our Island.'

'The Grand Wizard need do no such thing.' The King

looked utterly dejected. 'He put us all here in the first place. There's no reason why He can't take us away. He made the Disenchanted as well, didn't He?' Rosamile refused to answer. 'Who knows?' he continued. 'After we're all gone they might learn the true ways of Magic. In time they might even become the new Enchanted. Had you thought that that might be His purpose?'

'That's absurd – '

Before Rosamile could finish her sentence there was a loud knock on the door.

'Come in!' Septor boomed impatiently.

Sir Garador clanked in, his blond beard now stained by the blood pouring from a wounded cheek. 'Your Highnesses, we await your commands. I fear there's little hope for those in the bailey but – '

At the sound of terrible screaming Rosamile rushed to the window and gasped. Swimming across the moat were at least a dozen monsters. Now they really did look like tentagoths, as their tentacles splayed out in the water. Being dragged behind them were large rafts. Each raft was carrying at least a hundred soldiers. Her view from this window was limited, but she had no doubt that similar numbers were advancing on other walls. While the King and Queen gasped with horror, she turned to Sir Garador.

'All we can do is defend the Keep until the rest of the Island comes to our rescue.'

'I doubt if we can get everybody in the Keep,' the King said grimly.

There could be no argument with that statement. Neither could there be any argument against the statement Rosamile was now forced to make.

'We've no choice but to sacrifice the old and infirm,' she said solemnly. 'It is the young and fit who can save Sanctuary and not they.'

Sir Garador nodded but said nothing. He would not relish imparting such a cruel message. Rosamile hoped that their subjects would not hold this command against her. War had turned her into a tyrant.

Even despite such a harsh yet necessary decision, there

was little hope. By the time the rest of the Islanders had formed an army it would be too late anyway. It wouldn't be long before those here in the Keep came under attack. With their superior forces, the Disenchanted would gain a quick victory. She turned away from the window and studied, perhaps for the last time, the tapestry on the wall. How well it depicted the world she had known and loved for the joyful twenty-five years of her life. Then, head high, she returned her gaze to the window and prepared herself for what was surely to follow.

Chapter Sixteen

Below, those who were fit would be making their way to the Keep while those who had the courage to admit that they were too old or infirm to give of their best would be taking their places in the bailey with the wounded, preparing themselves to face certain death. The Grand Wizard would bless them for their sacrifice.

Rosamile would be spared the ordeal of witnessing that sacrifice. Her duty was to organise those in the Keep. Not that there was really any point. She was convinced that their own time for dying would soon follow. Unless . . . Wasn't attack the best form of defence? Cheeks flushed, she told her parents of her plan. Septor made a mild protest but Katrila soon saw the sense in it and persuaded him to agree, even though she realised that it could well mean the final parting from their daughter. Death would be coming to them all. The prospect now held less fear for her than she had expected.

If you reach the Wizardom before us, tell Ruthor that I will see him again.' Katrila's voice shook slightly.

'I too,' Septor put in. 'That is, if he's forgiven me.'

'Of course he has!' Rosamile touched her father's arm. 'Should we not just be grateful we aren't the Disenchanted with no Wizardom to go to?'

'Let no one accuse me of ingratitude to Him!' Septor smiled a smile that reminded her so much of those halcyon days when, as a little girl, she had sat on her father's knee. 'Life doesn't just end here, it begins all over again. Besides, if your plan does work and we do win, then, who knows? We might be spending a little more time together in this world.'

'No, Father. We'll be spending a lot of time together.' Rosamile hugged the King as best she could in her armour.

It should have felt like a goodbye but it didn't. This was no time for grief. It was a time for proving themselves. Like any mortal, Rosamile was fearing the process of dying. But not death itself for The Wizard was giving her courage. Unencumbered by steel, her mother was easier to embrace. Even through her own armour, the Princess could feel not only the loving warmth of her mother but also her deep courage. What was there to fear? Soon they would be reunited in a world of eternal Magic.

Then there was no time for anything but valour. She would ensure that everyone in the Keep played their part to the full. Outside, people were gathering. Children were asking why so many had gone there. The attempts by the adults to conceal what was really happening were pathetically sad. Trying not to hate herself for the cruel decision she had been forced to make, Rosamile made her way to the top of the stairs that overlooked the Main Hall. For a moment she wondered whether the Nameless One was down there amongst the multitude. She could not see him and there was no time to search.

'Listen to me!' she called.

They fell silent; even the children stopped their crying.

271

Then that silence was broken by the snorting of the Black Unicorn. Rosamile had almost forgotten about its being there. She would ignore it; the beast could do all the snorting it wished. Besides, was it not their ally? It hadn't harmed anyone except the rider. Perhaps it might even decide to attack the invaders. She could but hope.

'We have a choice,' she continued. 'Either we stay here in the Keep and try and defend ourselves as best we can or we give these Disenchanted a taste of their own poison.'

'Whatever you say, Your Highness!' a woman called, while others roared in agreement.

Glad of their support, the Princess continued. 'I say we let the Disenchanted think we're going to do nothing about protecting the bailey. Let them approach – then we charge out when they least expect it.'

Her suggestion was greeted by silence until someone shouted, 'What other choice is there? I say we make the charge!'

'Better to die fighting than be starved to death!' a spearwoman cried.

'And that would be our option,' Rosamile told them, her voice firm. 'The rest of the Island will be powerless to help us unless we play our part.'

'Then play our part we shall!' A female knight raised her glavor high into the air.

Another knight followed her example, then an axeman raised his weapon high above him, shaking it to left and right. Soon, wherever she looked, spears, axes, glavors, swords, and bows, were being held high, creating a clattering, angry forest of weapons. Rosamile felt a lump in her throat. Their valour could be surpassed by none but herself.

'If I am to die soon then I could not end my life in better company!' she cried when the clattering finally died down. 'I can but give you all the deepest blessing of not only myself, but of your King and your Queen. As for The Wizard's Blessing, I know from deep within my heart it will be upon you all.'

'Praise be to Princess Rosami – '

There was an interruption from outside. A messenger stood there, his face scarlet, his eyes bulging. The Disenchanted were within the bailey. In silence they listened to the pitiful, heartwrenching cries of the slaughtered. Rosamile's stomach churned as the sounds of her own people being murdered grew louder.

'Spearfighters will be first,' she commanded, her voice like steel. 'Remember, the five towers will have cast the bailey in shadow. Be careful not to kill a comrade, and that goes for you arrowshooters as well. Let the knights start their killing before axewielders finish off the job. As for the monsters they have brought – when have we been afraid of oxen even if they do have tentacles?'

Without delay, spearfighters and arrowshooters jostled their way to the front. Rosamile raised the sword a youth had passed to her before sweeping it down. The two great doors were swung open. Those at the front, flanked by arrowshooters, lowered their spears and charged out into the turbulent darkness. Then it was the turn of the second wave, the third, and the fourth. Not one of them hesitated. Then came the knights. Although slower moving of necessity, they too charged out just as fearlessly. Now all that was left were the axewielders. Rosamile would lead them herself. Donning a helmet, she took her place at the door. Before her was a black cauldron of death. Like her subjects, she did not falter. Waving her sword aloft, she charged forth.

A spiked helmet glistened in what little light there was. Smartly, she sidestepped as the Sangoran lunged at her. With perfect accuracy she drove her blade into the only part of him that was exposed – his neck. A stream of glutinous blood jetted over her before she turned her attention to dealing with another. This Sangoran had his back to her. Despite the dark frenzy of the battle, she thought carefully about her next move. Even spiked armour had its weak spots. As the Sangoran stretched forward, a gap would appear at his waistline. It was almost too dark to see but she made no mistake. She rammed her sword forward. Having severed his spine, the blade lodged in his stomach. Jamming her foot against his twitching body, she managed to pull it free. Blindly, she hacked and slashed at the advancing Moberane giants. To kill them would be impossible. She was satisfied with crippling two of them before avoiding a tentacle as she killed a deadly-tongued Clavitar. Then there were others to deal with – Goblins, strange, horse-faced soldiers, more Sangorans, and the spiked maces of the Moberane. She fought, she killed, and she survived. Then the shadows were gone, the Orb was shining down on her. Joyfully, she chopped off the hand of a murderous Goblin as the place became filled with benevolent light.

Suddenly Rosamile was standing alone with no one to fight. Too late, she saw the massive tentacle descending towards her. Remembering the fate of the young girl at the South Wall, she prepared to face her death.

The tentacle lashed up into the air again. The beast gave a deafening bellow. It was now light enough to see that something had turned its face into a bloody pulp. A golden shaft of Orb-light blazed down upon the Black Unicorn, its horn dripping with blood. Astride its back was the Nameless One. Seemingly in full control of his mount, he turned the unicorn towards another of the tentacled monsters. Rosamile had no chance to see anything else. She was being attacked. Usually their kneecaps were protected, but this giant's knees were exposed. One well directed slash was sufficient. His cries of agony were drowned by the sound of another dying beast. She left him clutching his bloodied legs, confident that someone else would finish him off. Now there really did not seem to be anyone else to fight.

All around her were the dead and dying. It was impossible to ignore such carnage but she forced herself to assess the situation. It was not difficult. Admidst the mountainous remains of the tentacled beasts and blood-stained bodies, only her own subjects remained standing.

Nearby, two women had taken hold of a Goblin and were hurling him high into the air. With skilled timing, a spearman placed his weapon directly beneath the falling body. As they watched their impaled victim's death throes they shouted with relief. No mercy was being shown to any of the Disenchanted, their slaughter would be total. Rosamile would do nothing to discourage this except –

'Don't kill him!'

The spearwoman turned and looked at her in astonishment, as did a wounded Sangoran who, having been knocked to the ground, was about to have the point of a spear driven into him.

There was an ill-concealed look of relief as he gazed up at the Princess with his almond-shaped eyes, his voice quavering, 'I must thank you.'

'Don't thank me too soon,' she said coldly. 'Your life is only worth something if you can tell me a few things about your master's plans.'

'And then you will attend to my wounds?'

Although the left part of his body was still covered by his shield, there was a deep gash on the right side of his chest. Blood was pouring from the wound. There would be little time to find out what he knew before he bled to death.

'Of course,' she lied.

Before she began her interrogation she told a young girl who, despite a bad cut on her neck, seemed fit enough, to fetch the King and Queen, together with any Magicians who could be found.

'Now tell me of your plans,' she said, returning her attention to the Sangoran, 'and I'll hear no lies. Our Magicians have a way of knowing whether you're telling the truth or not.'

'Does that mean I can lie as much as I like until they get here?' The Sangoran managed a sneer, despite the pain of his wound.

Rosamile kicked him hard in the thigh. He gasped with pain while she threatened not to deny the spearwoman the satisfaction of killing him.

'Point made.' His almond eyes slithered treacherously as he spoke. 'Besides, what have I to hide?' The High Lord Giraldo intends to kill you all. It's that simple.'

'I'm sure our victory here must have had some effect on

your glorious plans. Deny that if you can.'

'We can still lay this place to siege . . .' Momentarily they were interrupted by the screams of a woman staggering past, a Sangoran shield bolt jutting through her hand. 'After all,' he continued, 'we've got the city and dealing with the rest of the Island'll be no trouble, will it?'

Rosamile ignored his question. 'So what happened to your precious High Lord Talango then?'

'He's gone. Now we've got four High Lords instead of one. Not many rebels these days either. That's why we can afford to give you lot our full attention.'

'How flattering,' Rosamile said sarcastically. 'Now forget your bragging and tell me about those abominations.' She pointed to one of the monsters that lay dead nearby, its stench filling the air.

'The tentaoxen, that's what they're ca – ' The Sangoran halted, forced to cough up some blood. Rosamile was powerless to do anything but hope that he wouldn't die on her. To her relief, he was able to continue. 'Nym the Goblin made them. Somehow he managed to graft the tentacles of tentagoths onto giant oxen. Clever, eh?'

'Disgusting!' Rosamile was revolted by such deliberate evil.

'Well, they don't live for long, that I'll grant you. Even so, they did a good job in getting us into your City. Don't you agree?'

'They didn't do so well when they came up against the Black Unicorn,' Rosamile said.

'The Black Unicorn?' The Sangoran looked stunned. 'There's no such thing and that's official. The High Lord Talango used it as an emblem, nothing more.'

'Well, that emblem has just killed all your tentaoxen and probably a good many of your comrades.'

'That cannot be!' The Sangoran coughed up more blood before continuing. 'It was a tactical retreat, that's what it was.'

'There was no retreat. My daughter would not lie. Not even to scum like you!'

The words were spoken by King Septor. Beside him was Queen Katrila.

'That thing on your head must mean you were the ruler,' the Sangoran croaked, his voice growing weaker.

'I *am* the ruler!' Septor roared, stabbing the air with his finger.

'Well, now I can talk to someone in authority instead of some bitch of a female who doesn't know her place. I've got something very important to tell you.'

'The female happens to be my daughter!' Septor roared again. 'Just say what you have to say before it's too late.'

'I know I'm on my way out.' The Sangoran's face had now turned ashen. 'Even so, I might as well do someone some good before I go to the Nothing.'

'We all repent before death,' Katrila told him. 'Tell my husband your secret and who knows? The Grand Wizard might even take you into His Wizardom.'

The Sangoran retched some more blood. Rosamile told her father to hurry. The King knelt down and put his ear close to the Sangoran's mouth. Too late, Rosamile realised what was about to happen. Why had she assumed that all the bolts from the Sangoran's shield had been fired? She would be asking herself that question for the rest of her life.

The force of the deadly bolt took it straight through Septor's chest and out through his back. Rosamile and Katrila rushed to his aid. The King's blank, staring eyes and the limpness of his body were evidence enough. He was dead.

Katrila took the corpse in her arms and cried out his name over and over again. Wretched with her own grief, Rosamile turned to see that the Sangoran was laughing maliciously, blood bubbling from his mouth.

Angrier than she had ever been in her life, she wrenched the spear from the woman who by rights should have been the victim of that shield bolt. The Sangoran continued his malicious laughter until the spearhead was rammed through his teeth. Rosamile twisted it down his throat, gouging away until she was sure he was as dead as her father. Then she threw herself to the ground and wept strenuously. There was nothing else in her power to do.

'Can't you bring him back to life again?' Katrila pleaded to Barney Fowl when he arrived on the scene.

He did not answer. Instead, his mouth agape in horror, he stared down at the corpse of their King.

'Dead? he said, his whole body trembling. 'The King is dead!'

'Yes, but you can bring him back again,' Katrila said, still clutching her husband's armoured body. 'You've done it once – you can do it again!'

'Your 'Ighness, that was a calling from The Grand Wizard 'Imself. 'Is own Magic was flowing through me then. It was 'cause that rider's got a Destiny to fulfil.'

'And so has your King!' Katrila sobbed.

''E meant as much to me as anyone,' Barney insisted, as tears coursed down his cheeks. 'But there's nothing – '

'Just *do* something!' Rosamile screamed at him. 'Or are you – ?'

'The Wizard Without? Is that what Your 'Ighness was going to say? Well, it's true. All my Magic's gone.'

'Get away from here, you useless lump of filth!' Rosamile screamed at him again. 'Get away from here!'

Smarting from the Princess's outburst, Barney Fowl left them to their grieving. His own sorrow was just as great. There had only ever been two people in the whole of Sanctuary who had believed in him. One had been Orina, the other had been King Septor. Now both of them were gone. As far as he was concerned, the Disenchanted had already won. What did he have to live for? What did any of them have to live for now that their beloved King was dead?

Chapter Seventeen

It was a night for grieving and waiting, for the Disenchanted preferred to do their fighting by daylight. Some of the survivors had busied themselves by erecting a wooden plinth on which would be placed the King's corpse. Rosamile and Katrila stood silently watching their efforts while others cleared away the bodies as best they could. Barney Fowl went from corpse to corpse pronouncing The Wizard's Blessing upon all their own fallen.

The braziers around the walls of the bailey had now been lit. The darkness was eased by the fires. Soon, for a short time, it would be completely driven away when, as was traditional with a Royal personage, the bier would be set alight. The soul of their beloved King would then rise upon the flames, up towards the Magic Wizardom. When the work on the plinth was finally done it was the duty of the Royal Wizard to inform the Queen and the Princess.

The King's body had been so prepared that all traces of a sudden death had been removed. Now he appeared to be in a deep and peaceful sleep. The surviving knights, each bearing a candle, took their positions behind Queen Katrila and Princess Rosamile. Then, taking his place at the head of his dead King, Barney Fowl raised his arms up towards the Silver Orb.

'Beloved Creator of this land,' he began, 'I beg that you witness this, the sacred pyre of our most beloved King. Grant us the sight of 'is earthly body glowing and let us feel for the last time 'is warmth before 'is soul is taken to Your exalted Wizardom.'

Then began the Chant of Remembrance. Neither Katrila nor her daughter could join in. Following the chant was the Time of Silence. Still weeping, Rosamile reflected upon the kindest and noblest father who had ever lived. There had been times in her life when she had cursed him for standing in her way. How quickly those memories faded! Only his warmth and love now dominated her thoughts. That love would stay with her for as long as she lived, she knew.

When the bier had been soaked in oil, her mother too grief-stricken to perform the task, Rosamile took the burning torch and, with a trembling hand, threw it onto the bier. Flames exploded into the night sky as the fire roared into life. She was forced to retreat quickly. While she smelt his earthly flesh burn she remembered a warm Leaftime day when, as a little girl, her father had taken her out into the Island to pick some white pears to make his favourite Double Strength White Pear Wine. In later years she had criticised him for his indulgent drinking, reminding him that in her opinion members of the Royal Family should be sober at all times. She now hoped that in the Magic Wizardom he would be allowed to drink as much Double Strength White Pear Wine as he wanted.

Suddenly and inexplicably, the fire changed. There was a loud gasp as the flames turned to a brilliant blue – soaring up into the sky until they became as tall as trees. A knight emerged and, without faltering, stepped onto what remained of the pyre and stood in the centre of the flames.

Rosamile's reaction changed from wonder to rage. Who had dared to walk upon her father's ashes? Whoever this impious man was, he would be cast out from the Citadel to face certain death at the hands of the Disenchanted! To her astonishment, the knight stayed in the flames' centre. Whoever he was, he was wearing the official armour of the Nameless Knight – the suit which had always been regarded as too heavy and cumbersome for real combat. Her mouth dropped open. Could this armour be suitable for just one person – the Nameless One? It had to be him.

'He's blind and he's walked into the flames!' she cried.

'No, Your 'Ighness!' Before she could rush to the Nameless One's aid, Barney Fowl dragged her back. 'It's all part of 'is Destiny. Besides, 'ere comes the Black Unicorn.'

It was only then that Rosamile realised there was no heat coming from the pyre. Awe-struck, she watched the Black Unicorn take its place beside its master. Now both were oblivious of the flames. Humbled by the sight, she joined her people in falling to their knees and chanting, 'The Wizard is All, The Wizard is All!'

Amidst the weird, spectral flame of the Colidor-tree-tall flames, the Black Unicorn lowered itself to a kneeling position. Without the aid of any pulleys or servants, the Nameless Knight, despite the massive weight of his armour, mounted the beast. The unicorn then raised itself upon its cloven hooves with a graceful ease that none had ever seen before, and carried its rider out of the fire.

Silhouetted by the spearing blue flames, the Nameless Knight and the Black Unicorn created a terrifying vision. Rosamile knew that it would be one that would strike terror into the hearts of every enemy of Sanctuary. Not only was he wearing the strongest armour ever made, but he was also carrying the black steel glavor which, unlike the wooden facsimile, none before had ever been able to wield effectively. He was to be their salvation. No wonder she had fallen so hopelessly in love with him.

Rosamile's hope of saving the Island returned in force. By now the legend of the Black Unicorn would have swept through the ranks of the Disenchanted. Had it not been the symbol of their High Lord Talango? Perhaps they would assume that the beast was actually the reincarnation of that legendary creature? Perhaps it was. And now riding upon its back was an invincible knight. What better ally and champion could they have?

'Your 'Ighness – ' Barney interrupted her thoughts. 'I think I know what the blue fire means.'

'It is The Grand Wizard giving the Nameless Knight and the Black Unicorn His Blessing.' Rosamile said irritably. 'I don't need a Wizard Without to tell me that!'

'There's more, I reckon,' Barney sounded smug. 'It was The Wizard's Magic all right, but the Nameless Knight was receiving more than 'Is Blessing. I reckon that fire was sealing 'im in that armour for good.'

'Impossible!' Rosamile was angered at such foolishness. How could anyone live permanently sealed in a cumbersome suit of armour?

'Isn't it true that there are little 'oles for breathing but also openings for eating and – '

'There's no need for details,' Rosamile snapped. 'You know as well as I do those features merely save the wearer the inconvenience of getting in and out of such heavy armour during a tournament.'

'Have it your own way,' Barney said. 'But I know I'm right.'

'It's true.' Katrila was no longer weeping. Her face was alight. 'I saw many things in the fire. Now come with me and I'll show you a miracle.'

Baffled by this statement, Rosamile followed her mother to the Royal Chamber. Quite naturally, she had expected it to be empty. It was not. She could sense a presence even before the two pale shapes formed in the air.

'*Father*! *Ruthor*!' The shapes were now recognisable. Her veins turned to ice. It was unsettling to see in their spirit form two people whom she had once touched and loved. Part of her was gladdened by the sight – the other part of her was afraid.

'Aren't you going to ask us why we're here?' The ghostly voice echoed around the walls of the chamber.

'Of course she is.' Katrila seemed unafraid. 'Go on,

child, learn of your Destiny. I already know mine.'

'The Island must fall,' her father said gravely, speaking in a strange and distant voice that was not his own.

'Fall? But I don't understand.' Rosamile was devastated.

'Sanctuary has hidden from the rest of the world for too long,' Septor went on. 'I never realised it when I was alive but I do now. What right have we to live in such bliss when the rest of our brethren lives under such tyranny? The old ways must go. That's why the old Magic has gone.'

'*Gone*, Father? But how can it – ?' Rosamile almost began to argue with her father as if he were still alive.

'What did any of us ever care about those abroad who were conjured at exactly the same time as ourselves?' Although the King's voice sounded different there was still that unmistakable gusto.'

'Nothing, I suppose,' she admitted reluctantly.

'Nothing is right.' Despite the change of voice her father was sounding like his old self. 'Things couldn't go on as they were. There must be change.'

'So the Nameless Knight and the Black Unicorn are not here to help us after all?' She could not keep the disappointment from her voice.

'Of course they are! It's The Grand Wizard's Gift before the Magic of the Island is finally done.'

'I don't understand . . .'

'Tell her, Ruthor.'

The formless, pale shape which resembled her dead brother became even clearer as he spoke. 'The Disenchanted must be blessed with the Magic of Life. Mortals you may be, but you have the power within you to change everything. Let the Nameless Knight be your champion, let your love for The Grand Wizard be your strength.'

'So what are we to do?'

'Magic is fading . . . fading.' Ruthor's voice and image were growing fainter. 'You must find it again. The world cannot turn away . . . . Magic is for all . . . It . . . is . . . for . . . all . . . ' Then Ruthor was gone.

'Goodbye, my beloved Rosamile.' Her father gave his old warm smile before he, too, faded.

'Don't go! Don't go!' she begged at the wall before turning to her mother with tears in her eyes. Then, as realisation struck, she gasped, 'Mother, they didn't say anything to you!'

Katrila looked calm and serene, as if she knew some marvellous secret. 'They didn't have to. Very soon I'll be joining them.'

Rosamile went white. 'What do you mean?'

'Oh, Rosamile!' Katrila's eyes were glowing with some deep, inner knowledge. 'Can't you understand?'

Rosamile shook her head.

'Instead of becoming the salvation of one small Island you will become the salvation of the whole world.'

'But Magic has gone from this Island. That was what Ruthor was saying, wasn't it?'

Katrila smiled knowingly. 'Magic isn't just on Sanctuary, it's on the mainland too.'

'Do you mean that I must go to the mainland? But how?'

'Those fit enough must make a dash for it when the time comes.' Katrila hesitated, seemingly getting the plan clear in her mind. 'When the rest of the Island launches an attack, they will have no hope of defeating the Disenchanted, not even with our new champion.'

'We're bound to be outnumbered,' Rosamile admitted, 'but whatever happens we'll put up a good fight. We have no cowards on Sanctuary!'

'No.' Katrila took Rosamile's hands in her own. 'Putting up a fight isn't going to do anyone any good.'

'What then?'

'While the enemy is occupied with defeating the Islanders, those from the Citadel must make their way to the ships.'

'And occupy one and sail away? That's impossible!'

'It's not.' Katrila's eyes were full of determination.

'And you'll be coming with us?' Rosamile was dreading the answer.

'No, Barney Fowl can administer a herb to the children and myself. Better we die by our own hands.' There was no hint of fear in the Queen's voice.

284

'I want to stay with you!'

'You, the born leader?' How could that be? I doubt if many will survive the charge to the ships, but you have a better chance than most. You have a way of surviving in battle that has always filled me with wonderment.'

'What use is that when I have no mother or father?' Rosamile said bitterly.

'The Grand Wizard made the world and you've got the chance to save it. We'll all be willing you on from the Magic Wizardom. That is why we are going there.'

Rosamile was powerless to argue. This was a mother she had never seen before. One who was radiant-faced with determination. Through Ruthor and her father, The Grand Wizard had spoken. She had often boasted of the great Destiny that lay before her. Now she would have gladly traded that Destiny for the old way of life. Even if they escaped, what happiness could ever be found upon alien soil with only the memories of her family to sustain her?

'You know it is His wish.' There was The Wizard's Wisdom in Katrila's eyes.

Rosamile could hardly bring herself to say the words. 'When – when do you intend to take the herbs?'

'Go and fetch Barney Fowl now.' Katrila's voice sounded resolute.

'Am I to trust a Wizard Without to send my mother to her eternal sleep?' There were now tears in Rosamile's eyes. Her time for crying was far from done.

'If I am willing to place myself in his care, you must accept it. Now hurry!'

'But there'll be no time to prepare a funeral pyre!'

'There will be no time to bury the children either,' Katrila said. 'But what does it matter about our bodies? Only our spirits are important, and they will soon be in the Magic Wizardom.'

Rosamile found Barney Fowl in his chamber. When she told him what had happened he did not seem surprised. Amidst the chaos, he managed to find the necessary herbs and make the tincture. The Princess was grateful for the short delay. It gave her time to collect her thoughts: to come to terms as best she could with what was about to happen. At last her tears dried, to be replaced by a deep and overwhelming sorrow. Barney offered to administer the poison but she declined. It was something which she had to do herself.

Her sorrow became deeper still when her mother took the goblet and in one brave and unfaltering movement, drained the glass of its fatal contents. Then Katrila laid herself down upon the Royal Bed. She looked up at Rosamile and smiled. It was as if the Golden Orb was shining from her eyes. They were not only filled with peace but with Magic, too.

'I'll be with you very soon!' Rosamile vowed.

'No, you still have much work to do, but we'll be waiting for you . . .' Katrila's eyes closed. They would never open again.

Trembling, Rosamile kissed her mother's forehead as she fought back her tears. There was nothing else to be done but to leave the chamber and return to the Main Hall. So much loss had numbed her emotions; there was comfort in having tasks to complete.

First would be the dreadful task of putting the children to eternal sleep. Many parents would wish to die with their children, and such requests would be impossible to deny. There would still be a good hundred or so to fulfil The Wizard's Wish. The second task would be to lead a charge towards Blue Bay. She owed it to the family which was no longer by her side to set her mind upon taking one of the enemy ships.

The High Lord Giraldo emerged from the Silver Cone clad in his emerald-sheened armour. On his head was a full-faced helmet rising to a high point, and across his back was a silver cloak which flowed down from his spiked shoulders to the back of his knees. It was a pity that the two serviles he was using as steps were, like the rest of his army, denied the pleasure of seeing him so spectacularly garbed as he mounted Nym's latest creation, the spider horse.

Once astride, he flicked the reins and the six legs of the creature carried him up swiftly to the top of the nearby hillock. His whole army was now abasing itself. Surrounding him was a vast sea of backs. Never before had a force of such size, strength and variety been assembled. In addition to his own Sangoran troops, the Clavitars from Sudelia with their lashing tongues, the Moberane giants and the devious Goblins, there were the horse-faced Beletars of Nordag who used special scythes for their fighting. Despite the recent mishaps he had every confidence in them all.

Very soon they would be facing the rest of the Islanders, and the defeat of those misguided imbeciles would be little more than a mere formality. As for the Sanctuarites defending their Citadel? There was no real reason why they could not be allowed to stay where they were until they rotted away. What point was there in hurrying matters? The voyage to Sanctuary had been so smooth that he was now considering returning to the Supreme Fortress and waiting there in comfort for the final downfall. There was just one disturbing aspect to the present situation, but on that matter he would soon be putting all minds to rest.

'Underlings of my will,' he called through the mouth-piece of one of the Goblin inventor's devices, a twisting arrangement of trumpets supported by large stanchions which enabled all of them to hear his voice. 'Many of you will have witnessed the slow torture and excruciating deaths of those who failed to take the Citadel. Before they began their screaming there was mention of a Black Unic – '

The pipe which linked him to the trumpets suddenly fell away at the connecting end. It took an interminable time for the two serviles in charge of the instrument to replace it. If he had time he would have them put to death as well as whipping Nym for his carelessness.

'This so-called unicorn,' he continued when the pipe had been reconnected, 'was nothing more than a black horse to which a false horn had been attached. It was not – I repeat –*not* the High Lord Talango returning from the Nothing in the form of his own emblem! Be only afraid of my wrath and win this battle!'

Having delivered his speech, the High Lord Giraldo rode down from the hillock and returned to his Silver Cone. There he listened with pleasure to the sounds of his mighty army preparing itself for war.

Chapter Eighteen

From the fourth tower Rosamile watched the two armies clash, allowing the battle to get fully under way before blowing her horn as loudly as she could. Immediately the drawbridge was lowered. She watched the first group charge forth before racing down the stairs to join them.

When the Princess reached the bailey a female axewielder handed her the reins of a white Arildan. Despite her armour she managed to swing herself up into the saddle in one urgent movement. After wishing the woman The Wizard's Blessing she guided the assembled horde over the rotting tentacles of a tentaoxen. About her, all varieties of fighters were thronging towards the lowered drawbridge. Once more she mentally prepared herself for battle.

Those of the enemy surrounding the Citadel were easily outnumbered and soon dealt with. No doubt their leader would be assuming that the defenders would remain in the

Citadel. The advantage of surprise was certainly in their favour.

Along the Main Street she urged her mount past those on foot until she had joined the knights at the front who still had a Havelot to ride. Conveniently, the doors of the Main Gate had been left open.

She and the knights would forge a path through the mêlée while the rest followed behind. The fields surrounding the City were now unrecognisable, the battle raged everywhere. Victory would go to the Disenchanted, there could be no doubt of that, but her people were certainly giving them good reason to keep fully occupied while the rest made their escape.

Before she could lead a charge towards a gap in the fighting a shield bolt struck her horse in the neck. Mercifully, it died instantly and she managed to fall without injury, rolling aside to avoid being trampled to death by the thundering hooves of the Havelots behind her. This time she kept hold of her sword and quickly got to her feet.

She was now confronted by five giants. They would have to be faced. Maybe she would die here, after all? Then she thought of an alternative. A heavy spiked mace slammed down into the ground beside her as, on all fours, she scrambled between their legs, before getting to her feet and running as fast as she could.

Rosamile was congratulating herself on her escape when something hard and heavy glanced off the side of her helmet. Although dazed, she could see that the blow had been delivered by a Sangoran who was now staggering towards her, an axe embedded in his back. She was about to nod her thanks to the axewielder who had saved her life when a shield bolt struck him in the eye, killing him instantly. Rosamile's dagger slashed open the neck of an approaching Goblin. His companion died just as quickly when she drove the blade into his tiny chest.

Nearby, a beleagured knight was surrounded by three giants. It was her natural instinct to go to his aid. She ignored that instinct; there was a greater priority. She threaded her way towards Blue Bay. It was The Wizard's Wish that she do her best to reach those ships. His Will would be done.

Barney Fowl had never killed anyone before. Knowing that he lacked any fighting skills he had simply avoided any contact with the enemy. Even when such vicious slaughter surrounded him, some instinct of self preservation, aided by innate cowardice, helped him to avoid it all. True, he had nothing to live for and every good reson to die, but the painful and bloody process of dying in battle was too terrible to even contemplate. He had never been so afraid in his life.

The only way to survive the ordeal was to duck and weave his way to safety while arrows and shield bolts hissed through the air, which vibrated to the sound of clanging weapons. Once he almost fell over a Sangoran shield lying on the ground. Knowing that it would provide some kind of protection, he picked it up in trembling hands. His timing could not have been better. A weird, horse-faced warrior was charging towards him, waving a scythe-shaped weapon that could cut him in two with one blow. Instinctively, Barney raised the shield and pressed the trigger on the handle.

Relief was replaced by nausea at what he had done. Horrified, he watched the death throes of the man who now had a shield bolt jutting from his mouth. Blood gushed down upon his victim's breastplate as, with wide, horror-stricken eyes, the soldier gazed in disbelief at his executioner before crashing to the ground.

For a moment Barney could do nothing but stare at the writhing body. He had actually taken someone else's life! It was unthinkable! At last he reluctantly welcomed the possibility of death for the thought of the release it would bring. He kept on running, hoping that a stray arrow would end his miserable life. Suddenly, he was on open grassland with none but his own compatriots surrounding him. His wish was not to be granted. It looked as if he would be reaching the ships after all.

Trapped forever within the black suit of armour, the Nameless Knight sat astride the scaled back of the Black

Unicorn. He could not have explained what was happening to him, for he did not know. Why could he not return to the Magic Wood? Only his mind and body belonged to these people, for his heart was with Medila and her enchanted world, as it always would be. For some reason he could neither speak nor hear; he didn't even have a mind as such. Cocooned in a silent world of voiceless strangers, he had wandered into a place of weapons and armour. There he had seen his dark Destiny. Against one wall was a black suit which a voice from deep within his soul told him would serve as his protection. Although mute, he had managed to inveigle a stranger to help him into it. That same voice then told him to walk into the blue fire. He had obeyed, knowing that he would be sealed into that armour for the rest of his life.

He could remember nothing of his life before entering the Magic Wood, but whoever he had been he must have been very wicked. What else but wickedness could warrant such a cruel punishment as this? It was all for a purpose, but he was ignorant as to what that purpose was. As he stood within the blue flames he had seen what was to be done. His Destiny lay upon the decks of those great ships. The Unicorn would carry him to them. Many would try and stop him. All would be slaughtered, save one.

From the narrow viewing slit of the Silver Cone, the High Lord Giraldo watched as his mighty army slaughtered what was left of the Sanctuarites. His assessment had been perfect: they were imbeciles and very obliging ones at that. But what had possessed those defending their Citadel to join the battle? Now there was no need for any siege tactics. All the Islanders would be wiped out at the same time. It was most convenient. Very soon the Island would be his. He, the High Lord Giraldo, had finally conquered where all others had failed.

There were viewing slits all round the Cone. Rejoicing, he went from one to another, while the seething vista raged about him. Above, the sun was radiant amidst a clear and bright blue sky. Life had never seemed better. Jubilantly, he punched a fist in the air as he watched his spike-armoured Sangorans deal with what remained of an ill-equipped and incapable army.

Why should only his underlings have the pleasure of massacring the remaining Sanctuarites? Staying within the protection of the Cone was worthy of such cowards as his three brothers. He could imagine the bulbous Vestudio cringing at every sound outside, even though they had won. And what about the studious and pathetically effete Karabano? What lack of spirit would he be showing under these circumstancs? As for the hook-nosed Sigaraldo, who always seemed to be sniffing the air in search of some new illness to plague him, he wouldn't even have survived the voyage, let alone the sight of the massacre.

For a moment his thoughts wandered, as he tried to guess, not for the first time, when he would be launching the invasions of the other three fiefdoms. It had always been his destiny to rule the Supreme Domain as its total ruler. That old fool Talango had no right to deny him this. Now that he had conquered Sanctuary, he would need new challenges. Who would be his first victim? Vestudio or Sigaraldo or . . . ?

His thoughts were interrupted by what he suddenly saw. Did he have cowards in his army? There could be no other answer. A number of his men had obviously decided that their work for the day was done and that, unnoticed, they would retire to the safety of the bay. Well, they had been noticed! Their deaths would soon follow.

He had already decided to emerge from the Cone to perform his self-appointed task. The ringing of a bell summoned the Goblin, Nym, whose back was still bleeding from the whipping he had received. His instructions were to prepare the spider horse. Other serviles were to go outside and seek out any Combat Lord, Captain, or anyone else of reasonable authority, to form an escort of thirty mounted soldiers. Those in the escort were to be told that there was no need for them to abase themselves on all fours before him. However, it would be instant death for anyone caught failing to avert their gaze. As time was growing short, Giraldo decided to wait for them outside. Besides, he wanted to experience the thrill of battle at first hand. Quickly, he descended the spiral metal ladder and then, stepping on the backs of two serviles, climbed into the armoured saddle of the spider horse. The sliding doors of the Silver Cone were hauled open and the High Lord of Etania rode out upon his six-legged mount.

Never before had he smelt anything so exhilarating as that battle. The bracing stench was not only that of spilt blood but also of terror. Before him, a great carpet of blood and disfigurement, stretched the dead and the dying. Many of the bodies had been twisted into most interesting patterns, permanently frozen in those positions until they would begin to rot. Those still alive provided even greater interest. He chuckled within his helmet. Without realising that they were in the presence of their High Lord, a group of mischievous Goblins were gleefully torturing a Sanctuarite woman to death by jabbing and poking at her with their little swords.

By now very few of the tentaoxen were left. It didn't matter, they had served their purpose. However, one was still living and being put to admirable use. Those mounted upon the beast had actually managed to train it to deliberately use the sucker pads of its tentacles to kill. It was probable that in the process it had also killed some of his own troops. This was a small price to pay for its success. At a safe distance he gloated over the sight of a young Sanctuarite boy now attached by his stomach to a tentacle. A short scream preceded a sucking sound which could be heard even above the din of battle. While his limbs flailed the air, the boy's innards were drawn up into the great arm before what remained of him clattered to the ground, a heap of bones.

All these sights provided more than ample amusement before the escort assembled before him. Although he had decided against bringing any of their own horses, the men had been commanded to capture as many of the enemy's mounts as possible. As they formed a crescent around him, he noted that some were astride the heavy, shaggy breeds used by the so-called knights, while the majority were upon steeds which had already impressed him as being strong and fast, a selection of which he had already decided to take back to his own fiefdom for breeding. With studied exaggeration, all the riders stared down at the ground. It was instinct to raise the head when someone spoke. It would be amusing to see whether any of them made this fatal mistake.

'*Sangorans*!' he roared, but to his disappointment none fell for his ruse, all keeping their gaze riveted to the ground. 'Heading for the bay are men who are no longer your comrades! They are cowards fleeing from their duties on the battlefield! All of them must die!'

Giraldo enjoyed giving full rein to the spider horse which, despite the distance now covered by the cowards, soon enabled him to catch up with the men heading for the ships. It was only when he reached them that he realised to his astonishment that they were Sanctuarites. Worse still, there were far more of them than he had at first thought. With all his might the High Lord tugged at the reins of his spider horse. It was no use. They were travelling too fast. In the next moment he would be surrounded by them. He would have no other choice but to fight.

His only consolation was that the six-legged beast he rode gave him a decided advantage. Using a lethal combination of shield bolts and lance, he easily created a path for himself. He had also managed to spear a young boy and kill outright two wild-haired women wielding axes by firing shield bolts with perfect accuracy into their broad chests. The spider horse itself must have trampled to death at least two Sanctuarites.

Towering above him were the great masts of the Stormriders. Through the narrow slit of his helmet he could feel the cold spray of the heavy waves. It would be a rough trip in the fully enclosed transporter boats, but at least, thanks to Nym's engineering, the short trip to the ships would be reasonably safe.

An arrow whizzed past him, reminding him instantly that his current position was far from secure. The

Sanctuarites were still following him. Or were they? They had to be in the bay for a purpose. While he took avoiding action, the full realisation came to him. They were heading for the transporter boats.

Keeping out of range of their arrows, he urged the spider horse over the shingle until he was able to turn his mount back towards the battle. A riderless horse galloped past him before he saw that the ground was strewn with the bodies of his own men. All too many had been slaughtered, seemingly with ease. Then he saw others riding back to the battlefield at full speed. Cowards! Their deaths would indeed be slow and painful.

It seemed to appear from nowhere. The spider horse skidded to a halt before backing away in the manner of a real spider, drawing in its legs as if it would play dead. The black, shiny scales, the glaring, red eyes, the wickedly pointed horn . . . It truly was a Black Unicorn. Astride it was a figure of equal menace. This knight was covered from head to toe in glistening black armour. With both hands he held a massive saw-edged sword, crimson with blood. Nothing could have been more terrifying and fearsome than that beast – nothing more mercilessly implacable than its rider.

For the very first time in his life Giraldo was experiencing real fear. That fear turned to a leaping insanity when the Unicorn charged. The spider horse clattered the hooves of its six legs as it spun clear of the charge. There was no time to collect his thoughts. The Unicorn charged again. The black knight lowered the massive blade of his sword. Sword or horn? One or the other would surely impale him. Somehow, he managed to parry the thrust of the sword with his spear while the horn of the beast skimmed the neck of his horse.

Before they could be attacked again, his terrified mount turned on its six legs and galloped towards the sea. No other horse could travel as fast as a spider horse. At last the dumb creature was showing some sense. Above the clattering of its hooves and the sound of the shingle bouncing off his armour, Giraldo could hear the menacing thunder of the

Unicorn charging after them. The spider horse started to tire. The sound of the thunder grew louder. The black knight was now riding alongside. Giraldo was so afraid he could hardly breathe. The Nothing beckoned. Trembling, he raised his shield and fired a bolt. Incredibly, it didn't penetrate the black armour but glanced off the shoulder. This opponent was invincible! The High Lord's only comfort was that the six legs splaying out from the spider horse were preventing the blade of the massive sword from reaching him. While he remained in his saddle there was surely still some hope of survival.

That hope was eliminated when the knight raised his mighty weapon high above his head and brought down the saw-edged blade upon two of the spider horse's legs. There was a sickening crack as the legs fell away from its body like snapped twigs. The stricken animal bellowed in pain as it lurched on its four remaining legs, trying in vain to recover its balance.

Giraldo could do nothing to save himself. The spider horse collapsed, throwing him from the saddle. He lay on the shingle fighting for breath while the helpless creature's remaining legs flailed the air before the Black Unicorn drove its horn into the horse's belly, killing it instantly.

Despite the pain, and the sweat of fear that drenched him, the High Lord managed to get his feet. During the fall he had lost his lance and his shield. Once more, the Nothing beckoned. Frantically he searched the ground, hope his only protection.

None of this was really happening. There was no such thing as a black unicorn – no such thing as an invincible black knight. The lance! He could see it lying on the ground. It was just what he needed to rid himself of this appalling nightmare. One thrust and –

Now helmetless, he was able to smell the foul and strange odour of the Black Unicorn. Turning round, he saw the tall, ebon horn, its tip clotted with gore. The eyes were two raging fires, fires that did not burn the flesh but his very being. Avoiding their stare he looked up and saw the faceless visage of his executioner. Although smooth and shiny, the armour that he wore was as black as the Nothing. Reflected in the helmet was the image of his own wretched self. He felt as if he were being judged by a faceless icon. The teeth of that cruel sword would soon be sawing through his armour and into his own tender flesh. At that moment he could think of no more terrible way of entering the Nothing. Whimpering, he fell to his knees.

'Please!' he sobbed. 'I'll give you everything – everything! Just spare my life, I beg of you!'

There was no answer but the howl of the winds. The Unicorn gave a loud snort before turning its scaled head away. Although he could not see him, Giraldo knew that the Black Knight was staring down at him without pity. Then the Unicorn was turning. Still on his knees he watched the Knight ride away.

Why had he been spared? Giraldo looked up at the living sky and sobbed with joy. He was still alive! The air, the grass, the waves, he could see and hear and smell them all as if for the first time. His tears were replaced by laughter as he got up and staggered past the corpse of one of his dead soldiers, before looking out to sea.

His laughter stopped short when he saw a transporter boat bobbing its way towards the Stormrider ships. Another had its hatch open. Relieved, he watched the Black Knight and the Unicorn board the boat before it too was making its way through the surging waves.

Relieved? Why should he be feeling relieved when one of his precious, beloved ships was about to be stolen? Standing there, fists bunched, feeling more of a fool than he had ever felt in his life, he watched the Islanders escaping. But he would be avenged! And none would pay more dearly than the knight in black and his armoured horse. For, of course, it was nothing more than a mere horse dressed in some special kind of armour. Briefly, they had managed to trick him. There was no such thing as a black unicorn and soon – very soon – there would be no black knight either.

The High Lord Giraldo revived himself with the delicious prospect of what he would do to the horse and its rider when they were brought to him in chains.

Epilogue

Princess Rosamile stood on the rear observation deck of the Stormrider ship watching the frantic efforts of the Disenchanted to board the remaining landing crafts. If the wind stayed in their favour then one of those boats might stand a chance of catching them up. However, now that the Nameless Knight and the Black Unicorn were aboard and the Sanctuarites had mastered the complicated system of raising anchor and sail, they had little to fear. Even if one of the pursuing boats did manage to get alongside, there was not much that could be done to stop their escape.

The vessel lurched as the mechanically hoisted sail took the full force of the winds. Despite the swelling sea, the massive ship began to glide forward at speed. It was now obvious that none of their pursuers would stand a chance of reaching them. Her thoughts were confirmed by a voice behind her.

'I reckons we lost them for good, Your 'Ighness.'

Turning round, she saw a battered and bleeding Barney Fowl.

'You should get those cuts seen to, Barney.' She spoke to him like a mother, her voice almost tender.

'Nothing that won't 'eal.' He gave a shrug of his thin shoulders. 'Besides, there's only one Magician 'ere to tend to all the wounds. And that's me.'

Rosamile nodded in agreement.

'Where are we going?' Barney asked, staring at the mounting waves.

'I wish I knew. According to the Sangoran who killed . . .

Rosamile fought to banish the memory of her father's death. 'According to him, there are now four separate fiefdoms. We could land at any one of them, I suppose.'

Barney made no comment. Instead, he continued to study the waves.

'Barney?'

'Yes, Your 'Ighness?'

'Why didn't the Nameless Knight kill Giraldo?'

Barney thought hard before answering, his brow knotting.

'I suppose that 'e was showing us all that it's no good killing their 'Igh Lord if you don't destroy what 'e stands for.' He gave the Princess a broken-toothed smile. 'Now best I get back to tending the wounded. There ain't much Magic left in me but maybe if I try 'ard enough, I might be able to do something.'

Rosamile returned his smile, although her heart was heavy. 'Even if you can't, I won't hold it against you, I promise.'

'That's kind of you,' Barney said. 'That's real understanding, that is.'

Visibly cheered, he gave another broken-toothed smile before returning to the dark bosom of the ship.

Rosamile returned her gaze to the sea. The waves were now swelling higher, great cliffs of water, but above their foaming peaks she could just see the tall marblon cliffs of the place which had once been her home. Without tears, she mourned for the time when Sanctuary was.

All Futura Books are available at your bookshop or
newsagent, or can be ordered from the following address:
Futura Books, Cash Sales Department,
P.O. Box 11, Falmouth, Cornwall, TR10 9EN.

Please send cheque or postal order (no currency), and
allow 60p for postage and packing for the first book plus
25p for the second book and 15p for each additional book
ordered up to a maximum charge of £1.90 in U.K.

B.F.P.O. customers please allow 60p for the first book,
25p for the second book plus 15p per copy for the next
7 books, thereafter 9p per book.

Overseas customers, including Eire, please allow £1.25
for postage and packing for the first book, 75p for the second
book and 28p for each subsequent title ordered.

interzone

SCIENCE FICTION AND FANTASY

Quarterly   £1.95

- *Interzone* is the only British magazine specializing in SF and new fantastic writing. We have published:

BRIAN ALDISS	GARRY KILWORTH
J.G. BALLARD	DAVID LANGFORD
BARRINGTON BAYLEY	MICHAEL MOORCOCK
GREGORY BENFORD	RACHEL POLLACK
MICHAEL BISHOP	KEITH ROBERTS
RAMSEY CAMPBELL	GEOFF RYMAN
ANGELA CARTER	JOSEPHINE SAXTON
RICHARD COWPER	JOHN SHIRLEY
JOHN CROWLEY	JOHN SLADEK
PHILIP K. DICK	BRIAN STABLEFORD
THOMAS M. DISCH	BRUCE STERLING
MARY GENTLE	IAN WATSON
WILLIAM GIBSON	CHERRY WILDER
M. JOHN HARRISON	GENE WOLFE

- *Interzone* has also published many excellent new writers; graphics by **JIM BURNS, ROGER DEAN, IAN MILLER** and others; book reviews, news, etc.

- *Interzone* is available from specialist SF shops, or by subscription. For four issues, send £7.50 (outside UK, £8.50) to : **124 Osborne Road, Brighton BN1 6LU, UK**. Single copies: £1.95 inc p&p.

- American subscribers may send $13 ($16 if you want delivery by air mail) to our British address, above. All cheques should be made payable to *Interzone*.

- "No other magazine in Britain is publishing science fiction at all, let alone fiction of this quality." *Times Literary Supplement*

- -

To: **interzone** 124 Osborne Road, Brighton, BN1 6LU, UK.

Please send me four issues of *Interzone,* beginning with the current issue. I enclose a cheque/p.o. for £7.50 (outside UK, £8.50; US subscribers, $13 or $16 air), made payable to *Interzone*.

Name _____

Address _____

_____